REVENGE

ASSASSIN'S MAGIC
BOOK SIX

EVERLY FROST

DISCOVER THE EVER REALMS

Seven series. One world.

Suggested Reading Order:

Bright Wicked
Storm Princess
Assassin's Magic
Soul Bitten Shifter
Supernatural Legacy
Dark Magic Shifters
Kingdom of Betrayal

For the fury in all of us.

HUNTER CASSIDY - ONE HOUR AGO

Shadows sweep across the bookshop as dark clouds billow in the sky beyond the windows.

I drop the pile of books I'm holding on to the countertop, focusing on the sudden weather change, my senses prickling and my maternal instincts kicking into overdrive.

It's the end of a peaceful summer in Boston or, at least, the most peaceful that an assassin could hope for. I've spent the last five months clearing my ledger, crossing off missions, and tying up loose ends.

Only one mission remains incomplete and it's proving more difficult than most. But what worries me right now is the nature of the storm growing outside—and *inside*—the shop.

Electricity crackles in the air around me, charged blue streaks defying the laws of nature by arcing around my body. A whirlwind of sparkling light forms from my feet to my head, swirling around me a few bare inches from the surface of my skin, a biting force that compels me to remain completely still.

I fight the urge to release my wings and harness my full power to free myself. That would be a bad idea, not only because my wings are so strong, they would tear up everything in their path—including the priceless antique books in glass cases at the front of the shop—but because the lightning isn't forming to attack me.

It's forming to protect me.

Very carefully, I slide my hand up over my pregnant stomach. My daughter isn't due for three more months, but her power is growing wilder and more uncontrolled, stronger than any other unborn of my kind. She owes that to her father. Despite our ability to appear human, he and I are far from it.

If she's attempting to protect me now, it means she's sensed danger close by. That alone worries me because this bookshop, and the street on which it's located, is the safest place we could be.

Just as I close my eyes, rubbing my stomach to try to calm her, the shop door flies open. It hits the wall with a bang and the bell above it rattles so hard, it nearly flies off its hook.

Tansy Grey, the most powerful witch I've ever met, stands in the doorway, her dark blonde hair billowing in the stormy wind that tugs at her black dress.

Boiling clouds darken the sky behind her, casting the street into darkness. The shield around me is so strong that I don't feel the wind, even though it's wild enough to pluck open the ledger resting on the countertop.

The glowing electrical shield around me has been created by my unborn daughter, but the storm outside the shop is Tansy's.

They're both upset about something.

Tansy's olive green eyes glow with instinctive magic. She doesn't mince words. "A dark witch waits at the end of Saber Lane. She demands to see you, Hunter."

I ask the most important question first. "Can she breach the protective spell you cast over the Lane?"

Far too recently, the woman known as Lady Tirelli attacked my home here in Saber Lane and the consequences were devastating. During the attack, Tansy used her instinctive magic to cast an impenetrable spell over Saber Lane so that we can never be attacked again. Her spell protects everyone who lives here—humans and magical beings alike, all who escaped harmful pasts.

Tansy relaxes a little. "She can't."

I let out my breath. "But you're worried."

Tansy inclines her head at the light show still keeping me captive. "So is your daughter."

I can't deny it. If the dark witch came in peace, then she would be able to enter the Lane. The fact that she can't set foot beyond the entrance tells me she's truly my enemy. "Did she say why she wants to see me?"

"She demanded that you bring your ledger."

I startle. My ledger is the means by which people access my services. Assassins don't choose their own targets. I can only act if someone else writes a target's name in my ledger. "She requests an assassination?"

"I believe so."

My gaze narrows. "Who is she?"

"Nobody I recognize. She's young. Maybe twenty years old."

I allow myself to smile for the first time. If she's twenty, then she's actually not much younger than me, but I grew up quickly after my mother was murdered.

Tansy is several years older than me. For Tansy to describe this witch as 'young' means she's immature and has probably lived her life in a protected, privileged environment. Even if she controls dark magic, she won't know death like I do.

Even so... "I can't go anywhere until my daughter lets me."

Tansy steps inside the shop. "Let me help."

I sense her fighting her own protective instincts as she leaves the storm outside.

She kneels in front of me, closes her eyes, and slowly extends her hand, effortlessly breaching the electrical currents flickering around me.

Flattening her palm across my stomach, she exhales and all the tension leaves her body, her expression becoming serene.

Warmth and a deep sense of calm spread across my belly, easing out my worries. It's the most peaceful I've seen Tansy for months.

She always appears in control, but she hides her true battles. Her heart has been broken so many times that I'm worried she'll never heal completely. Somehow, she has already forged a bond with my unborn daughter.

The electrical currents around me fade and finally disappear.

Before she can remove her hand, I take hold of it. I'm not sure how to say what I want her to know. "This will be you one day."

Her focus doesn't return to my stomach. She withdraws with a small shake of her head. "Impossible. I lost my chance."

I want to argue with her, but I let it go. I can't reopen her emotional wounds.

Free to move around once more, I reach for my ledger where it rests on top of the shop counter next to the books I dropped. It's a wide book, bound in amethyst-colored leather with cream pages visible at the edges.

As I scoop it into my arms and prepare to leave the shop, I don't need to ask Tansy to watch my back. She and I have been protecting each other for months now. She's like a sister to me.

She turns on her heel, her shoes clacking down the shop's front steps. The storm clouds remain gathered in the sky above us, but I don't mind. It's good for this dark witch to see what she's up against if she tries anything underhanded.

I hurry along Saber Lane, my boots beating the cobbled stone walkway. I'm not exactly as graceful as I once was, but I'm managing to get around without waddling to accommodate my growing belly. Not yet, anyway.

The street is a tourist destination, a collection of rare and unusual shops. The road itself is paved and wide but not wide enough for vehicles. We head toward the brownstones that stand on either side of the entrance, passing the other shops along the way.

Farther back from my antique bookshop is an apothecary—the best in Boston—along with a dojo where I train every morning. On the other side of the Lane, a demure 1950s-style bakery sits beside a grocery store that shrieks every neon color from the 1980s. But my favorite place is Dean's Diner.

Dean himself stands outside it, his sleeves rolled up around his large biceps, accentuated as he folds his arms across his chest.

The bloodlessness of his cheeks tells me he's in pain.

It isn't a good sign.

He strides over to us, the muscle in his jaw ticking. "Be careful with this one, Hunter. She's more dangerous than she looks."

I place my hand on his shoulder. Dean is an empath. Anger, fear, sadness... The emotions that others carry with them resonate with him, sometimes causing him extreme pain. "Go inside. Keep away from us. I'll deal with her."

As he disappears inside the shop, I lean toward Tansy. "How powerful is she?"

Tansy gives me another shake of her head. "I can't place her power, Hunter. There's something incredibly dangerous about her, but it feels more like a foreign power, not her own. Something she's attached to herself—or has access to. We need to be careful."

Tansy is fiercely protective of every single human and magical being who lives here. So much so that she didn't trust me—an outsider—for a long time.

As we approach, I study the tall woman at the street's entrance. She huddles next to one of the dark gray lampposts, leaning into it, her coat pulled tightly around herself and her hood covering her hair, but she straightens as we approach.

Her gaze travels the length of my body from my mahogany hair to the tattoo inked into my right shoulder. I don't feel the cold so I'm wearing short sleeves. Her focus shifts to my rounded stomach. She can't conceal her surprise. I guess she didn't think an assassin would choose to have a child.

She has the aura of a witch, but Tansy's right... there's something else. A dangerous darkness clinging to her.

I push away any fears that might dictate my actions. I learned long ago to control my emotions, to act with reason, assess all threats, and deal with them quickly.

The wind whips at us as Tansy and I stop just inside the protective shield. Humans can't see or sense the shield, but to all magical beings who step through it, it feels like a waterfall descending across their bodies. We'll stay inside it for now.

The woman pushes back her hood, revealing blonde hair that is braided tightly across her scalp to end in a single braid that rests across her shoulder. I catch sight of jeans and a sweater beneath her coat.

Her eyes are more brightly blue than is natural and I sense the flickering remnants of a spell she can't quite get rid of. A glamor maybe. Possibly a spell that went a little bit wrong.

I stiffen as I recognize her, anger rising inside me.

Her photograph forms part of an evidence box containing proof of all the crimes she's committed. Assassins do not kill for the purpose of accumulating money, although it's true that we make a good living off our trade. Rather, we step in when the usual channels of justice fail, whether due to legal loopholes or because witnesses are so terrified, they won't come forward.

In this woman's case, fear of her family allows her to walk free.

Not for long.

Her name is written in the ledger of the Legion Master himself, Slade Baines.

In fact, the names of every member of her family—her

father, mother, and brother—are written into Slade's ledger by brave clients who trust Slade to keep them safe from retaliation.

If only Slade were here now.

He would cut her down in an instant, whereas I am not allowed to touch her because of the simple fact that it's not my ledger that her name is written in.

I follow the Assassin's Code. If I kill this woman now, I will break not one, but two rules.

First, all assassinations must be sanctioned by the Guardian. No matter how willing I might be to carry out an assassination, the Guardian has the final say. This rule guards against unjust assassinations. I don't have the Guardian's permission to kill her, only Slade does. To break that rule would result in excommunication, which I will never risk.

And second, an assassin must not interfere in an assassination—to touch her now would be considered an insult to Slade. As punishment, Slade would be entitled to fight me to regain his honor.

That could get a little awkward since I'm carrying his child.

A third complication is that the Guardian has elected me to take over her role when she retires in five months. I'm currently her Heir Apparent, but until I'm officially sworn in, I will remain a working assassin. My status as the Guardian's Heir Apparent certainly doesn't give me the power to sanction my own missions.

"Kaitlyn Hadrix," I say, unable to keep the chill out of my voice. "Why are you here?"

Her eyes meet mine, her expression darkening. "I come for revenge."

It's an interesting reason, but not unusual. She's the daughter of the man who trained all of Lady Tirelli's soldiers. Adrian Hadrix turned mere street thugs into skilled killers who terrorized innocent men, women, and even children in Lady Tirelli's name.

His name is also written in Slade's ledger, along with the names of at least forty other associates of Lady Tirelli whom Slade is yet to locate.

As for Kaitlyn's motives now, members of the underground are constantly at war with each other. Always fighting over territory. Lady Tirelli changed that by annihilating her competition, but she doesn't dominate the underground anymore.

Still, I'm curious about the emotion in Kaitlyn's voice. "On whom could you possibly want to seek revenge, Kaitlyn Hadrix?"

Her jaw tenses as she lifts her chin, petulant. "Did you bring your ledger or not?"

Unhurried, I turn to Tansy as I hold my book out in my hands. "If you don't mind, my friend?"

It would be dangerous to make any physical contact with Kaitlyn, so Tansy will float the book to her through the protective shield instead.

Always graceful, Tansy brushes the hair behind her ear.

Kaitlyn won't notice, but Tansy has written spells inside her palm so she can read them. Long ago, her power was irrevocably damaged and she still fights to recover it. Now she writes spells on slips of paper and across her body so she knows what words to say.

While I hold my ledger out, Tansy murmurs a simple levitation spell beneath her breath. As soon as my ledger glides from my arms across to Kaitlyn, she grabs the book and opens it to the page where the pen is wedged.

Hurriedly scribbling inside it, Kaitlyn only pauses once.

It's interesting to me that she hesitated. Judging by the progress of her pen across the page, she stopped around the place where she needs to write her offered payment. There must be something about what she's offering that troubles her.

Some clients pay with money, others with favors, and some with information.

She snaps the book shut and hands it back to me.

I smile when her hand can't cross the protective shield and the book sticks halfway between us.

As soon as Tansy floats it back to my waiting arms, Kaitlyn says, "We're done now, right?"

I shake my head. "Not even close. You've given me the target's details and made your offer. Now, I get to decide if I'll accept the mission. After that, we wait to see if the Guardian sanctions the kill. That won't happen if your grievance isn't justified." I glare at her. "Or if you're trying to target an innocent person."

She huffs, but genuine nerves enter her expression as she glances up the street, as if she's worried about being seen. Tansy's storm has chased most passersby off the street into nearby cafés and shops, but there are still some stragglers braving the suddenly chill wind.

Kaitlyn's lips press together, disgruntled. "Well, I don't have long, so make it quick."

I take my time opening the ledger, sensing her increasing frustration. "You either want this or you don't, Kaitlyn. It takes as long as it takes."

She huffs again and folds her arms across her chest, tapping her forefinger against her arm. Her fingernails are painted black, but each one oozes with magic.

A casual glance at Tansy tells me she's noticed them too.

I open my ledger and carefully consider what Kaitlyn wrote inside it. Each column in the ledger requires a different piece of information to allow me to make my decision: her name, the name of the target, her offered payment, and the reason why services are required. There's space for my signature if I accept the mission as well as a place where the Guardian's verdict will appear.

I look to Kaitlyn's offered payment first—the place where she hesitated. She wrote:

I will tell you where to find him.

I consider the cryptic promise with caution rising inside me. She must mean the target's location, but why would his location be of value to me...?

My focus flashes to the target.

Striker Draven.

My body suddenly becomes cold. Striker Draven is heir to the weapons manufacturing company that supplied all of Lady Tirelli's weapons.

While he himself never pulled the trigger, his guns and daggers have been used to strike down countless innocents, leaving them bloody and dying in back alleys or on their loved ones' doorsteps.

I myself felt the bite of armor-piercing Draven bullets that nearly cost me... too much.

Until now, nobody has come forward to write Striker's name in an assassin's ledger, not even in Slade's.

Striker Draven dropped off the grid over three years ago, his location unknown ever since. Even though he disappeared, his family trade has continued, supplying advanced weaponry that is used to terrorize innocents. Now Kaitlyn has promised to tell me where to find him.

In the 'Why?' column, she wrote:

Because he took away the only good thing in my life.

She could be lying. Playing me to make me feel sorry for her. There's no way for me to know if what she wrote is the truth.

In the column that asks when services are to be rendered, she wrote:

At a future time of my choosing.

I give her a hard stare. She returns it with a cold scowl.

Given that I can't kill Striker unless I can find him—and she is the key to his location—her timing means she can come back with his location when it suits her.

I don't like it. Not at all. It makes me a puppet on her strings.

However, she doesn't know how good I am at finding targets. I couldn't devote time to locating Striker before. Now that his name is written in my ledger, it's my chance to go after him.

Nothing can make me pass up the opportunity to wipe that man off the face of the Earth.

I pick up the pen she left in the ledger's fold and sign my name to accept the mission.

"Now we wait," I say. "The Guardian will take as long as she needs to determine the way forward. If she sanctions the kill, you will see her writing glow golden. If not, her writing will glow sapphire."

Now that Kaitlyn has finished writing in the ledger, she can't read her own entry in it any longer.

Only I will be able to see what the Guardian actually writes. Even Tansy, with all her power, can't read my ledger. She can't even read the target's information. This is to maintain full secrecy, which is essential to an assassin.

A light shines from my open ledger.

It's golden.

A smile breaks across Kaitlyn's face. "Sanctioned," she whispers. "I'll be back with the information I promised."

She taps the ring finger of her left hand against her arm. There's a flash from her fingernail and she disappears.

I blink at her sudden departure.

"A transportation spell," Tansy says, her eyes narrowed at the space Kaitlyn occupied. "Her own magic isn't strong enough to do that. She's conjured dark magic and adhered it to herself: on her fingernails and probably at pulse points around her body. You can't trust her, Hunter."

"I don't," I say. "Not for a—"

A sudden whoosh of air gusts around me, stronger than the storm. My heart speeds up but not in fear.

The air flickers with radiant silver light as Slade appears beside me. I'm tall, but he's taller, and right now he's looming over me in the most intensely protective way possible.

"Where is she?" he asks, his assassin's ring glowing and his eyes filled with silver that tells me his killing power is at full force.

His power is the same as mine and can't hurt me, but Tansy wisely takes a step away from him.

At least he's gotten better at not cracking the pavement when he arrives.

"Gone," I say, taking his arm. "We're okay."

His protective instincts must be in full swing because he doesn't relax. "What did she want? Did she threaten you?"

"She wants an assassination."

His gaze flickers to my ledger. Some of the tension leaves his body. "Did you accept the mission?"

If any other assassin asked me to divulge confidential information like that, I'd slug them in the face, but Slade and I… We don't have secrets. We learned the hard way that secrets can only tear us apart. Truth is at the heart of our relationship now.

"I did."

"Then she'll be back." He swings to Tansy. He's all business, in Master Assassin mode, but even so, his big hand finds the small of my back, stroking in slow, comforting swirls, easing out the tension in me as he addresses Tansy. "Can you trace the path she took to find her location?"

Tansy bites her lip. "Not now that she's gone, I'm sorry. But I can prepare for when she comes back." Her forehead creases in thought. "I can probably attach a spell to her—have it uncoil like a thread if she gets away—but it will have to be undetectable or she'll sever it." She nods to herself. "I'll start looking through my spellbooks so I'm ready next time."

"Thank you, Tansy."

As soon as Tansy heads toward her brownstone at the corner of the Lane, the storm clouds clear above us and the sunlight shines through.

Slade checks me over, his hands running over my cheeks and back. "Are you sure you're okay?"

I sigh, but not in exasperation. He's been busier in the last month than I would like. I understand why—he wants to make sure the Legion is in a good place so that he can focus on us when our baby arrives, but even so, we haven't seen enough of each other lately.

I soak up his touch, murmuring, "Dark witches should show up more often if it brings you to my door."

The corner of his mouth hitches up and the sudden heat in his eyes takes my breath away. He presses a tantalizingly gentle kiss to my lips, but when he draws back, I read the worry in his eyes.

I lean into him. "What is it?"

"We located another one of Lady Tirelli's warehouses—but this one was empty by the time we got there. Even the vault was cleaned out. Our targets are anticipating our moves better than they were before."

"What are you saying?" I search his eyes. "Does the underground have a new leader?"

"No," he says, but his denial is a little too fast. He sighs. "I don't think so. But Oliver Draven and Adrian Hadrix are both still out there."

"Still no luck locating them?"

Slade shakes his head. "Oliver and his daughter are demons. They can manipulate others to hide them. And Adrian keeps moving around. Every time I have his location, he's moved by the time I get there."

"You'll find them," I say.

Slade's hands lower to my stomach. "I want our daughter to grow up in a place where she has no need for her power."

Our power is death. Justice for those who can't seek it for themselves. I wish I could believe that such a place will ever exist.

I reach up to kiss him. "We won't give up."

Once he's gone, I carry my ledger back to the shop before I open it again and stare, perplexed, at what the Guardian *actually* wrote in it...

Hunter, we need to talk about Striker Draven. As soon as possible. I'll come to you.

Striker's assassination wasn't sanctioned. Not yet, anyway.

But the Guardian was smart enough to use her gold pen to deceive Kaitlyn and make her think she was successful.

The Guardian is an intelligent, remarkably compassionate, but strong-willed woman and I've always respected her.

When she asked me to become her Heir Apparent nearly two months ago, she told me she needed my help. She couldn't tell me much at the time, but now I flip to the pages of my ledger, where she has been communicating with me.

Five assassin's rings are missing. My mission to find them is most worrying of all. I was desperately hoping they were at the warehouse Slade hit today, but not so.

If we don't get the rings back soon—and quietly—it could impact the very existence of the assassin's Factions.

Lady Tirelli may have been defeated, but her legacy is far-reaching.

Closing the book, I turn my gaze to the plaque on the wall. It has the words my mother lived by:

Just because you are born into darkness doesn't mean you can't overcome it.

I've fought through a lot of darkness to find the light.

I want peace just as much as Slade does, not only for myself, but for my unborn daughter.

But the Guardian's message is a reminder that I'm not going to get it any time soon.

1. PEYTON PRICE

I know what I am now.

When I first arrived at Bloodwing Academy, my power was Unknown. I didn't know what I was capable of, but Striker Draven challenged me to face my true nature. He drew out every emotion of fury, violence, and determination that I'd caged inside myself and he woke the rage inside me.

I despise Bloodwing with every fiber of my soul, but this place has forged me out of fire and pain into what I am: a Fury.

The girl I was...

She's gone.

The sun dips behind the horizon and darkness creeps across the Academy's front entrance as I stand with Striker and the other students—Lucinda, Joseph, Ashley, Lachlan, Bree, Ryan, and the others.

We're surrounded by men wearing body armor and carrying an arsenal of weapons.

Moments ago, we made a deal with their leader, Adrian Hadrix, that ensures our mutual survival.

Outside these grounds, beyond the forest that surrounds the Academy, the assassins are hunting us.

We are their enemies, not because of anything we've done, but because of who we're associated with.

Bloodwing Academy was founded by Lady Tirelli, a woman whose criminal operations the assassins have vowed to destroy. We are her students. We were destined to be her soldiers. That puts us squarely on the assassins' kill list.

Hadrix offered to train us to prepare for their attack. In return, he, his family, and his men will take shelter inside the Academy, which is hidden from the assassins' eyes by protective magic.

Bloodwing is the last safe place for any of us.

Striker's body heat burns against my left side, heat that I welcome—can never get enough of—but his increasingly rapid breathing tells me he's struggling to stay in control.

Instinctively, I reach for his arm, wrapping my fingers across his bicep as far as they can go. Not far, as it turns out. Striker is a man of formidable height with bone-breaking strength, his black hair and piercing amber eyes a warning of his hellhound power.

I meet his gaze, demanding that he focus on me. Demanding that he ignore the woman standing opposite us—Hadrix's daughter, Kaitlyn. Her hair is an icy blonde and her eyes a bright blue. She's tall, slender, and part of the deal we made with Hadrix. She gets to stay here too, whether we like it or not.

Not.

Hell not.

I don't need to read Striker's mind to know what he's thinking. His incisors descend as his gaze rakes over her, the growing firelit glow in his eyes telling me he's seconds away from revealing his beast and taking a deadly swipe at her.

Kaitlyn taught Striker the meaning of betrayal. She clawed apart the last of his humanity and left him to piece together what was left of his heart. Hatred and fury are as much a part of him as they are of me.

I turn my back to Kaitlyn, catching her reddening cheeks when I deliberately ignore her. Moments ago, I warned her that I am her worst nightmare.

I intend to make good on that promise.

Striker, I mouth, barely whispering his name. *Do you hate me?*

His pupils dilate and his snarl shifts into a smile. His chest is splattered with blood. It's in his hair and sprayed across his neck, although there's only one smear across his cheekbone, the deep carmine color accentuating his jaw. His scent reminds me of cedarwood and balsam, warm and intense.

Always, he breathes.

I search his amber eyes for the fire he reserves only for me, finding it glimmering in the corners of his lips and the heat of his gaze, a slow burn that promises to ignite when I want it to.

I return the heat in his expression with a faint smile of my own. "Then trust me."

With a twitch of his lips, his incisors disappear, his arms stop thrumming beneath my grasp, and I sense he's in control again. Barely. But it's enough for now.

Leaning into his side, I maintain physical contact by pressing my thigh to his. Quickly tucking my whip into the top of my skirt where I hope it will stay put, I keep my hands free in front of me.

I hazard a glance at Hadrix and his wife—the teacher we know as Ms. Vulture. Vulture used to wear a glamor, disguising herself as an old lady so nobody would guess her true identity.

Now she stands tall with blonde hair and sparkling green eyes, wearing black leggings and a tight sweater. Hadrix's hair is also white-blond, his eyes a striking blue. Like Vulture, he appears to be in his mid-forties.

For now, they haven't stepped between me and Kaitlyn. That's probably because they're confident they can subdue me. Vulture's hand hovers near her wand and Hadrix's palm rests openly on the handle of a handgun clipped to his belt.

Neither of them saw me at my most dangerous, so they have no idea their weapons can't hurt me.

Projectiles will sail right through me. My body absorbs and dispels magic. As a Fury, I can survive any attack, healing myself instantly. I am built to withstand the attacks of even the strongest warrior and the most powerful supernaturals.

I am hell's executioner—the monster who judges other monsters.

Only Raptor knows the extent of my power. Remaining at a distance from all of us, he folds his arms across his chest, his blond hair falling across his eyes and a cruel smile growing on his face. As the teacher who was my primary tormentor at the Academy, he stabbed me multiple times during the fight, including once in the neck, blows that should have killed me.

I was preparing to end his sadistic existence when Vulture emerged from the building and Hadrix and his men arrived in trucks at the front gate, stopping me.

It's a little disconcerting to me that the focus of his cruel smile right now is not me, but Kaitlyn. It looks like he's content to sit back and wait for her to suffer the carnage I'll unleash.

Unaware of Raptor's gaze, Kaitlyn renews her smug smile as I return my attention to her. Her confident blue eyes descend in a condescending wave from the top of my head to my left shoulder, lingering on the patch of blood staining my white shirt above the location of my heart.

She leans a little closer, speaking in a loud whisper. "Someone who needs medical attention as badly as you do really shouldn't get in my way."

She must think the blood staining my shirt is mine.

I'm sure I look a mess, but she couldn't be more wrong. In fact, not a single drop of my own blood was spilled in the battle Striker and I fought against our compliance officers and teachers before Hadrix arrived.

Kaitlyn's focus remains on Striker, her sultry gaze dismissive of me. "Run along now, Peyton. Striker and I have a lot of catching up to do."

She flicks her hand at me. Her fingernails are painted black with sharp white runes etched across them. As she waves them at me, a sense of repulsion slides through me, a pushing sensation that tells me the runes are active spells. Dark magic.

Only one of her fingernails is normal, but the others are overly bright. I'm not sure what the spells are intended to achieve, but I'm suddenly wary.

She's had time to prepare for this moment. She must have a plan to subdue Striker. The spells on her nails could be anything from love spells to mind control. Striker can resist magic, but he's not immune to it like I am.

I slip directly in front of him, turning my body into a full physical barrier, keeping my voice clear and audible to everyone. "We're done here, Kaitlyn. If you value your life, you'll stay away from all of us."

She didn't only hurt Striker. She betrayed every student at the Academy.

Beside me, Lucinda's arms are lifted at her sides, her fingers outstretched. A mottled hazel sheen grows across her cheekbones that indicates she's about to summon her dryad power. I hope she turns the nearby rose bush stems into paddles and smacks Kaitlyn across the butt like she deserves.

Kaitlyn snarls. "We'll be done when you're screaming on the ground."

She darts forward and shoves the flat of her hand against my chest. A spark of light flashes where her pinky rests against my sternum. It's the smallest burst of power, but the impact hits me hard.

I gasp at the sudden agony in my chest as if a blade shot clean through me, ripping apart my bones from the inside.

I scream out the pain, expelling it from my lungs, harsh

screams that echo around the space all the way up to the hidden shield that rests across the Academy high in the sky.

To my shock, my feet become heavy, pinned in place so I can't jump back from her or levitate into the air to break the contact between her hand and my chest.

Striker mobilizes beside me, a moving mountain of muscle coming to my defense, stepping out from behind me before his fist swings at Kaitlyn's head.

"No, Striker!" Just in time, I extend my left arm out and across his broad chest, focusing all my strength into stopping him.

He hits the unexpected barrier of my outstretched arm and his swing misses Kaitlyn's face as he jolts off-balance. Attempting to push past me, the claws that extend from each of his fingers impale my forearm.

My eyes snap to his. "Don't touch her!"

He jolts backward, letting me go.

Blood runs from multiple incisions where he cut me. It's the first blood I've shed this afternoon.

I stare in confusion at the wounds. They should have healed instantly…

I can't worry about that now. I stopped Striker from touching Kaitlyn and that's all that matters. I throw out my other arm, waving Lucinda back. Her hazel eyes fill with worry, but she edges backward at my command.

Kaitlyn didn't even flinch when Striker took a shot at her. She remained exactly where she is, her hand pressed to my chest. A flicker of annoyance passes across her face when he steps away from her with a roar of frustration. Her reaction confirms that she wanted him to touch her.

His snarls echo around me as he begins pacing in a semi-circle. No doubt some of his rage is aimed at me because I stopped him. I asked him to trust me, but trust doesn't come easily to either of us.

Hadrix and Vulture have jumped closer to their daughter, Hadrix abandoning his handgun to reach for the semi-automatic strapped to his back while Vulture grips her wand. The men around the perimeter raise their weapons and aim them at me.

Vulture casts Striker a nervous glance, calling to her daughter with a warning tone in her voice. "What are you doing, Kaitlyn?"

Kaitlyn ignores her, pressing hard against my chest. Unable to shift my feet, I grit my teeth as the invisible blade twists inside me, cutting deeper.

I choke back my screams as I take stock of the situation.

Blood runs down my left arm. My chest feels like it's about to rip apart. My feet are glued to the ground.

Striker looks like he wants to kill me for refusing his help.

And thirty heavily-armed assholes are pointing their semi-automatic machine guns at me.

It looks like we're in for a wild ride.

2. PEYTON PRICE

Kaitlyn pastes a sweet smile on her face. "Now who's the nightmare?"

She has no idea who she's dealing with. I told Striker I wouldn't hide my power anymore and I meant it.

"Lucinda," I cry. "Get everyone inside!"

I'm grateful when Lucinda spins on her heel and a moment later I sense the student body backing away from me. I can't twist far enough to check their retreat, but I trust Lucinda to make sure they're safe.

My eyes water, tears leaking out when I squeeze them closed. I open them again as soon as Lucinda races back to me to take up position on my right side.

"They're safe," she says.

Kaitlyn smirks. "You'll never be safe." She runs her free hand up my arm, her fingertips playing across my shoulder. "Which torture should I use on you next, I wonder?"

I want to cut her threats from her tongue. I take a deep breath and focus on the pain inside my chest. At the back of my mind is the fear that I've already used up my reserves, that I have nothing left, that my power will fail me right when I need it the most.

But Kaitlyn has given me the gift of pain.

She's stabbed her power deep into my heart and that's where I find my rage. My fury. My power comes from pain. It comes from hatred. And right now there's a world of hatred all around me.

A crimson sheen drops over my vision as my power washes to the surface. It happens slowly and quietly.

A deep calm overtakes me and all the details around me fade into the background: the men, the rose bushes, Hadrix, Vulture, even Raptor.

Only Kaitlyn, Striker, and Lucinda remain sharply defined within my vision. I'm surprised when the other students do too. I'm suddenly acutely aware of their rapidly beating hearts all the way across the garden, the way they're huddled inside the Academy entrance, holding themselves together despite the new threat they're facing. All the guns that could turn in their direction without warning.

If the men carried wands, Lucinda could have used her power over wood to disarm them already. Not so for metal.

As soon as my power surfaces, the weight in my feet lifts and the pain in my chest eases. I'm aware of the damage Kaitlyn's spell is doing to my body, but it doesn't hurt and it won't last.

I wrap my fingers around Kaitlyn's wrist as though I'm about to try to push her away.

"That spell was your weakest," I say.

A crease appears in her forehead, her gaze flicking from my hand to my eyes. "No, it wasn't."

"Your strongest, then? That's a pity."

I give her a brief smile, the smallest warning, before I squeeze her wrist, twist, and drop my weight.

She screams with pain as her wrist turns in an unnatural

direction. She tries to wrench out of my grasp, but I hold fast, pulling her toward me and down before I shove her as hard as I can.

Tossed around like a leaf in a hurricane, she loses her footing, flies backward, and lands on her butt several paces away.

About a million metallic clicks tell me that the newest Academy assholes have primed their weapons, ready to fire at me. So has Hadrix.

"That's enough, Peyton," he warns. The grimace on his face tells me he's not happy right now. We're supposed to be allies. He made a rousing speech to that effect.

To hell with that. He brought his daughter with him, knowing the history between her and Striker. Knowing what she's capable of. He was never going to be my friend.

My claws descend with a snap. I stride toward Kaitlyn, ready to make my point, but Lucinda is way ahead of me. We haven't tested my power against guns and I guess she doesn't want to take any chances today.

Lucinda's skin transforms into a gorgeous woody sheen as her dryad power shimmers in the air around me. The nearest rose bush turns into a mass of vines that shoot out over Kaitlyn just as she's about to jump to her feet.

Kaitlyn screams curses at Lucinda as ropes made of greenery whip across her thighs and calves. The vines shoot around Kaitlyn's waist and twine around her torso despite her struggle against them. They pull tight and snake back to the ground, forcing her toward the earth to pin her there.

I tower over her, controlling my power. I made a decision in the fight with Osprey and Hawk that no matter what happens, I won't lose my honor. Fighting Kaitlyn while she's restrained would be a coward's move.

"Stay down," I order her. "And stay away from us."

I step away from her, ready to return to the other students.

A dark cloud of anger descends across Kaitlyn's face. She twists within the ropes, writhing to release her left hand. With an angry shriek, she rakes one of her fingernails across the rope around her waist.

Light flares as another magical rune in her fingernail activates. There's a *snap* as the vine breaks.

Kaitlyn jumps to her feet, but this time she launches herself at Lucinda. The ground at my feet trembles as Lucinda prepares to defend herself. Even the roots beneath the earth are at her disposal.

I can't help the smile breaking across my face. When Kaitlyn was at the Academy over a year ago, none of the students controlled their powers. Kaitlyn has no idea whom she's dealing with now.

But at the last moment, she changes direction, aiming for me instead.

The forefinger on her right hand flares with another spell. "Materialize!"

An object appears in her hand and power suddenly ignites around her, rippling through the air. More power than I've ever felt before.

The object she called to herself is a curved white wand, slender and bleached as pale as a bone.

The power radiating from it is foreign to me, but I immediately recognize its nature: raw and feral like a wild animal that refuses to be tamed.

Hadrix jolts away from his daughter and Vulture shrieks, "Kaitlyn! No!"

Vulture whirls on her husband. "You were supposed to lock it away!"

"I did!" he shouts back at her.

Kaitlyn pays no attention to them. Like me, her focus has become pinpoint.

"You think you're strong," she says to me. "But you're nothing compared to the power in this wand."

The wand glimmers, shimmering white and incandescent in the fading light.

Most wands are a conduit, a way for witches and wizards to channel and strengthen their power, but this one…

It's like being pulled by a tide, drawing me forward.

Unlike Kaitlyn's parents, I take an instinctive step *toward* the danger.

Kaitlyn's eyes shoot wide with surprise when I step right into the wand so that its tip presses against my chest.

She shakes her head, stammering. "What are you doing?"

I push so hard against the weapon that she stumbles backward, forced to adjust her grip to maintain control of it. I fight every instinct in my body that tells me to take hold of the wand, close my fingertips around it, and take its power into myself.

My voice is guttural, harsh in my own ears. "This wand doesn't belong to you."

Kaitlyn's parents brace, taking up position on either side of her, their focus darting from Kaitlyn to me and back again.

Vulture shouts, "Do *not* use that wand, Kaitlyn! Do you hear me? You're not strong enough."

Kaitlyn ignores her. Her knuckles turn white as she adjusts her grip again. There's no doubt in my mind that the magic in the wand is too much for her to control. Her power is like a weak flame compared to the fury raging through it.

She gasps when I lean forward again, pressing the wand's tip right against the location of my heart.

I welcome its rage, soaking it into my torso. Most wands leave me cold. In fact, touching them only reveals to me the horrifying memories of the damage their owners have caused.

But *this*…

This wand speaks to me like the heat of a summer evening…

a race through dark woods... the heady scent of green leaves after a rain shower... a quiet cave and warm lips...

I shiver.

The wand's power reminds me of Striker, a power that sends a thrill to my toes.

I want it.

3. STRIKER DRAVEN

I'm frozen beside Peyton, my heartbeat erratic, my beast's growls a low rumble in my chest, undeniable, near panic. Not for my own safety.

Peyton asked me to trust her, but she doesn't know the danger she's in right now.

She's pressed up against the wand, her hand rising toward it. Her dark lashes are lowered against her cheeks, her luminous brown eyes hidden from view. She leans forward at her waist, her long legs appearing even longer as she cranes forward.

The White Wand is supposed to be a myth.

Another of my stepfather's crazed delusions.

He told me that only a supernatural with a truly dark heart can wield it. Now Kaitlyn has it and she has no idea what she's doing.

A bead of sweat runs down her face from her temple to her jaw as her lips purse, trying to form sound. She doesn't look anything like she used to. Kaitlyn's appearance when she was here was a glamor for my benefit. Her big, brown eyes, sweet lips, and soft curves are gone.

Now she's all sharp angles, her hair as pale as ice and her

eyes as blue as her father's. When she came to the Academy a year ago, her purpose was to break me. She was meant to be the key to forcing me to reveal my power.

She succeeded.

I broke.

What's left of me is volatile, unforgiving, and heartless.

Peyton took my pieces and dragged them together with all the force of her fury, but even though my heart feels emotion again, I don't know who I am. Not even remotely.

All I know for sure right now is that Peyton is standing too close to the wand and I'm not about to lose her to its power.

A wary glance to the side tells me that the wand is having a dangerous effect on Lucinda. Her arms are lifted at her sides, her gaze fixed on the weapon. The thorns on the nearest rose bushes grow sharper as her dryad power ripples out around us. Her eyes are changing too, growing darker, glinting in the fading light.

I throw a glance over my shoulder to check the other students. In the distance, Joseph's gaze is fixed, not on the wand, but on Lucinda, a violent blush of indigo blue washing through his cheeks and down his neck as his draugr power surfaces.

Ashley presses her arm over her eyes. Her gorgon power is possibly the most dangerous of all. Her blonde hair will transform into snakes when her power is triggered. She drops to the floor in the doorway, curling her knees up to her face. As long as she doesn't open her eyes, she won't kill anyone.

I sense their fear and anger rising, wild like the wand.

I fight my panic, hating the unfamiliar feeling, taking deep breaths to calm myself and keep my movements controlled.

Peyton is an enigma to me, responding to force with more force. I can't see her face, don't know if she's in pain, can only try to guess her thoughts from her rigid shoulders. I want to grab her and drag her away from the wand, but if I make any sudden movements, she's likely to retaliate.

I already drew blood when I grabbed her before. I won't do it again.

My fingertips tingle with power—my hellhound power—as I step up behind her. Slowing my movements, gentling my hand, I wrap the fingers of my left hand carefully around her upraised arm, sensing whether she'll resist. I'm ready to pull her away from the wand if I have to…

She turns her head, her eyes meeting mine, and the expression in them is not at all what I expected.

Opposite her, Kaitlyn is barely in control, a sweating, stammering mess.

But Peyton is serene, her eyes and lips relaxed.

She's more alive than I've ever seen her.

She sees me and her eyes light up, a smile curving her lips, the heat in her gaze nearly more than I can take.

4. PEYTON PRICE

Striker's fingers scorch my arm like a brand, his power stronger even than the wand's as he steps close to me.

His power. My power. The wand's power.

His other palm presses flat against my lower back, making me arch against him, suddenly burning to kiss him.

"Peyton." He growls my name.

He only ever calls me by my first name when I'm in danger. I don't sense any threat from the wand. In fact, it makes me feel peaceful, but flames burn in Striker's eyes and the threads of his veins are running golden across his chest and arms, telling me his beast is surfacing.

He's worried. Really worried.

His concern brings me back to myself like a bucket of icy water.

I allow the gentle pressure of his hand to stop me from taking hold of the wand, allowing him to guide my arm back to my side.

Opposite me, Kaitlyn's mouth works to speak. "I will… kill… you…"

Her hands are shaking now, causing the wand's tip to vibrate against my chest. She's only held it for a few seconds, but the strain around her eyes indicates she won't be able to clutch it much longer.

At the side, Vulture points her wand at her daughter. "Kaitlyn!" she shrieks. "Don't do it!"

It looks like Kaitlyn isn't paying attention. Her cheeks flush red as she shrieks a spell. "Curse cut—"

At the same time, Vulture flicks her wand and shouts, "Righteous retrieval return to me!"

The bleached wand shudders as a wash of magic reaches out and tugs it in Vulture's direction.

Kaitlyn fights to retain her grip on it, her teeth clenched, trying to finish the spell. "*Curse... cut...*"

It's a cutting spell. Ms. Sparrow used it on me all the time, leaving me with hundreds of tiny cuts across every exposed part of my body—arms, legs, face, neck. They were papercuts. They stung with no lasting damage. Kaitlyn will cut deep.

Vulture's arms strain as her magic intensifies, trying to call the white wand to her. She's deathly pale, sweat dripping from her forehead.

"Let the wand go, Kaitlyn. You stupid girl!" she screams. "Before you kill us all."

I jolt at her scream. *Kill us?*

The fear on Striker's face chills me to the bone, telling me it's true.

Metallic clicking resumes around the garden as the men take aim. Not at me. They're aiming at Kaitlyn now.

Dear ancients. The wand must be so dangerous, they'll kill Kaitlyn rather than let her use it. Hadrix isn't even trying to stop them. His own daughter...

A deep, scary-as-hell part of me wants Kaitlyn to do it. If the wand will destroy her, then I want her to use it.

I fight my furious instincts, forcing myself to remain aware of everyone else around me, all the vulnerable students. It's time for me to draw on the only power that might work on Kaitlyn now.

The scent of wildflowers fills the space around us, my power of compulsion rising like a calming tide. I angle forward, reach up slowly, and place my hand on Kaitlyn's shaking shoulder.

As soon as she inhales the perfume of compulsion, her pupils dilate. Her knees wobble and her grip on the wand loosens. Her eyes glaze over, instantly unfocused.

I lean forward and murmur, "Let go of the wand, Kaitlyn."

She nods. "I'll let it go."

Without hesitation, she opens her hand, allowing the weapon to fly toward Vulture.

For some reason, Vulture's eyes widen even farther. With a surprised and fearful glance at me, she points her wand above her head, stopping the white wand in the air above her without touching it.

"Bring me the box," she cries. "Quickly!"

One of the soldiers is already racing toward us, carrying a wooden chest about the size of a shoe box with runes painted on all visible sides.

I'm disconcerted to realize that I didn't notice him break away from the others before. His running footsteps are lithe and agile, quiet, reminding me of a panther when it stalks its prey.

With his helmet and facemask on, I can't identify him.

He flips the lid open as soon as he reaches us.

Vulture drags her wand down in a sudden sweeping motion, and the white wand flies into the box. The soldier braces for impact as the weapon lands with a *thud*.

The impact causes the box to tilt and I catch sight of other objects inside it—shining silver and copper. I can't make out what they are before the soldier snaps the lid shut. Vulture waves her wand over it, whispers a spell, and the lid clicks as it locks.

Silence descends over the garden.

Kaitlyn's expression remains blank. She's still under my control.

I curve my fingers around her shoulder, fighting every destructive urge in my body. I could reach for my whip and end her now before she has the chance to do any more damage, but that would also bring an end to our precarious alliance with Hadrix. There's no doubt he's my enemy, but I'd rather keep him close for now.

Around the perimeter, the armed men slowly lower their weapons, quietly glancing at each other. Vulture is sickly pale, her gaze full of fear as she glances at me. It must be because of my power of compulsion. She knows I'm a Fury, but she probably didn't expect that I could use that power yet.

Hadrix holsters his weapon, his wary gaze fixed on me too.

He exchanges a look with his wife that I can't decipher before he steps up behind Kaitlyn and places his hand on her other shoulder.

I expect him to rage at me for causing the conflict with his daughter.

I'm surprised when he's subdued. "Remember our deal, Peyton. We all benefit if we work together."

We agreed to let Hadrix stay and train us, but we did so under pressure. There are more men with guns than students and only a handful of students know their true powers. I warned Hadrix that we wouldn't be treated like prisoners, that if he harmed any one of us, he would answer to Striker and me.

I grit my teeth as I lean toward him. "I'm amending our agreement. First, you keep your daughter the hell away from us. She doesn't train with us or sleep near us. Understood?"

Hadrix nods, his expression remaining deadpan. "And second?"

"The next time your men raise their guns at me, they'd better be prepared to meet their maker."

"Don't worry. They won't do it again."

I exhale slowly. It's the best I'll get. I return my full attention to Kaitlyn, feeling a little sick as I remove my hand from her shoulder. "You're free to go."

Released from my power, she jolts upright. Her eyes snap wide, her gaze immediately landing on her bare hands, growing wild as she discovers the wand is gone.

She inhales sharply. "You—"

Vulture dashes forward and grabs Kaitlyn before she can finish speaking. Vulture locks her arms around Kaitlyn's waist hard enough that the air whooshes audibly out of her daughter's lungs.

"Let's go," Vulture shouts.

Whatever protest Kaitlyn was going to make is lost as she gasps for air. Her mother drags her several paces away before she finally releases Kaitlyn to walk on her own two feet.

"Never pick an opponent you can't beat." Vulture's rebuke is loud enough to be heard in the silence.

"I can beat her." Kaitlyn smooths her braid and flicks a disdainful glance back at me. Even now, her gaze is filled with challenge. "Peyton's covered in blood. She's weak—"

Vulture yanks on Kaitlyn's arm. "*None* of that blood is Peyton's. That should tell you something. Now get inside!"

I catch sight of Kaitlyn's suddenly wide eyes before her mother pulls her up the front steps. The students part to let them through. I take some small satisfaction from the momentary shock on Kaitlyn's face, but it won't stop her from coming after me again.

Striker stands a few paces away from me, and I instinctively close the gap between us. His gaze is contemplative and wary where he wasn't wary before. It's the same expression Hadrix still wears and it stops me in my tracks.

I'm not sure what's changed in the last two minutes. Worry spears through me, but in the next moment, Striker shakes himself. He smiles, a deadly hitching up of one corner of his mouth, revealing the barest hint of a growing incisor. He inclines his head behind me.

I follow his line of sight to Raptor, who is oddly fixated on the box the soldier still holds.

Now that Vulture and Kaitlyn are gone, Raptor steps up to Hadrix. He keeps his voice low as he glances at the box. "You have what I need?"

Hadrix nods. "I do."

"Good." Raptor steps back again. Deepening shadows cast across his face and hide his thoughts, but it's impossible to miss the smile that touches his lips.

It sends a chill through my heart. I saw other objects in the box, things I couldn't identify. Raptor's interest in it tells me that whatever he wants is inside it.

Hadrix clears his throat before he begins shouting orders at his men. "Weapons down!" He gestures to the bodies in the grass. "Let's get this mess cleaned up before night falls."

Four soldiers peel off from the others and begin dragging the bodies toward the fence, laying them side by side. Our former Headmistress, Ms. Osprey, lies dead on the grass not more than a few paces away. Ms. Hawk also lies dead, her body fallen beside a rose bush several feet from Osprey. She and Osprey spent years hurting and killing Bloodwing Academy students, but Striker and I ended them.

The soldier holding the box hands it off to Hadrix. His voice carries a rumble that tells me he isn't entirely human, but I can't see his features beneath his protective gear. "Your orders, sir?"

Hadrix addresses him. "Harrison, mobilize the men and locate the other bodies. Bring them out here. They must be burned in order to avoid any unwanted revivals. Vulture will take care of the mess inside the building."

It's clear from his expression that 'mess' means blood and gore.

We fought the compliance officers hard. Striker and Joseph

ripped many of them apart. I take a deep breath and close my eyes. I'm not immune to shock. Maybe one day my heart will be cold to the aftermath, but not yet.

Harrison turns in my direction before he removes his helmet and face mask, revealing short, black hair, dark-rimmed brown eyes, and a faint wash of stubble across a strong jaw. His gaze is direct, but the rings around his irises are animalistic. He's definitely a shifter, but I can't tell what kind.

Harrison ignores Raptor as he steps toward me, but the sudden chill in the air between them tells me they know each other and they definitely aren't friends. I consider for a moment whether that could be a good thing for us.

Harrison's speech is overly formal and unemotional as he addresses me. "Ma'am, may I enquire about the other hotspots?"

It's such a detached way to ask about the dead.

"You'll find bodies in the dining room on the first floor of the east wing," I say. "They're mostly compliance officers, but there's another teacher there too. Her name was Ms. Sparrow. There are also two compliance officers bound and gagged on the fourth floor. They're still alive."

I guess my compliance officers will be set free now. All of these men, and our compliance officers, worked for Lady Tirelli before she disappeared. They're part of the same organization.

Harrison strides away from me, barking orders at the other men. Some of them stride to the trucks and begin unloading crates. The others head inside, where the students part for them quickly.

The remaining two soldiers take the only other living teacher, Mr. Mallard, inside the building, their guns pressed to his back.

Mallard was our history teacher, a slight man with a moustache and prematurely gray hair. He's harmless without his wand, which I broke—unless of course, they give him a new one. Raptor and Vulture were the only teachers in league with

Hadrix, sending Hadrix secret messages for the last few months. The guns held to Mallard's back indicate that they must see him as a threat.

Lucinda touches my arm, a light tug with a worried glance that says we need to get inside.

Hadrix hails me as I turn away. "Peyton. Striker. I'll expect you all outside in the old combat area by 6 A.M. tomorrow morning for training. Until then, get some rest. You'll need it."

He told us that his training methods are not for the fainthearted. I'm not sure what to expect, but I guess we'll find out tomorrow.

"We'll be there." I back up another few steps before I turn away from him.

I can finally see the faces of all the students as I approach them. They're all blank canvasses, each of them hiding their true thoughts just as they've done ever since they arrived in this hellhole.

As soon as I step into the mahogany entranceway with Lucinda and Striker beside me, the other students break off, moving silently up the stairs to avoid the soldiers swarming around the first level.

Ashley and Lachlan give Striker and me a quick nod before they leave. Bree and Ryan follow them. While Ashley and Bree know their power, Lachlan and Ryan are yet to discover theirs.

Lucinda and Joseph are the last to go.

Lucinda whispers, "Let's meet in the kitchen in an hour. I'll let the others know. We need to protect ourselves until we can get out of here."

I give her a nod.

Striker's amber eyes flare as soon as I meet his gaze. I can't imagine how messed up I look right now. The lights in the entrance flicker on and the blood on our clothing, arms, and hands is suddenly very confronting.

As Lucinda and Joseph disappear up the staircase, Striker

inclines his head in that direction too. He doesn't have to ask me twice.

My footsteps are increasingly heavy as I precede him up the stairs, taking them one at a time, returning to the attic in which I swore I'd never set foot again.

I stumble at the top. It's just one more stupid step, but until now I was able to believe that I was going to walk through the front gate after all. The Academy is no longer locked down, but it may as well have rows of barbed wire strung around it.

The assassins who wait for us outside these walls… I need to know who they are, what they're capable of, and how to defeat them. Until then, I choose to keep myself caged.

But I won't stay here forever. Hadrix is a means to an end. I'll take what I can from his instruction and use it to my advantage. We're allies for now, but one day, we'll be enemies again.

Striker's arms slide around my waist from behind and he pulls me close, causing us to teeter dangerously at the top of the staircase.

I'm not afraid. I give in to the pull of his arms, allowing myself to dare gravity to take us both down, spin us away from the attic and all its memories, good and bad.

His voice is a deep rumble as his lips brush my earlobe. "So begins another fucked-up game."

A deep burn begins in my heart as I make a promise. "This time they're the prey."

5. STRIKER DRAVEN

I don't know who she means. Hadrix. Kaitlyn. The assassins. Probably all of them. Peyton's angry as hell. This time, her rage isn't directed at me and I'm surprised by how uncertain that makes me feel.

She and I... anger is our safe place. It's where we're comfortable. We know each other's strengths and challenge them.

But this new place we're in now, with her leaning into me, trusting me not to drag us both down, fills me with pure and absolute fear.

My right arm wraps all the way across her stomach, my fingers curling around her left hip while my left palm flattens against her chest beneath her collar bone.

Her body fits perfectly into mine as she tilts her head onto my shoulder. Despite the blood coating her neck, her hair smells like wildflowers. It's the scent of her power of compulsion, lingering around her.

I want to tell her how good she smells. I want to tell her that we can leave right now, leave this place behind. We can take on the assassins by ourselves. They won't stand a chance.

Then there's the conversation I don't want to have. About the White Wand. My beast has been silent for hours—mostly because I merged with him for most of the day, becoming the hellhound that hides within my soul.

Now he growls a warning: *She doesn't know what she did.*

My heartbeat is suddenly erratic, but Peyton is oblivious, focused only on her determination to get us out of here.

She whispers, "I will kill them all."

The certainty in her declaration takes my breath away and calms my fears.

My arms tighten around her. For a crazy, insane moment, I want to tell her that we can. Right now. But my conscience is awake—she woke it—and it won't let me endanger the students who can't defend themselves.

I murmur, "Be patient. We waited before. We can wait again."

She's light in my arms, her power lifting her up. She spins to face me and pull me up the final step. "As soon as the other students know how to control their powers, I'm going after the assassins. I'll hunt them before they can hunt us."

I shake my head. A warning shake. "Peyton, you can't take them on—"

"They can't hurt me," she says, her gaze clear and certain. The whip she tucked into the waistband of her skirt is a deadly reminder of her new skills. "Nothing can..."

Her voice falters as her eyes meet mine. She just declared that nothing can hurt her, but now she doesn't look so certain.

She runs her hand across my face, her fingertips seeking the curve of my jaw, brushing across my lips before she traces what I suspect is a trail of dried blood that stretches from my cheekbone to my hairline.

She doesn't say it, but I know what she's thinking.

Me.

I can hurt her.

She doesn't mean physically. The worst wounds are hidden

deep within our hearts, rips and tears that scab over but never heal.

I wrap my arms around her, lifting her off her feet. She's so light, she could float out of my arms.

"I won't hurt you," I say, even though she didn't ask me to promise her anything.

Her fingertips rest lightly on the back of my neck. "Kaitlyn—"

"Means nothing to me."

"—wears spells on her body." The corner of Peyton's mouth hitches up as she registers my declaration, but her smile quickly fades.

She presses her palm to my cheek, urging me to listen. "She came prepared. Her fingernails are covered in dark runes. She only used three of them today. She might even have runes inked into her skin. She doesn't need to carry a wand to be dangerous. You have to be careful. She wants to hurt you. Don't underestimate her."

I can't deny the worry in Peyton's eyes, but its cause isn't what I thought. Peyton hasn't asked me for any kind of reassurance about how I feel. She hasn't questioned whether seeing Kaitlyn has changed anything for me, hasn't expressed any insecurity at all.

Peyton promised that she would protect me, defend me, and tear apart anyone who hurt me. She told me she would wait as long as it takes for me to trust her. I picture her stepping between me and Kaitlyn, the way she took on the threat herself.

Then the way she manipulated the White Wand…

Damn. I push my thoughts away again. I'm not ready for that conversation.

"I won't." It's the second promise I've made her.

She gives me a single, serious nod.

I slide my fingers into her hair, releasing her braid and stroking through the brown strands.

Crimson highlights glint in the light. I never noticed them before. They match the color of her fingernails and the sheen that clouds her eyes when she accesses her power to its full extent—a scarlet glow that makes her look as if she could be camouflaged in blood.

Her body has slowly changed over the last few months, but I'm certain that this change to her hair color is new.

She's still changing in ways I can't predict.

She sighs and closes her eyes as I continue to run my fingers through her hair.

It's time to stop thinking about the danger around us. She saved my life today. Twice. She fought for me in ways I never thought she would. Ways I don't deserve.

I've never been good at asking for what I need.

I've always been good at taking what I want with whatever force required.

"Peyton..." I swallow hard over her name. I used to reserve her first name for those moments when I didn't guard myself, only speaking it when my emotions got the better of me. When I was afraid for her.

I practice saying it again, but I stumble over it like a teenager. "Peyton, I want... I'd like... Will you...?"

Nope. Asking nicely is not in my repertoire.

I hoist her into my arms with an order. "Come with me."

She doesn't fight me as I hook one arm under her backside and guide her legs around my waist.

"Where are we going?" she asks, slipping her arms around my chest and dropping her head to my shoulder, pressing her face into the curve of my neck.

I stride past our bedrooms. I promised Peyton a bed far away from here in a place that belongs to both of us. Now, we're stuck here. Two rooms. Both with bad memories. No fresh start.

"I'm getting you cleaned up."

"So much blood," she murmurs as I carry her to the bathroom and nudge the door open with my foot. I lower her to the counter beside the sink, sitting her on the edge. When I move to leave her there, she tightens her legs around me, her arms closing around my bare chest.

She drops a kiss against my neck and my senses go haywire.

All my needs rush to the surface, and my body responds, but I push those thoughts away.

I'm determined to do this right.

Every second with her.

I may not always be polite, probably won't ever say 'please,' but I'm determined to treat her right.

She's my path back to myself. If I can just walk these moments with care and attention, with purpose, then maybe I'll find something good waiting at the end.

I brush my cheek against hers, deciding to give in just a little to my inner beast by nuzzling her soft skin, my lips lowering to graze the corner of her mouth. "I can't turn the shower on from here."

I test her strength by taking hold of her arms and gently disentangling her legs. She gives me a resigned sigh and lets me go.

Turning the shower on full, I check the water temperature, making sure it's not too hot before I turn back to her.

I freeze.

Her clothes lie in a pile on the floor, her whip resting on top of them.

She stalks past me, completely naked, and steps into the water.

She's perfect. From the curve of her full lips to the curve of her slender neck to the tantalizing curve of her waist above her hips to… all the curves that make my head spin.

Every naked inch of her body glistens as the water runs down her face, neck, chest, and her long, long legs.

Casting a look of pure challenge at me, she tips her head back under the water and closes her eyes.

I can't help my grin because she never fails to surprise me.

Stepping away from the shower, I remove my sweatpants but leave my underpants firmly in place. No matter what she does, I won't be swayed from my intended path.

Scooping up two washcloths, I step back to the shower to find her watching me with the first signs of uncertainty. I step in beside her, take a deep breath, and lean forward, sensing her quick inhale.

I don't allow our bodies to touch. "Let me take care of you."

Her lips press together. She is so fucking fearless, but when it comes to gentle touch, she wants to run away as fast as she can.

She has an irrational fear of receiving gentle touch, and I have an irrational fear of giving it. I need to change that for us both. Starting now.

She squeezes her eyes shut before she nods. "Okay."

I start with her face, carefully wiping away the blood from her cheeks, the side of her nose, and her ears.

When I'm certain her cheeks are clean, I drop a light kiss on them before I start on her neck, gently rubbing the cloth around her hairline, drawing her hair across her shoulder to reach the sides and back.

The water runs red below us, not only from her body, but also from mine. I refuse to touch her for any purpose other than to clean her until we're both free from the reminder of our battle.

I drop a kiss against her neck when it's clean and move on to her shoulders and arms, then down to her fingertips, cleaning between each one before I kiss them one at a time. I leave her chest alone for now, focusing on her hips and waist, then her legs.

She watches me carefully at first, only closing her eyes each time I drop a kiss on a clean patch of skin, but by the time I reach her ankles, her eyes remain closed, her eyelashes trembling with water droplets where they rest against her cheeks.

I kneel at her feet, rinsing away the final blood from between her toes, but I pause as I rise.

Her fingernails…

Resuming a kneeling position, I take hold of her hand, drawing her fingers closer so I can study her nails.

They're pale again. Ordinary. Completely normal. The crimson color of her power has faded.

I'm not sure what to make of it. I draw myself upright so I can run my hand through her hair. It's impossible to tell if the highlights are still there while her hair is wet.

She opens her eyes, her head tilted back to see me. Her eyes are a perfect chocolate color, perfectly clear.

She looks… *human*.

The smile she gives me is dazzling in the extreme, a contrast to the absence of power in every other part of her body.

"Satisfied?" she asks.

I shake myself, trying to ignore the worry growing in my mind. "Hardly."

She blushes. "I meant… am I clean enough for you?"

"Maybe." I shrug, indulging in a scan of her gorgeous body. I'm not clean from the battle, so I won't touch her that way, but I can't help admiring the view. "Maybe I'll start all over again now."

The color in her cheeks deepens, but her eyes fill with determination as she holds out her hand for both washcloths. "You're filthy. It's your turn."

I hesitate. I've maintained control of the situation until now. Handing over the cloths means I don't know what will happen next. Neither of us likes to lose control.

"Please?" she asks. Her expression is open. She seems to have forgotten that she's completely naked and totally vulnerable. She never would have stood like this in front of me before today.

She trusts me.

The realization freezes me to the spot.

Trust is a fragile thing, fleeting, easily broken. But Peyton's trust is like being punched in the stomach, doused in molten lava, and dragged back out of the fire.

I take a deep breath of steam-filled air as two opposing fears rise inside me. One tells me to get the hell out of her life because there's no way I won't screw this up. The other tells me to wrap her in my arms and dare fate to tear us apart.

I close the gap, pressing the two cloths into her open palm.

Her fingers curl around mine, drawing me closer. She urges me under the water, swapping places with me so I stand under the spray. Her lips curve into a smile before she sets about washing my face and neck, then my filthy chest, giving my arms, fingers, and even my toes the same treatment I gave hers.

Her touch is soothing. Not platonic, not even close, but calming, easing the worries that lurk at the back of my mind.

For a few moments, I forget about the White Wand, about the way I cut Peyton's arm when I grabbed her, about her absent power right now, even about my fear of screwing up her trust.

I open my eyes when the sound of the cloths dropping to the shower floor meets my ears.

She steps into my arms, her naked chest pressed to mine, her head tilted back. "Striker, can we—?"

Bang!

Peyton jumps.

My reflexes kick in and my arms close tightly around her.

The crimson sheen drops over her eyes again. "That was a gunshot."

6. PEYTON PRICE

I drag myself out of Striker's arms, my adrenaline spiking as the gunshot fades.

"It came from outside. We have to get down there." I grab the nearest towel from the floor, toss it around myself, and throw Striker the other one.

He catches it, raking it over his body to dry himself as we run from the bathroom.

I dash into my bedroom and snatch up clean clothing—underpants, a T-shirt, and workout pants. There's no time for a bra. I curse my wet skin because the clothing sticks, delaying me for precious seconds as I try to shimmy into my pants.

Just as I make it to my door, Striker appears wearing clean sweatpants, but his expression is dark and dangerous.

He tackles me, pushing me back inside my room, kicking the door closed behind him with his foot. "We're not going."

"What?" I shove at his chest, trying to get past him. "We have to, Striker. It could be Lucinda, Joseph, Ashley. Our friends could be in trouble. They could be hurt—"

"It's not them!" He pulls me off my feet, but he may as well try holding on to air. I slip his hold, levitating upward and toward the door.

My hand barely brushes the handle before he grabs my ankle and refuses to let go.

"Striker! What the hell?"

He shakes his head at me, digging in his heels as I try to pull away. "It's not our friends, Peyton. We don't want to get involved in this."

I take a closer look at his face, trying to clamp down on my panic. "What's going on?"

His hand tightens on my ankle. His claws appear and they drag against my skin so hard, it stings.

"Promise me you won't go down there," he orders me.

"I can't do that."

He squeezes his eyes shut. "Come to the window. See what they're doing. Then decide for yourself."

I lower myself to the ground, but he simply adjusts his grip, taking hold of my calf, then my thigh, then my waist, leaving little cuts all up my body as I descend.

I wince but ignore the pain. He told me he would never hurt me, but twice today we've both reacted out of panic.

His touch used to make me stronger—it triggered my healing power—but something's different now and I'm not sure why or what it means.

I tell myself I'll deal with it later. Right now, I need to know that the people I care about are safe.

As soon as he releases me, I dash to the window. Darkness has fallen since we left the front yard. Sharp lightning flickers in the distance, a storm raging far away, but it will take hours to reach us.

Above us, a half-moon glows brightly in the sky, but a brighter light is caused by the bonfire near the fence on the left side of the front yard.

It's a burning pyre.

Hadrix was serious when he told the soldiers to burn the bodies.

I hated the compliance officers. Not a single one of them showed me any empathy or kindness. Many of them were responsible for killing other students.

Even so, I can't watch. I look away from the pyre, my gaze veering right.

Striker plants a finger on the window, pointing directly down. "There," he says. He removes his finger and clamps his hand across my shoulder, a steadying force. "Look away when you need to."

With that, he steps back, his expression unreadable. The moonlight is so bright in my room that I only now realize I haven't turned on the light.

Striker steps back into the shadows as I turn to the window again.

Directly below us within the circle of light streaming from the open front door, Raptor and Hadrix stand in the front yard. Hadrix holds a gun and Raptor grips a sword. It's hard to see, but the sword looks bloody. Farther back near the rose bushes, Vulture and Kaitlyn stand side by side, as if they're waiting for something.

My eyes narrow as a soldier appears, pushing someone in front of him. As the soldier steps farther forward, I make out Harrison's face and silhouette. He's pushing a compliance officer wearing the standard navy blue uniform, although it's torn at the front.

I recognize the officer's scaled tattoos that look like snakeskin in the bright light below.

It's Colby, my old compliance officer.

He's still gagged with duct tape, the way I left him.

Harrison forces Colby to his knees in front of Hadrix, and the older man takes quick aim.

My eyes shoot wide. *An execution?*

My heartbeat has barely caught up, pounding as Hadrix presses the barrel of his handgun to the back of Colby's head and pulls the trigger without pause.

Before Colby's body falls, Raptor swings his sword at Colby's neck—

I stumble away from the window, clapping my hand across my mouth. The gunshot echoes through the air as Striker catches me, pulling me into the shadows beside my closet.

I crumple against his chest, slipping down into his lap as he curls around me, the strength of his arms a welcome restraint now.

"It's okay," he murmurs into my hair, stroking my back with soothing strokes. "You're okay."

"They already shot Collin, didn't they?" I suck in air, trying to breathe. "That was the first gunshot."

"I saw his body on the grass. I didn't want you to see it." Striker's arms tighten too hard, but I need the pressure.

"What about Mallard?" I ask. "Do you think they'll kill him too?"

"My guess? He's still useful. He knows a lot about the history of supernaturals and can help Hadrix understand our powers— our weaknesses, to be specific." Striker's fingers flex against my back. "It's okay. You'll be okay."

"No," I say, shaking my head. "Collin and Colby were assholes. Tormentors. But they worked for Lady Tirelli too. Now they've been executed by their own people."

Striker takes hold of my face, tipping my head back, his gaze burning mine as his voice becomes harsh. "Don't forget this, Peyton. Don't forget what Hadrix is capable of. We fought today to defend ourselves. We had no choice. *They* will kill anyone who gets in their way. Never trust them."

I meet his amber eyes. "I won't. Ever. All I have to do is touch Hadrix's weapons to know what he's done with them—who he's killed. The same way I saw Raptor's past when I held his dagger. The same way I knew about Kaitlyn..."

I stop. Press my lips together. *Dear ancients, I shouldn't have said that...*

Months ago, I picked up Kaitlyn's wand and saw her memories of Striker when he was a different person. Back then, his heart was still whole. He treated her like a guy would treat a woman he loved. He defended her, held her, comforted her. All of the things he will never do with me because that part of him is broken.

I don't fool myself that he will ever treat me the way he treated her, and I don't want him to. Cleaning the blood off me in the shower just before is the gentlest I will tolerate.

There may still be a small part of me that craves that kind of affection, but it is quiet compared to the fury inside me that demands to be fed.

Striker is frozen. He's still holding my face, his demand harsh. "What did you see?"

I force my eyes open. "I saw a different person. *You.* I saw a different *you.*"

He doesn't move, but the heat in his hands increases. I sense the distance he's already putting between us in his expression, the way he's shutting down.

"That person—the person I was—doesn't exist anymore," he says. "If you think I'll be like that again..."

My stomach sinks even further. He thinks I'm with him because I'm hoping he'll change, but he couldn't be more wrong.

I want the hellhound he keeps caged.

I choose my words carefully, needing him to hear me. "I don't want that person, Striker." Without pulling away, I slide my legs around him so that I'm straddling him, my palms pressed against his chest.

I'm grateful when he doesn't fight me or push me away. His body is still healing from his fight with the manticore in the pit that left him with a deadly gash from his right shoulder to his bottom left rib. He doesn't have the power to heal himself like I do. I saved his life by transferring my power to him for long enough to heal his wounds.

We've already fought too many battles today. The battle for Striker's life, then the fight to free the other students, then Kaitlyn…

We're still fighting Kaitlyn.

Right now, it's the memories that are our enemy.

I curl myself into him the same way I did today when I healed him. "I want the person you are now. Every dark, fierce, angry, broken part of you."

His arms slowly rise around me, his hands sliding under my shirt, tracing up my back in a way that makes me shiver.

He gradually relaxes within the circle of my arms.

His lips turn to my ear, his breathing suddenly ragged. "The next time you walk past me naked, don't expect me to hold back."

I smile, brushing my lips against his cheek, and dare to hover my lips above the corner of his mouth, challenging him to kiss me. "Promise me you won't."

He turns his lips to mine, but he doesn't claim my mouth like I hope he will. Instead, he pulls back far enough to meet my eyes. "If we start something right now, Peyton, we won't make it downstairs to meet the others."

Every time he says my name, it sounds different. He's gone from worried, to fierce, and now… the tone of his voice promises me a world of fire.

I lean forward but pause as a smile grows on my face. "Lucinda wanted to meet us in an hour. We still have twenty minutes left."

I'm worried for my friends, but they're smart enough to stay out of Hadrix's way until we're due to meet them. The gunfire has stopped. There are no more compliance officers to kill.

Striker takes hold of my shoulders, stopping me, but his lips curve into a lazy smile. "Twenty minutes? Price, when we start something, I promise you, you'll need to set aside a whole night."

A thrill passes through me, making me shiver. Despite what he said about stopping, one of his hands grazes down my side and across my thigh. He stops just as suddenly as he started, his fingertips hovering above my skin.

A hint of anger enters his voice. "I cut you again."

I glance down to the place on my thigh where he grabbed me to stop me leaving my room. The moonlight hides most of the wound, but my skin is visibly scraped.

All of the heat disappears from his voice, which is now ragged with worry. "Why is this happening?"

I shake my head. "I don't know."

A worried crease appears in his forehead. "You transferred your healing power to me this afternoon. Now you don't heal right away if I hurt you."

I ignore the question in his voice. "I'm stronger than ever, Striker. I can survive anything."

"But you might not survive me." He suddenly clenches his jaw, his chest rising and falling, his breathing increasingly rapid. "You'd better not have made yourself vulnerable to me, Price. That's the last thing you need."

"Why?" I challenge. "You're not going to hurt me."

"I already have!" He rocks forward, his hands curling around my waist, as if he's going to pick me off his lap and push me away.

He connects with my bare skin because my shirt is hitched up against his chest.

The moment he touches me, he stops, his palms flexing against my hips for a moment before they rise across my back, seeking my spine and my shoulder blades.

He growls. "I should push you away for your own sake, but I can't get enough of you."

He drops a light kiss on my jawline, trailing kisses to my collarbone.

"You told me you wouldn't hurt me." I sigh, melting into his kisses.

"I'm a fucking liar," he snarls, pulling back. "Don't you know that already?"

I break into a grin, making his eyes widen in surprise. "Yes, but you're *my* fucking liar."

I dart forward and press my lips to his, inhaling the scent of his skin and the taste of his mouth.

He responds with a heat I can't deny, his lips coaxing mine apart, tasting my mouth. I arch against him, pressing my chest to his, drinking in the fever of our embrace.

It takes all my willpower to pull away again.

I consider his serious eyes and stern mouth. He's worried, but it only makes me want to kiss him again because... he wouldn't be worried if he weren't opening up to me, and that gives me hope that he's lowering his defenses.

"If there's something wrong with your power to heal," he says, "we need to keep it to ourselves. Hadrix can't find out or he'll use it to his advantage."

"You're right." I draw to my feet, wishing I felt as certain as I sound as I flippantly declare, "He won't find out."

I don't know why this change in my healing power has come about or how it's going to play out, but no matter what happens, I can't show Hadrix any weakness.

I grab a bra from my closet, turn my back to Striker, and pull off my shirt. I quickly clip the bra into place. Striker keeps his distance while I get dressed. He can be a scary, volatile asshole, but he never crossed the line when it came to my body. He didn't even kiss me until I asked him to.

Before I turn around, I ask, "What do you know about the wand Kaitlyn had?"

It's a casual question, but there's suddenly silence behind me. I turn. "Striker?"

He leans up against the wall, his arms firmly folded across his chest. "I know too much," he says, his amber eyes glinting in the shadows.

"Okay, then." I lower myself to perch at the edge of the bed opposite him.

A poultice on the ceiling used to make my stomach turn, but I dragged my claws through it this afternoon, breaking its magic.

Even so, the sudden darkness in Striker's expression is making me feel a little sick. "Tell me."

"I heard about it from my stepfather."

"Oliver Draven," I say.

I don't know much about Striker's family history except that his stepfather controls the Draven fortune, and his stepsister, Zara, left Striker here to die despite claiming to care about him. They're both demons with the power of suggestion. They can manipulate others into doing things they don't want to do. Zara's power didn't work on me and I strongly suspect it doesn't work on Striker, either.

Striker nods. "Oliver told me that Lady Tirelli kept a box of treasures hidden among her possessions. The box contains magical objects of extreme power that she collected over the course of her life. One of those objects is the White Wand."

"What is it for?"

Striker unfolds his arms. "Death. Power. Anything you want and everything you could imagine, but there's a catch. The White Wand is an instrument of deception. It controls anyone who tries to use it."

He shrugs, but it's a falsely casual gesture. The tension in his shoulders is real. "You think you're in control, but you're not.

The wand controls you. Apparently, some supernaturals over time believed they were strong enough to use it, so they tried. The wand worked for them for a time, manipulating them into situations where it could do the most damage. Then it killed them and everyone around them."

I shudder. "So it really could have destroyed us today. But I…" I shake my head, struggling to describe how I felt when I saw it. "It didn't feel dangerous to me. Is that the deception you're talking about? It fooled me into believing I was safe?"

"Maybe." Striker's expression is unreadable.

I narrow my eyes at him. "What aren't you telling me?"

He speaks carefully. "Kaitlyn was completely under its spell this afternoon. Your power of compulsion… no matter how strong it is… shouldn't have been able to break through."

My forehead creases as my confusion grows. "You're saying I somehow controlled the wand."

"No." He stops and shakes his head. "Maybe." He exhales. "I'm saying you overrode it. Maybe that means you controlled it. Maybe you diminished its power somehow. Or maybe your power is stronger than the wand."

"That's a lot of *maybes*." I wipe my suddenly sweaty palms against my jeans. No matter how powerful I become, anxiety will always be my constant companion.

"What about the effect it had on everyone else?" I ask. "It was drawing out the other students' powers. I was worried they might all have flicker fits."

"You noticed that? I thought you were completely focused on Kaitlyn."

I shake my head. "I sensed their power rising."

"I can't explain it," he says. "I'll admit I wasn't exactly afraid of the wand, either. But I was afraid of what it would do to you."

He clears his throat and fixates on the window.

His body language tells me I've pushed our conversation as far as he's willing for it to go.

An eerie golden glow rises beyond the window now—reflections from the growing fire below. I don't want to look across the scene again, but I need to make sure it's safe to go downstairs.

The other students will be smart enough to stay well clear of the carnage, so I'm not worried about them. Yet. Time will tell how long Hadrix sticks to the terms of our deal.

I steel my breath before I step up to the glass.

Below us, Hadrix, Raptor, Vulture, and Kaitlyn have gathered near the pyre. Harrison isn't with them anymore and neither are any of the other men. Firelight flickers across their faces as Hadrix and Raptor stand near each other with their arms crossed.

Nearby, Vulture's arms are raised, her wand held in one hand.

Smoke from the fire flows directly upward, an unnatural direction, so I can only assume that Vulture is siphoning it upward so it doesn't wash across the yard and seep through the cracks beneath the doors and windows.

In addition to the smoke rising, a glowing stream of light flows from the fire, but it floats toward Vulture, lighting up her face and torso.

"What is she doing?"

Striker edges toward the window. I resist the urge to lean into him, sensing he needs space.

His lip curls in disgust. "She's stealing remnant magical power from the bodies. It's how weaker witches try to imitate instinctive magic. It will give her power without her wand. Not much, but enough to do damage if she's disarmed."

I sigh. "She's figured out that Lucinda can use dryad power to take her wand."

In front of the fire below, Hadrix suddenly claps Raptor on the back. I can't hear their conversation, but it looks like they're congratulating each other.

Kaitlyn is the only one who stands farther apart, rubbing her arms as she fixates on the fire, ignoring her parents.

I lean forward, suddenly focused on their hair... their features...

My stomach slowly sinks. I reach for Striker. "Tell me you see it too."

Striker's gaze passes across the four people standing in the yard, from one blond head to the next.

Raptor and Hadrix stand at the same height with the same military silhouettes, but the similarity between Raptor and Vulture is even more striking. They have the same eyes. It was never visible before because of Vulture's glamor.

"I see it," he says. "Raptor's one of them."

I shake my head in realization. "That's why Vulture made sure I didn't kill Raptor. It's why Hadrix bargained for his life. Raptor must be their son. He's Kaitlyn's brother."

Striker's incisors appear, deadly white in the moonlight. "They're one dangerous family."

7. PEYTON PRICE

My bare feet quietly slap the wooden floor as Striker and I make our way cautiously to the kitchen.

I left my whip in my room tucked under books at the bottom of my closet. I prefer bare feet to shoes now. The weight of shoes feels foreign and counters my ability to levitate. I've never been to the kitchen before—mealtimes were confined strictly to the dining room—so Striker leads the way.

I allow a little of my power to rise to the surface, expanding my senses. I sense Striker do the same. His hellhound power is a familiar force to me now—both dangerous and comforting, a confusing combination.

My senses tell me that most of Hadrix's mercenaries are located on the second level of the west wing. That's where the compliance officers and teachers used to sleep. It makes sense that they're preparing their sleeping quarters for the night.

Still, several soldiers stand guard at the front door when we reach the entrance area at the bottom of the stairs, including Harrison. I consider this a good thing. He won't allow any students to go outside tonight.

A stack of crates is piled at the side of the door. Each crate is marked with the Draven Industries insignia—Striker's company, the one he would control if his stepfather hadn't locked him up at Bloodwing.

The last delivery of supplies to the Academy was of uniforms and linen. There's no doubt in my mind that these crates carry weapons.

As we approach, Harrison steps forward and points toward the east wing. "The kitchen's that way."

He's certainly taking guarding the front door seriously.

I sense Striker sizing him up. Harrison is Raptor's height and build, but far more disciplined.

I breeze past Striker, veering out in front and between Harrison and him before turning in the direction Harrison points. "Thank you, Harrison."

His expression doesn't change. "A pleasure to help, ma'am."

Hmm. He calls me 'ma'am,' but every time he does, his voice carries a hint of challenge. I should keep walking, but I'm not sure how many opportunities I'll have to speak with him without Raptor or Hadrix around. I need to get a better handle on this guy's motives and state of mind. Or rather, I need to know if I can drive a wedge between him and his commanding officer.

I remain casual as I pause. "Oh, wait." I give him a smile, considering how I might best crack the military mask he wears and get at the man beneath. "I'd like to borrow your handgun."

It's a reckless request. Striker tenses beside me and I can only imagine the warning glare he's giving me right now. Thankfully, he stays put and turns his glare on the other soldiers in case they try to harass us.

Harrison's expression doesn't change. "It would be a bad idea for me to hand you a loaded weapon, ma'am."

"Why?" I ask. "Are you worried I'll take revenge for the deaths of my compliance officers?"

"Not at all."

"Then… are you concerned I'll use your weapon against you?"

Still, he isn't rattled. "You don't need a weapon to do a hell of a lot of damage, ma'am."

There it is. *Ma'am* again. With the same hint of challenge.

I try a different approach. I soften my voice and cast him a smile. "Then why?"

His gaze flickers to my lips, but he doesn't otherwise move. "Because you might hurt yourself until you know how to safely handle a weapon."

"So it's for my safety. Was killing Colby for my safety too?"

He appears thrown, a crease appearing in his forehead. "Who?"

My eyes narrow, hardening so fast, it must make his head spin. "My compliance officer."

He remains focused. His expression clears. "You mean Jarrod Peterson. The one with the snakeskin tattoos. No, it wasn't for your benefit. It was for the teenage girl he murdered before he took up his position here." His own eyes harden before he adds, "*Ma'am.*"

I consider him for another moment. My stare is sharp, but Harrison doesn't flinch. I've finally cracked the exterior, but what I found isn't what I expected.

My tone is scathing. "Do you really expect me to believe that Adrian Hadrix and his son, Raptor, killed Collin and Colby because of atrocities committed in the past?"

He shakes his head. "They didn't. They can't afford loose ends. But that's the only reason I was part of it."

"So you're a bad guy with a conscience?"

He steps up to me, but he doesn't hide the way his gaze flicks to Striker. "I never killed anyone who didn't deserve it."

"Then why the hell are you part of Hadrix's crew?"

He grinds his teeth. "None of your damn business."

I've gotten well and truly under his skin, but I only have more questions than answers.

I lower my voice, bringing the tension down a notch. "Continue to tell me the truth, and we won't have a problem."

I spin on my heel, sensing Striker relax beside me. I don't have to read his mind to know that he was prepared to jump to my defense if he had to—even though he knows damn well I don't need his help.

Striker draws level with me as I glide along the corridor. He sounds angry as he asks, "What was that about?"

"Harrison and Raptor don't like each other." I glance at Striker. "We can leverage that. But only if we engage Harrison and make him one of us."

He gives a short laugh. "I don't think he felt like one of us just then, Peyton."

"Probably not," I acknowledge. "But it's a start."

He gestures at the wood paneling ahead of us. "The kitchen is up ahead."

As it turns out, he didn't need to point it out. We stop at a wide-open space in the wall one door up from the dining room at the end of the hall. The door to the kitchen was previously concealed and spelled so we couldn't access it. They didn't want us feeding ourselves.

Now it gapes open.

Inside, the room looks like a commercial kitchen—multiple stainless steel work tables with stovetops, along with rows of pots and pans hanging along the wall. Five women busy themselves at one of the tables, preparing sandwiches.

Lucinda, Joseph, Ashley, and Lachlan sit on tall stools at the next table, facing the door. I was expecting more students, but maybe the others are on their way.

Lucinda jumps from her seat and rounds the table to give me a hug. She's earthy like her power and always the least afraid to show her emotions. I'm the polar opposite. She could have interpreted my physical barriers as cold and aloof, but Lucinda always saw through me.

I hug her back before she waves her hand at the opening behind us with a grin. "I did something about the hidden door. They won't keep us from food ever again."

As Striker takes glances from the broken door to Lucinda, the corner of his mouth hitches into a smile that, if I didn't know better, might be admiration. "You annihilated it."

"Yep." With a proud smile, Lucinda steps toward him as if she's going to hug him too.

Striker's smile vanishes, morphing into a *back off* scowl that freezes her mid-arm-swing. She arches her eyebrows in a pointed manner as she backs away. "You're welcome."

I interrupt them. "Where's everyone else?"

Ashley sighs where she remains seated at the table, her blonde hair lank down her back. A half-eaten sandwich remains on the plate in front of her. "After they heard the gunshots, most of the students wouldn't come out of their rooms. Bree offered to stay upstairs with them so they'd feel safe. She had a shower, so she's at full power right now."

As a siren, Bree can only access her power when she's in contact with water.

"She needs to carry bottled water with her at all times," I say.

"Way ahead of you," Ashley replies. "She came down here to get whatever plastic bottles she could find and fill with water before she went back upstairs."

"*And* she sang to the kitchen staff so they will give us food but not remember our conversation," Lucinda adds, guiding me to the nearest chair facing the others.

Bree's siren power is very similar to my compulsion power. I'm grateful that she's taken care of the kitchen staff so we don't need to worry about them.

Since my back will be to the door once I sit down, I allow my power to rise again, keeping my senses heightened so I'll know if anyone approaches.

"Good," I say, taking a seat as I greet Joseph and Lachlan.

Striker remains behind me, standing against the wall by the open door. I guess he's even less at home with this situation than I am. Planning is not our forte. We're both more comfortable reacting in the heat of the moment, making our decisions on instinct alone.

Lucinda jumps right in. "Our current sleeping arrangements make us vulnerable. We're isolated in separate bedrooms with no way to warn or help each other if there's an attack. We've spent years going to sleep at night fearing what could happen while we're sleeping and…" She takes a deep, shuddering breath. "I can finally do something about it."

Ashley closes her hand over Lucinda's in a comforting gesture.

I ask, "What do you propose?"

"I can use my power to take down some of the walls and rearrange them," Lucinda says. "Not the weight-bearing walls of course, but I've figured out that I can make two large rooms on either side of the corridor. That's four dorms. All the girls can move up to the guy's floor on the fourth level and sleep on one side of the corridor while they sleep on the other."

"That puts us the farthest from Hadrix's men as possible," Ashley adds. "We'll have a rotating guard throughout the night. We'll work in shifts, starting with those of us with powers."

Lachlan leans toward me. "We need your help to make it work."

"Of course." I pause as one of the women places a plate with a sandwich on it in front of me. She also hands one to Striker before going back to work at the other table. "What do you need?"

Lachlan takes a deep breath, his broad chest rising and falling. "We need you to discover our powers." He meets my eyes, his own open and honest. "I don't know what I am. Neither do most of the other students. Until I understand what I'm capable of, I can't protect—"

He glances at Ashley. He was always watching over her, quietly helping her without appearing to do so. In the fight with the compliance officers, she saved his life when an officer was about to break his neck.

"I can't protect anyone," he says. "And worse…" He clears his throat. "We're not stupid, Peyton. We know that you and Striker could break out of here in two seconds if you wanted to, assassins or no assassins. We know that *we* are keeping you here."

I start to object. "Lachlan… no… that's…"

Striker snaps at him. "Don't flatter yourself."

Lachlan grins at us. "The sooner we can defend ourselves, the sooner we can all get out of here and kick some assassin ass."

I smile. "Okay, then. I need to spend time with each of you. I'm not sure what kind of routine Hadrix intends to impose on us, but he can't demand every second of our day. I'll start with you, Lachlan. Tomorrow. Come see me the first chance you get. But you have to be willing to be honest with me. Answer my questions truthfully or I won't be able to help you."

He leans back in his seat, the tension in his face disappearing. "I can do that."

"We also need your help guarding the dorms until we have enough people who can take over that task," Lucinda says.

"Not a problem," I say. "Striker and I will take the first shift tonight."

Lucinda finally relaxes. "Thank you. Joseph and I will take the second shift. Ashley needs to sleep. Her power is more draining than mine."

The rings around Ashley's eyes are getting darker by the second. She sways in her seat, leaning into Lachlan. He wraps his arm around her shoulders and helps her stand. "I'm taking Ashley upstairs. Lucinda?"

She nods. "I need to get to work." She pauses in the act of rising. "One last thing. Do either of you know anything about that wand?"

I glance at Striker since he knows more about it than I do.

"Short version? It's called the White Wand," he says. "It belonged to Lady Tirelli. Basically, don't touch it or it will kill you."

Lucinda gives a short laugh. "Okay. I don't plan on it. But I need you to know that I can't disarm someone who's holding it."

"It's too powerful," Striker says with a nod.

"No, it's not that." Lucinda shakes her head. "I can't control it because it's not made of wood."

"What then?" I ask.

She shrugs. "Could be metal. Maybe resin. Possibly bone. I just wanted you to know."

She and the others rise, leaving Striker and me alone in the kitchen. He pulls up a seat beside me, places his plate on the table, and begins eating in silence. I focus on my food too.

Halfway through his sandwich, he suddenly puts it down. "Lucinda could change the attic for us. She could take down the wall between us and make a new room." He clears his throat, staring at his food. "For both of us."

It's a big step for him. And a new start for us. The wall between us isn't only a structural one. We're breaking down emotional walls too.

I try to keep my response casual. "That would be nice."

"Nice?" His gaze suddenly burns fiercely. "Nice is eating cake on Sundays. Nice is holding hands at a picnic. Don't think for one second that sharing a bed with me will be *nice*, Peyton."

I can't stop the smile breaking across my face. "I can't wait to find out."

I lean in and brush my lips across his, but I can't help the disappointed sigh I make as I pull away. "But not tonight."

"We have to guard the new dorm." He strokes my hair from my face, his fingertips lingering against my cheek. "Peyton—"

Beyond him, one of the women suddenly drops the butter knife she's using. The implement thuds onto the table. She stares at her hands as if she's not sure what she's doing.

"Bree's commands are wearing off," I whisper. I have no idea where the kitchen staff's loyalties lie, but I don't want to stick around to find out. I've had enough conflict for today.

Striker inclines his head at the door. "Let's get out of here."

We slide off our seats and step into the corridor.

I pull up short.

Kaitlyn peels herself off the opposite wall. She's changed into tight black pants and a plunging V-neck halter top, but she reeks of wood smoke and flecks of ash rest in her hair.

I sigh. So much for avoiding conflict. I thought my power would let me detect her approach. I shiver as I realize how human I feel right now, how tired and drained. I need to rest and recover from everything that happened today.

Even though Striker bristles beside me, I make up my mind to continue walking, taking his hand and tugging him along the corridor.

Kaitlyn steps right into my path. Her voice takes on a mocking tone as she says, "You haven't slept together yet." She side-eyes Striker with a snide smile. "How precious."

She must have heard the end of my conversation with Striker and drawn conclusions from it.

I force myself to relax, my heartbeat calming as I lower my voice. "I could reach out and snap your neck, Kaitlyn. Get out of my way or I won't be responsible for what happens next."

The faintest crease mars her forehead. The faintest worry enters her eyes. "You think you're invincible, but you're not," she says. "I *will* find a way to destroy you."

"That's doubtful," I say.

The female assassin with green eyes is the only person who ever killed a Fury. I'm not sure how she did it. I saw the memory of her encounter with the Fury when I picked up the Fury's whip, but I didn't see how the Fury died.

Boots thud quickly along the corridor, breaking the tension.

Harrison appears behind Kaitlyn. He grabs her arm, his hand tightening fast. "Kaitlyn. You need to come away."

She whirls on him. "This has nothing to do with you."

"Like hell it doesn't."

She tries to wrench out of his grip. "Fuck off, Harrison!"

He doesn't release her. His expression is far from deadpan, real emotion showing. I'm surprised by what I see. He looks deeply hurt.

"Really?" he asks. "That's all you've got to say to me?"

She sucks in a breath as if she's going to give him a tongue-lashing, but her shoulders suddenly slump. "Okay... whatever you say."

She lets him pull her away down the corridor.

I stay rooted to the spot for as long as it takes for them to disappear from sight along the far wing of the building.

"What the hell was that?" I ask Striker when he draws level with me.

He wears a perplexed expression. "They must have history."

"But what kind?"

He meets my eyes. "The kind that means we need to avoid them both."

8. STRIKER DRAVEN

The night passes without incident. We arrive upstairs in time to finish watching Lucinda work. It's like watching an artist create a masterpiece.

Walls come apart, a pile of boards grows in the hallway between wings, and the rooms on either side of the corridor open up.

Lucinda behaves like a mother hen around the other students and now that she's more powerful than most of them, they follow her. They sure as hell avoid me.

I take up guard with Peyton at the corridor's entrance, leaning against the wall while she takes up position on the other side.

Deep into the night, well after the lights have turned off elsewhere, I cast a glance at Peyton, only to discover that she's half-asleep. She jolts as if my gaze was a physical push. Not my intended outcome.

She takes a quick breath, blinking rapidly. "I wasn't sleeping."

I murmur into the silence. "You're too tired for this."

"So is Lucinda," she retorts. "She just rearranged the entire west wing. The longer I stay here, the more sleep she gets."

Peyton's stubborn, but I knew that. I persist. "You need to rest."

She fires back at me. "You died today. I'm not falling asleep before you do."

Her damn pride. She's swaying on the spot by the time I head along the corridor to wake Joseph.

The beds inside the guys' dorm are pushed up against the wall to the left, lined up in a row—eight in this room and seven in the other. Joseph's is positioned at the front of the room nearest to the door.

They've chosen to leave the curtains open so it's easier to see in the moonlight.

I bend and grip his shoulder, quickly planting my flat palm on the other side of his chest to subdue him if he doesn't remember where he is and why I'm waking him.

He lurches upward, his power surging. His skin flushes indigo blue, his dangerous eyes meeting mine. He grabs my wrist, twists, and prepares to put me on my ass before he recognizes me.

His voice is guttural, his power not diminishing even now that he knows it's me. The draugr are undead. He's impervious to death like Peyton is—unless someone deprives him of his head.

"Easy," I say, keeping my voice low. "It's your shift."

Joseph finally releases my arm to rub his eyes. "I'll wake Lucinda and meet you out there."

I turn on my heel and return to Peyton to wait. She leans against the wall, her hair spreading out against it. The moonlight streams across her body but leaves her face in shadow. If I didn't know better, I'd wager she was asleep on her feet.

I don't draw attention to her as Lucinda emerges, dragging her hands across her bleary eyes. "Damn. It feels like I went to sleep only a few seconds ago."

Joseph casts a gaze across Lucinda's messy hair and old, white T-shirt. She's wearing incredibly short shorts under it and he gives her a crooked smile.

She blushes and clears her throat, suddenly all business. "Okay, Draven. We're good here."

I catch the sideways glance and smile she gives Joseph, but my focus is on Peyton now. She hasn't spoken, confirming my suspicion that she's dead to the world. I cross the distance and scoop her into my arms. Her hair falls across my arms, and her face turns into my chest.

I carry her the entire flight of stairs to the attic before fear rakes over me like daggers.

Standing between our two rooms, my feet are leaden. I don't want to put her in her room where the bed is nothing more than a mattress, but I'm not sure how she'll react if she wakes up in my bed. I vowed I'd take careful steps and I didn't ask her what she wanted.

Fuck it.

I'm not spending another night without her. I paced my room for hours night after night while she slept in the room next door. She's sleeping with me from now on.

Nudging the door closed behind me, I awkwardly pull back the bed covers before I lay her carefully on the near side of the bed so she doesn't feel trapped against the wall in the morning.

I brush the hair from her face as her head sinks into my pillow. She draws her knees a little to her chest but otherwise doesn't move.

Damn it, Peyton.

I want to rage at her for not fighting me. She's completely vulnerable right now. I could be anyone. I could have taken her anywhere. With any intentions.

Staying fully clothed, I slide in behind her, wedging myself against the wall before I pull up the blankets, keeping my distance.

Her breathing remains even. Calm.

I close my eyes, but sleep is impossible. Her scent is even more alluring while she sleeps. I sense every small move she makes, the rise and fall of her chest, her soft exhalations.

I press my hands into the bed rather than reach for her, but the more I try to calm my heart, the faster it beats.

Sudden movement causes my eyes to fly open.

Peyton turns toward me, carefully shifting beneath the blanket.

Her eyes are wide open, a soft smile on her lips that makes my heart suddenly stop. She edges toward me, brushing her fingertips across my forehead, gently drawing her hand down my face so I have no choice but to close my eyes beneath her touch.

"Stop thinking," she whispers, pressing a light kiss to my lips. "And for goodness' sake, stop keeping your hands to yourself."

I don't move. "How long have you been awake?"

"Long enough to gouge your eyes out if you left me in my room."

My beast rushes to the surface, annihilating whatever shred of inhibition remains.

"Be careful what you wish for." I drag her toward me, hooking her upper leg around me before my hands slide beneath her shirt, finding her back and pulling her toward me so her chest presses to mine.

"Sleep," I order her.

She settles against me and this time when I close my eyes, I fall asleep.

Peyton and I are tangled around each other by the time we wake. She stretches against me before settling back into the crook of my arm.

My heart is quiet.

We did nothing more than sleep, but somehow I'm calmer, more whole than I've felt in a long time.

My thoughts are simple, uncomplicated.

She's warm. Soft. Part of my life.

After a minute, her breathing changes. More alert. Despite her closed eyes. "What time is it?"

I refuse to move. Refuse to break this moment. "Don't care."

Her eyes open a little, sleepy and serene. "We missed our morning run."

"Still don't care."

She relaxes into me again, but a second later, she's wide awake. "We *will* care if Hadrix takes it out on the others."

I groan, fighting the reality that's quickly rushing back in. "Dammit, Peyton. Don't wake my conscience."

She edges up to me and smiles against my mouth. "I didn't think you had a conscience."

My beast hijacks my vocal chords, growling. "It's growing on me."

Peyton pulls away from me to study my eyes. Whatever she sees, she smiles before she plants a light kiss on the corner of my mouth.

She shivers. "Ooh, sandpaper bristles. You need to shave."

She slips from my arms to rise from the bed.

I rub my chin—she's right—before I slide my legs over the edge of the bed and check the brightness of the sunlight glowing through the crack between the curtains. It must be 6 A.M. already. "No time, remember? You'll have to put up with them."

Pausing in the doorway, she gives me a smile before she stretches again. "Meet you out here in five minutes."

She darts away before I can reply.

I'm still dressed in yesterday's clothes so I pull on fresh ones —workout shorts and a sleeveless shirt—and head to the bathroom, meeting Peyton on her way out. Her hair is tied up in a messy ponytail. She's opted for workout gear like me.

My stomach growls, but we don't have time for food. The wide windows lining this side of the attic corridor give us a full view of the yard below and, judging by the number of students already milling around, it looks like we'll be the last to arrive.

As soon as I'm out of the bathroom, we hurry down the stairs and exit the building.

It looks like all of Hadrix's men are here, standing at intervals around the yard close to the fence line. I'm not sure whether they realize that if they take a single step back, they'll electrocute themselves on the fence. I don't plan to enlighten them.

Hadrix has positioned himself on the raised combat mat with Harrison and Vulture. I don't see Raptor or Kaitlyn anywhere, which is both a relief and a concern. I'd rather they were firmly in my sights.

Among the students, Lucinda and Joseph are both bleary-eyed. When Peyton offered to take the first shift last night I don't think she realized she was taking the easier shift. Both Lucinda and Joseph were woken from deep sleep and will have to function all day before they can rest again.

I make a mental note to watch them both for signs of fatigue that could jeopardize their safety.

Ashley at least looks much better today, the rings around her eyes faded. She clutches an opaque red scarf in her hand and begins tying it around her eyes, obscuring her sight.

Bree, also, is completely alert. She's somehow procured a small leather satchel, which she's wearing slung over her shoulder, a bottle of water peeking out of it. Her aquamarine eyes are clear blue in the sun, but when I look closer, the color in her irises ripples like waves.

When she catches me looking at her, she gives me a shark-toothed smile that would scare the pants off any rational person.

I snarl in return, allowing my incisors to descend. She grins before her gaze passes to Ryan. Like Lachlan, he doesn't know what his power is yet. He approaches her from the other side of the field, taking up position beside her.

Hadrix's sarcastic drawl forces my attention forward. "Good of you to join us, Draven. Price."

Harrison steps forward to take up position on Hadrix's left side while Vulture stands on his right. The silence thickens around us, but Hadrix waits another beat before he begins.

"From now on, your daily routine will be divided between learning practical skills and gaining theoretical knowledge. Your mornings will alternate between learning hand-to-hand combat and weaponry, starting with combat today and weaponry tomorrow. Harrison and I will take those lessons.

"Your afternoons will be devoted to theory. Vulture will continue to teach you anatomy. Raptor will teach you about the assassins: their code, how they think, and their weaknesses. Mallard, who is still with us"—he gives a smirk that tells me Mallard had a much worse night than we did—"will continue to teach you about the history of your powers."

Hadrix folds his arms across his chest. "Academy maintenance will still be a thing. This place isn't going to clean itself." He peers across at us. "Okay, then. Pair up. I want to see what you're capable of."

Peyton nudges me carefully. "I'm going with Lucinda. She's tired and I don't want Raptor to pick on her."

I give her a puzzled look. "Raptor? Don't you mean 'Hadrix'?"

She doesn't hear me. She's already dashing toward her friend.

Nobody will willingly pair up with me and that's for the best. There are an odd number of guys, so I can remain the odd one out, but... I also take Peyton's point. Hadrix knows that Lucinda and Joseph control their powers. It doesn't take a genius to see that they're tired. He also knows that the other students view Lucinda and Joseph as a line of protection—even more than Peyton and me. It's pretty obvious from the way the students avoid me that they don't trust me.

If Hadrix wants to dominate our group, he'll do everything he can to make Lucinda and Joseph look weak and vulnerable, not the protectors they need to be.

Joseph sighs when I stride up to him, shaking his head at me. "I don't have the energy to fight you today, man."

"That's why I'm picking you."

He scowls, muttering beneath his breath. "Fuck you."

I stand my ground. I could let him think I plan to beat him bloody while he's low—it's what I usually do—but I decide to take a chance on revealing my motives.

I keep my voice down as the other students move around us. "Think about it, Joseph. Who are they going to try to crush first? If they can destroy the strongest defenders among us, then they can control everyone else. If you fight one of the other students, it makes you look like a bully not a protector. If Hadrix makes you fight him or Harrison, they'll find a dirty way to beat you and make you look weak. I'm your best choice."

He remains still for a beat. I can tell from the way he studies the ground that he's thinking about it, and then—

He spins and shoves me in the chest, knocking me off-balance. His voice rises to a shout that makes the other students jump. "What the hell did you say to me, Draven?"

I regain my balance, bouncing back and getting in his face. We're the same height, although his power will allow him to increase his height and size, but that's the last thing he should do while he's exhausted.

Raising my voice, I knock shoulders with him hard enough

to bruise us both. "I'll wipe the mat with your worthless body, Simmons."

Hadrix calls from the combat mat. "Looks like we have two volunteers. Get up here."

I catch Peyton's confused look as I stride toward the mat with Joseph.

Her eyes are wide, her mouth turned down. She's confused *and* disappointed. *Oomph.* Her expression drives a knife into my chest.

I nearly miss a step. *Damn her.* A single look can squeeze the breath out of my lungs.

She stands beside Lucinda, her hand firmly clutching Lucinda's arm, visibly restraining her friend. Lucinda strains forward, her concern for Joseph written all over her face. The growing bond between them is undeniable, but the last thing Joseph needs is Lucinda coming to his aid. He needs to make a statement on his own here and now.

I give Peyton a sharp shake of my head, not sure how she'll interpret it, hoping she'll understand she shouldn't get involved.

She leans into Lucinda with a whisper as we pass them. I don't hear what she says, but Lucinda's gaze becomes wary instead of stab-me-through-the-eye angry.

Joseph takes the steps to the mat ahead of me and strides right up to Harrison, who remains next to Hadrix. Vulture has already descended to the grass.

Joseph's voice carries a hint of power as he addresses Harrison. "If you don't want your blood on the mat, get the hell off it, man."

Harrison inclines his head, unflustered. He sidesteps without a word and skirts around us, his dark eyes hooded.

Hadrix is slower to move, eyeing us, as if he's still determined to remain in control of this fight.

"You too, old man," I snarl at him.

Yesterday, Peyton took the brunt of dealing with Hadrix. I

need to get a handle on Hadrix's strengths and weaknesses—the chinks in his armor—to figure out what makes him tick.

He whirls to me. His lips are suddenly compressed so hard, they turn white.

Power rises behind his eyes, a glint of wild growing in his expression. The sudden strength growing around him makes the hairs on the back of my neck prickle.

I had him pegged as completely human, but now I'm not so sure. He doesn't have an aura, so I'm not sure what that makes him. I definitely don't want to contemplate the possibility that he could be magically repressed like us.

"You'd do well to focus on the fight in front of you, Draven," he says.

I stand my ground, staring him right in the eye. "I always do."

A muscle in his jaw ticks, but he takes a deep breath and I have to admire the way he gets his temper under control, quickly striding away from us and off the mat. He's definitely much more controlled than his volatile son.

I turn back to Joseph.

Joseph's fist flies straight at my face.

Smack.

He hits my chin like a ton of metal, stunning me and knocking me backward. My knees quit functioning and I can't avoid his follow-up fist that cuts up my shoulder, pain blasting through my upper arm and chest.

Damn. He's way stronger than he used to be.

My self-preservation instincts kick in and I lunge left, drawing on my power as I hit the mat and tumble. I rebound back to my feet, my legs functioning again with the influx of my hellhound's strength.

Joseph bounces on the balls of his feet opposite me, grinning, self-satisfied, fists up. "C'mon, Draven."

I return his grin with a challenging snarl. Until now, only Peyton has matched me on the mat. I don't think Lucinda,

Ashley, or Bree could match my strength in a fight—their power doesn't lie in combat—but Joseph definitely can.

Finally.

I spit blood onto the mat before I rip off my shirt. I release the careful hold I keep on my aggression, the hunger that I feed every time I throw myself against the electric fence, the anger that demands to be fed.

I let go of caution and reason and give in to my inner nature that craves destruction.

Joseph pitches his shirt into the grass. His grin grows sharper. He senses the shift in my aggression as I stride toward him, but he doesn't back down. He steps forward to meet me, the darkness gathering in his eyes.

The same darkness that lives in me.

I feint to avoid his swinging fist, ducking and planting a hit to his stomach that forces the air out of his lungs. I follow up with a throat punch with my right hand and a quick clip against his temple with my left, spinning him off his feet, but he uses the momentum to swing back at me with a hard kick in my side that throws me off-balance.

Dodging his next fist, I duck under his arm, switching positions and aiming a kick at his face.

He lurches backward, but I rage at him, knocking us both off our feet. We gain air before we tumble to the edge of the mat.

Joseph retaliates with superhuman speed, clipping my head with his fist before I can get up. I'm barely on my knees before he lands rapid hits to my face and shoulders.

Making it to our feet, we trade blows to every inch of our bodies: faces, chests, and sides. Warm liquid drips down my cheeks and chin. Even the skin across my shoulders is split and bleeding.

I'm going to have hellish bruises. But so is he.

Our punches are hard and bone-crunching, but neither of us

breaks. I'm vaguely aware of the soldiers wincing as we hit each other with blows that would crush a normal man's skull.

I'm also aware of the increasing scowl on Hadrix's face. He comes across all calm, but there's a deadly warrior hiding beneath his façade, a cold killer who put a gun to Colby's head and pulled the trigger.

He called us warriors, but I don't think he realized how strong we actually are.

With a roar, Joseph lands a final hit to my cheek that knocks me to the mat. I smile as my head buzzes, pushing up with my arms.

I ward him off with a raised hand. "You've made your point, brother."

Dragging air into his rapidly rising chest, Joseph looms over me. I take a chance to check the other students. They saw what Joseph could do yesterday, so they knew he was strong, unbeatable, but I guess they thought I'd crush him anyway, since that's what I always do.

Now, they're looking at him with trust and belief. They will follow him and Lucinda, and it's a selfish relief to me.

My place is not out the front, making decisions that affect other's lives. My place is in the darkness, waiting to rip our enemies apart.

I take the hand Joseph offers me. As I rise to my feet, I draw him toward me in a warrior's hold. "It's up to you now, Simmons. You have to lead them. You call the shots."

His forehead creases in confusion. "What about you?"

I take a deep breath and level my gaze with his. "When you need a killer, let me know."

His smile fades, his expression becoming grim. "I understand."

Maybe he does. I didn't mistake the darkness I saw in his eyes when we fought—death is at the center of his power—but unlike me, he will keep his darkness at bay.

His controlled behavior in the past tells me he won't feed his darkness like I feed mine.

He swings away from me and heads to the edge of the mat. I follow, but my foot hasn't even hit the top step when a scream makes my head snap up.

Peyton streaks toward me, her claws descended, her eyes crimson red with rage. "Striker!"

Confusion floods me. She must be angry that Joseph and I beat the hell out of each other. But Joseph won. He's fine and so am I, and I had my reasons.

She'll understand once I explain it to her—

She screams again, her cheeks pale. "Striker! *Move!*"

Her gaze is fixated on a spot beside me, but… there's nothing there.

A quick glance tells me Joseph is as confused as I am. So are the other students.

But I trust her and she's screaming at me to get out of the way. No way in hell am I going to ignore her.

My muscles bunch, ready to jump off the steps.

She launches herself at the empty space beside me, claws reaching, voice screaming, but before I can get out of her way, her claws slice across my neck.

9. PEYTON PRICE

I won't make it in time.

All my speed, all my power… useless.

Five paces from Striker's location, Raptor launches himself into the air, but Striker doesn't seem to see him.

Neither does anyone else and it's scaring the hell out of me.

Raptor was prowling around the combat area when Striker and I arrived. I thought he was going after Lucinda because he was standing near her when we first arrived, but since then he's paced around the combat mat, avoiding the other students while Striker and Joseph fought.

The harder they battled each other, the deeper the scowl grew on Raptor's face.

As soon as Striker hit the mat and yielded to Joseph, Raptor strode toward the steps as if he was going to confront them.

But it wasn't until Striker stepped down that I saw Raptor's dagger.

Raptor's feet leave the ground an impossible distance from the combat mat. He launches himself through the air at Striker, his dagger raised, both hands on the hilt, perfectly aimed to slice through Striker's throat.

Raptor's focus is unbreakable, his biceps bunching, his blade so sharp, it glints. And Striker…

Striker just stands there, staring at me, waiting to be slaughtered.

Wild thoughts shriek through my mind. Thoughts I don't have time to vocalize.

Doesn't Striker see him? Why is he just standing there? How does Raptor have the speed and strength to jump like that?

I'm screaming something. I don't know what.

My power rushes through me.

I push off the ground and leap, the air rushing around me, my claws fully descended.

I smash into Raptor just as his blade reaches Striker's neck.

Just in time.

Raptor roars as he flies off course. He tumbles through the air, impossibly agile despite my hit. He lands neatly on his feet on the mat, still clutching his dagger, adjusting his grip as his gaze snaps to me.

He rises up, focused on me now. "How the hell did you do that?"

I come to a ragged stop several paces away from him on the mat, regaining my balance slower than he does.

As much as I'd like to say I've mastered levitating, I'm not there yet, but my concern right now is for Striker, not my own ungainly landing.

Spinning on my heel toward Striker, I'm ready to race back to him, terrified that he's hurt. I healed him yesterday, but I don't know if I can do it again.

He clutches his throat, blood seeping between his fingertips.

My heart misses a beat until he removes his hand.

It's only a shallow nick across the side of his neck.

Striker stares at the blood on his hand and then at me. His voice becomes an angry growl. "Peyton? Why the hell did you do that?"

The way he looks at me...

He thinks *I* hurt him, probably with my claws as I flew past.

I don't know what the hell is going on, but it's clear that nobody can see Raptor except me. Even Hadrix and Vulture appear confused, exchanging looks as they stride toward the mat with Harrison close behind.

Hadrix gestures at the men around the arena, who pull out their weapons. He's taking my threat from yesterday seriously, though, because they don't aim at me.

Damn, they're preparing for it, though.

Somehow, Raptor has made himself invisible to all of them and now they think I've gone crazy.

Striker advances on me with a dangerous glint in his eye. "Peyton..."

It's unsafe for me to take my eyes off Raptor, but I need Striker to listen to me. I throw my arm up into the air between us, leveling my gaze with his. "Stop. Please."

Striker pulls up sharp, his power flaring in his eyes, his chest rising and falling rapidly. The visible tension in his body tells me he's fighting every instinct right now to grab me.

He's fighting every learned behavior, which is to attack first and ask questions later, that uncertainty calls for retaliation, not reason. The fact that he stopped at all tells me he wants to listen.

"Trust me," I say, keeping my voice low. "Stay. Back."

I can't risk looking at the other students—it's risky enough dividing my attention between Striker and Raptor—but I sense the rising stress levels among them.

Also a strange sort of buzz as Striker continues to stay put.

He has never respected anyone's wishes before, never obeyed a command. To see him do so now must be surprising to say the least.

But if they think I've somehow tamed the beast... *Hah.* He's only staying where he is because he's smart enough to know there's something he can't see.

Raptor's lips are curved into a derisive smile that fades as I return my attention to him.

"If you can see me, I'll cut out your eyes," he says, striding forward, his knife ready.

"Like hell you will." He cut me up once. I won't let him do it again.

He slashes at me, but my reflexes kick in hard. I block his downward cut, my arm thudding against his forearm, but he pulls back rapidly and slashes low instead, aiming for my stomach this time.

I deflect again and duck when he swings his other fist at my head, his blade arm flying across the space where my face used to be.

His movements are faster than humanly possible, his knife arm cutting through the air with a speed I can hardly follow.

What's worse, he's pushed me closer to Striker's location.

Raptor swings away from me, thrusting the blade straight at Striker's heart. My foot connects with Raptor's torso just in time, knocking him off course.

Striker responds by crouching low, making himself a harder target. If he can't see Raptor, I can't begin to imagine how this looks right now, but the shift in Striker's expression, the way his gaze moves wildly around the mat, tells me he's trying to see what I see.

Raptor laughs again. He flips the knife, spinning it in the air, catching it as he leaps forward. He slashes at me again and again, this time cutting my arms and cheeks.

The wounds heal instantly, but they sting badly. It's only because I'm moving fast that he can't stab deep.

There's no way I can avoid his blade. He's too fast and I haven't been trained in knife fights.

Hell, I have no choice but to make a sacrifice. I stop moving just as the blade glints across my chest, tearing through my shirt, scraping from my shoulder to my abdomen.

A scream rips from my throat, but I focus only on the knife's location.

My hand snaps out. I grab Raptor's fist, holding fast as my wound heals.

He was always strong, but now he's practically rabid, strong enough to flip me into the air if I don't immobilize him fast.

I squeeze tightly, sensing his knucklebones shift beneath my hold. He kicks and knees me in the stomach, but I retaliate hard.

My other fist connects with his face, cracking against his chin in a hit that would have broken his jaw before today. I hit him again. And again. His skin splits, bleeding, but he barely blinks, snarling at me.

He takes a swipe at me with his free hand—his left hand— and this time I catch sight of the ring he's wearing.

It's wide at the top, crafted into the shape of two silver wings. The magic in it is scorching as it connects with my cheek. It's as strong as the magic in the White Wand. A deadly force.

With a scream, I release my claws into his knife hand, ripping through skin and tendons, forcing him to drop the blade.

The dagger hits the mat and Striker shouts, tensing as if he's going to make a lunge for it. Now that Raptor's not holding it, I guess the knife is finally visible.

I shove Raptor away from me and kick the blade toward Striker.

Striker snatches it up, shouting, "Tell me what to do, Peyton!"

Raptor regains his balance, nursing his hand and examining the cuts across it. Despite their depth, he doesn't seem perturbed by them.

He gives me a grin a moment before his ring glints.

I can only assume that Raptor has made himself visible again because Striker's eyes suddenly widen, focused on Raptor's position now.

"Raptor," Striker growls.

At the same time, the other students gasp and Hadrix pauses on the step behind Striker.

Striker can't see Hadrix's expression—his cold smile—or the way Hadrix tips his chin at his son, who smiles back at him.

Striker quickly crosses the distance to me, gripping the knife so hard, his knuckles turn white. My blood is still on the blade.

He takes up position close behind and to my right before he leans in close to me, murmuring into my ear. "I'll kill him."

I tilt toward Striker, our sides connecting, drawing on his heat as I access my power to heal the wound the ring left across my cheek. My brow furrows when the pain continues and a trickle of blood slides down my face.

"Not if I kill him first," I whisper beneath my breath.

Hadrix stops in the middle of the mat, carefully positioned between us and Raptor. He gives Striker a hard warning glance before his features settle into an expression of military control.

"Well, I wasn't expecting you to begin your lesson this morning," he says, inclining his head at Raptor. "But it's never too soon to demonstrate the power of the assassins."

Raptor steps up to his father's side. "Invisibility is an assassin's greatest skill. They call it 'blurring.' You won't see them coming." He turns his grin on Striker. "Even your strongest can be killed."

Striker tenses beside me. The wound across his neck has stopped bleeding, but it's a reminder of how close Raptor came to killing him. Striker curses beneath his breath. I suspect that he chose to fight Joseph to prove how strong they are—how strong we all are—that we can't be broken.

Now Raptor has shattered his show of strength like it's a child's illusion.

"No," I say, raising my voice. "It won't happen."

Raptor's face reddens, but I ignore him, turning to the students. "I saw through this so-called 'blur.' So can you. I'm sure that's what Raptor intends to teach us." Turning to Hadrix, I give him a hard stare. "That's why you're here. Correct?"

The older man casts me a derisive smile. "Striker and Joseph will go with Harrison, who will get you started on drills. The next two combatants, to the mat!"

I take hold of Striker's arm and pull him from the platform.

He leans toward me before we join Joseph. "What just happened?"

"Raptor has an assassin's ring. It must have been in that damn box that the White Wand is kept in." I ignore my stinging wound as we move. It still hasn't healed, no matter how much my power rises. "The ring must be the thing he said he needed yesterday."

Tugging Striker to a halt as we reach Joseph, I address both of them. "Raptor's strength is beyond human now. Be careful about taking him on. I don't know how to tell if you can't see him. I need you to give me a signal if you lose sight of him."

Striker nods and taps his temple with the forefinger of his left hand. It's the same finger on which Raptor wears the assassin's ring. "Like this."

"Okay," I say.

Harrison appears behind them and further talk isn't possible. As I turn away from them, I catch the way Harrison looks at me, his brown eyes containing a hint of danger.

I quickly glance down. *Am I flashing everyone?* My shirt is cut across the middle and so is one bra cup, but it's intact enough that my breast isn't visible.

I scowl at him, expecting him to be on his way with Striker and Joseph, but he pauses for a beat. "You're still bleeding."

Striker turns back to me, flames rising in his eyes as he focuses on my cheek.

"I'm fine," I announce, firmly turning and striding away from them.

I'm determined to keep a close eye on the other students, especially Lucinda in her tired state. With every step away from Striker, my wound begins to knit, the skin sealing and the flesh healing.

Fear fills me with every step I take.

I didn't heal while Striker was touching me.

He was right. Something's wrong with my healing power and it has everything to do with him.

10. PEYTON PRICE

Raptor remains visible for the remainder of the lesson.

I keep close to the mat as the other students demonstrate their combat abilities.

Hadrix seems less and less pleased as we continue to show him just how skilled we are. I spent my first five months at the Academy learning as much as I could from Striker, and it looks like he taught us well.

Still, every time I casually glance in Striker's direction, where a growing number of students practice the moves that Harrison is demonstrating, Striker appears to be quietly taking on board the new instruction.

It tells me just how seriously he's taking our new situation. He won't let arrogance blind him to the possibility that he can learn his enemy's moves.

As more students join Harrison, he sends them off to work with the other soldiers one-on-one, which is a new approach. We're used to practicing new moves against each other.

It makes me wary that the soldiers will try to undermine the students, so I keep a close watch, dividing my attention between the students fighting on the mat and the ones practicing with the soldiers.

It's impossible to relax, even though the soldiers appear to be all business, talking through each move and taking the time to correct their students' technique.

Striker himself is paired off with a burly guy with multiple tattoos in the shapes of bones across his arms. So far, the soldier is holding his own, but that's only because Striker's following orders.

Every fight on the mat is between girls or guys, but there are fifteen of each, leaving Lachlan and I standing at the end. I could argue that I've already demonstrated my skills because of my confrontation with Raptor, but that leaves nobody for Lachlan to fight, other than Hadrix or Raptor.

Before Raptor can force Lachlan to fight him, I tip my chin at Lachlan. "You and me."

I haven't interacted with Lachlan much. I told him to come and see me today so I can help him discover his power.

He's quiet. A careful presence around Ashley. The gender segregation at the Academy was so strict, he barely talked to her, let alone with me. Even Joseph and Lucinda haven't had a decent conversation.

But love can grow from actions, more than from words, and it's clear that Lachlan cares for Ashley the way Joseph cares for Lucinda.

Lachlan gives me a laugh as he removes his shirt and approaches the steps. "I should probably yield right now."

From across the grass, Ashley watches him from the outskirts of Harrison's group. It's hard to reassure her from this distance that I don't intend to do any damage. At least… not yet.

I arch an eyebrow at Lachlan. "You never know. You could surprise me."

When I first saw him with Joseph and Ryan, I picked Lachlan for a compliance officer in the making. He's not a small guy;

he's broad-shouldered and chiseled. He doesn't have Striker's brutality, but from what I've observed of his fight moves in the past, his fists carry weight.

His gray eyes crinkle at the corners, suddenly light. I suspect he actually has a great sense of humor, but this place has beaten it out of him. "We'll see."

We ascend to the combat mat under Hadrix's watchful eye. Raptor stays off to the side. Vulture has long since left the combat area. Now that most of the students are training with Harrison, Raptor seems impatient.

I guess he's itching to tell us more about how the assassins will cut us to shreds.

Once we're on the mat, though, Lachlan seems more uncertain than before. His brow furrows and he scratches his chin.

I look at him expectantly. I was going to let him get in a hit, but now I'm wondering if I'll have to make the first move.

He clenches his fist but unclenches it again, shaking his head at me and taking a step back. "You know... my brain tells me that you're not going to get hurt no matter what I do. But my heart reminds me what my mom taught me."

"What's that?"

"Never disrespect a woman. That includes hitting her."

Damn. If I met Lachlan in a normal life, he'd be the honorable guy I'd trust with my heart and body, but we aren't in a normal world here.

I stride right up to him, keeping my voice to a whisper. "You see Raptor circling, right? You see the assassin's magic he controls? Either you fight me or he's going to rip you to shreds. So you can choose to get bloodied up by him or you can fight me knowing that you won't hurt me or disrespect me. Which will it be?"

Still, he hesitates.

I persist. "Fighting me doesn't mean anything, Lachlan. I'm

not a woman, I'm a Fury. But if you ever hurt Ashley, now that's when you and I would have a problem—"

My head spins as his fist cracks against my temple.

He looms over me as I lurch to the side, his expression a dark cloud of anger. "That's for suggesting I'd ever lay a hand on her."

I smother a smile. His reaction confirmed for me that he won't choose violence to defend himself, but he will choose it to defend others.

On the ground, Hadrix wears a smile, so I'm guessing the sight of someone beating me up makes him happy.

I duck Lachlan's next swing and he darts out of the way of mine.

Keeping my voice low, I say, "Tell me about your favorite childhood memory."

His forehead crinkles into a bemused expression as he bounces on the balls of his feet, ready for my next move. "Really?"

"Really."

He narrows his eyes at me, remaining focused on my fists. "Camping with my mom."

"What was the best part?"

His fists dart out, a neat combination of blows that I dance around to avoid. Rolling his shoulders, he tries again with a different combination, this time answering my question at the same time, as if he's testing whether I'll be distracted enough for him to get in a solid hit.

"Putting out the campfire."

"Huh." Not what I expected. My eyes widen as he nearly clobbers my nose. Darting to the side just in time, I ask, "Not the fire itself?"

"No." He pauses for a moment, rolling his shoulders. "That single line of smoke rising from the fire after it's doused. The fire's dead, but the smoke remains. Sort of like a memory, don't you think?"

"Maybe." What's more interesting to me is the way Lachlan's face changes when he talks about it.

Every time I looked for clues about another student's power, I started with their eyes. Lucinda's reminded me of tree bark, and Ashley's filled with swarming threads like snakes. I need to get closer to Lachlan to see his.

I suddenly go on the attack, the kind of rapid shift of tactic that Striker would employ to take his opponent unawares.

Harnessing my full strength and levitating at the same time, I hit Lachlan full in the face, following up with a roundhouse kick that sends him sprawling.

He tries to push up off the mat, but I drop onto him, straddling and pinning him.

"Peyton," he snarls, blood running down his face. "What the hell?"

For a second, his eyes turn white, filling with wisps of smoke the color of pristine snow.

Just as quickly, they clear again.

There it is. His power. But smoke could mean many things. He could be a fire mage or some kind of elemental…

Maybe I just have to light the fire.

I hit him again—completely unjustified and unwarranted— and this time, pure rage floods his face. He grabs my hands to stop me. He's stronger than before, his eyes filling and swirling with smoke.

Still, he doesn't hit back, so I lean down to him, snapping out my claws despite his hold on my wrists. "You couldn't defend Ashley yesterday. She would have died if it were left up to you."

"No." His gray eyes harden and soften at the same time. His skin flushes gray like the color of ash and his voice becomes a threatening whisper. "Nobody will ever hurt Ashley again."

His fingers squeeze around my wrist, unbearably tight as he jerks me forward, down, onto him, onto…

Pure, freezing cold air surrounds me as I fall through nothing.

My vision blurs, covered with white, as if I'm falling through a cloud. I try to breathe, but my lungs fill with acidic smoke that burns me from the inside.

I claw at the ground, my sense of place and time completely displaced when I land hard on the mat, my knees knocking its surface and my palms planting in front of me.

But Lachlan… he's not there, not beneath me anymore.

A large shadow spreads across me, blocking out the sun.

I twist and freeze, remaining crouched on the mat, trying to expel the smoke I inhaled.

Lachlan towers over me, nearly unrecognizable, his skin dusted with ash.

Gray smoke curls around his silhouette, a shimmering haze in the sunlight. His workout clothing is stretched tight over muscles that have doubled in size—not that he was a small guy to begin with.

His eyes are filled with white, so I can only tell he's looking at me from the angle of his head.

I stare up at him, suddenly registering how quiet it is around us. "Did you… just float through me?"

His voice is a deep whisper. "Get up, Fury, and save your mind games for the real enemy."

Preparing to stand up, I accidentally kick his shins.

My feet pass right through his legs.

He doesn't just look like smoke.

He *is* smoke.

His mouth curls up into a satisfied grin as he reaches down and grabs hold of my shoulder. To my surprise, his hand is completely solid, able to pull me to my feet, but when I try to touch him, my fingers pass through his wrist. "How…?"

He draws me close and I have to tilt back my head before I decide to levitate to stand eye to eye with him.

He asks, "What am I?"

I say the first thing that comes to my mind, suddenly knowing it as truth. "You're an Enenra. A monster of smoke and darkness."

"I can touch you, but you can't touch me," he says, a statement of fact.

I glance at his fist still curled around my shoulder. "It certainly appears so."

"I wonder, then… How would you kill me, Fury?"

Whatever elation I felt at figuring out his power fades.

I realize that I'm not talking with Lachlan anymore—I'm talking with the monster inside him, the same way Striker's hellhound takes control sometimes, the same way I give in to the Fury inside me.

"I can kill everything," I whisper. "That's what I'm built for."

Lachlan's monster pulls me closer, face to face, his other arm slipping around my waist to trap my chest against his.

It isn't a possessive move or a lustful one, but a pure show of control. I know without trying that if I attempt to hit back, I'll do nothing more than launch myself through smoke again and I've had a lungful already.

His eyes narrow. "How do you stop smoke rising from a doused fire?"

My brain tells me there has to be a way for me to beat him. Probably using my power of compulsion, if not harnessing my full physical strength, but for now I sense I should remain still. His monster has taken over for the first time and it's volatile, seeking to establish itself.

I remind myself that he is not my enemy.

I meet his challenging gaze, my own open and honest. "You will never give me reason to want to, Lachlan."

He nods, slowly and carefully, and I find myself lowering to the ground under the pressure of his arms as he shifts back into himself.

The smoke that was rising from his skin curls back into his arms and legs, his eyes clear, and ash falls off his skin, dusting the mat at our feet before it lifts in the breeze and blows away.

"I guess we won't need that discussion today after all," he says, finally releasing me.

He and I were going to try to discover his power today, but that task has been well and truly accomplished.

I incline my head with a nod. My lungs are still burning and I give in to the need to cough out the last of the smoke.

Ouch. It clings to the inside of my body, an uncomfortable burn, but he doesn't apologize and I don't want him to.

He turns away from me, a determined glint in his eye as he sweeps down the steps.

The other students have quickly gathered around the mat. Most of them are watching Lachlan—all smiling, although some appear envious, since they're all desperate to find out about their power—but Striker is watching me.

The glare in his eyes could be the sunlight. Or he could be unhappy with me right now. It's difficult to say.

But what I do recognize is the way he presses the forefinger of his left hand to his temple.

He can't see Raptor.

I cast a carefully casual glance around the area.

Raptor's gone, but he'll be back.

11. STRIKER DRAVEN

The dining room is pristine by the time we break for lunch.

Any sign of the battle yesterday is gone, every crevice cleaned and gleaming.

With access to the kitchen wide open, we collect our meals on the way through. The kitchen staff avoid us other than to point to the meals before they get back to work spooning out food onto—*what a surprise*—real porcelain plates with actual metal cutlery for the first time since I got here.

Once we enter the dining room, Lucinda touches Peyton's arm and whispers, "We're starting off how we intend to continue."

Gliding past us, she grabs both Ashley and Lachlan and hustles them along to sit at the same table with her. Joseph follows her with a grin.

No more gender segregation.

I find a quiet corner away from them. Peyton nearly tugs on my arm to join the others, but she takes one look at my face and follows me instead. I may have fought a battle on behalf of the other students yesterday, but a single act can't override three years of my aggression toward them. I growl at the three girls who look like they're about to join us at our table.

Peyton nudges my knee. Like me, she must be starving, but she's poking at her food. "We can't hog the whole table."

"They shouldn't get close to us, Peyton."

She sighs. "Is that why you picked a fight with Joseph this morning?"

I'm not the only one who picked a fight for complicated reasons. She actively provoked Lachlan into revealing his power. What he is... I'm not sure even Peyton could subdue a man made entirely of smoke and darkness.

I can't answer her straight away, my thoughts churning inside my head. I can't deny the worry that settled inside me when Lachlan towered over her. He refused to fight her until she demanded that he respond.

"You and I led the charge yesterday," I finally say. "But I can't be the one they look to for help. I have a massive target on my back. Not only our new headmaster and his entire family, but my stepfather wants me dead. It's far better that Joseph and Lucinda are their leaders."

Her gaze passes over her friends. The students need stable leadership. They're already congregating around Lucinda and Joseph, and now that Lachlan controls his power, he and Ashley will be a duo to contend with. Even Bree looks happy at the next table, talking openly with Ryan.

Even so, the moment Peyton meets my eyes, I know she sees through me.

I have a lot of enemies, but fear is at the heart of my actions. If the others start to trust me, then... eventually... I'll screw it up.

The darkness inside me will destroy their trust.

"You *can* be that person, Striker," she says. "You can lead them."

I shake my head, a violent back and forth. "Neither one of us can. I'm a hellhound. You're a Fury. There's too much darkness in both of us. We can't be the guiding light. We'll fail and take everyone down with us."

I take her hands in mine, a crushing grip filled with as much truth as I can manage.

"What we *can* do for them…" The heat between our hands builds and the burn at the back of my eyes is matched by the fire behind hers. "We can be the ones who carry out the dark, monstrous tasks so they don't have to wear those acts on their souls. We can do the cheating, the tricking, and the killing."

Our tangled fingers feel like chains tying us together.

"I don't want you to be right, but I've felt what's inside me," she says. "I've fought the darkness and failed—"

Sudden silence falls over the room.

My focus swivels to the door, my grip on Peyton's hand tightening.

Raptor saunters into the room. "Ten minutes," he announces. "If you're late, you'll regret it."

"Some things don't change," Peyton murmurs.

I don't like the way Raptor's gaze lingers on Peyton before he saunters out again. There's an edge of both tension and anticipation in his body language and the way his gaze passes across her as if she's some sort of challenge or worse—a creature to be dominated.

When we reach Raptor's classroom, he leans against the desk at the front of the class.

I take up my usual seat at the back with Peyton sitting at the desk beside me, but the other students choose new seats, reorganizing themselves. They must have talked about it at lunch, because those with known powers are positioned at strategic points throughout the room, ready to defend those without.

I suddenly feel guilty about staying so close to Peyton at the back. She and I should probably talk about positioning ourselves differently. Although, by sitting at the back, we can see the entire classroom and any threats in front of us, so I decide to stay put for now.

Ryan is the last to arrive. He surprises me when he ignores Raptor's glare and strides right up to Peyton all the way at the back of the class. His hair is shaved close to his head and his eyes are a dark hazel.

A narrow scar slashes through his left eyebrow and skims across the top of his cheekbone, as if someone once took a knife to him. He's never talked about it and I sure as hell haven't asked.

He says to Peyton, "I'll fight you tomorrow, Fury." He gives her a wink that makes her blink at him in surprise before he takes a seat three rows ahead of us.

Peyton shrugs at me, but it's obvious she's pleased. I am too. In a way.

The faster the others discover their powers, the sooner I can get the hell out of here and take Peyton with me.

Raptor takes a threatening step toward Ryan, his expression a dark cloud of anger, but Peyton quickly stands up, her clattering seat drawing Raptor's attention.

"Assassins," Peyton says loudly. "You're going to tell us all about them."

Raptor pauses, glaring back at Peyton while he twists the ring around his finger.

"The assassins are bound by a code," he finally says. "It's their greatest weakness."

He returns to the head of the room, leaning against the desk again. "There are three rules you can use against them. The first is that every assassination must be sanctioned by a woman they call 'the Guardian.' Unless she approves your death, they can't kill you. What's more, the approval is only given to a particular assassin."

Peyton opens her mouth again, but Bree calls out ahead of her. "What does that mean?"

Raptor's smile is cold. "It means that you can kill as many assassins as you want, but only one of them is allowed to kill you."

"How do we know which one?" Peyton asks, resuming her seat.

Raptor's gaze snaps to her. "Well, now, that's the trick, isn't it? You won't… until they kill you. But hopefully you'll have the chance to engage them first. They will either fight you or retreat. If they retreat, then you will have them at your mercy."

"You make it sound like they hunt in packs," Lucinda says from her desk at the side of the room.

Raptor smiles again. "They used to hunt solo, but lately, they've started backing each other up, forming unusual alliances. Enemies have become friends."

His expression changes, becoming serious, less cocky for the first time as he focuses on Peyton. "Unfortunately, this makes them even more formidable. The Master Assassins used to be at each other's throats. Now that they're working together, your chances of survival are slim."

"You said there were three rules we could use against them. What's the next one?" I ask, trying to draw Raptor's attention away from Peyton.

"A failed assassination can't be attempted by the same Faction again," he says, prowling down the center aisle toward us. "That means that if they attempt to kill you and fail, they can't try again. Neither can another assassin from the same Faction. There are three Factions so only three attempts can be made and then you're untouchable."

I watch him carefully as he approaches. His hands are empty, but that doesn't mean he isn't carrying a weapon. "So we're actually better off fighting them—letting them try to kill us—than running away," I say.

Raptor drops his hands down on my desk with a *bang*, his ring glinting.

The sound echoes around us, but I don't flinch. I don't like the way his gaze flicks to Peyton. It's as if he's carrying on a whole conversation with her inside his head.

"Only if you can defeat them," he says, his focus swiveling back to me, his blue eyes brighter than they should be.

I sense the growing power around his hand, the hazy silver glow from his ring.

"Every assassin is human," he continues. "But they train for years, and these rings give them supernatural powers. What's more, every ring has a specific power. Some rings increase healing. Other rings can form bullets from nothing. This ring—"

Without warning, he flicks his wrist and a gleaming rope snaps through the air toward me.

I don't have time to blink before it winds around my neck and pulls tight.

I jolt, shouting against my constricted vocal chords, and wrench backward as my power rushes to the surface, making the air around me sizzle.

My claws descend, ready to slice through the strand, but Peyton gets there first. I catch sight of her crimson eyes as she leaps across the space between us, her claws extended.

The magic disintegrates as she cuts through it, but at the last moment, I catch Raptor's smile.

He wanted her to do that.

Both of Raptor's hands snap out. He shoves her so hard into me that we fly backward. He leaps at us at the same time so that we fall together, Peyton wedged between us. Steel flashes at the corner of my eye.

A dagger is already clutched in Raptor's hand.

No!

He rams it into Peyton's chest at inhuman speed, pulling it out and plunging it into her again and again, five times as we fall.

Her blood splatters my face and shoulder as we hit the floor, the chair crashing and shattering beneath me, Peyton resting on my chest and Raptor landing on her.

I hear the air whoosh out of her lungs, the scream in her voice, the wet sound of blood choking in her throat.

My beast bursts into life, my body shifting so fast that my bones *crunch*, an awful snapping sound.

I shout, wrap my fiery arms around Peyton, and yank her to the side, kicking Raptor hard in the chest.

He flies off Peyton, gaining air before his ring flashes and he disappears. I don't see or hear him crash to the ground in the sudden chaos, don't know where he is.

All I care about is Peyton. We've rolled close to the back wall, where I cover her with my body, determined to protect her.

Lucinda screams behind us. I'm facing away from her, so I can't see her, but there's suddenly the sound of many running feet.

"Bree! Ashley!" she shouts. "Raptor's disappeared again. Get everyone out of here and protect them."

Peyton is limp in my arms, her breathing shallow. One of my arms curls around her head, protecting her; my other reaches for her face. "Peyton, talk to me."

Blood bubbles up through her lips and splashes the floor when she coughs.

Her eyes are clear brown. *Human.*

"Fuck."

Lucinda skids to her knees beside us, bumping into me. "Why isn't she healing?"

I glance up to see Joseph and Lachlan in full monster mode. Even in their monster state, they're frozen in shock as they stare down at Peyton and the mess of her chest, the cuts, the blood pooling across the floor, all over my arms and chest, seeping through my stretched clothing, staining my skin.

"Peyton!" I shout, but she doesn't seem to hear me. Her gaze is far away, her head tilted as if she's listening to something I can't hear.

Her arms twitch but don't rise, remaining loose against me.

She squeezes her eyes closed, her voice a scant whisper. "Striker... Let me go..."

All I can think about is how she felt in my arms this morning, about stealing a moment in time when nothing was wrong, when everything was right.

I can't help the raw response that tears out of me. "I'll never let you go."

Her eyes open. A thin splatter of blood rests across her cheek. Her voice is fading. "Before it's... too late..."

I stare at my hands gripping her head and shoulders, at all the places I'm touching her.

I'm killing her.

The others can't know it's because of me. I shout as loudly as I can, my voice a monster's roar. "We have to get away from her."

I carefully place Peyton's head on the floor, fighting every instinct that makes me want to hold her.

I am her worst enemy right now.

Only Joseph, Lachlan, and Lucinda have remained in the room with us. I have no idea whether Raptor's gone or is still here. I'd wager he's stayed to watch the outcome of his handiwork.

"Get away from her!" I shout.

"What? No! I'm not leaving her." Lucinda grabs me, but I shake her off, shoving her as hard as I can, pushing her into Joseph.

"Hey!" Joseph catches Lucinda, who stumbles to the side. He

makes a grab at me. "Stop, man. We have to help Peyton. We have to—"

"No!" My fiery fist punches Joseph's head.

Darkness floods his monster's eyes. He hits back, but I duck. It doesn't do me any good.

Lachlan barrels into me from the side, propelling me ten paces up the center aisle before I can thump him. Or try to. My fist passes right through him.

I try again, but it's useless. He deftly drops me to the ground, but his arm wraps around my neck, pulling me along that way, my feet dragging against the floor.

I'm facing the back of the room now.

Peyton stirs. Her arms move, then her legs.

Sickening relief floods me as her head turns, watching me with her increasingly crimson eyes as Joseph and Lachlan drag me from the room.

I keep fighting them, forcing them to pull me away, because if they don't...

If they don't make me leave her, I won't.

But if I stay, I'll be responsible for her death.

12. PEYTON PRICE

Raptor leans up against the wall beside me. His ring glints.

I'm lying against the back wall, my body covered in blood and Striker's arms around me, as if he can protect me.

Striker doesn't look at Raptor, which confirms for me that Raptor isn't visible to anyone else anymore. After Striker kicked him away from me, Raptor landed on one of the desks, cracking it down the middle. But the other students were already moving, chairs flying backward as they ran from the room, so nobody seemed to notice the oddly broken desk.

"I have a theory, Peyton," Raptor says calmly. "I want to know if I'm right, because if I am..." He smiles. "You're in trouble."

I try to warn Striker, but the sound only bubbles in my throat. Striker is gripping my head, his body curved protectively over mine. He's trying to shield me. So are Lucinda, Joseph, and Lachlan, forming a ring around me.

I try to speak, try to move, but all I hear is Raptor's voice as his gaze passes over Striker and me. "I want to know if you can heal when you're touching Striker."

Damn.

Striker's beast has taken over and right now he's the most beautiful thing I've ever seen.

A beautiful beast that I need as far away from me as possible.

I struggle to form sound. "Striker… Let me go… before it's… too late…"

I'm dying. I can't feel my legs. Raptor's dagger struck so many times and so deeply that it sank into all of my vital organs. He moved at a frenzy, but he knew exactly which parts of my body to hit. I can't see my chest for all the blood.

The power inside me is a dull flicker, a mere sputter, and the most reckless part is that all I want to do is kiss Striker. Not heal. Not worry. Just be a girl who loves a guy and likes to hold his hand and kiss him in the sunlight.

Striker stares at his hands around my face, at his body, and all the places he's touching me. He turns deathly pale.

He speaks, not to me, but to the room. "We have to get away from her."

"I'm not leaving her," Lucinda declares.

Striker places my head on the floor before he eases away from me, rolling to his feet. He towers over Lucinda, a threatening mountain of fire before he shoves her so hard that she loses her footing. "Get away from Peyton!"

Joseph jumps to Lucinda's defense. A sigh whispers from my mouth as I watch Lachlan and Joseph fight Striker, watch them drag him away.

It's exactly what he needed—to be forcibly restrained.

Violence is his constant friend.

I watch him go, even though I want to call him back, blinking away the tears from my eyes. They roll hot down my cheeks, but I can finally lift my hand to brush them away.

The farther Striker moves from me, the stronger I become.

Lucinda drops to the floor beside me.

I grab her hands, drawing her down to me. "You need to leave."

"But you—"

"Will be fine."

She eyes me as I draw my knees up and pull myself into a sitting position.

I tear off my torn shirt, running my hands over my chest.

My fingers slide through the blood, sloughing it off my freshly-healed skin. My focus zeros in on Raptor, who watches our interaction with a pleased smile. He flips his dagger in his hand as if he's impatient to use it again.

Despite all of the blood, I pull Lucinda to me, hugging her and whispering, "Raptor's still here and he *will* hurt you."

Her gaze snaps up, her power igniting, the nearest desks and chairs wobbling and threatening to rise into the air. "Where?"

I place a calming hand on her arm. "I'll deal with him. But I need to know that you're safe."

She gives me a nod before she backs away.

Raptor stays put until Lucinda steps out of the room. Then he picks himself off the wall and circles around me.

"Theory confirmed." He narrows his eyes at me. "But now I want to know why."

Him and me both.

I step carefully away from the bloody floor, lifting off the ground a little, buoyant in the air. "Your mother will have a cleanup job ahead of her," I say, gesturing to the pool of blood on the floor.

"My mother?" His confused expression clears. "So you figured that out."

"The family resemblance is pretty clear." I dart forward, grabbing his dagger arm, pushing him up against the wall, bashing his hand against the wooden surface.

He pushes back—but not as hard as I thought he would—before he allows the weapon to clatter to the floor.

I snarl. "Give me one good reason why I shouldn't kill you right now."

"Twenty-three reasons," he says. "All of the students who don't know what they are. If anything happens to me, my father will open fire on your defenseless friends."

I grit my teeth, fighting my rage. If he wasn't right, I would crush his bones right now. "That threat won't work on me forever."

He smiles. "But it will work for now."

He relaxes beneath my hold and it suddenly dawns on me that maybe I'm right where he wants me to be.

My chest presses against his. My bra was already cut through from my fight with him this morning and now it gapes open.

I should have replaced the damn thing at lunch time, but I was too hungry after missing breakfast and then I didn't have time.

His gaze runs from my eyes to my lips. "How does Striker Draven have so much power over you?"

I draw in a sharp breath. It's the question I desperately need answered.

Before I can push myself away from him, Raptor's free arm slides around my waist, pulling me far too close, his cruel eyes glinting at me between the strands of blond hair falling across his face. "I did everything in my power to hurt you, break you, trigger your rage, make you powerful, make you *furious*—"

I nearly choke. "What?"

"And yet Striker undoes it with a single touch." His arms clamp around me. "I *made* you, Peyton. You're strong because of me."

"Because you hurt me."

He returns my incredulous stare with the first sign of honesty. "I'll keep you strong. With every cruel, hurtful thing I do to you, every punch, every cut, every push and pull that triggers your rage, you will grow stronger. Because of me—"

With a shriek, I wrench myself out of his grasp, my chest heaving, but he grabs hold of my wrist before I can get away, holding on tight.

The more I tug, the brighter his ring glows, turning his hold into a vise.

Damn assassin's magic. I have to learn how to beat it.

"You're the only one who can kill her," he says, a sudden declaration that makes me freeze.

"Who?"

"Hunter Cassidy."

I narrow my eyes at him. "Who is that?"

"Only the most unbeatable assassin in known history. She's even more powerful than her mother. Except that we can't confirm her identity until you tell us about your vision."

My head is a whirl of confusing thoughts. Raptor has never spoken the truth to me. Every word out of his mouth has been intended to hurt me, manipulate me, but now…

"I want something in return," I say.

He becomes very still. "What do you want?"

"Don't blur again. You have to remain visible to everyone all the time."

"Done."

I laugh, shaking my head. "I'm supposed to believe you'll keep your word."

He strokes his chin with his left hand before he glances at the ring. Carefully, he bites the ring, drawing it off his finger with his teeth before dropping it into his upturned palm.

He holds it out to me. "Take it. I can't blur without it."

I stare at the offered ring. It feels like a test and I have no idea if I'm going to pass or fail.

I stop pulling away from him and dart forward, my hand closing around his, ready to take the ring.

His left hand closes around mine, his fingers digging into the back of my hand, clamping closed and dragging me close to him again.

Now both of my hands are trapped. He drags me up against him while I contemplate the option of using my compulsion power on him—or employing a savage kick to his groin.

I grit my teeth, anger roaring to the surface, my vision coated in crimson as I tell myself to wait.

I want this ring. Without it, he can't challenge Striker or the others. I can keep them safe.

Raptor's gaze runs over my face again, a pleased smile growing on his lips as he settles on my eyes. "Good. You're furious again. Tell me what I want to know and I'll let you take the ring."

"Mahogany hair," I say. "Green eyes with silver rims."

His smile fades. "Damn. The silver in her eyes indicates that she's more than human." He grinds his words. "Even though that should be impossible."

His grip slowly, reluctantly, unclamps from my arm and hand. My skin blushes with bruises before they disappear.

For an infuriating second, I think he's going to double-cross me and keep the ring, but he allows me to scoop it up as he releases me.

He lifts his arms as if he's helpless. "I'm at your mercy now, Peyton. But remember, I know about your weakness. I won't tell anyone—or use it against you—unless you force me to."

I stare at the magical object I now grip in my hand. The silver wings fashioned across its top are so finely crafted that they look like they could be beating in the air.

"Whatever you do, don't put it on," Raptor warns. "There's a reason assassins are always human."

I don't take my eyes off the ring. The power inside it is... intoxicating.

I inhale and exhale, sensing my heartrate increase, a thrill passing through me as the ring's power shoots through my hand, traveling up my arm like a drug through my veins. "But you don't think she's human—this Hunter Cassidy you're so afraid of."

"She can't be human, but we don't know how she doesn't—" He stops speaking, clears his throat, and swallows whatever he was about to say. "Did you see whether she wore a ring?"

I think back to the Fury's memory, replaying the image in my mind.

The woman—Hunter—wore fitted black clothing and carried a curved sword as she crept toward the Fury's cabin.

More than anything, I remember the pain I felt from her, as if she carries grief like a cloak around her heart the same way I carry fury.

I also remember the lies she told. Every time she opened her mouth, she lied with purpose.

Despite that, the man who was with her scared me more. I try to shake off the memory of his piercing blue eyes and the way he carried his daggers—even more comfortable with his weapons than Raptor is.

"Who was the assassin with her?" I demand to know.

"The Legion Master himself," Raptor says, scowling at the change of subject. "Hunter may be unbeatable, but *he* is ruthless."

I shiver, understanding it now. It's the male assassin's rage that I recognize, the same fire that burns in me.

"Her ring wasn't metallic," I say. "It looked like crystal."

Raptor gives me a dismissive shrug. "Assassins' rings are all colors and shapes. Hunter Cassidy is an enigma." His gaze settles on me again. "Like you."

An enigma.

Wow. For a few seconds there, we were actually having a relatively normal conversation.

I back away from him, clutching the ring tightly to my chest.

Raptor flips back to his usual sadistic self. "Don't think for a second that I'll go easy on you now, Peyton." His sudden grin makes me shiver. "You know I can hurt you even without that ring."

I turn and hurry from the room, gripping the ring hard in my fist, ignoring the pain that shoots through me, a burn I can't identify in my chest, as if Raptor sliced off a little part of me without me realizing.

As I exit the room, I catch movement to my right farther along the corridor.

A slightly open door quickly closes. For a second, I think I see Mallard looking through the gap—his moustache and graying hair—but the door closes too fast for me to be sure.

As I hurry away, I realize that touching the ring hasn't given me any visions.

This ring is pristine. Clean. An unexpectedly blank slate, as if it hasn't been worn before today.

I'll need to hide it somewhere that Raptor won't find it. Anywhere in my room will be too easy to find. My mind runs to the library on the fourth floor and a smile crosses my lips.

I have the perfect place, but I'll have to hurry.

I need to see Striker right away.

13. STRIKER DRAVEN

You're going to get her killed.

For once, I agree with my beast.

My heartrate is out of control as I back away from Joseph and Lachlan along the corridor beyond the classroom.

My power has receded. I've returned to my human form, but I feel less and less in control with every passing second.

If I don't get a hold of myself, I'm going to tear up this whole place and damn the consequences.

The guys keep glancing back at the classroom. They're worried about Lucinda and Peyton like the good guys that they are. I have to believe that Peyton's safe now. Not knowing is tearing me apart, but there's no way for me to find out without putting her in more danger.

Lucinda suddenly races from the room and runs toward us, speaking in a rush as Joseph grabs her. "Peyton's fine. She healed. She's alive."

Smoke rises from Lachlan's body, filling the space around us. "Does she need our help?"

"She needs us to stay away. Raptor's in there." Lucinda's

worried eyes meet mine. "We have to trust her to deal with him."

I back away from them. *Trust is the problem.*

I can't stay still any longer. Sprinting away from them, I run straight for the empty combat area outside, ignoring Lucinda's shout. "Striker!"

I don't know where Bree and Ashley took the other students, but I'm guessing they would have either gone to the dining room or the fourth floor dorms. They'd better not be outside.

The door hits the wall as I push through the exit. Tearing through the empty yard, my feet kicking up grass, I hurl myself at the electric fence, needing the crippling pain through my body, needing to knock myself out before I do something truly stupid.

Like take a knife to Hadrix and his whole family.

My back connects with the metal bars. The fence creaks and groans under my weight.

Nothing.

No electricity.

They turned the damn fence off.

With a roar of frustration, I spin and grab the bars, curling my fingers around them, pulling at them, dragging them apart as the metal shrieks in protest.

My heart is pounding. My chest is heaving. But now the gap is wide enough.

All I have to do is step through.

One little step and she'll be safe from me.

We didn't want to escape this way yesterday because of the creature that roams the forest that surrounds the Academy. We don't know what it is because Osprey didn't tell us, but right now, I don't care.

I'd rather fight a monster than face the fact that I'm the reason Peyton almost…

I stumble to the side, grabbing the bars to stay upright.

All the blood. *Her* blood. It's all over me and I suddenly realize it's all over the fence now, too.

I double over, bringing up everything I ate for lunch, throwing up into the grass on the other side of the fence. I've fought guys in the ring, broken their bones, shattered jaws, left my opponents screaming, but somehow none of it compares to the way Peyton lay bloody in my arms.

My beast is quiet as I rise up and stare at the gap in the fence. Every muscle in my body hurts and my chest aches badly.

For once, my beast doesn't seem to have an opinion. Or maybe he does because he hasn't told me I should stay.

You don't have a choice, he finally says. *You have to leave. The alternative is worse.*

I don't know what alternative he's talking about.

As far as I can see, I only have one choice.

Some shred of sanity must prevail because I know I can't leave without supplies. I need water and weapons. Medical supplies, too. Everything I need is in my room.

I tell myself I can make it up the stairs and get out again before Peyton knows I'm gone. It'll take me five minutes. After that, she can hate me, but she'll be alive.

I squeeze my eyes closed, remembering the way she sauntered past me naked in the shower, but I force myself to shake it off.

If I leave now, I won't have taken anything from her that I shouldn't have.

Energy shrieks through me and my beast's power bursts through my muscles as I pound across the yard, enter the building, and run up the first four flights of stairs.

I ignore the students on the fourth floor. My guess was right —Bree and Ashley stand guard at the entrance to the corridor while the other students gather behind them in the corridor and inside the entrance to the dorms.

They must still be waiting for the all-clear. It tells me that

Peyton hasn't appeared yet. Ashley wears her red scarf wrapped around her eyes, but I sense her gaze following me as I disappear up the final flight of stairs.

She takes a step toward me as if she's about to call out to me, but I don't stop.

Inside my room, I wrench the medical kit out from its hiding place in the wall. I leave most of it for the other students—Peyton will know how to use everything in the kit to help them —but I take a tube of healing gel.

The silver label on the tube glints in the light.

Funny the things I never noticed before. A silver star adorns the corner of the label with the words *Saber Lane Apothecary* across the middle.

Hurrying on, I stuff my duffel bag with a few sets of clothes before I reach once more into the cavity where the medical kit was hidden, angling my hand as far as it can go so that I reach the dagger I keep taped to the inside of the wall.

The Draven Industries insignia is etched into the black handle. The dagger is smaller than I would like, but it was the best I could smuggle in with me when I was first brought here.

If I'd had my power then, my stepfather wouldn't have had legal standing to take control of my livelihood, let alone take away my freedom.

Finally, I grab the bottled water from my desk, taking a deep drink, washing away my doubts.

I stride from the room and around the corner.

"Oh!" a soft female voice exclaims as I collide with her warm body.

My reflexes kick in before my mind catches up. Dropping the bag and jumping back, I immediately release my claws, ready to attack.

Kaitlyn catches her breath opposite me, her hand planted across her heart, overly dramatic, as if I gave her a fright.

She's wearing a white collared shirt that's open a few too

many buttons at the top, her lacy black bra visible beneath it. Tight black jeans hug her ass while her heels give her extra height.

Her wide eyes travel from my head to my toes, taking in all the blood.

"Dear ancients, Striker," she exclaims in a breathy whisper. "Who did you kill?"

Of all the things she could have said…

"Who did I kill?" A burning snarl rises in my throat and my incisors lower.

I grab her shirt front, my claws ripping through the flimsy material, popping off more than a few buttons as I thrust her against the wall.

What I really want is to throw her through the glass on the opposite side of the corridor, but I don't want to walk past her dead body on my way out through the yard.

"Who *won't* I kill?" I snarl.

She blinks away her surprise. I never threatened her when she was here. Not once until that final night when I tore up everything around us—except her.

I never laid a hand on her.

Unlike Peyton, whom I've ripped apart again… and again…

Never again.

My beast whispers a denial at the back of my mind—he knows I'll hurt Peyton no matter what—but I push his truths away.

Kaitlyn's lips part, a sultry smile settling onto them.

"I missed you," she whispers.

Her fingertip trails down my cheek. That nail is painted black with white runes and I suddenly remember Peyton's warning.

Damn. Peyton went to great lengths yesterday to keep Kaitlyn away from me and now I've willingly touched her.

I force myself to relax against her, closing the small gap

between us, slowly releasing her shirt. She settles against me, her back arching, one leg rising to curl around my hips.

My stomach turns as I deliberately reach for her hand—the one that lingers on my jaw. I start at her elbow and run my fingertips along her forearm first before gently taking hold of her wrist, my thumb circling her palm in slow movements.

Her eyelids lower, a provocative sigh on her lips.

Carefully, I reach for her other hand, skipping my fingertips along her soft skin, pressing my palm against hers.

I now cradle both of her wrists as she arches against me.

She melts into me. "I knew you'd remember."

I lean toward her, my lips hovering above hers, close enough to kiss her. "I'll never forget."

She smiles, shifting as if she'll wrap her arms around my neck.

Hell no. That's close enough.

I jerk backward, my claws descending into her wrists, pulling her arms out straight.

I make sure to miss all the important veins, cutting through the flesh around them.

She screams, her eyes shooting open, pain flooding her face.

I stop pulling before my claws would rip through her arms. Her fingers spread wide, but her spells are useless now that she can't touch me.

I've taken control of her hands and my claws have dug deep enough to do serious damage.

"Don't struggle," I warn. "Or you'll rip your own hands off."

She freezes, her wild gaze passing across her outstretched arms. She knows I'm not lying. Her lips press together, her face turning red with anger as well as pain. "You... asshole."

"Yep." I incline my head to her left. "Now move."

It only takes a little tug and she hustles to move in the direction I pull her. She shuffles to the side, wincing, until her back is clear of the wall.

"Come near me again and I'll finish the job," I say, retracting my claws and shoving her away from me down the corridor.

She lands on her butt...

...and slides right into Peyton's legs.

I raise myself up, suddenly unable to focus on anything but the blood splattered across Peyton's face.

She's coated in it, as if it's paint-on clothing drying across her bare shoulders and stomach. Fucking Raptor. Once again, he's deprived her of her shirt.

Kaitlyn clutches both her bleeding wrists as she looks up.

She shrieks, taking a single glance at all the gore before she jumps to her feet and backs away, pressing up against the fragile window glass.

"What the hell did you do to each other?" she screeches.

Kaitlyn's bloody wrists leave smears all over her white shirt, but it's nothing compared to the mess all over Peyton.

Peyton barely looks at her. "Get lost."

Kaitlyn pulls the torn pieces of her shirt together as she runs away as fast as she can, her heels clacking on the stairs.

The rapidly fading *tap-taps* fill the silence around us.

Peyton's perceptive gaze has already settled on my duffel bag along with the clothes hanging out of it. "What are you doing, Striker?"

I pick up the bag, firmly pulling the strap over my shoulder.

I wanted to be gone before she got here. This conversation is not one I wanted to have.

Focusing on the blood and not her face, I force myself to move until I draw level with her.

Her forehead creases in confusion. "Striker?"

I make myself speak. "You have to let me go."

14. PEYTON PRICE

e's telling me to let him go and his bag is full of clothes. My brain registers those two things before I piece their meaning together.

I step into his path as denial rages through me. "No."

He doesn't look at me, focused on my bloody cheek instead. His voice is hoarse. "You could have died."

"But I didn't—"

His voice turns into a shout, his amber eyes burning me. "You nearly died because of me!"

I flinch at the savage tone of his voice, but I don't retreat. "Raptor did this. Not you."

"He won't stop until you're dead." Striker's warning echoes in my ears, along with Raptor's accusation.

How does Striker Draven have so much power over you?

I shake my head. "No—"

Striker sidesteps me. "I'm your weakness, Peyton."

I can't deny it. "You don't have to leave."

I wrap my fingers around his arm, trying to make him stop, grappling to find solutions. "We can stay away from each other during the day. Sit separately during class. Never fight each other during combat—"

"Sleep in separate beds?" His humorless smile is full of wrath, the dangerous light in his eyes telling me he already knows my answer.

I grit my teeth. "You're sleeping with me. I'll stay safe in the day but I want you with me at night. I won't let them tear us apart—"

He wrenches out of my hold but just as suddenly grabs my shoulders, his expression like stone. His claws slowly extend, pricking my shoulders all around front and back. "Tear us apart? Raptor will sneak in at night and stab you to death in my arms."

I swallow a gasp of pain as Striker's claws very slowly cut my skin.

He isn't wrong. Raptor proved today that he doesn't need an assassin's ring to hurt me, but right now, Striker's hurting me more.

My power sputters inside me, trying to rise. Trying to heal myself. Failing. Worse, pain spreads across my chest, my heartbeat increasing with every unwanted word Striker speaks.

I grit my teeth through the pain, clenching my fists. "I'm not letting you push me away."

"One day," he says, ignoring my declaration. "One fucking day is all it took for Raptor to figure out how to hurt you. It won't be long before everyone else knows too. How many nights do you expect me to fall asleep wondering if you'll be alive in the morning?"

"Every night!" I shout back at him. "Because living means taking chances. We have to grab hold of what we love while we have it."

Love.

Wrong word.

Oh, fu—

He shoves me away from him so hard that I hit the wall. Pain shoots through my shoulder. Pain from the cuts. Pain from the impact against the wall.

I whimper before I can stop myself, and for a second, I imagine I see agony in his eyes, maybe deep regret, maybe rage, maybe a silent roar that he'll never utter.

I promised to hate him always, but somewhere between yesterday and today, my feelings got mixed up. I found a fragile place with him where we both opened up and trusted each other.

It was only for a few hours, but now it's destroying us.

Without another word, he spins and walks away from me.

He's… actually… throwing everything away.

The angry hunch of his shoulders, the clench of his fists—it's as if he's the one driving a dagger between my ribs and every beat of his boots on the floor is a shouted lie.

I hate lies.

Pure fury fills me, rage filling my head and speeding through my body like an electrical current.

I run, not after him, but to his room.

My whip lies curled up on the end of the bed. As soon as my fingers close around it, the crimson haze falls across my vision.

I remember what I am.

I'm not a woman. I'm a Fury, and he will never break me. Nobody will.

Gripping my weapon, I run from the room.

Striker has reached the end of the corridor, but I'm faster.

I scream at him. "Damn you, Striker Draven. I told you. I'm not letting you push me away."

My whip arm releases and the three deadly tips shriek through the air, biting the narrow space between him and the top of the stairs.

An inch farther to the right and I would have ripped the

flesh off his bones, but I'm not afraid of making a mistake. This whip is a part of me and my aim is precise.

Striker jolts away from the steps, dropping the bag and crouching to avoid the lashes. The furious, angry glint in his eyes tells me it's the last defensive move he'll make.

His gaze flashes to mine as the whip recoils. Its tips flick and *crack* between us before they *snap* against the floor, gouging little holes in the wood.

I test the whip's weight in my hands while I plant my feet, raising my chin in defiance.

"You refuse to let me go," he says, more statement than question.

"I do."

"So be it." His claws elongate from his fingertips, fully extending while fissures of molten lava crackle along his arms and legs, speeding up through his neck and down across his torso.

His shoulders shift and expand, broadening, his height increasing as he shakes out his upper body. Sharp bones release from his upper back and shoulders, tearing through his shirt.

He rips the torn material off his back as he stares at me with eyes that taper at the edges, golden amber, pure hellhound.

"Then stop me," says his beast.

15. STRIKER DRAVEN

There are no more careful steps.

I destroyed my new path, tore up all my good intentions, the moment I pushed her away from me.

Peyton's whimper is a lost echo that tears out a piece of my heart.

She levitates off the ground, her hair rising around her, blood-red strands floating across her face.

She is as she should be—wearing a mantle of blood, except that it shouldn't be her own. Her claws aren't as dangerous as mine, but they don't need to be, not while she's holding that whip.

Not while the scent of wildflowers grows around her and all I want is to obey.

Her monster is in control now and...

She is fierce.

There isn't a shred of humanity in Peyton's eyes as she looks at me.

I let my beast take control and pray I'll be alive when it's over.

16. PEYTON PRICE

I roll my wrist, stretch out my neck, and slowly rise off the ground.

My power is weightless. I may as well be a feather suspended in the air. Only my whip anchors me, its metal tips screeching and scraping across the ground as they rise with me.

The cuts across my shoulders knit together—not that the extra blood mattered.

I dismiss any confusion I feel about my power returning in full so suddenly. Maybe it's the whip. Maybe it's the way Striker pushed me. Maybe it was the sudden and pure hatred in his eyes when I spoke about love.

So many *maybes*, but answers can wait.

I allow a smile to rise to my lips as I float toward him, a single tip of my whip dragging a jagged shallow groove into the wooden floorboards below me.

When I reach his location, I veer left, positioning myself at the very lip of the upper step. "Oh, I will stop you. The question is whether I'll leave your soul intact."

His beast's eyes glitter. "I have no soul."

He casts a smile at my feet. A single push will send me tumbling down the staircase.

Maybe.

I arch an eyebrow at him, waiting for him to try.

He takes a step toward me, towering over me by a full foot, the heat from his body scorching me.

Sweat breaks out across my face and chest, but I remain where I am, anticipating every move he could possibly make right now.

"Come on, hellhound." I flick my wrist so that my whip snaps against the top step. Little chips of wood fly into the air as it cuts across the glossy surface. "What are you waiting for?"

His muscles bunch and he grabs me—maybe to push me, maybe to pull me. It doesn't matter. I'm ready.

Shifting left, the flat of my left hand connects with his ribcage above his waist, pushing him sideways up the corridor.

At the same time, I take a step forward and plant my foot against his stomach, kicking him farther back.

He grabs my ankle, yanking upward, trying to flip me, but I spin gracefully in the air, smacking my other foot into his shoulder.

My whip also flicks dangerously close to his face, forcing him to leap back even farther.

I settle to the ground as he growls at the growing distance between himself and the stairs.

Baring his incisors at me, his claws whip out to slash at my chest, to force me into a defensive position, but I spin again, whirling upward, my foot planting neatly against his jaw and kicking hard.

To my surprise, he absorbs the blow this time. With a treacherous smile, he leaps higher than I thought he could, ripping me from the air.

My seamless dance is over.

As I fall, I flip the whip handle around in my hand so I can use it as a baton.

Smacking it across his face, I follow up with my left fist, cutting across his shoulder before I ram the baton into his stomach as I touch the ground.

He barely flinches before his fists arch toward me, savage cuts aimed at my head and chest so fast that I only narrowly avoid them.

As I attempt to retaliate, he grabs my whip hand and squeezes hard.

My bones shift and crack. Every pop and break rips through me, even though I heal a second later. I used to cry when I was in pain, but my eyes are bone dry now.

He knows he has to disarm me, but I'm not having any of that.

I wrench my whip hand out from my side, yanking his arm with it as I press my body hard up against his.

At the same time, I flick my wrist with all my strength. The long, black lash lifts into the air behind him, flying left. His eyes widen as I push my left arm past his chest under his arm and grab the swinging lash before it tears his back to shreds.

Before he realizes what I'm about to do, I lean back from my waist, our lower halves pressed far too close together, the heat between us unbearable as I yank the whip toward me and wind it around his chest, securing the middle of the lash around the handle before I dart into the air holding the tip end.

He struggles and tries to grab me, but he isn't quick enough.

I soar upward over his head. Faster than he can shout, I whip the rest of the lash around his neck, yanking it taut as I land on the other side.

He lands on his back with a heavy thud and a roar, choking as I pull the tips of the whip tight and drag him along the corridor at speed.

He hacks at the lash with his claws, but he can't cut through it. Other than the handle and the tips, my whip is made from the long, black tails of nightmare carnivorous horses. I wasn't sure if the hair could be cut, but it looks like it can't. At least, not by his claws.

He twists onto his side, the jagged bones on his back ripping up the floorboards until I pull him past his bedroom and dump him outside my old bedroom.

The room inside is cold and gray, not a home, not comfortable like his room. No chance of falling into warmth and happiness here.

I rapidly wind the end of the lash around the door handle, pulling him partially upright against the door. He has no choice but to wrap his hands around the rope to keep it from closing completely around his neck and choking him to death.

I watch his legs as I round him, since he can still kick me.

Pausing a beat, I wait to see if he can free himself. Flames rise around his hands as he tries everything, his frustration growing. The rope is wound tight, but not tight enough to kill him. Assuming he doesn't let it go.

"A trapped beast," I murmur, hardly recognizing the melodic tones of my own voice as I carefully kneel, straddling his legs and settling down across his knees, a strategic position in case he decides to employ his legs as weapons.

I'm vaguely aware of the scent of wildflowers filling the air around us.

His pupils constrict as he inhales and shakes his head, rapidly trying to shake off my power of compulsion.

So that's why subduing him was easier than I expected.

He was battling my power the entire time.

"You won't fight me," I say, easing forward, daring to reach out and place my palms flat against his stomach.

His skin varies in temperature. Where my fingertips cross molten fissures, they burn, while the in-between patches of muscle are hard but cool.

My touch plays across his chest up over his shoulders, feathering the backs of his hands where he grips the lash. He stops struggling and studies me instead, his breathing settling down, the rapid rise and fall of his chest easing.

He's a caged predator, more Striker right now than when he's in his human form.

The moment his gaze falls to my lips, I know I have his attention.

"Hellhound," I whisper, addressing Striker's beast. "Tell Striker to stop being an idiot."

His gaze burns across my lips, his own parting softly. "If I stay, I'll hurt you," his beast says. "Worse than anyone ever has."

I arch a disbelieving eyebrow at him, considering the way I've got him tied up. "I don't see how."

"Not your body—"

"What heart?" I ask, cutting him off. "A Fury doesn't have a heart."

"But Peyton does."

I recoil. "No."

He pulls against the rope, but this time, he tugs closer to me, tightening the lash around his own neck as he tries to close the gap between us. "Now who lies?"

"Maybe," I whisper. If I lean an inch forward, I could brush my lips against his. "Maybe I'll hurt you back."

His beast grins at me, an enigmatic smile that draws me closer. "You will. Worse than anyone has ever hurt me before."

"Well, then," I say. "If we're going to destroy each other, what are we waiting for?"

With a single nod, he lets go of the rope, cupping my face in his enormous hands.

My eyes widen in surprise as his fiery fingers tangle in my hair and he tugs forward to kiss the corner of my mouth.

Now that he's not keeping the lash at bay, it tightens around his neck, even more so as he leans toward me. The muscles in his neck tighten visibly, fighting the pressure while his hands remain firmly around my face, refusing to let me go.

He shifts his palm so he can nuzzle my cheek, but... if he keeps going, he'll choke himself.

"Striker, what are you doing—?"

"Destroying you."

Damn him.

I wrench out of his hold and slide forward as far as I can, my chest a scant inch from his face as I reach up and quickly unwind the whip from the door handle.

As his hands find my waist and his lips press warm kisses between my breasts, I realize with shock that—*damn, damn, damn*—he could have reached up and freed himself the whole time.

His arms are long enough. He's strong enough. He could have even wrenched the door handle out.

No matter how I might try to compel him, he can beat me.

Remaining raised on my knees, I carefully unwind the lash from around his neck and chest, sensing the pressure of his palms as he allows me to move around him—but only as far as he wants me to go.

The moment the whip unties, he tugs me down so that I'm firmly straddling him while his hand strokes upward to cup the back of my head.

He turns me onto my back on the floor in the middle of my bedroom doorway, his big body looming over me, his biceps bulging at my eye level as he shifts to push himself off me, a dangerous smile on his lips.

Dropping warm kisses over my cheeks and mouth, his lips whisper across my ears and trail down my neck, sending shivers to my toes. He inhales when he reaches my collarbone, his nose wrinkling as he draws back. "Blood."

I grip his shoulders. "It doesn't matter."

His smile is brutal. "But I want to see your skin."

He presses down on me for a mere second, his body connecting with mine for an agonizingly short moment before he scoops me up, his movements commanding as he carries me to the bathroom, grabbing a washcloth after he kicks the door closed.

Whatever blood was on his body has burned away with his emerging power.

I'm the only one who needs to wash.

He heads straight for the shower and manages to turn it on without putting me back on my feet. The water runs hot, but every droplet that hits his body turns to steam. The air quickly becomes dewy white around us, filling my chest with humidity.

Water flows down my body and I tip my head back into it, my legs still wrapped around his waist. He reaches up to angle the water to the side of the shower, pushing me up against the tiles on that side so he can balance me there and free up his hands.

There's nothing gentle about his movements as he cleans the blood from my face and hair. Nothing gentle and everything demanding.

I'm determined not to make it easy for him.

I run my hands across his chest and shoulders, marveling at the way the fire in his body moves in all directions, rippling out through his skin wherever I explore his muscles.

With a growl, he hooks a claw beneath the center of my bra and snaps it. Then he cuts the straps so that the broken pieces fall away.

I close my eyes, relaxing against the oddly cold tiles, a stark contrast to Striker's heat. Every firm stroke of his hands, every swish of the cloth both soothes and agitates me, a deep need building in my center, and I find myself arching into him, trying to find relief.

As he scrubs away the memory of this morning, tears burn at the backs of my eyes. I don't know why I'm crying. I don't hurt.

His sudden growl sounds in my ear, sending a shiver down my spine. "Stop compelling me."

My eyes fly open. His pupils are constricted and his fist rests against the tiles beside my head, his gaze burning me as water cascades from the dripping cloth he grips.

The scent of wildflowers fades as I force that part of my power to stop.

I refuse to diminish my other powers because the moment Striker senses that I'm human again, he'll turn and leave, but compulsion doesn't belong in this moment. I don't want to go on wondering if he's not here of his own free will.

As the heady scent disappears, Striker's features relax, but if anything… it seems that my compulsion was restraining him.

He hooks a claw around the waistband of my shorts, ripping neatly through them. My underpants meet the same fate. He pulls me away from the wall so that my clothing falls away, the wet material slapping against the tiled floor.

Placing me on my feet, he kneels at my feet to clean my legs, but unlike last time, his gaze passes over all my curves as he works, the cloth raking across my thighs down to my calves and then up again.

I gasp as he nudges my legs apart to clean the sensitive skin inside my thighs, my legs turning to lava beneath his touch. I grip the side of the shower to keep myself steady as his hand passes roughly across the top of my thighs so close to my center that my head spins.

With a last sweep of the cloth, he stops cleaning me, leaning back on his heels, the now-clean water swirling around him.

When he looks up, his eyes are mid-shift, resuming their usual shape, even though the fire inside them doesn't die.

He rolls his shoulders as the bones along his back retract and the molten tracks across his chest and arms fade, leaving his torso chiseled and smooth.

His features may be human again, but as he rises to his feet, he is no less a predator.

He pitches the washcloth into the corner of the shower before his arms close around me, his hands raking through my sodden hair as he pulls me close, tipping my head back but stopping right before our lips would touch.

His breathing is ragged and out of control. His voice is hoarse, a hint of anger in the way it catches. "We have nowhere to do this. A bathroom, a desk, a room with bad memories, another room with worse memories. Our options are no better than the fucking floor."

I tip my head back, arching into him. "All of them. One at a time. Starting with the bathroom, ending with the floor, and then we'll start over again."

His lips part in momentary disbelief and then curve into dangerous agreement.

Still without kissing me—still while holding me against him with his right arm—his left hand sweeps down my side to the curve at the top of my hip, his thumb drawing across my stomach between us before it moves lower toward my center.

My breath catches and my lips part as my breathing rapidly increases.

I'm determined not to close my eyes, not to give in to the overwhelming fire he's stroking, to remain in control, but...

Dear ancients...

He doesn't take his eyes off me. A droplet of water runs from my forehead to my chin and he dips his head to follow its path with his lips, tasting the skin across my temple, cheeks, the corner of my lips, my jawline, neck, and shoulders. Just like his left hand, his mouth follows a trail lower, finding all my curves and exploring them.

My head spins and the hand I brace against the wall suddenly becomes completely insufficient, especially when he lets go of my back to grip my hips with both hands.

As I sway, he catches me against him, drawing himself upright, his lips finally crashing against mine.

I drown in the taste of his mouth and all the sensations of his hands stroking every part of my body. Soaking up the remnant heat from his power, I kiss him with a fever that grows in my body and mind until moans break from my lips.

He sweeps me off my feet, wraps my legs around his waist, and carries me to the counter, propping me on the edge of it.

The last time we were in this position, he held back and ended up pushing me away, but this time…

He swiftly removes his own clothing, completely naked with me for the first time, before he grips my hips and pulls me close. I burn with need, wanting all of him, wanting to connect, but for a moment, he hesitates.

It isn't doubt that I see in his eyes, but a fierce certainty.

He leans forward, captures my mouth with his lips, and says, "I choose you."

My senses go wild as our bodies connect. My claws extend and my power rages through me, just like it would have the last time we nearly had sex. I thought I'd be afraid my first time—at least for a moment—but I have no hesitation as he starts to move.

My body fits perfectly to his, every part of me, the curve of my chest, the reach of my arms around his back and shoulders, my legs around his hips. My power flows through me and every move I make responds to him, as if I know exactly what he wants when he wants it.

I fall into a heady rhythm of movement as the heat in his hands burns a trail across my skin until I sense he's close to letting go.

But if anything… my own need grows more elusive.

Fear strikes through me for the first time. What if this is all I can feel? What if I can't go any further than this?

I'm a Fury. I'm built to beguile and seduce, to lure and please… until I attack.

My power tells me to draw my lips across his to make him shiver, to arch my back a certain way to make him go wild, to press my claws against his shoulders as if I want more.

But it's all about controlling his responses and not about me. Not about what I want or feel.

Maybe I'll always be left wanting, always furious about the true happiness that's kept from me.

Now I understand why I started to cry before.

All I can give is what he can take.

Striker groans against my ear, the sudden sharp bite of his mouth telling me his incisors are descending.

I close my eyes, prepared to accept what I can't have, when he slows and stops.

My eyes fly open. I'm confused. I'm sure he wasn't done.

Tension fills every line of his body. His breathing is ragged and fast, but the brush of his fingers is light as he draws his thumb across my cheek. "Peyton?"

I meet his gaze and all the fire in it. I'm shocked by how much control I see in him. His lips press into a gentle line as he searches my eyes.

"You have to do this with your heart," he says. "Not just your body."

I shiver, rocked by fear.

Human Peyton chose Striker. Human Peyton gave him her heart.

I can't be her. I can't be human because that means being vulnerable.

He strokes my cheek again. "Look at me."

I shake my head. "You'll leave," I say, hating how human I sound, how small and lost.

He exhales slowly and carefully. "I messed up. I couldn't see another way to keep you safe. But I'm not going anywhere. Not unless you tell me to go."

I search his eyes for a lie, but there isn't one. His beast said he would hurt me, but right now, all I see is truth.

He presses a kiss to my lips, resting his forehead against mine. "You have to choose me too."

Fighting my fear, I force my claws to retract and my power to recede. Not completely, not wholly, but subduing it enough that…

I gasp and grab his shoulders, jolting as my heart burns, beating so fast inside my chest.

I couldn't feel it before. As I drag a deep breath into my chest, I shift against him and the sharpest sensation runs through my hips and stomach, a strange mix of pain and pleasure.

My human body hurts, but it also *feels*.

I shift again, testing my own responses, careful as I move closer to him.

He remains completely still. I didn't think that the flames in his eyes could rise higher, but they do.

His lips curl up into a smile as I move against him, gasping as my heart expands and intense pleasure ripples through me. It's no longer outside of me, no longer observed and controlled, but part of me.

And part of him.

A cry rises to my lips as I crash into him, letting go of my fears, finally giving in to what I feel.

17. STRIKER DRAVEN

It takes all my willpower not to tell her what she means to me.

Peyton trembles in my arms, her head resting in the crook of my neck, her chest rising and falling rapidly. We haven't moved apart. Her legs remain wrapped around my hips, her body as close to mine as she can be.

This isn't what I would have chosen for her first time. The shower's still running. The air's thick with steam. Sweat drips between us, our bodies slick with it, but beneath it all, a deep, driving need still remains.

The tiles to the left of the bench are cracked. So is the wall behind her. At some point, I shoved my hand against the tiles to brace against the need raging through her at the end.

She was the one who broke the wall, arching back into it.

I sense the smile of her mouth as she kisses my collarbone without removing her head from its resting place. "You're thinking too hard, Striker Draven."

I'm thinking that I want her again. I told her she'd have to set aside a whole night, but I'd partially lied.

I intended that we'd take our time, but once was always enough for me. Not with her. I have no idea what time it is or what could be going on beyond the attic, but, selfishly, I don't care.

All I want is to start over.

She raises her eyes, a rare twinkle in them. "You promised me a desk, two bedrooms, and the floor, Striker."

I stare at her in surprise. As her smile grows wider, she arches up and kisses me, the tip of her tongue touching mine.

"We'll start with the floor," I say, reaching for the nearest towel so she has something to rest her head on.

She surprises me with a determined push and I end up with the towel bunched behind my own head.

A long time later, we leave the bathroom with a few more cracked tiles than it had before.

Peyton drops her towel on the floor of my room, drags on one of my shirts, and slides into my bed, but her eyes don't close, a crease settling in the middle of her forehead. "I'm hungry."

I grin at her. "I'll get some food."

"Don't be long."

I pull on clean clothing. In the last two days, my clothing supply has been seriously depleted what with the number of shirts I've ripped apart. I'll have to be careful with what I've got left.

Closing the door behind me, I head down the corridor. It's dark outside, pitch black actually, much later than I thought.

As I approach the fourth floor, I slow my steps, the silence making me wary.

Ashley stands alone at the entrance to the dorms. She wears the same red sash around her eyes, the crimson color contrasting starkly with her pale skin and white-blonde hair. She's casually dressed in jeans and a pale green T-shirt, but she's anything but relaxed.

Her face turns in my direction as soon as I appear. I remind myself that she can see me even with her eyes closed.

"Striker," she says. "Is Peyton okay?"

A stab of guilt strikes me that Peyton and I aren't guarding the dorms tonight. Also that her friends would have been worried about her.

"She's fine, Ashley."

The tension leaves her shoulders. "That's good."

I consider her lonely figure. "Is anyone standing guard with you?"

Her lips curve into a wry smile. "It's too dangerous if I need to use my power. I need to keep everyone I love behind me. Only my enemies will approach from this side." She clears her throat and hurries to add, "Except you and Peyton."

"You won't be able to hurt Peyton." As I speak, I fight the memory of the way Peyton rocked in my arms before she let her heart take over.

Her Fury has no weaknesses, not even to put her own needs first.

"I think you're right." Ashley's smile changes. "But only her."

She means she could kill me if she wanted to. She takes a step toward me. "Don't hurt her, Striker. Or you and I will become enemies."

I swallow and give her the most honest answer I can. "I have every intention of keeping her safe."

Just as I swing back to the stairs, Ashley calls out softly. "Striker?"

"Yeah?"

Her lips curve into a bemused smile and a curious crease forms in her forehead. "You're sort of... glowing around the edges."

I can't help the laugh that breaks out of me. "Don't tell anyone or you'll destroy my reputation."

She seems more startled by my laugh than anything else. I guess I never do that. I never laugh.

"I won't," she says.

I take the steps lightly, conscious of the quiet everywhere else, checking down the corridors on each level before I proceed to the kitchen. The lights are out on the first floor, but my power allows me to see easily.

I like dark places, feel comfortable in them.

Blending into the shadows, I head down the east wing and raid the fridge for leftover sandwiches, piling a plate high with them, along with some grapes. Returning to the stairs, a light catches my eye from the west wing.

The door to Lady Tirelli's old office is ajar and voices spill from it. Hadrix's voice is closest, the shadow at the door making me think he was about to open it and step outside but he must have stopped.

Vulture's voice from farther inside the room arrests me, the tension in it palpable. "But will she do it?"

The door clicks closed again and I creep closer, harnessing my full power to disappear completely into the shadows. I did it the night that Lady Tirelli last visited. My power to become part of the darkness is possibly akin to what the assassins call blurring, but I can only do it at night and only while I remain still, whereas they can disappear in sunlight.

The voices inside the room are muffled, but I close my eyes and expand my senses to make out what they're saying. It's three of them: Vulture, Hadrix, and Raptor.

"We'll find a way to persuade her to kill the assassins for us," Hadrix says. "Peyton will come to understand that it's the only way she can gain her freedom."

"You won't be able to lie to her," Vulture warns. "She'll see right through it."

"Then I'll tell her the truth. She'll have to agree." He adds, "Despite the risks."

Raptor's voice cuts across them both. "Leave it to me. I've broken her before. I can do it again. She won't have a choice."

"Fine," Hadrix replies. "But proceed carefully, son. Giving her your assassin's ring was a risky move. We don't know how that will play out."

My forehead creases a little. Peyton didn't tell me about the ring and I don't remember seeing it on her.

Leaning close again, I hear the shrug in Raptor's voice. "She just needs to be angry enough. I know how to trigger her rage. She won't think twice about the risks."

Vulture takes a deep breath. "And what of the creature in the forest?"

"We can convince Peyton to kill him," Raptor suggests.

Vulture sounds unconvinced. "What about Kaitlyn?"

"Kaitlyn can't know anything about it," Hadrix snaps. "She must never know the truth about that creature."

Raptor's tone is matter-of-fact. "Even if she finds out, she'll blame Peyton."

Vulture suddenly laughs. "Oh, that's cold, Jake."

"I am what you raised me to be, Mother," Raptor says. "It was a nice touch not letting Kaitlyn heal herself tonight."

Vulture sounds satisfied with herself. "It's an important lesson for her to learn. She's so irritatingly emotional."

"I can understand why she's confused," Raptor scoffs. "First you send her here to mess with Striker and now you're trying to teach her *not* to mess with him—"

"Enough talk." Hadrix sounds annoyed. "The creature will be dead soon and we can close the door on Kaitlyn's problems."

Footfalls sound, coming toward the door again, thudding boots like the ones Hadrix wears.

I quickly dart away from the room, hurrying back to the attic.

When I reach my room, I find Peyton propped up on my

pillow, her hair spread out around her. Her eyes are sleepy. The photograph of my sister and me is held loosely in her fingertips. She must have pulled it from the back of my door.

"How can Zara leave you here?" she asks.

I place the food on the bed between us, sinking onto the soft mattress. "It's complicated."

She gives me a wry smile, sitting up to eat. "Which is code for *don't ask.*"

I can't stop the smile that breaks out across my face. "If I ever meet your brother, I'm killing him."

She laughs. "Oh, so my family's fair game, but yours isn't?"

"If you want to take out my stepfather, go for it."

She snorts. "I need a kill list already."

Like an assassin. I become still. "You have Raptor's assassin's ring."

"I made a deal with him," she says, only making me more tense. She glances up at me. "It's okay. Really. I told him what the assassin looks like and in exchange, he gave me his ring so he can't blur again. It seemed like a fair trade. Especially since they were bound to figure out her identity eventually."

As she eats, Peyton tells me what she knows about the assassins—that the woman's name is Hunter Cassidy and the man is no less than the Legion Master himself, Slade Baines.

"We need to be careful," I say. "And not just of the assassins. Hadrix is planning something and it involves the creature in the forest."

Her eyebrows rise. "Do you know what it is? The creature?"

I shake my head. "What I heard was too vague. Promise me you'll treat everything they do with suspicion."

"I already do." She's deadly serious.

She drops the food she was holding as if she's suddenly not hungry, but then her expression changes. Softens. Her gaze runs across my naked chest.

As she leans forward, my gray T-shirt pulls across her sexy-as-hell curves. She slowly removes the plate from between us and places it, and the photo, on the floor, my T-shirt rising up to her waist as she moves.

I reach for her, my hands finding the naked curves above her hips, sliding her toward me so I can taste her mouth. She draws back a little as soon as I kiss her, timidly pressing her fingers to her own lips.

She blushes. "Bruised. I'll do something about that in the morning."

I keep my kisses light, exploring every inch of her body from her shoulder blades to her thighs and ankles and all the way to her center, over and over, an exploration that she returns, driving every other thought from my mind as her hands roam across my body.

Before she takes control, demanding more, she bites her bruised lip and asks, "Tell me where we'd be if we weren't here."

I smile as I pull her up and over me. "A summer house with a massive bed, the softest sheets, and candles burning in every corner of the room."

She closes her eyes, sighing. "Then that's where we are."

Afterward, I stroke her hair until she falls asleep, sensing the last of her power fade until she's completely human, completely vulnerable in my arms.

I finally allow myself to feel the pain and fear that storm inside me.

When I hurt her, she heals.

But when I love her, she hurts.

My beast is subdued inside my mind. *You gave up the kindest option when you stayed. Now you only have the alternative.*

No.

He doesn't give up. *If they come to kill her, you know what you have to do.*

Inside my mind, I take my beast's truths and tear them apart with my claws, shredding them into tiny, bloody pieces until I can convince myself he's wrong.

I won't hurt her, I say.

But his response is irrefutable. *You won't have a choice.*

18. HUNTER CASSIDY

Kaitlyn Hadrix hunches beside the lamppost at the end of the lane, shivering beneath her hooded coat.

Her icy eyes can't hide her pain, but I'm not sure where she's hurt.

It's difficult to feel sorry for her, given the blood on her hands.

It's only been two days since she was last here, but we're ready for her.

Tansy meets me silently at the edge of the protective shield, taking up position a step behind and to my right. She gives me a nod to indicate that her spell is in place. The moment Kaitlyn leaves, Tansy will be able to trace her path to its end point.

"Kaitlyn Hadrix," I say, addressing the blonde. "Back so soon."

"Fuck them all," she says, peeling herself away from the lamppost and reaching up with shaking hands to push back her hood.

Her sleeves rise as she moves, revealing wide bandages wrapped around both of her wrists. Blood seeps through them.

The anger in her eyes indicates the wounds weren't self-inflicted.

Hmm. Literal blood on her hands.

"Are you ready to tell me where Striker Draven is?" I ask.

She reaches into her pocket and extends her hand, offering me a slip of paper.

I can't see all of her fingers, but it looks like she's already used up most of the spells she painted on her nails. She might only have two or three left. I guess she didn't think to make any of them healing spells.

I don't reach for the paper, so she shoves it toward me, releasing it into the air. It catches for a second before it passes through the protective shield and floats onto my open palm. It wouldn't pass through if it carried a dark spell intended to harm me.

As my fingers close around it, Kaitlyn exhales, slumping as if she has nothing left.

"I've done it now," she says. "His coordinates are written on there."

Curious, I consider the numbers scribbled on the paper. It's ripped at the edges as if she tore it out of a book in a hurry.

"Coordinates?" I ask. "Not an address?"

She snorts. "This place isn't on any map. It's also very difficult to get into." Her eyes harden. "I've given you the location, but you'll have to gain entry on your own."

I shrug, as if nothing daunts me. "Consider it done."

Tansy shuffles a little beside me. She knows my mission isn't sanctioned, but she of all people should know by now that I have no qualms about lying to a liar.

Kaitlyn's blue eyes turn impossibly icy. "My name can't be written in your ledger or you would have killed me already. You can tell Slade Baines that he'll find me where hell exists on earth. That's where Striker is and that's where I'll be waiting for my end."

She taps her finger against her arm and disappears.

I whirl to Tansy. "Have you got her?"

Tansy closes her eyes and smiles. "Yes." Then her forehead crinkles in a thoughtful expression. "Uh, maybe."

"*Maybe?*"

"Her path ended, but there's… nothing there." She opens her eyes. "Give me a few minutes with a map and my spellbook. I'll have her last known location for you soon."

"Okay. I'll meet you back at the bookshop."

Her smile becomes grim. "You need to return to your visitor."

My official visitor. Not Kaitlyn, who turned up unannounced.

I hurry back to the bookshop and the woman who waits in the little kitchen that forms part of the apartment above the shop.

The Guardian arrived only minutes before Kaitlyn did, so I barely had time to greet her before I had to head out to the street.

Taking the internal stairs isn't as easy as it used to be now that my stomach extends beyond my normal center of balance. It would be easier if I could use my wings, but the stairs are too narrow. Not to mention, the Guardian doesn't know what I am.

She rises from her chair, her glossy caramel hair falling straight to her waist. "Is everything okay?" she asks, her luminescent brown eyes radiating concern.

I slide into the chair opposite her and push the slip of paper across the table. "She gave me Striker's location."

The Guardian sinks into her chair with a soft exhalation. "Indeed."

I lean forward. "You need to tell me what you know about him."

She nods and reaches into the satchel she placed carefully on the table when she first arrived.

Sliding a slim folder across to me, she says, "This is everything I have on Striker Draven."

My eyebrows rise at the thinness of the folder. A large part of the Guardian's job is to collect evidence on all mercenaries. I still don't know exactly how she does it, but I suspect she has a network of spies in every city.

Once she sanctions an assassination, she sends everything she knows about the target to the relevant assassin. Most targets have a whole box filled with copies of police reports, photographs, video, and audio evidence—even objects such as weapons or DNA evidence carefully packaged up in bags.

The folder in front of me is the slimmest I've ever seen.

I was expecting a box filled with evidence of his every misdeed. "That's..."

"Not much." She nods. "I know very little about him."

I pull the folder to me and open it, flipping through the information at the top—family history, including the suspicious death of his mother—to his history of cage fighting.

I pause at the images of bloody and beaten opponents.

Not much fazes me, but this sort of damage was caused by one very angry man.

"All part of the game," the Guardian says. "The combatants sign waivers before they get in the cage. Brutal, but not criminal."

"Any deaths?"

She shakes her head. "Not in the cage but read on."

The final pages in the file start with a photograph of a young man—maybe twenty years old—with dark hair and brown eyes. His eyes are noticeably dark-rimmed, distinct and piercing. "Who is this?"

"His name was Jesse Anderson. He was a panther shifter. He went out one night and didn't come home. You'll see in the file that his older brother was in the military but disappeared off the grid a few weeks before Jesse went missing."

I scan the file, but it doesn't have the answers I seek. "What happened?"

"All unsubstantiated, which is why it isn't in there. I only include verified information in my files. You'll need to take the same approach when you're Guardian."

I give her a nod before she continues. "In this case, the story is that Jesse and Striker were partying that night. Things went wrong and Jesse ended up dead."

"An accident?" I ask.

"Not according to the rumors."

I rub my forehead in frustration. "Is there *any* evidence that Striker killed him?"

The Guardian shakes her head. "Striker disappeared on the same night. Nobody's seen him since."

"Then how do we know Striker's even alive? Kaitlyn could be hatching some sort of plot—"

The Guardian takes a deep breath. "Two reasons. The first is that she wouldn't risk coming to you unless he was alive. Her whole family is written into Slade's ledger."

"I don't know." I cross my arms across my chest with a shake of my head. "She said she lives where hell exists on earth. She practically invited Slade to come and kill her. I think somebody hurt her, or allowed her to be hurt, and now she wants revenge more than she wants to live."

"Hmm." The Guardian taps the table with her finger as she considers my argument. Her assassin's ring is the most elaborate I've seen. A large emerald sits in the middle of smaller emeralds that drip to each side in the shape of leaves interspersed with glittering diamonds.

"What's your second reason?" I ask, when she remains silent.

"It's only a rumor," the Guardian replies. "Again, it isn't substantiated."

My stomach swirls, sudden worry making me tense. I hope

my daughter doesn't do her protective trick again because I'm not sure how I would explain it. "Guardian?"

"I believe Lady Tirelli was attempting to train her own assassins."

I lean back in my chair, unsettled as I recall Lady Tirelli's threat before she died. She told me she was building an army of assassins to crush the people I love.

The Guardian studies me. "You don't appear entirely surprised."

I grimace. "It was something Lady Tirelli said, but I thought she was referring to all the brutes and assholes she already had at her disposal."

The Guardian shakes her head. "Do you remember how I mentioned the Unknowns?"

I nod. "Young men and women born to magical families, but the children themselves don't exhibit any magical power until it's too late for everyone around them."

The Guardian reaches into her satchel again. "I finally acquired this picture."

She pushes a photograph across the table. It's an aerial shot of what appears to be the remains of a school, multiple buildings burnt and scorched, roofs and walls blown apart.

"What did this?" I ask.

"An Unknown." She meets my shocked eyes. "Their power is catastrophically repressed. It finally bursts out of them and destroys everything—and kills everyone—around them. Have you heard of Bloodwing Academy?"

I think for a moment, sifting through my memories. "Maybe. I'm not sure."

"Bloodwing Academy was established to keep Unknowns isolated from the general population. To keep *us* safe from *them*."

"Damn," I whisper. "That would make for a bunch of very angry students."

"The Academy's purpose is to help them control their power before it's too late. However, I've had my suspicions that Lady Tirelli was behind it."

Dread builds within me as Lady Tirelli's long ago threat echoes in my memory. She said her army would be made of supernaturals who had been rejected and shunned by everyone around them.

My voice is strained. "Lady Tirelli was cunning and strategic. She would have recognized the potential in these Unknowns. At the very least, she could use them to do a lot of damage."

The Guardian doesn't disagree, her eyes filled with worry.

Trying to gather my thoughts, I lean away from the photograph. "What does this have to do with Striker Draven?"

"I believe he's an Unknown."

I blow out a breath and press harder into the back of my chair. My wings burn within my back and my daughter suddenly kicks hard inside my stomach, making me wince as she drums a quick beat with her feet. "You think he's at Bloodwing."

"I do."

My eyes narrow in thought. "But you don't know for sure?"

"Nobody knows where it is. It's hidden from sight and even the families have their memories irretrievably wiped the moment they leave the grounds."

I grab the note Kaitlyn gave me, needing to take action to deal with the dread growing inside me. "She said it isn't on any map. She gave me the location."

"Perhaps. But you're forgetting I haven't sanctioned the kill."

I pause. "What's stopping you? His stepfather gave Lady Tirelli every weapon she could wish for—every type of gun and grenade. Even missiles. His stepsister has knowingly funded weapons production for years. His entire family is complicit."

"He is not his family." She presses her lips together in a stern line. "Their sins are not his."

I fight to contain my frustration as my daughter kicks hard again, her fear igniting my own. "Then… you won't sanction the kill?"

The Guardian sighs, folding her hands on the table. "Striker Draven's history proves that he is capable of extreme violence. The fact that he's also Unknown makes him an extremely volatile individual." She pins me with a hard stare. "But based on the evidence in front of you, should I sanction his assassination?"

I stare at the file. She's asking me what I would do. I've already agreed to be her replacement and now she's rightfully testing me.

I take a deep, calming breath, at which my daughter settles immediately. Perhaps it was *my* fear unsettling *her*.

What I've learned more than anything else over the last year of my life is that judgement is fraught. I've always had the luxury that the Guardian made these decisions for me.

Now I'm catching a glimpse of how hard it is for her, and how hard it will be for me.

I exhale slowly, the air leaving my lungs. "You need more evidence."

"I do."

"Then I'll get it. Do I have your permission to do that?"

A smile breaks across her face. "I was hoping you would ask." She leaves the files and Kaitlyn's scribbled note on the table as she rises. "How is your other mission?"

It's my turn to sigh. "We located the missing rings in a warehouse in Boston's south, but it was empty by the time Slade got there."

The Guardian's lips purse into a worried line. "You know better than most people how dangerous assassin's rings can be in the wrong hands. Even a trained assassin will struggle to control a ring that wasn't assigned to them. These rings are pure. They've never been assigned to anyone, which makes them extremely volatile."

She gives a heavy exhale. "Not to mention the problems we'll have if the Magical Magnate decides we can't control our own assets."

"I will find the rings. I promise."

"Thank you, Hunter." She gives me a firm nod that conveys her trust. "Give my regards to Slade."

I twist my glass ring around my finger as I listen to the Guardian's receding steps followed by her brief conversation with Tansy as the powerful witch enters the shop downstairs.

Within minutes, Tansy sweeps into the kitchen. "Kaitlyn is at the same location as the coordinates she gave you for Striker. But it's like she's been swallowed into an abyss. According to the map, there's nothing there but a cemetery."

I tap the files in front of me. "Bloodwing Academy," I say. "It's there, hidden somehow. It has to be."

Tansy looks at me expectantly, but her gaze passes to my stomach. "What do you want to do?"

There was a time when I was fiercely independent. I still am. But now, I have more to lose than I ever did before. "I need to talk to Slade. I can't do this alone."

We need a plan.

I have Bloodwing Academy's location, but what danger waits for me there, I don't yet know.

19. PEYTON PRICE

My body aches in new places. Bruised lips are just the beginning. Every other part of me feels new and alive.

As the sunlight grows behind my eyelids and Striker's deep breathing continues—soft inhalations where he sleeps curled up around me—I allow myself to be human, to feel the wildly pleasant discomfort of a night spent with him.

He's quieter beside me than I've ever seen him, fast asleep, his upper arm heavy across my torso. I fight the urge to run my hands through his hair and kiss his resting mouth, but I don't want to wake him.

A pleasant shiver runs through me as I remember just how little sleep we got last night.

I reach for my power to heal, testing whether I can ease the tingle in my lips.

My power rises, sputters, and… dies.

Damn.

I thought I might have fixed it when Striker and I fought yesterday. Fighting him was the first trigger for my power and that remained true yesterday. I don't plan on getting into it with him right now, though. Not in the slightest.

Striker stirs beside me, tugging me close and dropping kisses across my cheeks, nose, and eyes. His sandpaper bristles leave my face tingling. Even biting my lip to smother my laughter doesn't work. I only end up wincing instead.

"You're wearing too much," he growls, finding the base of the shirt I borrowed, his big hands skimming my ribcage.

"You can have your shirt back right now if you want," I say with a sultry smile, shimmying out of his hold to sit up, present him with my back, and take the shirt off. I'm completely naked from the waist up, only a pair of underpants covering my lower half.

I turn my head to find him wide awake.

"You're going to kill me, woman," he says, watching me rise.

I cast a smile back at him as I drop his shirt onto the bed and reach for my whip where it rests on his desk. Its familiar weight is a comfort and I grip it hard, hoping that it will trigger my healing power like it did yesterday.

I can't make my claws extend.

Still nothing.

Another shiver runs through me, but this time, it's worry.

Damn, damn, damn. I really thought I'd fixed this.

Striker moves like a panther, rising quietly to stand behind me. Shifting my hair to the side, he kisses the back of my neck. "We can't be anywhere near each other today."

My hand grows warm where my palm presses against my whip. "I'm taking this with me. From now on, I don't separate from this whip."

"Except in my bed."

I spin in his arms, the whip resting against his hip as I narrow my eyes at him. "*Our* bed. *Our* room."

He laughs, a husky sound. "Our bed," he agrees. His eyes crinkle at the corners. "Our desk. Our floor."

A blush grows on my cheeks, but the heat in my face is nothing compared to the warmth spreading through my chest. My heart expands as I tip my head back and accept his kisses.

"I hate you a lot right now," he whispers.

I sigh, soaking up the warmth of his hands, the strangest melting sensation spreading through my arms and legs as I lean into him, trusting him to keep me upright. "I love you, too."

No, that's not right.

My eyes fly open.

He inhales sharply.

I can't move, frozen in his arms as the tension in his body increases. His hands flex against my back in a way that tells me his claws will appear at any minute. Telling him I love him is one thing, but the way I spoke assumed he said it first.

My mouth is completely dry. I swallow and try to find my voice as I push out of his arms. Getting out of here is the only sensible thing I can do.

I turn and reach for the door handle. "I'll see you at the end of the day."

Striker hangs back, watching me go as I push away the tornado of emotions racing through me. Human emotions. I need my power back ASAP.

Dressing quickly, I consider what to do with my whip. I need some kind of clip. There aren't any belt loops on my workout shorts, so I decide to wear a skirt over the top of them.

For now, I use a hair tie wrapped around one of the belt loops on the waistband of the skirt, winding up my whip and securing it with the tie.

With every step away from Striker down the stairs from the attic, I sense my power growing again. By the time I reach the kitchen, my lips don't tingle and not a single other part of me aches.

I sigh with relief as I head inside the kitchen, finding Ryan staring at the plates of bacon and eggs lined up on the nearest table.

"Fuck it," he says when I reach for the plate next to him. "Want my bacon?"

I stare at him, surprised by his outburst. "Sure, but aren't you hungry?"

"Starving, but I'm vegetarian. They don't exactly cater for that here."

The woman preparing food at the next table looks up sharply. "Who says we don't?" she asks, giving Ryan a hard stare.

She's a thin lady with graying hair tucked into a tight bun at the nape of her neck. She relaxes a little as she scoops bacon rashers from a frying pan onto another plate. "How do fried mushrooms on sourdough bread sound?"

Ryan narrows his eyes at her as if he suspects a trick. "Fried in vegetable oil?"

She scowls at him, appearing insulted. "Of course."

"Sounds good, then."

"Coming right up."

She shouts an order to one of the other ladies, who responds with a grin and says, "Finally, something other than bacon and eggs."

Ryan's jaw drops when the other ladies smile at him too.

I take another look at them. They don't have auras, which makes me think they're human. They're all older, probably in their fifties, and their motivation for choosing to be at the Academy is a mystery to me.

"Why are you here?" I ask, directing my question at the woman with the bun, who appears to be the head cook.

She pauses but doesn't look up from her task. "You're Peyton Price, aren't you?"

"I am."

"I was told to be careful around you."

I shrug, even though she isn't watching. "You should be."

She finally looks up and gives me the same hard stare that she gave Ryan. "I've been serving meals to hungry people all my life. I know a caged tiger when I see one. The best thing they could do is let you go free."

I blink hard as she returns to her work.

Ryan grins at me, folding his arms across his chest. "I like her," he whispers.

"Enjoy your mushrooms," I say. Somehow this human woman summed up my life in a couple of sentences—and still avoided telling me anything about herself. Clever. And unexpectedly perceptive.

Carrying my plate to the dining room, I'm surprised when I meet several of Hadrix's men coming out on my way in. They step aside with watchful looks as they allow me to pass before they continue outside.

Inside the room, most of the students are already eating while a number of Hadrix's guys still sit at the back table. They aren't paying any attention to the students and there certainly aren't men lining the room with guns—or wands as our compliance officers used to carry.

I make a beeline for Lucinda, Bree, and Ashley, taking the spare seat beside Bree. A water bottle rests on the table in front of her—her weapon. She casts a wary glance back at the men before she greets me.

"It looks like we'll have company at meal times from now on," she says.

Ashley's wearing a red scarf tied around her eyes, the same one she was wearing yesterday. "Apparently, most of them ate before we arrived, but those guys aren't morning people."

I give her a quizzical look. "How do you know that?"

She tilts her head with a perplexed smile. "They told us."

"Like in a conversational way," Lucinda adds, giving me wide eyes. "The one on the end really doesn't like mornings."

I consider the guy she singled out. He's burly with a shaven head and tattoos in the shapes of bones crisscrossing his arms. I remember him as the one who was training Striker yesterday. He's a typical scary-looking dude, except that he's hunching over a coffee cup, as if it's a lifeline.

Lucinda gives me a meaningful look. "His name is Hugo. The guy beside him is Henry. And the other guy is Hodges."

I sigh. "Not their real names, then."

"I'm guessing, they're all 'H' after 'Hadrix,' which means Harrison is an alias too," Lucinda says, returning her attention to her meal.

I try to relax until Ashley asks, "Where's Striker?"

I poke at my food, realizing I should have come up with a story. I hate lies. They're like ash in my mouth, but I tell myself that the truth is dangerous for everyone.

I opt for truths that don't reveal our real reasons. "He and I have decided to split up during the day. We want to make sure we're around if we're needed. Like you did in class yesterday."

I'm not sure if they'll buy it, but Bree and Lucinda nod their heads. Ashley's the only one who doesn't. Even with the scarf covering her eyes and much of her forehead, I sense her thoughtful expression.

Bree nudges me. "I've been practicing using my power so I can figure out my limits."

"And?"

"So far I can only control short-term actions. I can convince someone to stand up or sit down. But I can't tell them to walk around the yard all day. My control wears off unless I reassert it over and over."

"Hmm. I guess that's why sirens have a reputation for luring people to their deaths."

She gives me a nod, her aquamarine eyes suddenly bright. "Kill them quickly before they can recover. But it means that if the shit starts to fly, I'll have to act fast. It'll be brutal." Concern fills her eyes. She takes hold of my hand before I can stab another piece of bacon, her voice suddenly an urgent whisper. "I don't want to kill anyone unless we're out of options. I don't even know who my enemies are right now."

I know what she means. It's hard to hate the guy hugging his coffee or the kitchen ladies frying mushrooms. Even Harrison is a mystery to me.

My only clear enemies right now are Raptor and his family. And the assassins.

Another question dawns on me. "Wait, Bree… how have you been practicing using your power?"

Her cheeks flush red. "Ryan let me test it on him yesterday."

Speaking of Ryan, he saunters into the room, looking pleased about his breakfast. Less pleased when he sees the men at the back table.

His quick gaze homes in on us. As soon as he sits down on the other side of Bree, she leans over and presses a kiss to his lips. He immediately abandons his plate on the table, giving her —and her lips—his full attention.

My jaw drops before I raise an eyebrow at Lucinda and Ashley, who grin back at me. It's one of the first open shows of affection I've seen at the Academy.

Bree catches my disbelief as soon as she scoots her chair closer to Ryan's.

"Hey," she says, mildly defensive. "You didn't see Lucinda and Joseph after dinner last night." She waggles her finger at Lucinda. "You did us a disservice when you took down the walls between bedrooms."

Lucinda clears her throat, innocently poking at her nearly clean plate. "Our old bedrooms on the third floor still have walls."

"But not beds," Ryan grumbles.

I laugh. "Who needs beds?"

They all stare at me. The silence is suddenly oppressive. My smile fades and my defenses fly right up. "What?"

Lucinda reaches across the table. "Be careful, Peyton. Striker will always be brutal."

I slide my hand out from under hers. "So will I."

"You need to take care with your heart and your body—"

Even Striker's beast insisted that I have a heart, but right now there's nothing but anger beating inside my chest. On a human level, I understand Lucinda's concern. But she doesn't understand that I am just as much a danger to Striker as he is to me.

In fact, I'm a danger to all of them.

We're all monsters at the Academy, but Striker and I are the only ones who have embraced our true nature. Even Bree is afraid of using her power to hurt someone and Ashley wears her scarf as if it's part of her body, making sure others are safe around her.

I push my chair back before Lucinda can finish speaking, addressing Ryan. "I'll see you on the mat, Ryan."

Picking up my plate, I stride from the room and deposit my dirty dish in the kitchen without speaking with the ladies.

Right outside, I find Hadrix waiting for me.

My power was already surging, but I force my claws to retract.

"Peyton. A word, please." He spins on his heel before I can answer.

Cautiously, I follow him to Lady Tirelli's old office. Just before I enter the room, I catch sight of Striker at the bottom of the steps, but he doesn't look up at me before the office door closes behind me.

I find myself inside the room with both Raptor and Vulture. Raptor is dressed in his usual distressed jeans and a T-shirt that clings to his torso, while Vulture looks like she just stepped off a runway in three-inch heels, designer pants, and a tight sweater.

Kaitlyn is the only member of the family not present. She doesn't spend as much time with her family as I expected, although it could be that Hadrix is respecting my demand that she be kept away from us.

Folding my arms across my chest, I allow my claws to descend a little so they know I'm not vulnerable.

Hadrix leans against the front of the desk, casually assessing me. "I understand you decided to tell Raptor what the assassin looks like."

"If you're trying to make me give back the ring—"

Hadrix waves his hand dismissively. "You can keep it for now."

A glance at Raptor tells me he isn't perturbed about losing his ring. Vulture appears relaxed also, moving to her husband's side, her heels clacking on the polished floor.

"I want you to know I'm very pleased that you've decided to work with us and not against us," Hadrix says. "Now that you've confirmed Hunter Cassidy's identity, we can finally plan our attack."

I remain on guard. "What do you propose?"

"Her home is protected by powerful spells. The Legion Master lives in a protected Realm. We don't know whose ledgers our names are written in, so we need to lure them both out and kill them." He holds up his finger. "*But* we must kill them one by one. Taking both of them on at once would be suicide."

A shiver settles at the base of my spine. "How do we lure them out?"

Hadrix smiles. "We're all potential bait. When we're ready, we'll leak someone's location and be waiting to ambush them."

"Whose location?" I ask, glaring at him, guessing one of the students will be bait.

Raptor doesn't bat an eyelid as he speaks up from the side of the room. "Mine. The Guardian's been trying to wipe me out for years. Whoever's assigned to kill me won't hesitate to come out after me."

It's not exactly what I was expecting, but I can see a major flaw in their plan. "What do the silver rings around Hunter's eyes mean?"

In Magical History class, Mallard started telling us that the silver rings around a supernatural's eyes could be significant, but I never got to finish that lesson.

"We think she's Valkyrie," Hadrix says.

Vulture adds, "Even though the Valkyrie should be extinct."

"Then she can't be killed," I say. "Valkyrie are Class A monsters. You can lure her out, but you can't end her."

"On the contrary." Hadrix smiles. "We have the weapon we need. And *no*, I don't mean you. The problem is that it's dangerous. Like the White Wand, this weapon comes with risks to the person who uses it."

"What is this weapon?" I nearly held the White Wand, felt the power inside it. If this new weapon is anything like the wand, then my Fury power might allow me to use it. It's a big question, but one I won't ignore.

Hadrix's smile widens. It's as if he reads my mind. "All in good time, Peyton. You need to become stronger first. You must have complete control over your powers. Your levitation skills are only fledgling, whereas Hunter has been flying her whole life. You must be able to fight her in the sky as well as on the ground."

He lifts himself away from the desk. "This afternoon, you are to see Mallard in the library. He can help you understand the nature of your power so you can build on it. You and the other students have already proved your skills in hand-to-hand combat, so this morning we're starting weaponry. Harrison will train you personally."

I narrow my eyes at them. Personal training and special treatment doesn't sit well with me.

Hadrix grins. "Don't worry. I won't neglect the others. In fact, I want you to set aside time every day to meet with them."

He approaches me slowly, ending up closer to me than I would like. He's close enough that I can see the icy flecks of white in his blue eyes.

"You have the ability to bring out their power," he says. "We need you to keep doing that. When it's time to lure Hunter and Slade to their deaths, it will take everything we've got."

I give him a nod, refusing to step back and give him any ground despite how much he's encroaching on my personal space.

Just as he's about to dismiss me, Vulture speaks up. "I'd like a private word with Peyton, please. Woman to woman."

"Of course, my love," Hadrix replies, giving Raptor a sharp nod toward the door.

As soon as it closes behind them, Vulture pastes a smile onto her face. Beneath it lurks an edge of tension in her unsmiling eyes.

She isn't carrying a wand and I can't see any runes painted on her nails or skin—although that doesn't mean they aren't there—but for now I'm comfortable that I can beat her if she tries anything.

She clears her throat. "You always speak your mind, so I'll be clear too. I know there's history between Striker and Kaitlyn, but what he did to her yesterday is the limit of what I will tolerate."

When I arrived in the attic yesterday, it was to find Striker shoving Kaitlyn away from him. The flash of his claws and the way she nursed her wrists told me he'd hurt her.

I keep my expression blank. "Why are you telling me instead of him?"

She licks her lips as if they're dry. "You have some influence over him. You can make him see that working together is best for all of us."

I consider the way she picks at her shirt, the tense lines of her mouth, and her sharp inhales before she speaks Striker's name, as if she's mentally preparing herself.

"You're afraid of him," I say.

"I am," she replies, surprising me with her admission. She steps up close, her eyes wide. "You don't know the true violence he's capable of. I was here the night he killed the beast in the pit. Attacking his compliance officers may be understandable, but he would have hurt the other students if we hadn't stopped him."

I give a quick shake of my head, a confident denial. "That isn't true."

I want to believe that if push came to shove, Striker would never harm the other students, but his motives are always complex, driven by the need to survive. Violence is his backup plan. Always.

First Lucinda, now Vulture. Both of them warning me to be careful around Striker. Lucinda was motivated by genuine concern but Vulture can only be trying to sow seeds of distrust.

"Believe what you will," Vulture says. "Striker Draven is capable of greater brutality than my son. I think you know that's saying something."

She sweeps past me before she hesitates at the door. "Kaitlyn has learned her lesson. She won't bother you again. Please make sure Striker stays away from her, too."

She's gone before I can tell Vulture where to stick her request. Of course Striker will stay away from Kaitlyn. Vulture should worry about her daughter.

I sigh into the quiet. I don't believe for one second that Kaitlyn has given up. Not by a long shot.

20. PEYTON PRICE

*H*arrison approaches me the minute I appear at the Academy's back entrance.

He looks well-rested and crisp in combat gear, his dark hair appearing darker in the sunlight, even though he still wears a wash of stubble across his jaw.

"You and I are training inside this morning," he says, gesturing toward the door I exited through.

I'm immediately on my guard. Hadrix told me that Harrison would train me personally, but he didn't say I'd be isolated from the other students. "Why not out here?"

He gives me a half-smile. "Because you're a fast learner. The others don't need to be discouraged."

In the distance, Ryan is heading in my direction too. I told him we would fight this morning—the best way to discover his power.

"I need to speak with Ryan first," I say, ignoring Harrison's disapproving look. "I'll be right back."

I leave Harrison at the door and meet Ryan closer to the combat mat.

"You ready to fight?" he asks, his demeanor relaxed despite the hint of anticipation in his eyes.

I give him an apologetic smile. "Apparently, I'm not training out here this morning."

"Oh." His disappointment is palpable, the slump in his shoulders immediate. I understand his frustration. He's the last of his friends to find out what his power is.

"Come and see me this evening instead—before dinner," I hurry to say. "We can take a run around the perimeter and figure things out then."

A wary crease settles onto his forehead. He glances at Harrison, who waits at the back door with his big arms folded across his chest and the intensity of his scowl increasing.

"Is everything okay?" Ryan asks.

I'm impressed that Ryan's forgotten about his own disappointment so quickly and now appears concerned for my welfare.

I put on my most confident face. "Nothing I can't handle."

"Well, that's a given." Ryan suddenly laughs, his hazel eyes brightening. He gives me a wink like he did yesterday, but it suddenly feels... intense. Like his eyes are a little too bright. Slightly feverish.

Hungry.

I shiver at the emptiness I see when I look into his eyes, as if he's a hollow chasm that needs to be fed.

I suddenly find myself asking him, "Are you sure you ate enough for breakfast this morning?"

He side-eyes me. "Uh. Yeah, Peyton. I did."

"Of course." I laugh, trying to recover from my own weirdness. "Okay, then. But just to be safe, please ask Lucinda to come find me if I haven't reappeared by the time you finish up here."

"I will." He glances left, and I'm suddenly aware of Striker's burning gaze.

Striker's waiting for me to come out to train too. Our agreement to separate during the day didn't include losing sight of each other for long periods of time, but maybe it's for the best.

Simply standing in Striker's line of sight makes my stomach flutter.

Ryan turns away with a nod. "Be careful, Peyton."

I stride back to Harrison, determined not to hurry in answer to his commanding glare. "I'm ready now."

Striker's gaze follows me until we disappear inside the building. I'm momentarily confused when Harrison guides me down the east wing on the first floor in the direction of the kitchen, but he quickly veers into one of the rooms on the right-hand side.

The room has been set up with tumble mats, but it's the table of knives that draws my attention. It's like stepping back in time except that there are at least ten daggers lined up in a row on the table instead of one like there was during my lesson with Raptor.

"What is this?" I demand, freezing in the doorway.

I'm not defenseless like I used to be and I won't hesitate to fight back if I have to.

Harrison turns carefully, focusing on my hands, where my claws are extending. He follows my line of sight to the table. "Your choice."

"Of what?"

"Dagger," he says, keeping his voice low, still watching my hands before his focus shifts to my whip. "You need to choose one that suits your grip and the size of your hand."

I should be able to tell the truth from a lie, but right now, his honesty is confusing me. "You want me to choose a weapon. Why?"

"So you can practice with it," he says, as if he's speaking to a child.

"Whom did these knives belong to in the past?"

He relaxes as if he finally figured me out. "You're concerned about the memories attached to them. You have nothing to worry about. They're brand new. We only have a limited number of spares, so you get first pick. We thought it best to avoid any unintended consequences of training you with a used weapon."

Taking his word at face value for now, I move carefully toward the table, eyeing the daggers, but my voice fills with threat. "If you so much as lean toward this table, I will shred you to pieces."

He gives me a frustrated growl, the confusion returning to his face. "What's going on, Peyton?"

When I continue to glare at him, he folds his arms across his chest. "I don't know what happened to you in the past—"

"Raptor happened."

"Right." His expression clears, somber now. He exhales slowly, studying the knives and then me. "Well, I'm here to train you, not hurt you. If you follow my instructions, we won't have a problem. Is that clear?"

"What kind of shifter are you?" I ask, evading his command.

He appears thrown by the change of subject. "What?"

"You heard me."

"I'm a panther."

"Huh." I tap my finger against my thigh. "Most of the guys out there… they're human, aren't they?"

"Most of them," he says. "Not all."

"'Harrison' isn't your real name."

He returns my frank expression with his own. "It isn't."

I nod. "It's refreshing to have an honest conversation," I say. "So, yes. We're clear."

He breaks into a smile before he tries to hide it. *Too late, Harrison.* He might be a panther, but he definitely has a human side and right now, he must be mentally claiming victory that he got me to agree to anything.

"Then let's get started," he says, his expression controlled again. "Pick up each knife and test its weight in your hand. You should know pretty quickly which one suits you."

"My whip suits me," I fire back.

His response is so smooth, he could have practiced it. "Then choose a dagger that reminds you of the handle of your whip."

I step three knives down and pick up one with a handle the same length and diameter of my whip. "This one."

He waits a beat. "You're sure? You don't want to try any others?"

"No."

"Okay, then. The next part of your training requires that I touch you. I'd like to retain all of my limbs, so is that okay with you?"

"That depends where you're going to touch me."

He misses another beat. "Arms, legs, torso—that includes your back and waist. Also your neck and head."

My voice softens. An unexpected warmth spreads through my chest. "So… pretty much *everywhere.*"

The corner of his mouth curls up. "Not everywhere."

I inhale, start to speak, and then stop. The scent of wildflowers wafts around me, faint but unmistakable. *What the hell?*

Harrison takes a step toward me, his features relaxed, but the way he moves confirms his assertion that he's a panther shifter. He doesn't step so much as *prowl.*

Confusion strikes through me. *Why the hell is my body compelling him to come to me right now?*

I close my eyes, fighting my basic instincts, but it's like trying to stop lava flowing down a volcano.

I am a Fury. I want to…

Dominate. Allure. Seduce…

Control.

If I give in to my inner nature, I could end up on the table with Harrison doing something that has nothing to do with knives.

But I don't want that! Damn this Fury inside of me.

I dig the claws of my free hand into my palm hard enough to draw blood. Warm liquid pools inside my closed fist and I focus on it with all my might.

I open my eyes to find Harrison standing right in front of me. He was so quiet that I didn't hear him close the gap between us.

His eyes are unfocused. He's compliant.

"Peyton?" he says. "Tell me what you want."

I grit my teeth, my chest rising and falling rapidly, fighting every instinct to unfurl my fist, put down the knife, lean forward, and kiss the stubble on his jaw.

I could whisper things to him, tell him to kill Raptor for me, tell him to murder Kaitlyn in her sleep, but I plant my feet and force stern sounds from my mouth. "I want you to train me and never touch me except for that purpose."

His eyes clear. His forehead creases with apparent confusion as he assesses the very short distance between us, but he doesn't take a step back. "Then let me show you how to hold your weapon."

His hand closes around mine and my training begins.

21. PEYTON PRICE

Training in weapons requires a lot more physical strength than I thought it would.

Learning how to use the dagger is just the beginning. Harrison is determined that I move with it efficiently—that means not cutting myself as I duck, roll, and tumble. Even kicking my leg can result in a savage wound to my standing thigh if I'm not conscious of where the blade in my hand is also moving.

Halfway through the lesson, I ditch my whip and skirt, stripping down to my bra and boyshorts so that I can move more freely in my workout gear.

Harrison doesn't blink an eyelid, but when I emerge from the training room, sweaty and tired, I find Striker directly in my line of sight.

He pauses at the end of the corridor thirty paces away, his gaze raking over me from the sweat dripping down my face and chest to the rapidly healing cuts on my legs—all self-inflicted.

I pushed myself harder and faster, finally succeeding in running, levitating, spinning, and tumbling back to the floor without cutting myself.

Striker's burning glare is for Harrison as he steps out behind me.

"Water," Harrison orders me, ignoring Striker. "You worked hard. You need to hydrate."

He strides past me, along the corridor, directly facing Striker, who doesn't say a word as Harrison passes him.

Now that I observe them from a distance, I sense the same chill between Striker and Harrison that passed between Harrison and Raptor.

It's more intense on Harrison's side than Striker's. I remember the way Harrison looked at Striker when he said he never killed anyone who didn't deserve it.

A sudden shiver courses down my spine. If it weren't for the glitch in my power, I would cross the distance between myself and Striker right now and reassure him that none of my wounds were caused by Harrison. But I'm already struggling to heal now that Striker is in my sights.

Dammit.

I spin on my heel and stride away from him toward the kitchen, where the head cook has placed a large pitcher of water on the table.

I cast her a curious glance, wondering if she's somehow a mind reader.

"We heard you training," she says. "It sounded like you'd need this sooner or later."

"Thank you." I take a long sip before I ask, "What should I call you?"

"You're not supposed to call me anything, but my name is Alison."

"Thank you, Alison."

She gives me a quick nod before she turns back to her work. I drink the entire pitcher, then I check my wounds again.

All healed. Just as well, because I don't know what to expect from my lesson with Mallard this afternoon.

~

The library is quiet as I approach and take a cautious look inside.

Mallard sits at the table farthest to the left, his focus fixed on the window on that side of the room, his gaze following the specks of dust floating in the sunbeams. He doesn't seem quite present, which is strange because he was always one of the sharpest teachers.

A book lies open in front of him.

I recognize it, even without seeing its front cover.

"You found the book about me," I say, taking a careful seat opposite him.

His head turns slowly and his eyes finally become focused on me. He sports a black eye and a cut across his lip. Bruises dot his neck and shoulders beneath his collar. Hadrix has not been kind to him.

Mallard's gaze is a little too bright, his shoulders a little too tense, and I'm not sure how to read the sudden change in his posture.

"It's the most important book," he says, speaking normally, as if his behavior moments before wasn't strange. He turns the book toward me. "I'm supposed to talk to you about your killing power, but there's something much more important to discuss."

"What is that?"

He taps the illustration.

"They are three," he says. "Always together. Never alone. They are synonymous. Their thoughts are the same. Their actions mimic each other. Even their voices—they sound and speak as one." His eyes meet mine. "They *never* cohabit with anyone else."

The full-page illustration backs up his assertions.

The three women have identical features; even their legs are the same length. They wear the same diaphanous clothing, carry the same black whips. Snakes coil around their bodies, winding around their shoulders, curling around their thighs, each reptile extending from the Fury's neck and coiling down her body. Only the color of the Furies' hair differs.

He turns the page and taps the very first sentence written at the top of it. "Read this for me."

I already know the sentence in the book that he's pointing at.

A Fury is incapable of love.

I refuse to look at the page. "I know that part. Talk to me about something else."

His forehead creases in a suddenly furious expression. "But do you understand it?"

"What is there to understand? I'm only capable of pain and torment."

His lips press into a stern line. "I overheard you and Raptor yesterday. You're vulnerable around Striker. You need to know why."

I freeze in my chair. I'm struggling to believe that Mallard of all people has the answers I need so desperately.

"What's your theory?" I ask, maintaining a deadpan expression.

"A *Fury* is incapable of love. But you are not only a Fury. You're also human. *Humans* are capable of love."

I try to speak. "What are you trying to…?" I take a deep breath, clear my throat, and try to regain my composure. "What are you saying?"

"I'm saying that it's really quite simple. The only way you can feel love is to be human. You must choose to be human when you're around Striker because you—"

"Stop!" My claws snap against the table. "That is not for you to say."

"Then know the truth in your mind," he says, unperturbed by my show of aggression. "You react to Striker on a powerful subconscious level and completely without volition. Right now, it takes touch to trigger your reaction, but soon, it won't even take that. You won't even need to *see* him. The moment your heightened senses detect his presence, you will react on the most basic chemical level. You can't feel love as a Fury, so your human side takes control."

Could he be right? But that would mean that my need to love and be loved is greater than my survival instincts.

And it means that my vulnerability is only going to get worse.

"Hadrix and his family will use Striker against you as soon as it suits their purpose," he says. "You must understand what's going on so you can prepare and protect yourself."

I stare at the book in front of me, refusing to give Mallard the satisfaction of knowing that his theory has rattled me.

If he's right, then I have no solution.

I already told Striker that I love him. In my most human, most vulnerable, moment, I felt love glowing in my heart and mind and I was sure he felt it too.

No. I give a shake of my head. Mallard's theory doesn't hold, because I'm not always human around Striker. Yesterday I picked up my whip when Striker wanted to leave me, and I found my power again. I fought him tooth and nail to stop him leaving.

I lift my chin. "Your theory's flawed. I *have* accessed my power around Striker."

He clasps his hands in front of him, unworried. "How did you feel toward him in that moment?"

I close my eyes, not wanting to remember how betrayed I'd felt. "I was angry with him."

"Consciously?"

I open my eyes, dreading the truth I'm about to speak. "With all my heart."

Mallard nods. "Then you *can* override your humanity, but

only if you're genuinely angry with him. Your Fury will only prevail if your love turns to hate."

He leans so far forward that I'm worried he's going to try to take my hand, as if anything he could do would comfort me. "You can only be a Fury around Striker when you feel hatred deep in your soul. You're going to have to hate him if you want to survive."

A cold sweat suddenly breaks across my face and neck.

I remember Raptor telling me that he made me. That his brutality would keep me strong. Striker always triggered my power because... I hated him. More than I ever hated anyone. But now...

Love is my poison.

My voice is hoarse, a scratchy sound in my throat. "Why are you telling me this?"

He takes a deep breath, exhaling it slowly. "I used to think I was here for research. Now I know I'm here to die."

I consider him carefully, wary of his quiet declaration. He wasn't the most harmful teacher—he rarely raised his wand in aggression—but he also never stepped in to stop the other teachers from hurting us.

"They're going to kill me and you're the only one who can stop them." He leans forward again. "You're too smart to believe that I would do anything out of kindness. My actions are about self-preservation."

I nod. "The assassins are coming for you. You want me to stop them."

He looks surprised. "I don't fear the assassins. They're honorable. I would welcome death at an assassin's hand. It will be quick and merciful. They don't kill for the enjoyment of it."

He pulls his collar away from his neck, revealing multiple puncture marks across his collar bone. "Hadrix's mercenaries torture and kill because they like it."

"But—"

"Don't be fooled!" Mallard suddenly thumps the table. "They have their orders from Hadrix not to touch any of you. To be *nice* to you. But the moment Hadrix tells them to, they will hurt every single one of you. Look into my eyes and tell me you don't believe me."

I don't want to believe him. I want to believe that the men training us are ordinary, honorable soldiers. Soldiers who need coffee in the morning and ask permission before they lay hands on us.

"Your Fury has the power to tell truth from lies." Mallard speaks through gritted teeth. "Your purpose is to seek vengeance on those who have done wrong. Liars, murderers, thieves, abusers. People like me. People like Hadrix and Raptor and all his soldiers."

He grabs me and it takes all my willpower not to scratch my claws across the hand that holds me to make him let go.

The only thing that stops me is the crisscross of existing cuts and fresh scabs across the back of his hand and along his wrist.

I don't want to acknowledge the truth right in front of me—Mallard is taking the brunt of their aggression instead of us. But that won't be true for long.

"I only have one more thing to tell you," he says, holding me with a hand that suddenly shakes, as if he's running out of strength. "You must remember that your mother—your *true* mother—was the primordial deity Nyx. She was the mother of death. She's also the mother of the Valkyrie."

My eyes widen in surprise at this revelation.

His gaze bores into mine. "That makes you and Hunter Cassidy sisters. Don't forget that."

His shaking hand slowly unfurls from my arm before he sinks back to his chair and focuses on the sunbeams again. The change in his demeanor is so sudden that it's like a light switching off.

I study him a moment longer, allowing my senses to expand,

deliberately seeking truth from lies. My truth-seeking power is sluggish, as if it's also damaged.

Finally, a faint shimmer catches the light around Mallard's form. A dark spell clings to him, thicker around his head. He must have been fighting it the entire time he was speaking with me.

He said he was supposed to teach me about my killing power, but he told me something much more important instead.

"What has Vulture done to you?" I ask him, even though I know he won't be able to answer.

The spell around him is absolute once more. It's the same spell Vulture used on the students the day that Hadrix arrived, keeping them compliant and subject to her will. She must have set it to release him when I arrived, but only for a short time.

Mallard exists at her whim now.

How can I trust anything he told me? He acted as if he was telling me something they didn't want me to know, but he also told me I would have to hate Striker to survive.

Just this morning, Vulture tried to make me afraid of Striker. She wants to drive a wedge between us. She could be using Mallard to do the same. That means his theory about my healing power could be lies… or it could be the truth.

What really scares me is that I can't tell the difference.

In my vision of the Fury, she and her sisters lived in a cabin far away from everyone else, far away from the liars and cheaters, a place where peace might be possible.

I'm surrounded by liars, murderers, and assholes here. My ability to see the truth is dying because I can't face the evil around me.

I close my eyes against the quiet scream at the back of my mind, the deep fury that I keep at bay.

If I recognize the evil around me, I'll kill them all.

22. PEYTON PRICE

I stumble from the library, desperate for fresh air.

I need to get my head straight before I see Striker again. I also need to carry through with my promise to meet Ryan before dinner.

Hurrying outside into the crisp early evening air, I start running around the perimeter while my whip thuds a calming rhythm against my thigh. If I were human, it would bruise me with every hit, but I heal instantly.

A few minutes later, Ryan joins me, easily keeping pace at my side.

Before I can focus on the task of discovering his power, he asks, "There's more to it, isn't there? You and Striker, I mean."

I focus on my breathing, the air rushing in and out of my lungs, and the thudding sensation through my legs as I deliberately plant my feet on the ground instead of levitating. "Not open for discussion."

I catch the humorless grin he throws in my direction. "Yeah, I thought Lucinda stepped into some deep shit this morning. I don't want to force information out of you, but everyone noticed your separation from Striker today. Even Hadrix's guys were talking about it. It's one thing to separate during class, but you didn't eat meals together, either. After Raptor's attack on you yesterday, there's talk."

I jolt to a stop, plowing up the grass as I dig my feet in. "Okay, spit it out. What are they saying?"

He pulls up beside me. "That Raptor has it in for Striker because Striker beat the crap out of him. Raptor's targeting you to get his revenge. Now you're pretending to hate each other so Raptor won't target you anymore."

My blood boils, but not because the students are talking about me—or because their theory is partially true, or even because it makes it sound like I'm the weaker one and that's why Raptor is picking on me instead of taking his revenge out on Striker. It's because...

Damn wildflowers.

I asked Ryan a question and my power of compulsion rose without me even realizing it, forcing him to speak.

What really scares me is that it feels so natural. Unlike my truth-seeking power, which is fading, my urge to dominate is growing.

Just like my interaction with Harrison today, using my compulsion power is becoming easier than subduing it.

Ryan's chest rises and falls in my vision. Every time he sucks in air, the movement pulls me toward him. The scar across his eye is suddenly like a yawning chasm, a twisted rope, a need for answers.

The dizzying desire to control him floods through me and I struggle to fight it.

I don't want to fight it.

I take a step forward, reaching up to touch his face.

My voice softens as my fingertips rest against his forehead. "How did this happen?"

He jolts a little on contact, but his pupils constrict as he inhales.

"You can tell me," I whisper, shifting closer to him.

His features relax and the tension leaves his shoulders. "My mom tried to hide the fact that I was Unknown. My uncle found out and attempted to kill me. She pulled me out of the way before he could do more damage. Except that he…" Ryan takes a shuddering breath and stops speaking, shaking his head.

"It's okay," I murmur. "Tell me everything."

Ryan's eyes glitter and the hunger in them grows, a swirling darkness filled with gleaming specks that look like…

I squint, trying to identify the flecks in his eyes. Not stars, not petals. Nothing so pretty. They're sharp and dangerous.

Ryan swallows before he speaks again. "His arm was still swinging and he slit her throat."

Ryan takes hold of my hand and runs my finger down the cut across his left eyebrow, following the way it sweeps down and to the side of his cheekbone.

I gasp, a deep horror filling me, along with a need for revenge. "What kind of supernatural is your uncle?"

"He's a bear shifter."

"I promise you, Ryan," I say. "I will find him and kill him for what he did."

"You don't need to," Ryan says, his focus on my face becoming intense. "I already killed him. Then I contacted Bloodwing and waited for them to come for me. The compliance officers got to me before the Magical Magnate did." He shifts closer to me, so close that his arms brush my sides.

"Now," he says. "What do you want from me, Peyton?"

"I want to see your power," I whisper into the narrow space between us.

He jolts away from me, as if revealing his power is harder than telling me the secrets of his past. He shakes his head, pressing his fingers to his temples. "No."

I'm surprised by his sudden reluctance, let alone his ability to push back against the compulsion thickening around him. "Don't you want to find out what you are?"

"I can feel it inside me. It isn't good. *I'm* not good."

"Neither am I." I take a step forward, dogging his steps as he backs away from me, my voice becoming stern. "Show me."

He stumbles backward, his feet catching in the grass, but I grab him, filling the air around us with the sweet scent of wildflowers. Sickly and thick, the fragrance clings inside my nose and throat.

When he struggles, I shout at him. "Show me!"

He lifts his head and roars. "*No!*"

As he shouts, his voice changes, becoming deep and guttural until the sounds are unintelligible and the flecks in his eyes brighten.

I suddenly realize what they resemble.

Shards of bone.

Ryan rises up before me, his torso elongating, the muscles on his arms and thighs thinning and constricting closer to the bone. Multiple fingers join together to leave him with three thick fingers on each hand, each digit ending in a heavy claw. The skin of his face tightens around his skull, his hair recedes, and his eyes hollow out into dark chasms.

He tilts his head toward me, his lips stretching apart to reveal rows of sharp teeth, surrounded by bloody gums.

Oh... damn.

"You're a wendigo," I say.

Bending to my eye level, he hisses beneath his breath, the hollows of his eyes burning into me as he looks me over like I'm his next meal.

"I'm hungry." He licks his lips. "You won't mind if I take a bite, will you?"

"Actually," I snarl, "I would."

I snatch my whip from its holder, snapping the hair tie that holds it against my waist as I dart out of Ryan's reach and leap back toward the fence.

My whip unravels, striking toward him.

As he charges at me, darting around the deadly lash, I flick my wrist. The tips *crack*. It's intended as a warning, but Ryan's thin arm snaps out and plucks the lash right out of the air.

The tips tear through his flesh, hitting the bone with sickening pops.

I'm sure his bone is broken, but he snarls at me again, gripping the lash and refusing to let go, as if nothing's wrong with his arm.

My eyes widen as he wrenches the weapon toward him, pulling me with it.

I dart up into the air, trying to stretch his arm up over his head and yank the whip out of his hold that way.

A grin breaks across his face as he watches my flight path and just as I ascend above him, he drops to his knees, pulling with all his weight.

I have no choice but to let the whip go.

It thuds to the grass as Ryan drops it, his arm hanging loose now, blood dripping down to his fingers.

He still doesn't seem to notice his wound.

He tilts his head back to see me. "Come down, little morsel. If you don't, I'll have to satisfy my hunger elsewhere."

Fear drives through me. I can't let him attack the other students.

I forced Ryan's power out of him. Now I have to control him.

"You will remain still," I order him, lowering myself carefully to the ground, testing my power of compulsion, but to my shock, the perfume is lighter now and I don't understand why.

Instead of wildflowers, the overpowering scent of cedarwood and balsam fills my lungs, striking at me with oppressive force.

It's Striker's scent.

Oh... hell...

Ryan shakes his head, the sounds from his throat long and drawn out. "I don't think I will."

He leaps for me.

My fist crunches against his skull, but he accepts blow after blow as he forces me down toward the ground, his hands closing around my shoulders and his head bending to my neck, his teeth a mere inch from the surface of my skin.

I scream as I struggle against his hold. "Let me go!"

I sound like Peyton, not Fury.

My knees buckle, Ryan's weight falls on me, and his teeth sink into my shoulder. The world turns to fire as pain shoots through me and my screams fill the air.

Striker's blazing hellhound thuds into Ryan from the side. Ryan's weight lifts, his teeth tearing through my shoulder as he flies off me.

Striker... he wasn't even near me this time.

A new shadow drops over me and Lachlan's concerned face appears—his Enenra face, smoke swirling in his eyes and around his torso.

"Peyton!" he shouts. "Focus on me."

A garbled response leaves my mouth. I'm shaking and I can't seem to stop. I taste blood in my mouth and smell it on my neck and shoulder.

Lachlan twists to the side, speaking to someone else now. "She's going into shock."

"There must be poison in Ryan's bite." Lucinda kneels beside me, her skin mottled like tree bark and her eyes hard and wooden. "See the color of her skin around the wound—tinged green. But why isn't she healing?"

I can barely form thoughts. Maybe it's true about the poison because somehow I'm less able to comprehend what I'm experiencing than I was yesterday when Raptor attacked me.

Struggling against Lachlan's hold, I twist to see Striker's hellhound tear into the wendigo. Claws and teeth flash. Blood splatters the grass and fear rises inside me.

"Stop," I whisper. "Stop them."

Ryan kept functioning despite the damage I did to his arm, which tells me he can either heal rapidly—or he doesn't feel pain and might not know that he's hurt. Striker could kill him. Or the other way around.

Lucinda focuses beyond me, whispering beneath her breath.

Just as Striker punches Ryan back toward the fence, the tree branches shoot between the bars. Vines whip around Ryan's torso and pull tight, trapping him against the metal poles.

Another figure races past me, shouting at them. It's Bree. "Get back, Striker!"

As she runs, she dumps a bottle of water over her head. Striker leaps out of the way as Bree's voice rises into the air, singing to Ryan.

She's just in time as Ryan slashes at the vines, cutting through most of them in one slice, but he focuses on her—the first time he's calmed down—his expression shifting from desperately hungry to confused.

Finally, he becomes silent and still.

I can't make out what Bree's saying, but even I feel calm. Or maybe that's the poison numbing me. I'm not sure.

Lucinda suddenly grabs my face. "Peyton? *Dear ancients. Striker!*" She screams for him, but at the edge of my vision Striker backs away, farther and farther until I can't see him anymore.

Lucinda calls after him, but he sprints into the distance and I can only guess that he's trying to get as far away from me as he can.

She gapes after him before she returns her attention to me. "Peyton? Can you hear me?"

My head begins to clear. Then a little more. My vocal chords resume functioning and the strength returns to my arms and legs. I sigh with relief as the pain eases in my shoulder and I sense the wound knit.

Lucinda's relieved exhale meets my ears. "Oh, thank the ancients. You're finally healing."

I grab her arm, my fingers closing tightly as I struggle to get to my feet. "I have to talk to Ryan."

She tries to stop me. "You need to rest."

"I'm okay. Really. Just a glitch—"

"That was not a glitch." Her firm gaze meets mine. "That was a major malfunction."

I press my lips together. "I can explain, I promise. Right now I need to know if Ryan's okay."

The pressure of her hold eases as she reluctantly lets me go, supporting me as I find my feet.

Across the yard, Ryan is crouched over his knees, throwing up into the grass while Bree rubs his back. She hands him the water bottle and he gulps down its remaining contents.

As I venture toward him, he thumps the grass. "I'm a fucking vegetarian!"

When I reach his position, his eyes meet mine before his gaze lowers to my shoulder.

He leans back on his heels to grip his forehead with one hand and his stomach with the other. "I hurt you, didn't I?"

My shirt is torn. I'm not a pretty sight right now.

"It's okay," Bree murmurs to him, hugging him from the side. "Peyton's fine."

I kneel in the grass in front of Ryan, my voice small. "I'm sorry, Ryan. I pushed you too hard."

I gave in to my Fury and it backfired on me.

He gives me a determined look. "I'm never turning into that thing again."

Bree's arms tighten around him, a cautious smile on her lips.

"I don't know…" She drops a kiss against his cheek. "I sort of like that we both have sharp teeth."

He considers her smile and the rows of shark teeth still filling her mouth.

"I can't control it like you can," he says.

"We'll find a way," she answers. "We'll go through the books in the library and find out everything we can about your power." She squeezes his arm. "Together. Okay?"

He exhales a shuddering breath as she helps him stand. "Okay."

They pass Lachlan, who stands at the side with Lucinda. Both of their powers are fading fast now that the threat is over.

Ryan fist-bumps Lachlan unhappily as he passes. "Looks like I got the butt-end of powers."

"You're okay, man. You'll figure it out," Lachlan says.

Both he and Lucinda wait expectantly as I draw to my feet.

Lucinda's expression is especially stern. She plants her hands on her hips. "Okay, Peyton. What's really going on?"

I'm tired of telling half-truths. Trying to keep the problems with my power a secret might have been the worst thing I could do.

If more people know about it, then they'll be aware when things go wrong. They'll be ready to help.

It's been so difficult for me to accept help in the past—it still is—but I'm slowly learning to ask for it when I need it.

"There's something wrong with my healing power," I say. "I can't heal when Striker's touching me. And now it seems to be getting worse."

Lachlan considers me carefully while Lucinda exhales slowly. "So that's why you separated today," she says.

"It's why we'll have to separate every day. Even training in the combat ring, I could get badly hurt if Striker's around. It didn't matter so much when we were all human, but it matters now."

"Who else knows?" Lucinda asks, but her face quickly pales. "Raptor knows. Doesn't he?"

I nod. "Yesterday was his idea of a sick test."

"So this morning when I said that Striker might hurt you… *Damn*. I'm sorry, Peyton. I didn't realize it would strike so close to the truth."

"It isn't something he chooses to do," I say, unable to keep the defensive tone from my voice. "It's all about me—how I react around him—but until we figure out a solution, I have to be careful."

Lachlan is quiet as usual, but he says, "You can't be alone when you unearth someone's power. From now on, I'll come with you."

I arch an eyebrow at him. "You?"

One corner of his mouth curls up into a smile and his gray eyes fill with wisps of smoke. "In case you haven't noticed, nothing can touch me. But most importantly, nothing can escape me, either."

"Yeah… okay," I say, even though I feel reluctant about it. I shouldn't be monopolizing his powers when there are so few with powers to protect the others. "I guess that makes you the perfect bodyguard."

He takes hold of my shoulder in a firm grip, genuine concern filling his eyes. "From now on, I'll follow your steps. If you're near Striker, I'll watch over you."

I seek my power and search Lachlan's eyes for truth.

Quiet honesty meets my gaze. He wants to help me without any ulterior motives.

The back of my eyes suddenly burn with hot tears. Damn, he's like the big brother I never had.

"Thank you." I swallow and clear my throat, blinking hard to chase away my emotions.

Lachlan turns to Lucinda. "I'll let Ashley and Joseph know that everything's okay. See you inside."

"I'll come with you," she says. "I think Peyton needs to be somewhere right now."

I do. I need to see Striker. Right away.

I hurry to the attic—the most likely place he'll be.

I find him slumped against the wall outside his bedroom, his head in his hands.

For a mere second, my power remains under my control.

Before it's washed away, I sense everything from Striker… fire and danger, the threat of pain and suffering. Far, far beneath it, something much more fragile—a mirror of my own feelings, an ache for something he can't have.

Then my human heart beats inside my chest, I can't sense his thoughts anymore, and I feel more at peace than I do when my power rages.

It scares me that Mallard could be right. I can't feel love when I'm a Fury and… I need to feel it.

Love might kill me, but I want it.

23. STRIKER DRAVEN

I lean against the wall outside my bedroom, the farthest I can get from Peyton and still see her through the wide windows.

Her response to me is getting worse. I wasn't even touching her just now. I was approaching her with ten paces still between us.

She's okay now, but every time she gets hurt, the cracks in my future deepen.

Not today, I tell my beast before I drop my head into my hands. *Just give me a little longer with her.*

Her soft footfalls meet my ears sooner than I expected. "Striker?"

I straighten as her arms wind around my chest, her thighs press against mine, and her lips find the hollow at the base of my neck. She draws my hands away from my head, her palms gentler than I've ever felt them as she presses my arms around her waist.

"I'm sorry," she whispers. "I didn't realize you were close by or I never would have taken such a risk."

I inhale the scent of her hair. It's soft against my cheek and her skin is very, very human.

"I came to find you when you didn't come to dinner," I say. "When I saw you with Ryan, I thought it was safe to be around you. I didn't think he would be a threat to you. But then he changed and I froze. I've never frozen like that before." I push at the rise of emotions, the fear I felt when she tried to use her whip against him and failed. "I couldn't get away from you fast enough."

"You helped me."

"You wouldn't need help if it weren't for me."

She draws back to peer into my eyes, her own becoming stern and grim. "I wouldn't need help if it weren't for *me*."

I run my hand through her hair, catching in the clumped ends, tangling in the torn material clinging to her shoulder.

How many more times will I wash blood off her body?

"I can't do this, Peyton," I whisper, hoping she won't hear me, but speaking my fears is the only way I can control them.

She doesn't know I don't mean staying with her. Her eyes narrow at me, a hint of fire growing behind them, the faintest tinge of crimson. "Don't even think about leaving, Striker. If I have to fight you with my human hands, I will."

"I won't break my promise," I say. "I'm not going anywhere until you tell me to go."

"Good." She relaxes against me. "You don't have to worry about me. I won't get hurt again. Lachlan will keep an eye on me from now on. He can get in anyone's way without getting hurt himself."

I grit my teeth. I want to rant and rail and punch Lachlan's lights out for offering to help because protecting Peyton is *my fucking job.*

She presses a kiss to my lips before she fits her head to the shape of my neck, not asking for anything other than my presence.

I breathe in and out.

Is this what love feels like?

I have nothing to compare it to. Even my relationship with my stepsister, Zara, has carefully constructed walls around it, truths we don't face. She picked me up after Mom died, but she didn't fight for me like Peyton has. Kaitlyn was like poison sapping everything I had, taking more and more, delivering suffering with every game she played, but Peyton… she only gives—even when her form of giving is facing me head on.

I don't have anything to give her in return.

For a moment, I lose myself in a fantasy of what our lives would have looked like if I'd met her out in the real world. I would have taken her to parties, showered her with expensive gifts, bought her anything she wanted.

She probably would have burned all of it. She sees through everything superficial.

She arches back to see my smile. "What is it?"

I groan as her body presses against mine in unbearable ways.

She answers my questioning kiss by drawing me into our bedroom.

Hours later as she lies in my arms, she tips her head back. "Striker?"

I stroke her hair down her naked back, trailing across her shoulder blades and spine. "Hmm?"

"What if we're the bad guys?"

I'm not sure what prompted her to ask me something like that. I guess it's a valid question, given the company we're keeping.

Maybe we are. Maybe we aren't. Only the future will tell us.

Whether we are or not, I'm determined that she'll survive.

My lips curve into a dangerous smile. "The end isn't written yet."

She settles into my arms, her eyelashes lowering toward her cheeks, half-asleep. "They'll come for us," she murmurs. "We have nowhere to run."

She must be talking about the assassins, but I'm not completely sure. Either the assassins will come for us or Hadrix's men will turn on us. It'll be a bloodbath. We'll stand and fight. Even escaping through the forest is fraught—

I jolt upright, grabbing hold of Peyton so I don't hurt her. "The fence."

She's wide awake. "Striker?"

"Yesterday, I bent the bars open near the side of the building. If I could get out through it, then something else could get in. Especially now that they've turned off the electricity."

"The creature," she whispers. She's suddenly on the move, sliding lithely out of the bed and snatching her clothes and her whip off the floor. "We have to close it."

I'm right behind her, hurrying to pull on my sweatpants before we race along the corridor and down the stairs.

We run past Joseph and Lucinda on our way. They're standing watch at the entrance to the dorms.

"What's wrong?" Lucinda calls.

I give a second's thought to whether we might need backup, but it's far better that they remain here protecting the others. "Stay where you are," I order. "Everything's fine."

For now.

The front and back doors are closed against the night, but that doesn't mean that the creature isn't already inside. It's only as we burst through the back door that I realize Peyton shouldn't have come with me.

I reach for her, ready to tell her to go back inside, but even in her human form, she's agile.

"I'll check the front yard," she calls, darting away from me. "You guard the opening."

At least if she puts distance between us, she'll be stronger.

The open bars are located at the side of the building where they aren't conspicuous.

They're still bent open, but I won't close them until we're sure the creature isn't inside with us.

My heartbeats crowd my chest as I expand my senses and listen carefully to the sounds around me. Peyton's running footfalls. Muffled voices inside the building. The whispering breeze through the trees.

A shadow shifts four paces away from me outside the fence just inside the tree line.

A pair of yellow eyes glint in the darkness, a hunched form crouching in the dark.

I sense its breathing—shallow and sharp with a strange growl in it.

My beast rises, glowing trails of lava forming across my torso and down my arms. As my chest expands and my back shifts to allow my bones to release, harnessing my full power in case I need it, the yellow eyes rise higher in the darkness, matching me in height, its silhouette changing, but I can't identify its shape.

It remains too far inside the darkness where the moonlight doesn't reach.

It whispers through the dark. "Striker Draven."

I take a quick step forward, reaching for the open bars, my hackles rising, my threat level high. My fingers close around the metal, muscles bunching, fear rising that the creature will attack before I can close off the opening.

I don't fear much, but there's a level of danger in those yellow eyes that I've never seen before. The fact that it knows my name…

Its eyes lift again, glancing up toward the moon resting high in the sky behind me.

Peyton's running footfalls approach from the side, but confusingly, the creature wasn't focusing on her.

Even so, my head snaps in her direction. "Stay back!"

She skids to a halt, but when I look back into the trees, the creature's gone.

"I saw it," she says, keeping her voice low as she reaches for my hands still wrapped around the bars.

She carefully presses a fingertip to a part of my hand that isn't glowing with fire. I'm shocked to realize that I could burn her while I'm like this.

"You closed it," she says. "We're safe."

I struggle to let go of the bars, needing to reassure myself that nothing can squeeze between this gap now. "Metal won't keep that thing away." My voice becomes a snarl. "Hadrix knows it. It must be why he turned off the electricity. If the creature becomes a threat, then you'll try to kill it."

I force my beast to back down, worried about harming Peyton.

I tell myself I can call on my power again quickly if I need it. My greatest fear right now is that Hadrix will use the creature against us.

Peyton raises her eyes to mine, her human face pale in the moonlight. "Striker—"

"He's waiting for a chance to use the creature to his advantage," I say.

She doesn't seem to hear me.

Her line of sight has shifted to something in the sky behind me. It's the same spot the creature was looking at.

The scent of fear increases around her and my threat levels rise to critical again.

I turn to see what she sees—what the creature must have seen—but there's nothing there.

"They're here," Peyton whispers, a visible shudder running through her. "The assassins are here."

24. PEYTON PRICE

They're flying.

Oh, dear ancients. They're really flying.

Not one, but two of them.

The breath catches in my throat as the woman and the man soar overhead and stop, hovering above the trees on the far side of the fence at the edge of the combat area, their silver wings beating slowly.

The woman's lithe form is surrounded by silver light that swirls around her torso from her chest to her upper thighs, obscuring most of her body. Her wings are like silver weapons, stretching wide on either side of her body.

The man's powerful silhouette is lit up by the shimmering, silver mass of his wings that extend as far on either side of him as the woman's, except that his are like electricity. His wings look just like the silvery blue light swirling around the woman's body.

Where Striker stands beside me, his body heat is a burning furnace, his hellhound ripping through him so suddenly that I'm buffeted in the heat wave that rushes over me.

His gaze is wild and his voice is urgent, breaking through my shock. "I don't see them!"

I realize that I've dropped into a defensive crouch. I rise, surprised that the assassins continue to hover above the forest, not moving toward us, almost as if they're waiting for something. Or they're confused...

I grab Striker. "They must be blurring. But they aren't attacking. They're just floating over there. They aren't even flying above the building."

His claws are fully extended. "You have to get away from me. You need your Fury. We have to warn the others!"

"No." My fingers tighten on his arm. I drag in a pained breath when the contact with the fiery seams along his skin sears my palm. "Wait. Please. Something isn't right. They aren't... They aren't doing anything."

I twist to see the assassins, peering at them as they continue to hover in the distance. The shield around the Academy—the boundary of the Realm—shimmers in the night sky between us and them, and I suddenly realize...

"They're outside the Realm." I exhale, speaking rapidly now. "Hadrix said the assassins couldn't find the Realm—which they clearly can—but he also said that it can't be breached."

I face Striker again. "I don't think the assassins can get past the shield. I need to get up there and hear what they're saying."

Even from this distance, I can tell that they're speaking to each other.

"No." He shakes his head at me.

I reach up on tiptoes, trying to draw Striker down to me. He's right about one thing: I need my Fury. "If I go over there— and you stay here—I'll be a Fury again. I'll be fine. You can't fight them in the air anyway. I'll scream if I need you. Okay?"

"I don't like it—"

"Trust me. *Please.*"

His entire body is shivering, growls breaking from his

throat. He's ready to fight. His own fury is barely contained. He and I are cut from the same cloth, both children of hell and death. I'm asking him to go against his entire nature and all his training right now.

"Please," I repeat.

The muscles in his fiery jaw clench as he gives me a single nod. It's the best I'll get. He won't stay put for long.

I race away from him, sensing myself grow stronger as the impact of his presence weakens.

Ten paces from the fence, I run and jump, grateful when I rise into the air. The farther I travel from Striker, the clearer the air grows.

For a second, I remember Mallard's assertion that I react to Striker on a powerful, subconscious level. Inhaling the crisp air, I realize that his scent has left my lungs, leaving me both empty and angry.

My Fury rages through me.

I'm positioned directly beneath the assassins, but they don't react. They don't even look in my direction, confirming my suspicion that they can't see through the shield.

For the first time since I came to the Academy, I rise toward the shimmering barrier. I've never approached it before and I make sure to stop before I accidentally touch it or break through it.

I've always levitated upright, but now I tip myself backward so that I'm floating horizontal to the boundary, my hair falling away from my face and gravity pulling at my clothing.

Slowly, very slowly, my body tips so that I'm parallel with the assassins, facing them.

The breath catches in my throat at how beautiful they both are. Hunter's eyes are even brighter than the dead Fury's memory, the silver rings around her irises mesmerizing.

Despite the way her body is obscured by the light around

her, I sense her smaller movements, the power of her muscles, her agility even greater than mine.

I grit my teeth as I determine that I will become as powerful as she is.

The man with her is the same one from the Fury's memory. I can only guess that he's Slade Baines, the Legion Master.

Up close, I'm surprised to see that his eyes have changed since I saw him last. Now they're shot through with silver—not ringed like Hunter's—but streaked like the electrical currents in his wings.

His features are just as harsh as I remember them: dark hair with a wave in it framing a face with a strong jaw and a slight cleft in his chin. He is unforgiving in the same way that Striker is brutal.

He carries a multitude of weapons in belts around his body, along with a row of narrow pouches about the size of my forefinger. They look like they could contain bullets—big ones —but I can't be sure. The woman must carry them too. I can see the edges of the straps across her shoulders along with the handle of a sword at her back.

I shiver as the breeze from their wings billows across my cheeks, bringing with it the scent of danger.

They're so close. Our faces and bodies are only a few feet apart as we hover in the air, and my fingers tingle with the urge to reach out, close the gap, and touch them.

They have no idea that I'm here, so close to them.

Hunter's gaze passes over me as if she's seeing beyond me to the ground. "We can't be in the wrong place, Slade. Tansy checked and double-checked the coordinates. The Academy has to be here."

Slade is quiet, his surprisingly intelligent gaze also passing over me and everything around me, but his scrutiny is slower, carefully assessing. A crease appears in his forehead. "My eyes only see trees and gravestones, but there's something else in this location. I sense it."

My claws slowly descend, preparing for discovery. Preparing to fight.

He becomes very still as he coasts in the air, as if he's accessing all his senses before his voice turns to a rumble that reminds me scarily of Striker. "It's a Realm, Hunter."

"A Realm." Her eyes grow wide. *Damn.* A Realm so close to Boston."

Boston! My head spins. That can't be possible.

When I first arrived here, I thought we'd traveled in the other direction toward the west coast.

It's impossible that we're in Boston, but how would I really know? My memory was wiped and since I didn't have access to my power then, I couldn't overcome the spell.

"Lady Tirelli must have created it," Slade says. "It would explain why Tansy couldn't sense what was here."

My forehead creases as I wonder who he's talking about.

Hunter's response is a whisper. "Can you sense anything inside it?"

For a second, his gaze settles on me. A shiver runs through me at the look in his eyes—deadly and controlled.

I'm shocked to discern that beneath his outer appearance of control, a rage simmers as violent and uncontrollable as Striker's. But the heart of Slade's rage is different. Where Striker's is like fire that turns everything around him to ash, Slade's anger is like a polished stone carefully hewn into an efficient weapon.

The kind he would use to crush my skull with a single hit.

He slowly reaches out his hand, palm up, not quite touching the shield.

At the same time, my whip rises at my waist, suddenly no longer pulled down by gravity but floating toward Slade instead. The metal tips rise first, then the handle, the rope middle the last to move.

What the hell? Is he pulling it?

I grab it before it strains so hard against the newest flimsy hair tie that it flies upward and gives me away.

"Power," he says, lowering his hand. "I sense immense power in this location. How many students did you say are imprisoned here?"

"Thirty," Hunter says. "I know all of their names now."

"Including two Unknowns?"

She nods. "Striker Draven and Peyton Price. I'm still digging into their histories."

I check Striker's position, grateful that he's staying clear of me, even if he's pacing like the caged beast that he is, roaming the length of the fence on the opposite side of the yard.

Above me, Slade beats his wings faster. "I can breach this Realm, but we can't proceed alone."

I draw a quick breath at his assertion that he can breach the Realm after all, but I force myself to focus as he continues speaking.

"We can be certain that there are thirty students here, who may or may not control their powers, along with Kaitlyn Hadrix and her family," Slade says. "I'm determined to end Kaitlyn and her family and fulfill my ledger, but we don't know how many of Lady Tirelli's old followers are also hiding out here. We can't be sure who is written into my ledger and who isn't. We need backup before we strike."

Hunter's wings give a sudden, strong beat. "I'll contact Cain and Archer. Alexei too. He has a stake in this. They can all be here in a week—"

"No." Slade's protective rumble stops her mid-speech. "We're not doing anything right now. In fact, all of this can wait."

Hunter pauses in the act of resuming an upright position. Her wings beat the air around me, making my hair slap my face.

"For how long?" she asks.

He gives her a smile that takes my breath away. It's so full of warmth, so suddenly and unexpectedly gentle and intensely protective.

Oh, damn. My power burns inside my mind, the brightest glow I've ever felt and it's not because Slade's a threat to me—possibly the greatest threat I'll ever face.

Slade loves Hunter. More than anything.

The love I sense between them is so strong that it ripples through my body, making me gasp for air.

I'm built to see the truth, to feel it in my heart, the good and the bad.

There is no greater truth than love.

I clutch my chest as tears burn at the back of my eyes. *How is so much love possible?*

I've never seen or felt anything like it, never dreamed it could exist, yet here it is in front of me. These two deadly, powerful creatures share an unbreakable bond that I could never imagine ever experiencing for myself.

"You know how long," he says quietly, his gaze passing across her face like a whispered caress.

For a moment, she smiles, her eyes brightening before they close as if she's soaking up his touch. Then she shakes herself, plants her hands on her hips, and gives a dramatic huff.

"Three months," she says, glaring at him in challenge.

"Five."

"Four... and a half," she counters, as if she's daring him to disagree now that she's given so much ground.

"Okay. After the next meeting of the Ambassadors then. We can talk with Cain, Archer, and Alexei and form a plan. This is the safest way."

Hunter gestures at the nothingness that she must see beneath herself. "What if they leave? You'll lose Hadrix. Along with his wife and daughter. Not to mention his son. You know how much Alexei wants Jake's head for betraying the Dominion. You might not get another chance like this."

They must be talking about Raptor. At my first 'lesson' with him, he told me his real name is Jake.

I guessed he was an assassin with the Dominion. My best guess is that this Alexei person they're talking about could be the Dominion Master.

Slade takes a deep, patient breath but doesn't give any ground. "I'll station Legion assassins around the edges of the Realm. If there's movement, they can alert me. Now…" He rises up alongside her until they're both upright. "It's time to go home."

The inflection at the end of his speech indicates a question. At no stage in their negotiation has he ordered her to do anything. The equality and respect between them stabs at my heart like little daggers, the sharp sensation forcing me to press my hand to my chest, trying to ease the ache.

She gives him a small smile that brightens as their wings start to beat in time with each other. My chest constricts at how connected they are in their thoughts and moods. How much love there is between them.

I squeeze my eyes shut against the onslaught of emotions that make me tremble.

Forcing my eyes open again, I remind myself that they're my enemies. They are not to be envied or liked.

Hunter gives Slade a quiet nod before she turns, a single beat of her wings carrying her a powerful distance from him in an instant, the strange electrical force around her body leaving a trail of light behind her.

At the last moment, Slade glances down again. An assassin's ring on his finger glows brightly, a flash of silver that makes me shiver.

His features harden like stone as he floats right down to the shield, facing me once more.

"Whoever you are," he says, making me freeze, "if your name is written in my ledger, be ready to meet your maker. If not, don't get in our way or our laws will make you our new target. We'll have no choice but to kill you. Consider this your only warning."

I jolt away from him, shock driving me toward the ground.

My hair falls around me as I alight on the grass, my heart thumping in my chest.

High above me, Slade takes to the sky, leaving me to try to pull myself together.

He can't have seen me—the angle of his gaze told me so—but he spoke directly to me.

I shudder as I drop all the way to the ground, crouching there, my claws digging into the earth. He said he sensed my power. He also said he could breach the Realm and it sounded like that power is unique to him. Hunter certainly didn't offer to help.

Hadrix promised us that the Realm couldn't be breached, but what if Slade Baines can tear a hole in the shield?

A thumping sound reaches me from the other side of the yard. Striker presses his back against the fence as if he wishes it were still electrified, banging his fist against its bars.

His agitation tells me he's done waiting for me to come back.

I hurry around the combat mat, breaking into a run, my power fading the closer I get to him until I collide with him. At the last moment, his beast disappears, so he doesn't burn me before his arms close around me.

"They're gone," I say, inhaling his scent like my life depends on it. Cedarwood and balsam, the same scent I inhaled before I lost my power today.

Dammit, it's no wonder he can affect me from a distance; his scent is as strong as the smoking embers after a fire.

"What happened?" he asks, burying his face in my hair, his voice muffled.

"I have to speak with Hadrix." I force myself to pull back. "And this time, I want you to come with me."

He pushes at me, already arguing against me.

"Striker," I say firmly. "They won't hurt me right now. I have information they need and I'm going to tell them everything. We can ask Lachlan and Joseph to come with us. Lucinda, Bree, and Ryan too. Someone needs to stay with the other students, but I want them to hear this, too."

He searches my eyes. "I can't see what you see. Promise me that you'll be safe."

"I will."

His jaw ticks—he's unhappy—but he nods his head. Just once.

"Thank you. I'll get Hadrix. You get Lachlan and the others. Meet me in the dining room as soon as you can."

I dart away before he can object.

My eyes harden the farther I get from his knee-weakening scent, a plan forming in my mind.

Striker won't like it, but I have only one path now and I intend to walk it.

25. PEYTON PRICE

My Fury power is fully under my control by the time I raise my hand to bang on Raptor's door.

The sound echoes down the west wing on the second level where Hadrix's family sleeps. I'm not afraid of waking them all up.

The door cracks open to reveal Raptor, bleary-eyed, blond hair falling across his face, dressed only in a pair of shorts.

He opens the door wider when he sees me, looking me up and down with a growing smile. "I figured you'd come to my door sooner or later."

I give him a cold smile as wildflowers fill the air around us.

His smile broadens and he inhales deeply, willfully dragging the scent into his lungs. "I'll do whatever you want, Peyton."

Ignoring the inuendo in his remark, I lean forward, my voice a whisper. "Your name is written in Slade Baines's ledger."

His smile fades, but he's already inhaled too much compulsion to retreat from our conversation. He won't be able to lie to me now. "I thought Alexei Mason would come for me."

"Is that the name of the Dominion Master?"

"Yes."

I file that piece of information away, confirming that the Alexei the assassins spoke of is a major threat to us. I don't know who the other men are—Cain and Archer—but I can only assume they will be just as dangerous. "What did you do to anger Alexei Mason, Raptor?"

"I betrayed him by feeding information about the Dominion to Lady Tirelli. I didn't think he'd pass on the contract to kill me."

He's trying to hide it, but fear lurks behind his eyes, a deep, gnawing fear that will eat away at him.

"You're afraid of Slade Baines," I say.

He fights his response, gritting his teeth and gripping the doorframe. "I am."

I'm genuinely curious. Slade Baines struck me as merciless, but surely all Master Assassins would be cut from the same cloth. "Why do you fear Slade Baines more than Alexei Mason?"

"Alexei Mason could crush your skull in one hand, but Slade Baines can crush Alexei Mason."

I shiver. "You will wake your father, mother, and sister, along with Harrison, and bring them to the dining room. Only once you do that will you be released from my control."

I swivel and stride away from him, satisfied to hear him leave his room and knock on the next door. He won't be so happy to see me at his door next time. Not that I plan on visiting him again.

Hurrying to the dining room, I find Striker and the others already there, converged around the table at the front on the left-hand side of the room. I'm glad to see that Ryan has recovered from this afternoon, the color back in his cheeks.

The loss of my power isn't as much of a shock to me now that I'm getting used to the rapid changes around Striker. He looks relieved to see me, quickly rising from his seat to tell me that only Ashley has remained behind to guard the sleeping students.

Lucinda also jumps to her feet. "What's this about, Peyton?"

I hold my hand up for her to wait, listening as footsteps sound outside the room.

Hadrix, Vulture, Raptor, and Harrison stride into the room, all fully dressed, although their clothes are crumpled.

Kaitlyn walks more slowly behind them, her gaze darting between me and Striker. I consider the bandages around her wrists, wondering why she hasn't healed herself.

"What's going on, Peyton?" Hadrix demands, striding right up to me.

"Take a seat," I reply, standing my ground.

With a disgruntled huff, he follows my request. He and his family find seats at the table on the righthand side while I remain standing.

Kaitlyn chooses a seat at the table behind them, once again separated from her family, although this appears to be by choice.

I catch Harrison's brief glance back to her. He appears genuinely concerned about her wrists as he takes up a position standing guard at the end of their table like the soldier that he is.

Striker moves to stand behind me on my righthand side, and I wait another beat to make sure I have everyone's attention. "The assassins were here."

Suddenly, everyone's back on their feet.

"What?"

"Where?"

"How did they get in?" The last question is from Vulture. "The Realm can't be breached."

I raise my hands for silence. "They didn't get in. They flew over us. They couldn't see past the shield. I was able to listen to their conversation without them realizing I was there."

One by one, everyone sinks back to their chairs, but Vulture remains the most tense-looking. She seems to be the only one who fully comprehends what I just said.

Her icy eyes couldn't become colder. "*They* flew?"

"Slade Baines and Hunter Cassidy," I say, keeping my response carefully calm. "They're both Valkyrie."

"Impossible!" Hadrix shouts, his face red with anger. "Valkyrie are women."

"I'm only telling you what I saw."

Vulture grabs her husband's arm before he can jump to his feet again. "Well, then, did they fly past by chance?" A hopeful light enters her eyes. "Was it accidental?"

"No," I say. "They know we're here."

At the back table, Kaitlyn flinches, but her gaze is fixed firmly on Striker now. I keep her well within my sights as Hadrix thumps the table.

"Realms can't be detected," he shouts. "And they can't be breached."

"Actually, they can," I say.

Deathly silence falls around the room.

The color fades from Hadrix's face as he presses his lips together in an increasingly angry, disbelieving line. Even without my power, I sense a threatening change in him, a simmering danger lurking behind his narrowing gaze. "What did you say?"

"Slade Baines can breach the Realm."

"Now I know you're lying."

I meet his gaze. "Do you take me for a liar?"

His nostrils flare and his fists clench on the table as he chews over his response. Vulture wraps her hand around his hand, casting him a warning glance. She gives him a nearly imperceptible shake of her head.

"It's not all bad news," I continue. "They won't be back for four and a half months."

"That's an oddly specific timeframe, Peyton." Vulture's tone is clipped as she gives me her attention. "Why that long?"

"I don't actually know. But they argued fiercely about it. Hunter didn't want to wait. Slade said they had to. They finally agreed to the delay." I hold up my finger. "However, they will station assassins outside the boundaries of the Realm to watch in case anyone comes or goes."

"Dammit!" Hadrix thumps his fist again, throwing off his wife's hand. "That means we're under siege."

I give him a humorless smile. "I estimate we have no more than a few hours before their assassins are in place. Especially since it turns out we're located near Boston, which is the Legion's stronghold."

Hadrix's expression couldn't become angrier. The Academy's location has been a long-held secret and it won't suit him that I know about it. Or that I've just told everyone.

"I thought we were on the west coast," Bree says, taking a deliberate drink from her water bottle. She and the others have been on edge ever since Hadrix and his family entered the room. "The winters here aren't cold enough for Boston."

They all nod and I'm glad that I wasn't alone in that belief.

"The Realm must be weather-controlled," I say. "The assassins were clear about it. They were unhappy to find a Realm so close to their home."

Harrison speaks up for the first time, remaining remarkably calm. "We need to get supplies in and out somehow. We'll run out of food and bullets otherwise. Vulture, can you use magic to transport supplies without detection?"

"Kaitlyn and I can transport ourselves in and out and bring things back," Vulture says. "But we'll only be able to transport what we can carry on our backs. We'll need to ration food. No more tearing up your clothing."

"I'll remember that in training," Harrison says. His

expression hardens as he turns to Raptor. "Raptor? Do you understand that too?"

Raptor hasn't said a word until now. He brushes off Harrison's pointed question, narrowing his eyes at me. "Whose names are written in their ledgers, Peyton?"

I remain expressionless. "The names of your whole family are written into Slade's ledger, *Jake*." My gaze passes over Hadrix, Vulture, and finally Kaitlyn.

Oddly enough, this news doesn't seem to be a surprise to her.

"It's you he's after," I say. "Not us."

At my declaration, Hadrix pushes his chair back so it crashes to the floor, making Kaitlyn jump so hard that she grips the table in front of her.

His mouth works around his angry words. "Do not forget, Peyton. What endangers us endangers you."

"I won't forget," I say. "Which is why in exactly four months, you'll allow me to leave the Realm."

"Why the hell would I do that?"

"Because Slade Baines is the only one who can breach the Realm and let the assassins in. That much was clear from their conversation. Without him, they can't hurt you. Without a Master, the Legion would withdraw their forces from around the Realm. They would have bigger problems to face."

I cover the distance between us, plant my hands on the table in front of Hadrix, and meet his cold eyes. "You will let me leave because I'm going to kill Slade Baines."

Behind me, Striker freezes, his reaction so intense that I sense it even without my power.

I can't see his face from where I'm standing, but his gaze burns my back, the physical heat beating at me telling me he's moments away from going full hellhound.

I force myself to remain focused on Hadrix, to stay the path I've chosen.

The older man's blue eyes are cold before a disturbing smile breaks across his face, chasing away his anger. "Very well. You have four months. Then I'll let you leave. But be warned, Peyton. If you double-cross me, everyone you know will pay the price."

I return his cold smile. "I wouldn't expect anything less."

26. STRIKER DRAVEN

It's hard to sleep.

I pull Peyton close, listening to her quiet breathing, hoping that her nearness will settle me, but it's impossible to chase away my dread.

The creature's sibilant voice and Peyton's plan keep rolling around in my mind.

Relief and terror wage a war inside me. On the one hand, Peyton is headed for freedom. Hadrix and Raptor are more likely to leave her alone while she's training.

She'll be safe for the next four months.

But after that…

The Legion is the most brutal Faction and Slade Baines has been confirmed as superhuman. If anyone could kill her, even in her Fury form, it's him.

I clench my fists around the blanket, feeling like I'm hurtling toward a future I can't control. I want to find another way.

A reckless part of me wants to speak with the assassins, try to make them see that we aren't their enemies. Just like Peyton said—they're after Hadrix, not us.

Maybe, if I could make it past the creature in the forest, I could exit the Realm and speak with the Legion sentries who are being posted outside the Realm.

That's if the shield will let me out. I don't even know how the Realm works in that regard. And assuming the assassins won't kill me on the spot. My slate isn't exactly clean.

There are no guarantees I'm not written into someone's ledger.

I fixate on the moonlight streaming through our window as I try to weigh the risks. I finally have to acknowledge what I've fought inside my mind: I would do anything to save Peyton. Even destroy my own future.

I just need to figure out a way past the creature.

When sunlight finally breaks over the horizon, Peyton slips out of bed and I let her go without asking for her kisses, but she turns back to press her cheek to mine.

"You hardly slept," she says. Even without her power, she's perceptive.

"You've chosen a dangerous path." It isn't what I meant to say.

She nods, her cheek brushing mine. "Hadrix said I'll train alone from now on—morning and afternoon."

"You'll be safe from me."

She pulls back with a dark scowl. "I'll be separated from you. I'll be safe from *them*."

She still refuses to acknowledge that I'm the most dangerous person in her life. My hands rise to rest on either side of her face.

I could make her hate me, but not yet. Not unless I have to.

I have no answer, so I kiss her instead.

"I'll see you tonight," she whispers, finally pulling away.

I hang back until she's gone, choosing to eat breakfast after her. She will spend her mornings with Harrison, her afternoons with either Vulture or Mallard, and her evenings with one of the students, trying to unearth their powers. It was the one concession Hadrix made regarding her training schedule when it was decided last night.

Even so, she's determined she won't be separated from me at night. My mind fights my body on that. I want her with me, but she's making herself vulnerable.

When I emerge onto the first level, I catch sight of Peyton disappearing into her training room with Lachlan by her side. I'm grateful now for his offer to watch over her—the only other concession that Hadrix will allow.

Hadrix argued that Peyton would be perfectly safe—what could she fear since we're all friends?—but Peyton insisted that Lachlan will go with her everywhere.

Setting my mind on this morning's training with Hadrix's men, I eat quickly and head outside to find Raptor standing on the combat mat, hands folded behind his back in a military stance.

He's wearing proper combat gear rather than workout gear, consisting of supple-looking pants and a black shirt. He carries a dagger at his waist and I have no doubt it's the one he cut Peyton with.

His father has taken up a position slightly behind him. Their men are lined up all around the perimeter like a guard. They're also wearing combat apparel. Somehow, the whole combat area doesn't feel so friendly anymore.

Casually finding a spot at the back of the group where I can keep an eye on the other students, I check Joseph's and Lucinda's positions. They've also stationed themselves where they can see the others—and where they can see me.

Bree and Ryan are standing together, but Ashley stands apart, wearing her red scarf, her lips pressed together in a hard line.

When I look again, Ashley has inched toward me, casually crossing the distance until she's only a few paces away.

She keeps her voice low and the general hum of voices

around us covers her speech. "I sense their dark intentions. We need to be alert."

"Noted," I snap, unhappy to have my fears confirmed.

She flinches at my clipped response, quickly inching away from me again.

I swallow and attempt the most apologetic tone I'm capable of. "Peyton isn't here," I say. "They aren't afraid of the rest of us, even though they should be."

She pauses in her escape, a small smile shadowing her mouth. "You're more perceptive than you appear, Striker Draven."

Before she can resume her getaway, I clear my throat. "Ashley?"

She faces me directly and I know she sees me through her scarf. She probably sees more than I want her to. "Yes?"

I choose my words with greater care than I would have in the past. "I would appreciate if you continue to tell me what you sense."

She gives me a short nod before she quietly slips in among the students again.

Up on the combat mat, Hadrix raises his voice to address us. "From now on, your training will be overseen by Raptor. This will continue as long as Harrison is training Peyton. You will obey every command Raptor gives you." He glares directly at me. "Even if you don't like it. If you defy him or me, you will face the consequences."

The men around the perimeter snicker, a sound that grates on my nerves. What consequences? Hadrix and Raptor are both human. They don't have our power, agility, or stamina. I've already proven I can pummel Raptor into a bloody lump, but their confidence right now is making me nervous.

Raptor steps forward. "Striker Draven. Up to the mat."

Now I'm definitely wary. Raptor would never challenge me to a fight unless he has something up his sleeve.

I catch Joseph's warning glance as I ascend the stairs and take up position at the end of the mat while Hadrix steps off with a smile.

Raptor appears relaxed, arms loose at his sides. He tilts his head before he strides toward me.

He swings his left arm, there's a flash of silver light across his knuckles, and—

He disappears.

Oh... fuck.

I barely register the shocked shouts from the other students as I attempt to duck under the anticipated arc of his fist, but he reappears behind me and thumps my lower back.

It's a savage blow that feels like a brick cracking against my back ribs before he disappears again.

He was never this strong before. I saw Peyton try to crush his face while he controlled the first assassin's ring and he hardly flinched.

I've barely taken a step to regain my balance before his fists knock into my chest, one after the other, hard as boulders against my muscles and collarbone, then my stomach, forcing me to double over.

He flashes in and out of view so fast that I can't even get my fists up.

My beast rages to the surface, but I force him away. Raptor wants me to fight with my beast because he wants to beat me in my strongest form and crush all hope of defeating him.

He's sending a message to all of the other students: It doesn't matter how strong they are—assassin's magic can beat them. Only Peyton is able to fight it. Despite her assertion that we would learn how to see through an assassin's blur, we haven't.

His boot cracks into the back of my legs. I try to swing but grab nothing but air before another blow forces me to the ground.

I freeze as cold steel bites my neck a second before Raptor reappears.

His whisper meets my ears as his arms appear already in position, his free hand gripping my hair and pulling my head to the side to expose my neck. "Assassins can kill any supernatural," he says. "Even one as strong as yourself."

I remain as still as I can while the blade kisses my skin. "You have another assassin's ring."

"I have several." There's a pleased smile in his voice. "Don't tell Peyton."

Damn. Peyton was sure we'd be safe now.

Raptor waits a beat as if he expects something to happen. "What, no beast? I'm disappointed."

"I know what you're doing," I say, keeping my neck as still as possible.

"Of course you do," he murmurs softly. "You've played this game yourself."

"Fuck you."

"Dominate the strongest and you can control the weakest." He smiles against my cheek, a drastic invasion of my personal space, before he shoves me away from him.

I tumble and roll to my feet, assessing my next move.

I could go on the attack, but he'll simply disappear again. I have no countermoves. Peyton beat him because she could see him. When he disappears, I can't even sense him. There's no sound, no sight, no shifting air to accompany his movements. Nothing.

His arms are relaxed. The blade rests at his side, his clutch on it deceptively casual again. "Will you obey my orders, Draven?"

An oppressive dread builds inside me.

Even when Osprey and Hawk ruled the Academy, I knew how to work within the rules, how to use violence to counter their moves, but Raptor changes the rules with every encounter.

He's unpredictable and that makes him ruthless.

"It won't matter if I do," I say, a sick feeling sliding through my stomach.

A cold smile grows on his face. "Now you're learning."

I eye the dagger, picturing in my mind the cuts on Peyton's body that day I found her wrapped in my blanket in her room. "Then get the hell on with it."

"With pleasure."

He sheaths the dagger in his belt and blurs in and out of view as he strides toward me.

I guess he's content to use his fists for now. I can't protect myself against the rain of blows he lands on my chest, back, legs, and shoulders. Fists. Boots. It doesn't matter. I try to grab the knife, but it's impossible.

He's stronger and faster than he should be, driving me to the ground until the world is pain and fire in every limb of my body —except my face.

When he kicks my back, nearly breaking my spine, I roll with the force of the blow, ending up half on my side, trying to push up off the mat, my arms shaking.

I've given enough beatings to know I should stay down, but my instincts compel me to get back up, my vision blurring as I take in the rest of the combat area.

Several girls kneel mere paces away on the grass, guns held to their heads.

Farther back, it's taken four mercenaries to restrain Joseph. They're pinning him to the ground on his stomach with his hands wrenched behind his back. A fifth soldier holds a sword against his neck—Joseph's one vulnerability. A clean swipe will kill him.

Bree is also on her knees, gagged so tightly that the binding cuts into the sides of her mouth. Blood trickles down her chin as she tries to scream around it, but she can't form speech. She's fighting her bindings despite the gun held to her head.

Lucinda appears to have gotten further in defending herself—the welts across several men's faces tell me she whacked them, maybe with vines she conjured from the rose bushes.

Too bad she now lies unconscious on the ground beside Ashley, whose face is also pressed into the grass. Hugo, the big guy who hugs his morning coffee, rests his boot against the back of her head pressing her face into the grass.

Ryan alone remains unbound, but his head is lowered, his shoulders sunk low. He must be trying to control his breathing. Hadrix's men haven't seen his power. They might not even know what he is. But it's dangerous for everyone if he lets it out. Nobody is safe around him.

Lachlan's the only one who might have evaded capture, but he isn't here.

Hadrix's men are finally showing their true colors and there's nothing we can do about it.

We've entered a new hell.

Raptor crouches down to me, not even bothering to blur anymore, his left hand clutching my shoulder. The assassin's ring burns my skin. The contact feels like it steals seconds of my life.

Despite my pain and fuzzy thoughts, I'm aware that he only attacked my body from the neck down.

"Come on!" I shout. "Hit my face!"

He smiles. "No."

Collapsing against the mat, I give in to the pain and how angry it makes me. "Why the hell not?"

"Because if I only bruise your body, you can make a choice."

I press my fists against the mat, too beaten not to bite. "What choice?"

"Whether or not to tell Peyton."

He's crazy. That isn't a choice. She'll see the bruises across my chest and back the minute I take off my shirt.

But as I stare at Raptor, I suddenly realize that's the game he's playing.

"You want to control her," I say.

The twist of his lips tells me I'm right.

Peyton was his plaything. Now she's out of his reach. His father is smart enough to know that Raptor should have nothing to do with her training, but if I tell her what's going on, she'll jump right back into this mess.

Raptor will force her to respond to his orders again, react to his taunts, compromise her own safety for the sake of others.

He'll continue to control her that way.

But if she strays from her path, from her training, what chance does she have to kill Slade Baines? Surely, Raptor needs him dead.

I stare at him in confusion. "How will that help you kill Slade Baines?"

His fingernails dig into my bruised shoulder so hard that my beast roars inside my mind.

Let me out, Striker. I will crush him.

I can't take the risk that he won't.

Raptor laughs in my face. "Anyone who thinks Slade Baines can be killed is delusional. Peyton's headed to her death and my father's very happy to send her. She's a thorn in his side and this is how he can get rid of her. But me? I think it's a shame to waste a woman like Peyton. You have the power to stop her from leaving."

His words are like bricks, harder than his fists. He's telling me that Peyton can't win in a fight between her and Slade, no matter how strong she is.

Fear settles in the pit of my stomach, but I shake it off. Raptor's playing with my mind. He wants me to doubt, to make Peyton stay, to play his game again.

But all that tells me is that Raptor knows nothing about Peyton. If anyone can kill a Master Assassin, she can.

If anyone can survive a battle with a Master Assassin, she can.

And maybe… maybe instead of fighting Slade, there's a chance she'll leave this place and simply run. Seek her freedom and never look back.

For the last three years, I haven't had a purpose beyond surviving each day and keeping as many students alive as I could. But now…

Peyton is my purpose. My only purpose.

What scares me more than anything else is the lengths I'll go to protect her now. Even if one day, it means hurting her more than anyone ever has.

"Forget it, Raptor," I snarl. "The assassins are coming. They'll rip this place apart. If Peyton can't stop them, how do you plan to survive?"

He smiles as if he has a secret. "You'll have to wait and see."

He kicks me one last time before he straightens. For the last few seconds, our conversation kept the pain at bay. Now it bursts through me and I can't stop the groan that passes my lips.

If Raptor thinks I'll lie down without a fight, then he needs to think again.

With a roar, I launch myself upward, catching him just before he blurs, allowing my beast to rip through me for the split second it takes for my fist to collide with Raptor's cheekbone.

I fly through air as he disappears.

Fiery pain strikes my back before I land. Fist or boot, I can't tell.

I smack the mat, sensing my bones shift, my beast rising again to stop my bones breaking at the last moment.

I try to stand, but a heavy weight presses down on me.

Definitely a boot shoving me into the mat.

Raptor shouts across the combat area as he continues to immobilize me. "Every single one of you will do exactly what I tell you to do, when I tell you to do it. Every skill I teach you will be used on my enemies. You will live, breathe, and die in service to us. But if you think for one second about using your powers against me, my family, or my men, I will end you."

Striding onto the mat to stand at Raptor's side again, Hadrix looks pleased. A real father-and-son team. I guess Raptor made Daddy proud.

Raptor reaches down, drags me across the mat, and pushes me off the edge. I thud onto the grass, managing to get my knees under me, even though my arms buckle.

He stands at the mat's edge, looming over me. "Get up, Draven. It's time to train."

The next two hours are grueling but made worse by the thick blanket of fear that covers the students.

I'm lucky I don't have any broken bones and haven't dislocated anything, but holding a rifle to the shoulder that Raptor pummeled is agonizing.

He takes every opportunity to shove me, even ramming the butt of the rifle into my stomach before giving it to me. I get through the morning by calling on my beast, giving him enough control that I can operate on auto-pilot, going through the motions while my mind tries to find a solution.

Every plan I come up with seems doomed. I could try to steal the ring, but Raptor said he has more and I have no reason to disbelieve him. I could try to fight him, but I can't fight what I can't see or sense. I could tell Peyton...

Hell no.

At the end of training, I know only two things: how to fire a rifle and that I won't tell Peyton what happened.

As soon as Raptor dismisses everyone, the men head inside with all of the weapons, but the students hang back.

Raptor pauses at the door as if he's going to break us up, but he disappears inside with a smile on his face.

He knows exactly the fight we're about to have among ourselves.

Lucinda strides right up to me. A black bruise is already forming on her forehead. "We have to tell Peyton. She needs to know that they've broken their promise—"

"No."

She recoils at the anger in my voice. "But, Striker—"

"It's *Draven* to you. And nobody's telling Peyton."

Her face falls. In the last few days, I opened the door to friendship between us and now I'm shutting it firmly in her face.

Barely an hour ago, I asked Ashley for help and now I'm turning on her and the other students. Behind Lucinda, Ashley stares at me with eyes hidden behind her scarf, but she will discern more than the others.

Whatever glow she saw around me the other night is long gone.

Now she's looking at me the same way she looked at the soldiers. Now she senses *my* dark intentions.

I knew that if they started to trust me, I'd screw it up. Now I have no choice.

Joseph stands protectively behind Lucinda, his hand pressed to her shoulder. A thin cut at the side of his neck tells me how close he came to losing his head.

Beside him, Bree rips off her gag, spitting blood onto the grass. The other students crowd behind them, all of them waiting for me to change my mind about the future to which I'm dooming them. Another hell to replace the one we thought we'd escaped.

Lucinda's voice is small. "But Raptor's targeting you."

I grit my teeth. I want to roar at her that there isn't anything Peyton can do about that. That's the reality I have to face.

I make her weak and in return she can't use her strength to—

I laugh at myself inside my mind.

Protect me?

I've lived my whole life protecting myself. Now, suddenly, the idea of someone standing in my corner, fighting for me, caring about what happens to me is a possibility that I can't face, can't acknowledge, and won't demand.

I'll protect myself like I always have.

"*Me,*" I say. "His men are assholes to you, but he's targeting me. That makes it my choice whether or not to tell Peyton."

"He could kill you, Draven," she says quietly.

She's right. He didn't take his dagger to me today, but it's only a matter of time.

The longer I refuse to draw Peyton back to him, the angrier he'll become. He wants her back, even if it means she fails to stop Slade Baines. He implied that he has something up his sleeve to deal with the assassins, but battle seems inevitable to me.

I give Lucinda a cruel smile, casting my eye around the rest of the group as they watch me with expressions varying from disbelief to fear and even—*fuck them*—pity. "Killing me will only make Peyton stronger. It would be better for her if I were dead."

Lucinda gasps, shock turning her face pale. "But—"

I grab her shoulder, making her wince. "I may not be able to defeat assassin's magic, but I can sure as hell rearrange your face, Adams."

Pushing her away from me, I take a step back to address them all. "Know this: If you tell Peyton—if anyone tells Peyton—I will rip your heart out with my hellhound's claws and leave you for dead. It doesn't matter what Raptor does to me. Focus on what I'll do to you. Do you understand?"

Nobody nods, but they don't argue anymore, either.

When I turn on my heel and stride away from them, Joseph mutters behind me. "And Striker's back."

It's better that they steer clear of me, especially if Raptor's targeting me. In fact, it's better that they actively hate me like they did before.

Lucinda and Joseph will take care of the others. I will take care of myself.

It was already my goal to avoid seeing Peyton until nightfall and I succeed for the rest of the afternoon and evening. Even after dinner, I roam around outside instead of going upstairs.

My purpose isn't only to stay away from her.

The fastest way to exit the Realm would be through the front gates and down the road, but when I head in that direction, I find that Hadrix has stationed men at the gate.

It would be foolhardy to get into a fight with them right now. I should assess all my options first, so I head around the back instead.

I've run the Academy's perimeter so many times over the last three years that I've memorized the patterns in the trees. There's an opening on one side that forms a path through the foliage. I've seen Peyton eyeing it too.

As the darkness thickens around me, I approach that side of the yard with the combat mat behind me.

I peer into the darkness, finding the gap between the trees. The path is barely perceptible, but it stretches as far as I can see, which unfortunately isn't far.

The path is the best way through the forest, but the creature is bound to walk it too.

The difficulty is knowing where the Realm ends, which is important because it will dictate how long I have to run and survive before I can get to the other side. It could be half a mile, two miles, or even more.

Peyton seems to be able to see the shield around the Realm that marks its boundaries, but I struggle to see what she sees. I thought I saw the shield once through her window, but it's even harder from the ground.

The darkness within the forest is oppressive. It isn't surprising that the creature has lived there undetected for so long, especially if the forest extends for miles before it ends. There are many places to hide. Even at the tree line, the branches are so thick that the moonlight doesn't reach the ground.

I freeze as the nearby leaves rustle, scanning the foliage for any sight of the same eerie yellow eyes I saw last night.

I call on my beast to heighten my awareness.

As soon as I do, I regret it.

I've been blocking out the pain all day and now I went and welcomed it in. Gripping the iron bars, I take deep breaths, trying to get past the agony that floods my body.

My plan to exit the Realm just got much harder. I can't begin to figure out a way through the forest until I have a sense of what threats lie within it, but if Raptor targets me every day, I won't be able to use my senses because I'll be blocking the pain.

I thump my fist against the bars in frustration, trying to convince myself that I can bend these bars right now and dare the creature to come for me, even if I'm wounded.

After five agonizing minutes, I accept reality and defeat. I should have packed ice on my bruises hours ago.

Hobbling away from the trees, I force myself to climb the stairs inside the building, raiding the ice chest on the third floor on my way past and filling my arms with cloths packed with ice. The chill against my chest and ribs from the ice is a welcome relief from the throbbing pain.

I find Peyton pacing the corridor when I arrive, the crimson glow in her hair disappearing as I approach.

"What happened?" she demands to know.

The lie is ready on my tongue. "Joseph and I fought each other today. Don't worry. It wasn't anything I didn't deserve."

The crease in her forehead tells me that maybe—for a second—she suspects I'm lying, but her misgiving fades with her power.

She's human again and that means I can lie to her as much as I want.

She points to our bed. "Lie down. I'll pack the ice around you and get more if you need it. Where are the worst bruises? Chest or back?"

"Hell," I say, telling the truth this time. "Everywhere."

I'm sweaty and smelly, but she doesn't seem to notice. Applying ice is more important than showering or I won't be able to move tomorrow, so I comply with her orders, easing down on to my side of the bed, but she tells me to lie in the middle.

It's been a long time since I came off the worst in a fight, but I leave my pride at the door.

"I'll sleep on the floor," she says, bending to tug at the base of my shirt. "You need space around you for the ice." Her eyes widen as she carefully lifts the material, freezing and staring at my chest. "Dear ancients, Striker. Were you human when you fought Joseph?"

She's assuming Joseph was in his draugr form, which is how he could do so much damage. I manage a deceitful nod but speak the truth. "Nothing's broken."

"You're lucky, then." She presses her lips into a disapproving line. "We'll need more ice."

She quickly sets to work packing the ice around me that I brought with me, her fingers light and gentle.

When she's done, she briefly rests her palm against my forehead, running her fingers through my hair in a way that sends an unexpectedly pleasant shiver down my spine.

I close my eyes against the ache growing in my chest at the way she's caring for me.

"I'll get more ice now," she whispers, rising up again. "I'll be back as soon as I can."

"Peyton," I say, stopping her in the doorway. "This won't be the last time I look like this at the end of the day. They're working us hard. But we…"

My mind swims with everything I won't say.

I need your help. I can't fight assassin's magic.

I can't do it alone. I don't know how to beat him.

I need you.

"We need to be stronger," I finally say.

She has no way to know that I will lie to her from now on. No power to detect my lies tonight or any night after this.

She has come to trust me and I will abuse that trust.

I will continue to tell her that my fights are with students, and she will have no power to see through my deceit.

"Then I'll be ready with ice each day," she says before she slips away.

27. PEYTON PRICE

For the next four months, I am single-minded.

My one and only goal is to control every element of my power, including every capability of my human body.

If I'm going to kill Slade Baines, I have to be stronger, faster, and more brutal than him. I have to reach into every facet of my power and draw it out to its full extent.

Just as he promised, Lachlan becomes my shadow, a constant protective force. Like the trailing smoke that rises above a dying campfire, he quietly and unobtrusively follows me everywhere I go during the day. He waits for me at the bottom of the staircase every morning and doesn't let me out of his sight until I return to the attic at night.

Despite that, I catch his non-verbal communications with Ashley whenever she passes us in the hallways. There isn't a moment that I don't feel guilty that I'm taking up all of his attention—the attention he used to spend protecting her—but I justify it in my mind. Once the assassins are no longer a threat, I will rid us of Hadrix and his family once and for all. Then Lachlan and Ashley can be together like they want to be.

During my lessons with Harrison, I learn how to handle a dagger like an expert. After that, a sword.

He talks me through all the different kinds of firearms, finally offering me two state-of-the art handguns that he tells me will fire reliably no matter what conditions I find myself in —extreme heat, water, you name it.

The Draven insignia on the handle doesn't escape me.

Harrison's smile is cold. "Draven's company designs the best."

Soon, I'm not only able to shoot a gun, but also fire accurately while running, jumping, and levitating. The room is large enough for me to carry out nearly any maneuver, and Harrison insists that I know how to move in more confined spaces because the fight with Slade will be at close range.

I also train using my human strength in case my power fails me at any time.

Slowly adjusting to the weight of carrying heavy weapon belts around my body, I learn how to draw, use, and control my weapons with lightning speed when I need them, even as a human.

My strength and stamina increase so that every combat move I perform while I'm a Fury, I can also carry out while I'm human—except levitate of course.

In the afternoon, I have individual lessons either with Mallard—although his eyes are glazed and he only teaches me about my power now—or Vulture, whose presence I grit my teeth and bear because she tells me everything I need to know about Slade Baines and Hunter Cassidy: from the layout of the street where Hunter lives to the supernaturals she and Slade have been seen with.

She also reinforces what Hadrix said: Slade lives in a Realm that I won't be able to get into and there is a protective shield around the street where Hunter lives.

If I'm going to fight Slade, I have to draw him out.

Every evening, I walk around the perimeter with a student to talk with them about their power. One of the guys discovers he's a cyclops. He transforms to Striker's hellhound height and strength while both of his eyes morph into one. Another guy is a yeti, also increasing in height and strength, but instead of fur, ice forms across his skin, burning cold when I stand too close.

I'm grateful that nobody has any flicker fits while I'm away from them, although I make Lachlan promise to check with everyone at the end of each day and it's the first thing I ask him to report the next morning.

Identifying their powers isn't always as easy as it was for Lachlan and Ryan.

One student takes a week, although that's mostly because I don't realize what she is until she turns around. At first I think she's another gorgon because her hair turns black, lengthens, and forms four distinct ropes that can twine around any object and bring it to her. But they aren't in the shape of snakes exactly and her eyes don't change, which stumps me, especially since she has the same aura of hunger as Ryan. The second mouth at the back of her head is a surprise. I finally find a name for her species in the same book in which I found Lachlan's: she's a futakuchi-onna, otherwise known as a woman with two mouths.

Slowly, but surely, the other students discover their powers until there are only a few left.

Despite all the gains in my physical strength and my power, and despite drawing out the other students' powers, there's an ever-widening gap between me and them.

At first it's the way they fall silent when I pass them in the hall.

Then it's the way they actively avoid passing me at all.

Then it's the way some of them choose to deliberately walk past me casting me silent angry looks, a confusing combination of disapproval and resentment on their faces.

When I try to speak with them, they suddenly find somewhere they have to be.

Even Lucinda, Ashley, and Bree become like ghosts in my life, seen from a distance before they're gone again.

I try to follow them one day, even call out their names, but they disappear around the corner. They're gone by the time I get there, leaving me confused and disheartened.

Striker is increasingly quiet too, withdrawn in a way I've never experienced before. He was always angry, aggressive, the first to lash out, but he was never subdued.

Some nights he barely speaks before he crawls into bed pulling ice packs around himself.

The idea of Lucinda combining our bedrooms into one room becomes a distant dream. My nights on the floor multiply until it becomes my normal resting place.

If he does speak to me before he falls asleep, Striker tells me he fought one of the students that day. It's usually someone whose power I've just identified.

He tells me they need to know their strength and it's his duty to help them.

For some reason, he never has a mark on his face.

When he comes to bed one night with cuts across his arms, a sharp worry settles in my stomach.

"Claws," he says, turning away from me, but he doesn't push me away when I apply healing gel to the wounds.

"It's all part of the game," he mutters, exhaling a relieved breath as the gel does its work.

The wounds are still raw, but the healing gel acts quickly. I wait a moment for the redness to subside around them, checking each one carefully before I dare to stroke his back, winding my fingers up into his hair and dropping a questioning kiss against his earlobe.

It's been a long time since we did anything more than sleep in our room and I crave his nearness.

When he doesn't immediately push me away, I trail kisses along the side of his neck, my hands seeking the hard planes of his chest, resting across his heart.

He moves so fast, it shocks me. Grabbing my hand, he twists, places his free hand flat against my chest and shoves me away from him hard enough that I crash to the floor. My shoulder and hip collide with it, the pain sudden and sharp.

I manage to push myself up to a sitting position, stunned at the deep gashes across my hand from his claws.

I'm numb from shock, but the pain will kick in soon.

He watches me with eyes full of fury. "Don't touch me like that again."

Nursing my hand, I glare back at him, deeply confused. "Why not?"

"Focus, Peyton! Any distractions will make you weak and get you killed." His voice is cold and hard. "If you want to heal, go sleep somewhere else."

He turns his back on me, leaving me with a choice, but I'm too stubborn to leave.

I pull the tube of healing gel to me before I stop, assessing how much is left in it. Not as much as I would like.

I don't need it. I'll heal in the morning.

Nursing my hand, I lie down on the floor and pull my blanket around me. I hate my human heart that hurts at his rejection and my human skin that bleeds at his touch.

I also hate my Fury heart that tells me he's right: I need to conserve every bit of my energy to train and fight.

The next morning, I throw myself harder into my training, taking more risks with a dagger while I'm in human form than I would have taken before.

Halfway through the session, Harrison stops me with a stern rebuke, taking hold of my arm and removing the dagger from my hand. "What's wrong?"

I scowl at him. I guess it shouldn't surprise me that after

training with him for months he would learn how to read my moods. I myself have become attuned to the fine distinctions in his tempers—the different ways his lips press together when I'm performing a maneuver, depending on if I'm doing it right or entirely wrong.

The wounds along my arm and hand healed as soon as I left the attic. I didn't even have to hide them from Lachlan.

I shake my head. "Nothing you need to worry about."

He narrows his eyes at me. "Recklessness is something I need to worry about. You have to control every action. Emotion has no place in battle. Right now, your anger is making you sloppy."

"Sloppy?" I snarl, my irritation rising.

"*Sloppy*. Now tell me what's wrong." His fists slowly clench as I remain silent. "It's Striker, isn't it?"

My shoulders slump. "I don't know where he's gone."

"Hmm." Harrison considers the dagger he holds in his hand, turning it over.

A series of emotions pass across his face fast, as if his thoughts scatter in all directions. I didn't mistake the hatred with which he looked at Striker on the first night Harrison arrived. Even so, when he looks up again, it seems that he's willing to put that aside.

"I hate to suggest it," he says, "but fear makes people do stupid things, even push people away that they care about."

"You think he's afraid?" I scoff. "Striker isn't afraid of anything."

Harrison steps up so close to me that he could ram the dagger into my heart if he chose. Not that it would kill me.

"The chances of you beating Slade Baines are slim to none," he says. "We all know it. I will give you a fighting chance, but you need to give everything to your training. No distractions. Striker's smart enough to know that too."

After that, I welcome the discipline of training and the long hours I can spend as a Fury, but beneath it all the worry and pain continue.

The only time I touch Striker is to pack ice around him.

Sometimes, I wake up and he's gone from our room. At first, it confuses me. My imagination runs wild about what might be wrong until I locate him through the wide windows lining the hall outside our room.

He prowls around the perimeter under the moonlight. Sometimes, I'm sure I see another shadow at the edge of the trees, but I can never be sure if it's the creature.

My humanity prevents me from using any of my powers on Striker to make him tell me what's going on, but as the days pass, I consider trying my power of compulsion to force the truth out of one of the students.

The only thing that stops me is that I'll lose their trust if I do that. I can't force them to speak with me.

My only other option is to open my senses to see the truth, but I fight that option, because the stronger my power grows, the more dangerous truth-seeking becomes. In fact, I've had to lock my truth-seeking power away, because if I don't, the crimes of Hadrix and his men will drown me in rage.

On the last day of the fourth month, when I emerge from my afternoon lesson with Mallard, one of the female students glares at me in the hallway. She's yet to find her power—a young woman with strawberry-blonde hair and freckles whose name is Tabitha.

She mutters under her breath as she passes me. "Special fucking cupcake."

I give her a furious glare. "What did you say?"

"I said *go to hell*, Peyton."

I grab her, not caring that she winces at the strength in my hold. "Why?"

Beside me, Lachlan edges toward me as if he's going to run interference.

At the same time, the color drains from Tabitha's face, and I can read her thoughts as clearly as if she's speaking to me: She wishes she'd never opened her big mouth.

Desperate to know what's going on, I allow a small trickle of my truth power to flow through me.

The minute I open my power, the evil around me hits me so hard that I crash against the wall.

Lachlan grabs me, slapping his hand over my mouth and pressing me against the wall to smother my ear-splitting scream.

"Peyton! Focus!"

As my scream echoes around us, his silhouette vibrates with the sound. His body swirls into smoke before I tear him apart, while his hand remains firm.

I inhale rapidly through my nose, clamping my lips closed, vaguely aware of every student and soldier around me crouched low with their hands over their ears.

A thin trickle of blood descends from Tabitha's ear and her gaze is even more full of hatred as she glares up at me from the floor where she landed when Lachlan grabbed me.

Damn.

I can never use that power again in this place. But if everyone refuses to speak with me, then how else can I figure out what's going on?

I relax beneath Lachlan's hold so that he slowly removes his hand.

"Under control?" he asks.

"Not until you tell me the truth," I snap.

His expression becomes blank. "What truth?"

I glance at Tabitha, who jumps to her feet and hurries away from us.

"What the hell is going on, Lachlan?"

I fill the air with wildflowers, but he morphs instantly, his entire body becoming smoke again so that my compulsion has no effect on him.

"Only Striker can answer that question for you," he says, inclining his head toward the end of the corridor.

Striker stands at that end of it, his expression as blank as Lachlan's. Tabitha gives him a wide berth, hissing something beneath her breath at him as she passes by.

He's close enough that I sense my power fading, but his focus is on something beyond me. Swiveling, I see Raptor standing at the opposite end of the corridor, closer to me than Striker.

When I turn back, Striker's gone.

Gritting my teeth, I shake myself free from Lachlan and stride straight toward Raptor. The soldiers on either side of him scatter. So do the students.

Raptor stands his ground, a smile growing on his face.

It only broadens when I shove him against the wall.

"Speak to me!" I order him. It's been a long time since we interacted and I haven't missed him.

My claws dig into his shoulder, but his smile doesn't slip. I guess he knows that Mommy will heal him no matter what I do.

I see his right fist coming from a mile off, block it without losing my grip, and yank him forward to wrap his arm behind his back before ramming him against the wall again so that he's awkwardly pressed against his own fist.

"Your training's really paying off," he says, wincing.

"Harrison's a good teacher."

"Unlike me," he says with a pleased smile.

The scent of wildflowers is so natural, I hardly notice as it wafts around me. "What are you playing at, Raptor?"

His pupils dilate. "I'm trying to distract you from your path."

"Why?"

"Because you're going to get yourself killed and then I'll be bored."

I screw up my face in disgust. "You're a dead man breathing your last air."

"I have a few tricks up my sleeve yet. At least my final days will be interesting." He grins at me again. "Striker gets the woman, but I get the Fury. I like it."

I'm not going to get any real answers from him. I shove him away from me in disgust.

He stumbles, rights himself, and shouts after me. "Open your ears, Peyton. You'll hear the screams."

I freeze. *Whose screams?*

I storm back to him. "Explain."

"I missed your anger," he says, smiling at me like a happy puppy.

My fist cracks against his cheek and he doesn't try to defend himself.

"Speak!" I shout.

He laughs, rubbing his jaw. "Don't you think it's strange how your training room is so quiet? How you never hear sounds from outside? Maybe you never questioned it because it lets you concentrate. No distractions, right? My parents are very helpful in that regard."

My stomach suddenly turns as I have an unwanted revelation. I've become so skilled at placing a boundary around my power to avoid seeing the truth—I've constructed such a strong set of shutters around my senses over the last four months—that I didn't fully comprehend until now how much has been hidden from me.

"Vulture seals the room." I grab his shoulder again, pressing the wounds I made before. "Doesn't she?"

"It's soundproof," he whispers. "Imagine everything you're missing."

That would be why I never hear any of Striker's fights. I thought it was because my training room is on the other side of the building, buffered by the nearby kitchen.

Dammit. Every other facet of my power is stronger than ever, but my ability to sense the truth is squashed and bruised, practically useless.

I turn on my heel and stride away from Raptor, evading his clutching hands.

Lachlan might not be susceptible to my power of compulsion, but the other students are. At this time of the afternoon, most of them will be in the dorm, so that's where I plan to go.

I want answers, and I want them now.

"Peyton." Lachlan steps right into my path with a warning tone.

"What the hell have you been keeping from me?" I try to get around him while he continues to block me.

The muscle in his jaw ticks. "Like I said—"

"It's up to Striker to tell me?" I can't contain my rage "Get out of my way."

He shocks me when he grabs me and shakes me hard. "Everything we're doing is so that you can get us out of here. If you lose your focus now, then it's all for nothing. Striker's the one taking the worst of it. It's his decision to ask for help or not. If he hasn't, then he has good reasons. You have to respect that."

Striker's taking the worst of it.

Everything we're doing is so you can get us out of here.

I promised everyone their freedom and I've failed to deliver it. But what's worse…

Anger swirls inside me because I hate that they need me. I hate that their freedom is dependent upon me.

More than anything, I hate that their freedom is dependent on me killing a man who is capable of terrible violence but also incredible love.

And then, if I sink even deeper into the mire of my thoughts, I find a Fury whose only goal is to cause pain and torment because that's what I am.

And that's…

…what I've done.

I've caused pain and torment around me and went on with my life, oblivious.

I am a Fury who was never meant to live with anyone, love anyone, or protect anyone, because that's not what I'm built to do.

I close my eyes. "You're right."

Lachlan is one of the strongest in the Academy. He has chosen to watch over me at the expense of protecting others.

I place my hand on his arm, turning my face up to his. "Thank you for watching my back. I'll be fine on my own from now on."

"That isn't what I meant." He stares down at me, shaking his head, but I can't keep putting myself first. Not when I question exactly what Lachlan's protecting: a future murderer.

"I don't know what's going on," I say firmly. "But I know you're needed elsewhere."

Turning away from him, I return to my training room, picking up my knives and tearing up the target on the other side of the room.

I was training to face Slade, to become strong enough to take on the man who crushes other Master Assassins, but first I need to fight for the truth.

28. PEYTON PRICE

The next morning, Striker's long gone from our bedroom before I wake.

Anger swirls inside me at how successfully he's distanced himself from me over the past months, tiny changes that I didn't notice until I was suddenly going to bed alone and waking up to an empty room.

The distance between us ends today.

I deliberately hang back after getting dressed to make sure the hallways are empty before I emerge. For the first time in a long time, I clip my whip to my waist. I've trained without it, but I'll need it today.

I'm satisfied to find that Lachlan isn't waiting for me at the bottom of the stairs. With quick steps, I head to my training room, where I find Harrison pacing impatiently.

I stop at the door. "I have to take care of something. Training can wait."

In fact, I don't intend to train again.

Harrison's perceptive brown eyes graze over me. "Is everything okay?"

I can't keep the venom from my voice. "I don't like being deceived."

He gives me a wary onceover. "What do you believe I've kept from you?" It's been a long time since he called me 'ma'am,' but I sense it on the tip of his tongue now. It's what he calls me when I inadvertently insult him in some way.

"Why don't you come with me while I find out?" I turn on my heel, not particularly caring if he follows me, slowing when I approach the back door.

I sense the spell now. Vulture was smart. She knew I wouldn't go outside while Striker was out there, so she placed the spell on this door. Not on the surface, but between the cracks like a magical filler, making it soundproof.

Inside the building, everything is quiet. The faint clangs from the kitchen float down the corridor. These are the peaceful sounds to which I've trained for the last four months.

Now, I'm about to hear the truth.

As soon as I go out there, my power will fade, but right here, right now, I'm strong.

Before I touch the door, Harrison plants his hand on it right at my eye level. "It's too quiet," he says.

To my surprise, he removes one of his weapon belts and hands it to me. It holds two daggers and two handguns, both loaded. I strap it across my chest, where it won't get in the way of my whip.

"You're as skilled in human form as you are as a Fury," he says, betraying nothing of his emotions. "But it's important to me that you know, I'm not part of whatever might be going on. Raptor and I aren't on speaking terms."

He could be lying about not knowing what's behind this door, but he's speaking the truth about his relationship with Raptor. I've witnessed the friction between them.

He steps back from the door, waiting for me to make my move.

I fantasize about cracking the wood apart with the strength I've developed over the last four months, but instead I push gently, sensing the resistance and then the *snap* as the spell breaks.

Sounds rush in as I push the door open and creep outside while my power flows through me, a crimson haze covering my vision.

A gun range has been set up on the righthand side of the field. Students line up in three columns with handguns held at their sides. Shots ring out when the three at the front fire, the sounds echoing through the forest so suddenly that blackbirds rise up from the trees.

The scene would look moderately normal except for the men aiming their own weapons at the students.

The big guy, Hugo, who can't function without his morning coffee grabs Tabitha, who just shot her gun, before she can return to the end of the column.

"Not good enough!" he shouts. "Do it again."

He yanks on her arm, pushing her back to the front of the line.

I narrow my eyes, incredulous, because her shot was a perfect bullseye on the paper target twenty paces away.

He circles behind her, grabbing and pawing all over her chest and butt as she tries to aim.

For a second, I think she's going to tilt her weapon and shoot him in the face, but the men surrounding her prime their guns.

I can't see Tabitha's face, but her shoulders are rigid and I can feel her skin crawling from here.

At the back of the line, Lachlan and Joseph stand with their fists clenched. The tension in their bodies as they watch the guards is so sharp that it stretches me beyond endurance.

When Lachlan steps in their direction, Joseph grabs his arm and shakes his head. In front of them, Lucinda stands glaring at the grass at her feet. Beside her, Bree wears a gag around her mouth—not that there's water in sight.

A glance around the combat area tells me that many of the students are bound or gagged in some way that hinders their power.

On the left side of the field, Vulture stands watching one of the soldiers, who is in a knife fight with a student. Ten other students stand waiting their turns, including Ashley, whose red scarf is oddly dirty. I'm not close enough to make it out for sure, but it looks like there's a boot print across her cheek, as if she's been kicked in the face.

The knife fight is fast and brutal and the student—the guy with yeti powers—falls to the ground with wounds on his chest while the soldier grins cruelly down at him.

Vulture waves her wand, the student's wounds heal, and she screams at him to get up. "Again! Until you don't get cut."

Rage billows inside me as I turn my focus to the combat mat.

Striker stands with his back to me, shirt off, a long cut bleeding across both his shoulder blades as if he's been slashed from behind.

He jolts and falls to his knees as Raptor kicks him with his boot.

The sound of crunching bones is sickening, but Striker doesn't make a sound. His silence makes my heart stop and my head spin.

Vulture waves her wand again, this time a nonchalant motion in Striker's direction. The bone jutting from his leg visibly heals as she forces him to his feet, lifting him like a ragdoll, his shoulders slumped over, his knees bent.

He wobbles to the side, far enough that I can see his face.

Blank.

He's somewhere else. Maybe his beast is keeping him numb, maybe he's simply shielding what's left of his mind.

Four months.

Four fucking months.

He's been coming back to me at night and telling me lies to protect me.

Well, fuck that. I didn't need protecting.

I don't make a sound as I glance at Harrison to find him focused on me. A storm grows across his features, his brown eyes shifting, the color in them lightening as I sense power flow through him.

He'll have a choice now. He's either with me or against me.

I point to the gun range first.

He nods.

I guess that means he's with me.

Silently, I speed around the back of the students, my feet barely touching the ground as I ready both of my daggers, holding them firmly in my fists as I run.

Harrison is right behind me, as lithe and quiet as the first day we arrived when he ran to the truck for the box that would contain the White Wand.

I've trained for this and even with my power beginning to drain from me, I'm fast and strong.

I duck and slice my blade across the back of the first guard's knees, then spin and drive my second dagger into the thigh of the next guard, then wrench it out and throw it into the chest of the guard across the way. The blade slices through the air between the standing students and lodges neatly into the guard's shoulder.

I spin and kick the next guard in the throat, following him down and stabbing him in the stomach before I leap off his chest and impale the next one in the throat.

Spinning and crashing into the big guy holding Tabitha, my arm hooks around his neck and my blade finds his jugular, tearing through it.

Blood sprays droplets like crimson jewels across the air.

As the droplets hit Tabitha's face, her mouth opens, but

whatever scream she was about to utter is smothered by my shout. "Down!"

The students drop and I fling my remaining blade into the heart of the man behind them who aims his gun at my head.

His finger pulls the trigger as he falls, but the bullet flies upward and way off the mark. The blast it makes crashes through my hearing, but I ignore it.

My first gun is in my hand at lightning speed.

An enemy bullet speeds past me, a slow blur in my powered vision, followed by another. I turn and duck, my own gun firing into the second last guard's thigh before I crash into the final man, my shoulder hitting him in the chest.

I twist and pull the trigger against his chest as he falls with a shout.

All of the men around the gun range now lie on the ground, but I run on, aware of Harrison taking his knife to the ones who dare to get up, severing tendons to immobilize them as he follows my footsteps.

The whole thing took mere seconds, short enough that Vulture is still blinking at me across the way. She must be trying to come to terms with what her eyes are telling her.

Yes, bitch. I figured out your game.

I speed around the perimeter, arm outstretched, aiming my weapon as I run toward the back of the man with the dagger who is about to ram it into the shoulder of the same student he was fighting before. The other students were already practicing with firearms—he would have been expecting to hear gunshots —so the blasts that have already rung out haven't startled him.

Now, he jolts as my shot echoes and blood spreads across his back.

He drops to his knees, but I'm already aiming at my next target. I squeeze the trigger in rapid succession, my arm shifting marginally with each shot. One. Two. Three more times. Four. Five. Six. Seven.

The men fall to the ground at Vulture's feet like cut wheat.

She's suddenly screaming and, up on the mat, Raptor has frozen.

For a split second, my Fury takes over and I want nothing more than to pull the trigger and put a bullet between Vulture's eyes.

She raises her wand at me, a scream on her lips. It's been so long since I was a threat to her that she must have forgotten her spells can't touch me while I'm a Fury.

Just as she finishes her spell, a body of black fur, sharp teeth, and silver claws speeds past me in a blur.

A panther launches through the air, claws outstretched, knocking into Vulture. She lands hard on her back and her wand flies wide. It rolls to a stop in the grass.

The panther tumbles to the side but circles back in an agile move—faster than Vulture can recover. He lands on her chest and pins her, snapping his teeth at her neck before thumping a paw across her cheek and forcing her face toward the ground.

The panther turns to glare at me with the brown eyes of the man who has spent every day training me for the last four months. A pile of clothes lies next to the fence.

Damn. Harrison. He's well and truly chosen a side now. I hope it doesn't get him killed.

I swivel and point my gun at Raptor on the combat mat.

His eyes widen as I squeeze the trigger without hesitation.

There's a flash of silver across his hand and he leaps to the side just in time. He moves faster than he should be able to and the reason is painfully obvious.

Assassin's magic.

I should have known. I should have fucking guessed. It's the only way he can beat Striker. It's the reason Striker wasn't fighting back.

The bullet flies wide, but I continue on my path, leaping

onto the mat and skidding to a stop on my knees in front of Striker.

"No more!" I scream.

It's a human scream, but it doesn't matter. I can aim just as well with my human eyes and hands now. As Raptor rolls across the mat, I empty my clip after him, cutting up the surface mere inches from his moving body.

Beside me, Striker groans, telling me he's coming back to himself. "Peyton... *No...*"

I swivel and check his eyes, waiting a second for him to focus on me before I run my hands over his arms and legs. Nothing broken that I can see or feel. The cut across his back has also healed. Vulture was thorough. She mended him so they could break him all over again.

Despite my desperate need to protect Striker, I'm also deeply angry at him.

He lied to me. For months. But worse than lying, he didn't trust me enough to tell me what was going on, and for that...

I hate him.

I hate Striker right now.

I grab his face, my teeth clenched. "You lied to me, Striker Draven. *You fucking asshole!*"

Without another word, I leap back to my feet, sensing my power flowing through me as his still-blank eyes meet mine.

My power isn't as strong as it can be, but it's there all the same, powering my actions and ensuring I'm not completely mortal right now.

Throwing my empty weapon to the side, I grab my second gun and follow Raptor's path. He's reached the edge of the mat, where he drops to the grass and backs away from me toward the rose bushes at the back of the area.

He doesn't have a gun, but he's carrying his dagger. No matter. I know how to disarm him.

I follow him, prowling across the grassy area, my hair rising around me and my feet light as air as my power increases again as Striker's scent fades.

Farther behind me, Harrison forces Vulture into submission and the other students have rallied and are pointing their guns at the men who dare to so much as twitch on the ground.

I grin at Raptor. "It's just you and me now."

That is until Hadrix and Kaitlyn get here with backup—there are still at least ten soldiers inside the building—but I'll deal with them when I have to.

Raptor grins right back at me. "Just how I like it."

Despite his confident statement, his gaze becomes increasingly alarmed as it travels an arc from one side of the combat area to the other, passing across all the wounded men.

They aren't dead, but only thanks to Harrison's precise training. He taught me how to aim between vital organs, how to immobilize without killing, because sometimes death is not the goal. Right now they're all in agony and that's how a Fury's vengeance works.

As Raptor's gaze passes over them, his confidence fades. "You did all of this." The inflection in his voice makes it sound like an incredulous question, as if he doesn't really believe it's possible.

My weapon hand is steady as I consider all the points on his body where I can shoot him to incapacitate him. Just like Harrison taught me—emotion doesn't belong in battle.

"You thought I was playing at war with the assassins," I say. "You thought I was furious but not precise. You thought I couldn't be an efficient killer."

He swallows. "I thought you were playing a game."

I scoff. "You think you've got me figured out, but you never will."

Raptor's focus flicks to the combat mat. I can't see Striker right now, but I trust Harrison enough to help if Striker's in trouble.

Raptor begins to speak, but I squeeze the trigger.

He roars with pain, his right leg collapsing as blood pools across his thigh. I wasn't sure if assassin's magic might help him heal, but it looks like it doesn't.

Retaliating instantly, he grabs his dagger faster than I can blink and flings it at me. It's a rapid and true shot at my shoulder, but its arc is slow within my powered vision.

With my free hand, I snatch the blade right out of the air and pitch it back at him.

It sinks into his other thigh.

He roars out a string of curse words, collapsing completely to one side, trying to prop himself up with his left arm while he presses his right hand to his thigh and attempts to stop the blood flow.

Striding over to him, I kick him in the chest, forcing him onto his back with my boot. I point my gun at his head right between his eyes. "Convince me, Raptor. Why should I let you live?"

"Ashley," he says, groaning as he grips his thigh.

I narrow my eyes at him, puzzled. *Ashley?*

A scream splits the air behind me, forcing me to spin on my heel, backing away from Raptor so I can keep him in my sights and see the combat area at the same time.

Hadrix stands on the other side of the combat mat, his thick arm wound around Ashley's neck as he drags her toward me. Her scarf floats to the grass behind them, leaving her eyes exposed.

She's squeezing them shut furiously, clawing at Hadrix as he forces her to move.

Kaitlyn trails behind them, a wand in her hand, her focus shifting from Striker, who's struggling to get to his feet, across to Harrison, who hasn't let Vulture get up, to finally settle on me.

Kaitlyn's expression is closed off, unexpectedly shuttered,

but it changes when she sees Harrison. It's only then that she misses a step and a flicker of honest emotion passes across her face. It's the same way she looked at him on the first night they arrived and he chastised her for the way she spoke to him.

Regret is a strange emotion to see on Kaitlyn's face.

Hadrix stops several paces away from me—far enough that it will take me more than a second to get to him. He presses his dagger to Ashley's temple, his thick arm unyielding around her neck as he kicks the back of her knees to unbalance her.

"I think you know how bad it'll be if I force her to open her eyes," Hadrix calls.

Ashley controls her power by containing it. Her power doesn't discriminate between friend or enemy. Whoever she looks at will die.

Right now, Hadrix points her in the direction of the students in the gun range, including Lachlan. Lachlan leaps forward, placing himself in front of the others, his palm held up as if he could shield them all.

Ashley whimpers, a strained sound forced out of her. The way Hadrix is gripping her, her vocal chords will already be damaged. She'll be able to see Lachlan standing in front of her, even with her eyes closed.

She knows he'll take the worst of her power if her eyes are forced open.

"Put your gun down, Peyton," Hadrix orders. "Do it! Now!"

Without lowering my weapon from Raptor's head, I try to calm the suddenly rapid beat of my heart. "Let Ashley go."

The scent of wildflowers fills the air. Hadrix inhales, shakes his head, and coughs, but he doesn't release her.

"I'm under a protection spell, Peyton," he says. "The strongest spell that Vulture could place on me. I'll admit it won't last forever. Your power of compulsion will break through, but I can do a lot of damage in the meantime."

My weapon swings from Raptor to Hadrix, aiming at his

head as my finger moves on the trigger, but I'm a split second too late.

Kaitlyn shrieks a spell and the gun flies from my hand, landing on the grass several paces away. She backs away from me, sheer terror written all over her face as I turn my furious gaze on her.

Damn. Her spells can't touch my body, but it looks like they can impact my weapons.

Ignoring her, I prowl toward Hadrix, unperturbed by the spells Kaitlyn flings at me to try to slow me down.

My claws descend and I calculate the distance I need to cross to swipe them at his neck, but he shouts at me. "I warned you, Peyton!"

Dropping his knife, Hadrix drags his thumbs up across Ashley's eyelids, making me freeze.

She struggles, but for a second, eerie emerald light spills across the yard. Every blade of grass between Ashley and the other students turns to stone.

"The next move you make will kill them," he shouts.

I change course, circling around Hadrix instead. I have to get in between Ashley and the other students. My body has to be the shield between them.

If I can be.

Spells and projectiles sail right through me. I have no guarantee that her power won't simply pass through me to whomever is behind me.

I throw myself forward just as Hadrix pulls at Ashley's eyes again and a stream of emerald light floods the space in front of her.

I'm close enough that her gaze lands on me.

Her eyes glitter like precious jewels, mesmerizing, slowing my movements, making my feet feel like lead. The veins in her neck twist and twine like writhing snakes while her golden hair clumps together into thick, hissing strands, the sound echoing in my ears.

I hurl myself against Ashley and reach for her face to free her from Hadrix's grasp, but I hit something else. Another body. This one is harder than stone.

I was so focused on Ashley—her gaze also on me—that I didn't see Lachlan move.

The scent of woodfire fills my lungs as he throws himself between her and me, one fist swinging and punching Hadrix so hard that Hadrix's nose cracks and the older man falls to the ground, finally releasing Ashley.

At the same time, Lachlan's free arm scoops around her and pulls her against his chest.

He presses Ashley's face hard against his heart, his left arm covering one side of her eyes, his fingers cupping the other side.

"I've got you," he whispers.

Her eyes are open against his chest. Her hair writhes with reptilian bodies.

A hiss screams from her mouth, so high-pitched that it shrieks through the air.

The other students drop to the ground, blood streaming from their ears. Across the way, Harrison writhes in agony and shifts rapidly back to his human form, his panther's ears undoubtedly too sensitive to the excruciating sound.

He scrambles for his clothes and his weapons.

Lachlan shudders as the emerald glow from Ashley's eyes intensifies against him, a dull glow spilling through the cracks around his arm.

His eyes meet mine, but I can't do anything to stop her killing power as it does its work.

He drops his gaze to the top of her head and his expression says everything.

No regrets.

His chest stops rising and falling. The scent of woodfire fades as his gaze turns to stone.

29. PEYTON PRICE

*S*ilence falls over the yard.

Or maybe I'm blocking out the sounds now because Ashley's sobs are breaking my heart.

The emerald glow around her face fades and her eyes finally close, her power exhausted.

She's caught in Lachlan's arms, her hair cascading across his frozen forearm as her golden tresses separate and soften.

"Peyton." Her throat is lacerated, her voice a whisper. "Please."

I don't make it more than a step closer when the dust covering Lachlan's arms and face rises from the surface of his skin, lifting into the air.

I refuse to inhale it.

Ashley grabs at his torso, struggling to free herself, her tears attracting the grit as she begs him to be alive.

I reach out to help her, my movements sluggish. My finger swipes across Lachlan's bicep before I pull away.

"Ash," I whisper. "Not dust." I press my hands to Ashley's back, my power of compulsion filling the air without even meaning to. "Wait. Stop."

She stills at my command.

"Close your eyes." I pull off my T-shirt and wrap it around her eyes as best I can while Lachlan's arms are tight around her, the material barely slipping between the gaps. "There."

I step back, holding my breath.

White ash blossoms across Lachlan's face, an unstoppable ripple that spreads through his cheeks and down his neck, flowing across his arms.

Woodsmoke chases away my wildflowers.

He shifts his shoulders, his arms gentling around Ashley, before he lowers his head to hers, pressing a kiss against her hair.

"Lachlan?" she whispers, tilting her head back.

He smiles down at her. "You can't turn smoke to stone." His arms tighten around her. "You don't have to be afraid of hurting anyone anymore. I'm with you."

Her tears track through the ash covering her cheeks, seeping past the bottom of my shirt. "I thought I would hurt you too."

"Is that why you've avoided me?" he asks.

She nods, telling me I wasn't the only one being kept at arm's length lately. She rises up on her tiptoes to press a gentle kiss to his lips.

I back away and close my eyes with relief, finally allowing myself to feel my own grief at the thought of losing him.

He stood by me for the last four months, quietly watching over me despite the cost to himself and to Ashley.

Now that I know he's okay, my focus quickly shifts to the continuing threat around us. On the other side of the combat mat, Vulture has taken advantage of Harrison's moment of shift to scramble for her wand, snatching it up before he can grab her again.

Swinging the wand in his direction, she rises shakily to her feet, forcing him to back away from her as she makes her way toward Kaitlyn, who is pulling her father away from me.

At the same time, ten more soldiers run from the back entrance, heavily armed, and head straight for Hadrix in the center of the yard beside the combat mat.

Suddenly, our enemy is regrouping. That includes Raptor, who drags himself toward his family. His mother diverts her attention from me just long enough to cast a healing spell at him.

His bleeding stops, but the way he limps tells me the spell is quick and dirty—the kind she must have used on Striker. It doesn't appear to have taken away any of his pain and the healing on the dagger wound on his leg appears fragile.

I'm not about to give her more time to heal him thoroughly.

Lucinda runs toward me with Joseph, Bree, and Ryan close behind. I've hardly spoken to any of them for so long, but this is not the time for reconnecting. Whatever anger I feel about being kept in the dark will only fuel my power. I'll need all the fury I can get to overcome whatever humanity still lingers inside my body.

Although… I suddenly realize that my power is stronger than ever, which can only mean…

The combat mat is empty.

Striker must have left during my confrontation with Hadrix.

I wish I could give Ashley and Lachlan longer to recover, but I need them to fight now.

"I want our enemy immobilized," I say. "The men on the ground are to be kept down. That's all I ask of you. I will subdue Hadrix and his family and give them one chance to leave. If they don't, I will kill them."

Lucinda reaches for me, her eyes full of worry. "On your own? Peyton, you'll need help…"

"Don't," I snap. "I understand why Striker didn't trust me, but you were the first friend I had. You let me live a lie for months."

Her face is ashen. "Striker forbade us from telling you."

"Since when has that stopped you?" At some point my vision has turned crimson, but I'm so used to it now that I barely register the haze. "You walked away from me, not the other way around."

Her lips part and her eyes widen, but she shakes off her reaction, backing away from me. "We'll make sure the wounded soldiers don't get up."

Ashley and the others hurry after her, heading back to the fallen men in the gun range. On the other side of the yard, Harrison is commanding the remaining students, who have also disarmed and subdued the men on that side.

In the center of the yard beside the combat mat, Hadrix's soldiers have formed a circle around him and his family.

I rise into the air and float toward them, remaining high above them to draw any fire into the sky and away from the students. I may have trained within a room during the day, but I practiced flying in the evenings. Hadrix told me that I'd have to meet Hunter Cassidy in the air, so that's what I've been preparing for.

I'm wary of using my compulsion from the air in case it affects the students too. Ten machine guns point at me, but I smile down at the soldiers holding them.

"You'd better shoot me while you can," I say.

Raptor's upturned face is full of expectant pleasure as the men open fire. Bullets rip through my clothing and it's a good thing I already gave away my shirt or it would be a shredded mess.

I feel the pain of every bullet, but my healing power is fully alive, dispersing the pain as soon as it happens.

I swoop toward the first man, taking bullets through my chest as I collide with him and wrench his weapon from his hands before I return to the air with the gun.

I shoot five men before Vulture disarms me. As soon as the

gun flies from my hands, I dart toward her, snatch her wand away from her, and break it in half.

Holding her wand is like swimming into the darkness of her mind.

I drop its broken pieces, as if they're made of venom.

Her wrists are my next target. I grab hold of them while Hadrix attempts to slash at me with his knife and Kaitlyn cowers at the side.

Vulture screams in pain as my claws impale her arms. I'm taking a leaf out of Striker's book on this one. Vulture's eyes shoot wide and she tries to yank out of my hold. At least Kaitlyn was smart enough not to move when Striker did this to her.

I push upward, wrench Vulture off her feet, and dart into the air still holding her. It's such a quick down-and-up movement that she doesn't have time to scream.

I rise high enough that she can't touch the ground, dangling her below me, her bleeding arms raised above her head.

The hatred in her eyes has no impact on me. She begins whispering spells beneath her breath, but the increasingly grey pallor of her skin tells me she's using her magic to keep the pain at bay, not to attack me.

I guess the power she stole from the dead compliance officers is coming in handy now that she's lost her wand.

I register the sudden silence around me. The machine guns have finally fallen silent since the soldiers can't afford to hit Vulture.

Hadrix shouts at me. "Put her down, Peyton. Or I'll put *you* down."

"How? You can't hurt me."

He swings to his son. "Where the hell is Draven? We need him to make her weak!"

Raptor shakes his head. "You're the one he got past."

I'm done listening to them. "You broke your promise. Now

you will leave this place. Or I will kill you all, starting with your wife."

Hadrix's expression turns as hard as stone. "You don't want to do that, Peyton. You need us."

"What could I possibly need from you?"

"We have the weapon you need to defeat Slade Baines. Without it, you don't have a chance. He'll tear this place apart—"

"Looking for you!" I shout back at him. "He's coming for you. Not *me*. Not *us*. I will welcome him if it means your death."

Hadrix splutters, but he must know it's the truth.

Sudden movement shifts my focus to Kaitlyn. She rises to her feet but allows her wand hand to lower. The look she casts her father is full of unexpected fear.

"They're coming for you too," she says. She's still looking at Hadrix, which makes my forehead crease in confusion, since that's what I just said.

She tilts her head back to see me. "Hunter Cassidy is coming for Striker."

I narrow my eyes at her. "What did you say?"

"Striker's name is written in her ledger."

Hadrix grabs Kaitlyn hard enough to make her wince, his hands clutched around her biceps as his eyes bore into hers. "How do you know that?"

"Because I wrote it there."

Hadrix freezes. He grips her so hard that his knuckles turn white and her watering eyes tell me he's hurting her.

"Did you tell them where to find Striker?" When she doesn't answer, he shakes her hard, his voice rising. "Did you tell them where to find us?"

"Yes," she whispers.

His fist strikes out so fast that it's a blur.

Kaitlyn cries out, clutching her cheek as she stumbles into Raptor. "I want Striker dead! No more games. No more pain," she screams. "He deserves to die!"

Raptor grabs hold of her tightly, but to my shock, he positions her directly in front of his father's next fist. "Bad choice, sis," he says without any hint of sympathy.

"Stupid, useless girl!" Hadrix's knuckles crash against her temple.

Kaitlyn slumps in Raptor's arms, bent forward with her braid falling across her cheek. Blood drips from a cut above her eye onto the grass.

Striker deserves to die? Kaitlyn is the one who came here and deceived everyone, who crushed Striker. Now she's screaming that she wants Striker dead? That he deserves it?

Assassins only accept targets they deem to be truly evil and beyond redemption: murderers, abusers.

Striker may be the most brutal man I've ever encountered, but for an assassin to accept him as a target? I never sensed evil like that in him, not like I sense it in Raptor.

My heart is sinking and cracking, but at the same time I'm shocked at the brutality Hadrix is showing his daughter. I should be happy about the punishment he's giving her, but I'm not.

It reminds me too much of the treatment my family gave me.

He grips her by her hair, pulling hard enough to make her cry as he shoves his face into hers. "You're the reason the assassins know where we are." His mouth works around his speech. "You're also the reason... Peyton will let us stay."

He shoves Kaitlyn away from himself and swings in my direction. "If you want Striker to live, you will kill Slade Baines *and* Hunter Cassidy. Slade can breach the Realm, which will allow Hunter to come in and kill Striker. Both must die. The only way to kill them is with the weapon we hold."

I consider him carefully, testing my power of compulsion. "The protective spell you cast around yourself won't last much longer. I'll compel you to give the weapon to me, whatever it is."

"You can try, but the weapon is guarded by spells built to

resist tampering. You won't be able to access it unless Vulture voluntarily releases it to you. Compulsion will only lock it away. No more charades, Peyton. You will follow my commands now."

He takes a step closer, his gaze passing over his wife, who still dangles from my hold. It looks like she's used up her magic now because her head lolls as if she's going to pass out.

Hadrix's voice is a command. "You will bend to my will and do as I say."

I consider all my options. I can kill Hadrix now and take my chances when I face the assassins. Or I can kill Slade Baines and Hunter Cassidy with Hadrix's help and then return to annihilate him and his messed-up family.

Of the two choices, I have to take the one that gives me the best chance of success, even if it means breaking my own nature.

It's time to lie.

I drop Vulture to the ground, where she snatches at Kaitlyn's wand to heal herself. Kaitlyn lets her take it without a fight.

Floating to Hadrix's feet, I take a knee and bend my head. "I will do whatever you say."

The lie is acid on my tongue, but as I speak it, I remind myself of the vow I made on the day Hadrix arrived at the Academy.

I will kill them all.

30. PEYTON PRICE

*H*adrix wastes no time ordering me to bully the other students into submission.

I was already angry with them, so I cloak myself in hatred as I approach them.

They're confused. Scared. Their hope has been shattered over and over. Too many times they've tried to fight, have touched freedom, only to have it ripped away.

Just moments ago, I promised them once more that I'd free them and now the tables have turned again.

No matter what I do, Hadrix manages to manipulate the situation to his advantage. The students are barely holding themselves together, but I speak to them without apology.

"Do as Hadrix says. Whatever he says," I say to Lucinda and Joseph. "Make sure the others fall into line or you'll answer to me."

I swing away from her, ignoring the tears glistening in Lucinda's eyes. She must think I'm punishing her, but it's easier to let her believe it.

My plan is my own. A path I made for myself months ago

without realizing the battles I would have to fight along the way.

I was born to be one of the bad guys, so that's what I'll become. Maybe, if I succeed, Lucinda will forgive me. Maybe she won't.

I return to Hadrix to find him gripping Harrison and forcing him to his knees. Harrison is dressed only in pants and his weapons are gone.

Oh, damn.

"Traitor." Hadrix snarls before he holds his hand out to Raptor for a gun.

As Hadrix presses the weapon to Harrison's temple, Harrison gives me the same look Lachlan gave Ashley. *No regrets.*

My muscles tense. I'm about to leap between them when Kaitlyn races forward.

"Dad! I might be an idiot, but even I can see that Peyton compelled Harrison to move against you. Harrison was clearly under her spell."

Hadrix turns to me with a questioning stare.

"Of course he was," I say, as if he'd be stupid to believe anything else. "Harrison tried to fight me every step of the way."

Hadrix continues to press the weapon against Harrison's head. "Release him from your power, then."

I place my hands on either side of Harrison's face, my pinky brushing the barrel of the gun pressed to his temple. "You're free."

Harrison does a good job of jumping to his feet and glaring at me, but beneath his outrage is concern. Apparently not only for me. He swivels to Kaitlyn, who gives him a rebellious stare.

I don't believe for one second that she thought he was being compelled, but for some reason, she chose to save his life.

"Your orders, sir?" Harrison asks, swinging back to Hadrix.

"Round up the students," Hadrix tells Harrison. "Confine them to their dorms until Peyton returns with news of Slade's death."

Harrison gives a curt nod before he shouts orders at the soldiers who are still able to stand.

Vulture rushes past him with a terse order thrown at Kaitlyn. "Help me heal the other men."

Blood still trickles down Kaitlyn's face and it doesn't escape me that her mother hasn't healed *her*. Nobody else in her family seems to care about her wound, but I track Harrison's watchful gaze on her.

"Come with me, Peyton," Hadrix says, interrupting my thoughts.

I follow him inside the building, up the stairs, and along the west wing on the second level.

Raptor follows close behind me, but he breaks off along the way.

I've never been to Hadrix's room, and I don't particularly want to step inside, but he orders me to enter.

A large desk dominates the left side of the room and a poster bed sits on the right. The desk has multiple objects on it, including a strange-looking slim canister about the same size as the White Wand that appears to be made out of bone shards pieced together.

My skin crawling, I steer clear of both the bed and the desk as Hadrix steps up to a panel in the wall, removes it, and produces the same chest, covered in runes, that he used to contain the White Wand.

He places it on the desk, resting his hand on the lid. "We have to wait until Vulture gets here to open this box, but in the meantime, you need to know one last piece of information."

Hadrix turns to his son as Raptor shoves Mallard into the room.

The teacher stumbles. He's grown much thinner over the last few months, slowly wasting away. He told me he wanted me to protect him but I sense that whatever mind he had is now gone. Vulture's control spell has been destroying his consciousness for months now. During my last few sessions with him, he barely spoke at all.

"Speak," Hadrix orders.

Mallard mumbles beneath his breath. "The Valkyrie and Keres died because they went to war with each other. Only a Keres can kill a Valkyrie. Peyton is not Keres."

My lips press together. *Well, that's stating the obvious.*

"However," Hadrix interjects, tapping the box. "We have the next best thing."

Vulture appears at the door at that moment with a cold glint in her eyes. "I've left Kaitlyn to heal the others, but I've spelled her so she can't heal herself. She can suffer for what she's done." She looks at me brightly. "Has Mallard told you about the Keres yet?"

"He just did," I say.

"Good."

My brow furrows. "I don't see why you didn't tell me yourself."

Vulture smiles as she grabs Mallard by the shoulder and propels him over to the desk. "Oh, we could have, but it seemed fitting to have him teach you one last thing before he dies."

"No!" My shout comes too late.

There's a flash of steel across Mallard's throat and he sags against the desk, his blood flowing across the box.

I cover my mouth as my stomach turns. I had no love for Mallard, and I shouldn't be surprised by Vulture's cold-hearted brutality by now, but there's a part of me that's horrified.

How many more people will die in this place before we gain our freedom?

"Since my daughter proved that nobody can be trusted around this box," Vulture says, "I sealed it with the blood of the dead on the evening we arrived. Your old compliance officers were very useful for that task. That means that only the blood of the dead can open it. Ah. There."

There's a *click* that tells me the seal around the chest just broke.

Vulture shoves Mallard's body at Raptor. "Take this away, will you?"

Raptor scowls but drags Mallard's body outside while Vulture grabs a towel from the bed. She wipes the top of the box before she unlatches and opens it.

Pulling a copper object from inside it, she closes the lid quickly, but not before I catch sight of two more assassin's rings. That makes four.

I study the new copper object from a distance.

It's a feather, perfectly formed, glistening in a way that tells me it's supple as well as strong. The power resonating from it is so intense, it feels like it's both pulling and pushing me.

"This is a Keres feather," Vulture says. "It was plucked from the wing of a Keres woman and contains all the killing power you need to end Slade Baines and Hunter Cassidy."

"Where did you get it?" I ask.

"I wish I knew the full story," she says. "All I know is that Slade Baines had it. He gave it away when he was a boy."

She holds it out to me. "Poetic, isn't it? That he should be killed by the thing he gave up."

I hesitate to reach for it, worried about what I'll see when I touch it.

"Go on," she says. "Whatever vision you have can only help you."

I'm not so sure.

I take a deep breath as my hand closes around it.

I'm sucked deep into the past, into darkness, my vision clearing as the dingy walls of an alley form around me, lit only by the weak light of a lamp at the corner.

Two figures struggle in front of me. One is a young man about eighteen years old, tall and strong, with glinting blue eyes that look like Slade's. For a moment, I think he *is* Slade, but this man is beautiful in a way that Slade isn't. The woman he fights remains in the shadows, her features concealed in the dark.

A shout from the alley entrance makes me start. "Foster, stop!"

A boy not more than ten years of age with pale blue eyes and dark brown hair darts toward the fight. It's Slade. He's just as fierce as a child as he is as a grown man, except that his body hasn't settled into the powerful muscles and deadly angles with which he holds himself now.

He must be shouting at the man—Foster must be the man's name.

Slade doesn't make it more than a few steps before the woman flings a gleaming dagger at him. It thuds into the wall at his eye level, a mere inch beyond his temple. He jolts backward to avoid it and crashes against the wall.

The woman screams, drawing my focus back to her as she arches in pain.

Light flashes and the silhouette of wings become visible. I can't see her facial features but I assume she's the Keres whose feather I hold.

My mouth suddenly fills with smoke and the strangest scent of lingering death and decay, of both power and weakness. Also, the scent of roses, most unexpected of all.

With a scream of rage, the woman grabs the young man's head and presses her hands to either side of his face. "Die, Ringmaker."

His knees buckle and his eyes lose their focus as death streams around me. I sense it like a black river washing through my mind, forcing me to step backward, even though logically, I know the vision can't hurt me.

The woman allows Foster to drop to the ground as she steps back into the shadows.

Lying on the filthy ground, Foster groans, barely alive.

"Foster!" Slade's anguished cry squeezes my heart in a way I never expected. The resemblance between them is unmistakable. Foster is too young to be Slade's father, so the only conclusion is that he must be Slade's brother.

As Slade cradles Foster's head in his arms, Foster pulls him close and presses a gleaming copper object into Slade's hand.

It's the feather.

Foster must have torn it from the woman's wing.

Slade stares at the feather with eyes that grow cold and dark, and I sense the pull around him, a growing power, the same power I identified when he dragged at my whip on the night he and Hunter flew above the Academy.

The feather floats into the air an inch above the surface of his palm.

The way he looks at it... with hunger and destruction... the same hunger on his brother's face when he fought the Keres woman...

A shiver shakes me.

Slade closes his eyes and the feather settles onto his palm again.

The life leaves his brother's body at the same time as Slade lowers his head, touching his forehead to his brother's.

I sense Slade's refusal to cry, but I also discern his growing rage.

Of one thing I *am* certain: He isn't a Valkyrie on this day. He's powerful, but he's human. Something made him Valkyrie later in his life. How that could be possible is a mystery I might never solve.

Stumbling back to his feet, Slade's footsteps are heavy as he makes his way over to the woman in the shadows.

I feel her growing desire to kill him and then her shock as he holds out the feather to her.

"Take it back," he whispers. "I don't want it."

She is frozen.

I am too.

Then her hand extends beyond the shadows and her fingers close around the feather, taking hold of it once more.

I'm pulled back to the present, reading the hunger for answers in Vulture's eyes. "Well?"

"It's as you said. He gave it away."

She narrows her eyes at me, but when I don't elaborate, she huffs.

"How do I use it?" I ask, ignoring her annoyance.

"That's where things get tricky. The power in the feather must be harnessed into a weapon. But it can't simply be beaten into shape. It has to be molded by the same race of people who made the assassin's rings."

The tension in the room rises and I'm not sure why. Raptor twitches where he stands leaning against the door. His father is suddenly deadpan, both of them deliberately blank.

"Who are these people?" I ask.

"They're called ringmakers. You will need to seek out the last ringmaker and convince her to make a ring for you out of this feather."

Vulture's hiding something. I read the deception in her shifting gaze and the way she wipes her expression carefully clean.

She just told me to have a ring made, but an old memory resurfaces.

When I took the first ring from Raptor, he told me not to put it on, that only humans can wear assassin's rings. It doesn't look like he's going to repeat that warning now, but I repress my concerns. I'll deal with that problem when I come to it.

"Tell me where to find the ringmaker," I say, anticipating what Vulture wants to hear. "I'll compel her to make a ring and I'll wear it to kill Slade Baines and Hunter Cassidy."

She smiles, reaching into the box again to retrieve a small card. "This is the ringmaker's address but be warned. She doesn't like unexpected visitors."

"It won't be a problem," I reply.

Hadrix appears far from satisfied. "If you fail, Striker dies." He grabs my arm as I pass and holds me tightly. "I will kill him."

"I understand," I say, refusing to react. "The next time you see me, Slade and Hunter will be dead."

"Good." He steps away from me. "To exit the Realm, you only need to walk out. But to get back in, you'll have to find the stone gateposts at the entrance to the cemetery. Prick your finger, press it to the gatepost, and the Realm will appear to you again. The Realm is already configured to recognize you. Don't allow anyone to hold on to you when you enter or you'll pull them in too."

My stomach flutters, but not because I'm about to leave this place for the first time in nearly a year.

It's because of what I have to do before I go.

"I'll get changed now," I say, more conscious than before that I'm only half-dressed. "Then I'll leave."

Raptor's gaze rakes over me as I walk past him gripping the feather in my fist.

His parents remain behind, but he stalks me out after me.

As I exit the room, the boundaries of my future, the prison bars lining the path I'm walking, become more sharply defined with every step I take.

I sense Raptor's indrawn breath as if he's about to speak, but I lift from the ground and turn to face him, my hair swirling around me. Unlike the battles I fought before, this one left me pristine. There isn't a drop of blood on me. I have nothing to say to him and for once, he seems speechless as he stares up at me.

He remains silent as I float away. The next time I see him, I intend to strike him down once and for all.

On my way up the stairs, I pause on the third floor, a cold scrunching sound drawing me around the corner. Levitating so I don't make a sound, I pause as soon as I see Kaitlyn filling a cloth with ice.

She presses it to her head and sighs with relief into the quiet, one hand braced against the wall as she leans up against it.

Only one of her fingernails remains painted with a rune. I'm not sure what the spell will do, but it surprises me that she didn't use it against me during the fight. She must be saving it for something.

I remember her cry of rage about Striker. *He deserves to die.*

Striker's name is written in Hunter's ledger for a reason, but I don't want to know why. I can't. Not now.

I've lived in this place surrounded by people whose past deeds make my skin crawl. I can't look at Striker and wonder if he's just like them. I have to block it out and take the only steps that are available to me.

Continuing up the stairs, I wonder if this is the last time I'll climb them. The fourth floor is crowded with soldiers standing in rows in the corridor. Harrison takes command at their head.

As soon as he sees me, he stills. He's being watched now, so he can't make a move toward me, but he shifts a little so I can see through the open door into the nearest dorm. Lucinda and Joseph stand with Bree and Ryan, and Ashley and Lachlan. They're safe for now.

The need to say goodbye to them is strong, but I push it away and continue to the attic.

It's quiet once I reach it, but I sense Striker's presence like the heat of a volcano.

I cling to my power as long as I can before I become human,

extending my senses in the last precious seconds to assess the power growing around him.

His beast is close to the surface.

Perhaps I should be afraid, but I'm still too angry—even if my anger is rapidly becoming human.

He steps from our room as I approach, the fire in his eyes glowing brighter than it has in months. He hasn't changed since this morning. His sweatpants are still bloody. The way his gaze follows all my curves from my face to my neck, chest, waist, hips, and all the way down to my toes makes me shiver. He hasn't looked at me like that for far too long.

He nods as if he's answering his own question. "You're strong now. Even as a human."

I stop outside of his arm's reach, my head held high. "At what cost?"

"The cost doesn't matter."

I narrow my eyes at him. "The cost always matters. You lied to me."

"It was worth it."

My anger flares. "Was it?" I take a deliberate step within his reach. "Even if you lose me?"

"If you die, I'll lose you," he says, his voice rising. "You left me with limited choices the moment you decided to fight Slade."

"There are always choices!" I grit my teeth. "Like right now, I'm deciding if I should turn around and walk away from you, Striker."

"Then do it!"

Pain shoots through my heart. He was the one who wanted to leave, but I wouldn't let him. Now he's telling me to go.

It doesn't matter what I do; he's determined to push me away. But worse than that...

I made him stay. Because he stayed, he became Raptor's

target. That's on me. In fact, all of Striker's choices since then are on me.

How do I face my own guilt? How do I quiet the voice at the back of my mind that tells me Striker and I will always hurt each other?

The knowledge of what I've done is too heavy on me to speak.

Quietly, I walk past him into my old room and retrieve my discarded duffel bag—the one I brought with me when I first arrived.

I slip the feather inside it along with my whip. There's nothing else of value to take with me.

Pulling on a clean T-shirt and jeans, I try to fix my hair, tying it back into a tight ponytail. I'm a mess, but this isn't a beauty contest.

When I exit the room, I find Striker exactly where I left him. He stares out of the window, his gaze distant.

Pausing beside him, I keep my speech short. "I'll come back and kill them. It's up to you whether or not you're here when I return. You're free to choose."

He jolts, his gaze suddenly burning mine.

When I step past him, he grabs my arm to stop me. "I never promised to tell you the truth, Peyton." His beast appears in the golden veins beneath the surface of his bare arms. "In fact, I recall warning you that I'd lie to you."

I inhale an angry breath, but mostly because I'm angry at myself. He told me he was a liar and still, I wanted more. I hoped for more.

Stupid, hopeful, human heart.

Fierce, destructive, Fury heart.

How can both beat inside me?

I refuse to look away. "Tell me one truth, Striker. Just one. Why didn't you ask for my help?"

His response is too smooth, too practiced. "You needed to focus."

I shake my head in a slow, angry side-to-side motion. "Still a lie."

A crease appears in his forehead. "You didn't need the distraction."

"*Lie!*" I scream, shoving him away from me, tears burning behind my eyes. "Why can't you give me one truth?"

"Because I love you!"

Silence settles around us as his shout echoes in my ears.

I can't speak, can't process his declaration.

He exhales and drags me close again, pressing his forehead to mine, the heat from his body seeping through me like sunlight from which I've been deprived for too long.

"I fucking love you, Peyton," he whispers. His hand cups the back of my head, tangling in my hair, loosening my ponytail and sending shivers to my toes. "Please don't leave like this."

He never said *please* before. He never told me he loved me before. My human heart is shattering quietly inside my chest because I never expected him to tell me that he loves me.

He ducks his head to steal a kiss, the briefest touch of his lips on mine as he waits for my response.

I sense the breath he's holding, waiting to exhale.

It's been too long since he kissed me. Too long since he bruised my lips in the best way. I've kept every desire at bay, locked down, and put away. I've hived off my emotions, become a soldier, and now with a single declaration, a single brush of his lips on mine, the fire in my heart is rising and threatening to consume me.

I was prepared to walk away, to remain a soldier, intent only on the brutal task ahead of me, but now I can't.

Closing the fragile gap between us, I press my lips to his. I fill my kiss with all the emotions of love and need raging through me.

He responds with fierce hunger, claiming my mouth and dragging me up against him. I gasp, shiver, and press closer, every inch of my body coming alive, a suddenly desperate ache in my center that I can't ease.

I urge him back toward our room, kissing him and inhaling his intoxicating scent.

We don't make it to the bed before I rip off the shirt and bra I just put on, tugging at the waistband of his pants to remove them.

He follows me as I drop onto my back on the bed, pulling off my jeans and underpants once I'm there.

Our bodies join and I arch against him, wrapping my legs around his hips and drowning in all the sensations raging through me as he moves.

He kisses me with a fever, his fingers curled into my hair, stroking down my side, finding all my sensitive places before coming to rest on either side of my face.

His breathing is ragged beyond control as he captures my gaze. "I want you. All of you."

The hunger in his voice, the flame in his eyes, triggers the deepest sensations inside me.

My world breaks apart, shattering through me, dragging a cry from my throat. I hold tight to him as we both crash and tremble, our chests rising and falling rapidly together.

We collapse into each other's arms, breathing heavily.

My heart pounds as I come back to Earth. I feel like my whole world is spinning out of my control and I want to grab it and hold it in this moment before it breaks.

I'm still shaking as Striker gathers me up against him, sitting me up so I'm straddling him, my legs wrapped around his hips as he presses kisses to my cheeks and lips.

"I'll do anything to keep you safe." He strokes the hair from my face, his fiery amber gaze burning across my eyes and lips. "I kept you safe from Raptor and now I can keep you safe from the assassins. Let me do this for you, Peyton."

I don't know what he means. "Striker?"

"Let me talk to the assassins. There has to be another way through this."

A cold chill passes through me. He wasn't there when Kaitlyn told everyone she wrote his name in Hunter Cassidy's ledger. He doesn't know he's a target.

"No, Striker. That won't work—"

"I don't care what it takes to protect you, I'll do it."

My lips part as a cold sensation creeps inside my heart and a sneaking fear grows, clawing at my insides. "Just like you protected me from Raptor."

"As long as Raptor was focused on me, he wasn't hurting you."

A painful, cutting sensation slices through my chest.

Suddenly, all I can see is Kaitlyn's memories of Striker standing between her and the torture she contrived. Of Striker protecting her with his body, taking the lashes, the cuts, surviving the pit.

His pain. All for her.

Now he's acting as if I'm her, taking punishment on my behalf, making himself a physical shield between me and my tormentor.

Suddenly I see: I'm no better than her.

My heart is slowly turning to stone.

No matter how hard we try not to hurt each other, Striker and I are born from hell. Hell is what we inflict on each other.

"That isn't love," I whisper. "It's self-destruction."

His lips part, his eyes searching mine. "But... Peyton... you have to believe..."

"I may as well be her. I may as well be Kaitlyn." A bitter laugh tears from my throat as I push away from him. I can't stay in his arms. "You nearly killed yourself for her. You nearly killed yourself for me. That isn't love."

His expression hardens. "I'm not allowed to protect you?"

A wail breaks out of me as I stumble from the bed, catching hold of one of his shirts to clean up my thighs before I turn on him. "Love is believing in my strength! Love is allowing me to fight beside you. Love is asking for help and knowing I'll answer your call. Love is trusting me."

I pitch the shirt into the corner of the room.

I want to hate him. I want my Fury. I want to not feel.

He is ashen. Frozen. The fire fades from his eyes and his silence is like fragile glass that I can shatter if I choose.

I back away from him. "You don't know what love is, Striker."

He suddenly bursts into action, leaving the bed and dragging me against him as I fight him. I push at his chest and arms, but he doesn't let me go.

"You're right," he cries. "I don't. I don't know what love looks like. I don't know how to show it. I don't know how to ask for it. I did it wrong." His chest heaves against mine. "I did it all wrong."

I tip my head back, tears leaking down my cheeks like little lines of acid.

The storm of emotion in his eyes cuts through my heart, but I'm so empty right now. Even when he was protecting Kaitlyn, she remained in his bed. He didn't turn his back on her like he did to me.

He pushed me so far from his heart and body that now I don't know how to make my way back to him.

"Let me go," I whisper.

For a moment, I think he's going to refuse. Then, his arms open, dropping to his sides.

I step back from him, one pace at a time, scooping up my clothes and rushing to pull them on, unable to speak.

The emotion in his eyes dies with every move I make until he's blank. "You could run free. Leave and never look back. Why won't you?"

"Because your name is written in Hunter Cassidy's ledger. I will kill her before she comes for you."

I don't wait for his shocked expression to clear before I turn on my heel, but his murmur stops me dead in my tracks.

"We're not so different," he says, his voice flat. "We try to love each other in our own messed-up ways."

I pick up my dropped bag and run, my power surging through me the farther I get from him.

31. PEYTON PRICE

 burst through the front door to find Harrison waiting for me at the open gate.

I expected Hadrix or Vulture to watch my departure closely, but apparently not.

He stands holding a weapon belt in his hands, his feet planted on the pebbled path that turns into a road behind him. His expression is hooded and dark, the tension in his body like a warning, but he relaxes as I approach.

"You'd better not be here to stop me," I say.

"I came to give you this." He hands me the belt, which I quickly place in my bag.

As I straighten and step past him, he reaches out, not quite touching me, but enough to make me pause.

"You asked me why I came here. Why I got mixed up with Hadrix," he says. "I want to explain before you leave."

The corner of my mouth hitches into a cynical smile. "In case I don't make it back?"

He inclines his head and my smile fades.

That would be a *yes*, then.

"I trained you well, but this fight will be more brutal than anything you've ever experienced," he says. "If you make it back, I want you to know why I'm here and where I stand."

I try to ease out the rising stress in my body. The road is so close and the need to move is killing me.

I lift my chin. "Walk with me to the edge of the Realm."

He gives me a nod of agreement and we step through the gate.

Just like that, I'm outside the Academy's fence. It seems so easy now, accomplishing this step that I desperately needed for months, but the weight of what's ahead of me beats down any elation I might otherwise feel.

Harrison keeps pace with me. "I didn't join Hadrix willingly. My younger brother got mixed up with him four years ago. Before Jesse knew it, he was stealing, threatening people, and breaking into homes. He came to me covered in blood one night —" Harrison swallows and clears his throat. "I told him to get himself away from Hadrix, but it was too late. Hadrix had him."

Harrison shrugs and sighs. "Maybe he didn't really want to get out. I don't know. I got involved trying to save his skin and then, I was in too deep to get out too."

"What happened?" I ask.

"Jesse was killed."

I miss a step. "How?"

Harrison's lips press together. For a moment, I don't think he's going to tell me. "Hadrix sent Jesse to a party one night. I don't know what he was supposed to do there, but he never came home."

I narrow my eyes at Harrison. His explanation doesn't clarify why he was reluctant to tell me. "How did he die?"

"The details are murky." Again, Harrison pauses. "It was Striker Draven's twentieth birthday party and Striker had a bad reputation for putting guys in hospital."

I speak carefully. "You think Striker killed him?"

"Hadrix told me he did." Harrison presses his lips together in an unforgiving line. "I have no proof either way, but I know for a fact that Jesse went to that party and he didn't come home. I saw for myself one of Striker's cage fights. I know the violence he's capable of. I'm sorry, Peyton. Hadrix is a liar but I had no reason to doubt his word at the time."

"And now?"

"I don't know what's true anymore. I don't trust Hadrix's word, but I wouldn't trust Striker's either."

My heart is in my throat as what Harrison told me. His brother goes to Striker's birthday party, ends up dead, and Hadrix claims Striker did it. There's a reason Striker's name is written in Hunter Cassidy's ledger and this has to be it.

I don't know how to feel about it. If Hadrix sent Jesse to the party, then he wasn't there as a friend. Things had to have gotten out of hand and Striker might not have started it. But the assassins don't target people who act in self-defense.

I shudder and close my eyes against all the possibilities, too cold and numb now to feel rage or betrayal.

Harrison's expression changes. Bitter. Defeated. "Kaitlyn wasn't the same after Jesse died."

I consider him carefully. "Kaitlyn?"

"She wasn't always like the rest of her family." Harrison's honest eyes meet mine. "In fact, she was trying to get away from them when she met Jesse."

I'm puzzled. "I'm sorry... I don't follow."

"Kaitlyn was the reason Jesse got mixed up with Hadrix," Harrison says. "Jesse met her and fell hard. He tried to help her find her own place, but her parents wouldn't leave her alone. He thought he could bargain for her freedom—he would do some work for Hadrix and in return they'd let Kaitlyn go—but it all went wrong. I believe she truly loved him back. More than anyone realized. I was there when Hadrix told her that Jesse died..." Harrison's gaze becomes distant. "It broke her."

Kaitlyn's screams repeat on me. *I want him dead! He deserves to die.*

Striker came here on his twentieth birthday. The day Jesse died. Then Kaitlyn followed him here and systematically broke him too. Revenge for Jesse's death.

I stumble on the pebbles. *How long will the cycle of hate continue?*

"I need to tell you something else," Harrison says. "If you don't come back and end Hadrix, he and Oliver Draven plan on rebuilding Lady Tirelli's empire. They will break every student in this Academy and use them as their tools. As you've discovered, they have a way of manipulating any situation to their advantage. If you kill Slade Baines and Hunter Cassidy, you will remove the two people able to stop that from happening. You will open the door for Hadrix to do what he wants."

I grit my teeth, but not in anger. Despair wells inside me. "What choice do I have?"

He holds his hand up in a placating gesture. "You have only bad choices. You can kill Slade or you can let Striker die."

My response is bitter. "But of the two, you think I should let Striker die."

Harrison gives me a hard stare. "I think that the assassins take justice seriously. They don't kill without reason." He suddenly grabs my arm, forcing me to stop despite the warning glare I give him.

"I was guarding one of Lady Tirelli's warehouses that the assassins hit," he says. "I came face to face with Hunter Cassidy."

"Then you're lucky to be alive," I snap.

"No," he says, surprising me. "She used tranquilizers. Even when we returned fire with armor-piercing bullets. I shot her clean through her shoulder. A lucky shot, I'll admit. Despite that, she left me alive."

I search his eyes. "What are you trying to say?"

"That they're honorable. They play by rules that keep the blood from staining their hands. If they come here, they will kill your enemies and not your friends."

I pull away from him. "Striker isn't my enemy."

Harrison stops on the road as I continue on without him. "Peyton?"

I turn back, but his gaze passes across the space where I stand, as if he can't see me anymore.

Shocked, I realize that I must have stepped through the shield.

A new road stretches out behind me perpendicular to the one that leads up to the Academy's gate.

In front of me is now a very different gate. Two stone posts sit on either side of it with identical inscriptions that read: *St. Michael Cemetery.*

Between Harrison and me, a glittering force shimmers in the air—the edge of the Realm. But contrary to what Hadrix and Vulture told me, I can still see the Realm too.

The two images sit on top of each other. One image contains the Academy in the distance and the road leading up to it. The other is the outside world—a lush landscape of tall trees and a paved driveway leading up a slope into what I can only assume is the cemetery.

Both landscapes appear to me as if they're transposed over each other.

As I blink and try to focus, the inside of the Realm begins to fade and the outside world becomes sharper. A car passes by behind me, startling me, but the proximity of the road explains how Hadrix was able to drive whole trucks directly into the Realm.

Inside the Realm, Harrison's silhouette begins to disappear.

"I'll be here when you come back," he says, as if he hopes I can still hear him. "You'll have to give everything you've got, Peyton."

The Realm fades away completely and I'm surrounded by the outside world.

I shiver as the sounds around me grow louder.

I'm not prepared for how cold it is out here. The climate within the Realm hardly changed through winter. I tilt my head as birds chirp in the trees, a foreign sound compared to the dark silence that filled the forest around the Academy.

The outside world smells like spring and new life—despite the fact that I'm standing outside a burial place.

I inhale the crisp air deep into my chest as if it can fill the pit that widens inside me.

Harrison said I'll have to give everything, but I'm already an empty shell.

I have nothing more to give except my life.

32. STRIKER DRAVEN

The silence in the attic is absolute. Peyton's absence is like sharp barbs pressing into my chest.

I have only two choices now. The first is to wait for death to come for me. The second is to stride right up to death and look her in the eye before she strikes me down. Only one of those choices saves Peyton's life.

Fuck death. I was destined to meet Hunter Cassidy sooner or later.

It may as well be now… even if I don't know what I did to deserve her wrath.

I cast my mind back to all the fights in my past. Did I go too far in a cage fight one night? Did someone I sent to hospital end up dead?

Did I drive away from an accident because I was too drunk on adrenaline after a fight that I didn't realize I'd hit and killed someone on the road?

What did I do?

My beast wasn't awake then to help me with my memories of that time, but he's well and truly awake now.

You messed up, he says. Maybe he's talking about my past or maybe he's talking about Peyton. Either way, he's right.

Peyton doesn't believe that I love her and she's smart not to. She was right to walk away, even if I was ready to beg her to stay with me. I will never be what she wants me to be. I will never fully trust her, the same way I can't trust anyone. I will never ask for her help because I can't even form the words in my mind, let alone speak them.

But she's wrong about one thing. I believe in her strength.

Every single one of Hadrix's men is afraid of her. Even Hadrix and, ironically, Raptor fears what she is now and what she can do. She was smart while she trained. She didn't become reliant on her Fury; she built up her human strength as well.

She might actually be strong enough to kill Slade Baines. Even Hunter Cassidy.

But if she succeeds, the assassins will pin a target on her and they'll never stop coming. One day, somewhere, somehow, one of them will end her.

I have the power to stop it all from happening.

I consider every object in my room, deciding if I should take anything with me. The only thing that mattered to me was Peyton and now she's gone.

I pull on a clean T-shirt and change my pants, but that's all I do before I leave emptyhanded.

Creeping past the fourth floor, I wait for the soldiers to turn their backs before I dart down the flight of stairs. Pausing at the third floor, I listen carefully for any sounds before I step into the corridor and prepare to hurry down the next flight of stairs.

I freeze when I see Kaitlyn resting against the wall beside the ice chest. She's pressing a pack of ice against the side of her forehead where her father hit her.

Before I can slip away, she twists and sees me.

Whatever veil she wore over her emotions before, it's gone.

Pure hatred meets my eyes, but behind it is the deepest pain, the kind that Peyton hides.

Kaitlyn turns fully, blazing mad as she throws the ice pack

against the wall with a *smack* and strides toward me, her feet bare, her heels discarded at the side of the hallway.

I allow my claws to descend. I seek my beast in case I need him, but she stops outside striking distance, her chest rising and falling, her buttons done all the way up to her throat this time.

"Why did you do it?" she cries.

The tears in her eyes shock me. I jolt, uncertain and confused, watching her carefully in case it's some kind of trick.

"Why, Striker?" She searches my face as if she's desperate for answers. "Jesse was all I had. He was the only good thing in my life. Why did you take him away from me?"

I don't know what she's talking about. I start to shake my head, but she crosses the distance and thumps her fist against my chest.

"Why? Dammit, tell me!" She wraps her fingers in my shirt and tilts her head back. "Tell me so I can understand!"

I can't stop my confusion, don't try to defend myself, my arms kept carefully at my sides. "I don't know what you're talking about. I don't know anyone called Jesse."

"You don't know?" Her pain turns to rage. "You killed him and you don't even know his name. You messed-up asshole!"

I grab her fists before she thumps me again, dropping my face to hers. "I didn't kill him, Kaitlyn. I don't even know who you're talking about."

"*Liar.*"

She fails to keep her balance, wobbling like she's drunk when I push her away from me so I can turn back to the stairs.

"I wrote your name in Hunter's ledger," she says, stopping me in my tracks.

I cast an angry sideways glance at her. "For something I don't remember doing."

She folds her arms across her chest, her shoulders slumped, as if she's trying to protect herself. "I thought if I came here and hurt you, I would feel better. But I can never hurt you enough.

Even when you're dead, the pain won't go away." She looks across at me. "Will it?"

I exhale a soft breath. A resigned sigh. "You'll know soon enough."

Maybe my death will take away whatever pain she's feeling —a pain I can't remember inflicting on her. Maybe it will wash away her own culpability for the jagged pieces of who I am now.

A confused crease forms in her forehead. "What are you talking about?" Her expression clears and she takes an angry step toward me. "You'd better not think about running. You don't deserve to be free."

I step away from her. "You can't stop me."

"No—"

Her cry fades as I race down the stairs, deftly avoiding the soldiers patrolling the hallways.

I make it out the front door before I knock right into Harrison.

He immediately points a gun at my head and I don't doubt his aim. He trained Peyton to do everything she did this morning, taking down twenty soldiers within the space of seconds while she was part-human.

He scowls and makes the same assumption Kaitlyn did. "Running away?"

I fight my beast's desire to fight back.

"Pull the trigger," I say, remaining as still as I can despite my instincts to disarm him. "But if you kill me, you'd better make sure the message gets to the assassins before Peyton fights them."

His eyes narrow at me. "You're going after her."

I shake my head. "I plan on getting there before her. Once I'm dead, she has no reason to fight them. Then they'll come here and kill what I can't."

He exhales. "Your friends will be safe then."

I don't bother telling him I have no friends, which is just as well because only Peyton will miss me when I'm gone. Maybe my stepsister, Zara, will spare a thought for me, but my death will free her from any guilt she feels about putting me in this place.

Harrison keeps his weapon trained on me for another second before he lowers it, his expression carefully blank. "You'll have to go through the forest. It might not look like it, but Hadrix is watching the road. The road is the shortest way out of here, but he'll shoot you down before you make it to the gate. He doesn't trust me anymore, either. He doesn't fully believe that Peyton compelled me to help her this morning."

I tip my head at him. "Of course she didn't. You're not one of them."

Harrison gives me another nod. "I won't stop you from leaving."

He holsters his weapon, but the moment he does, I grab him and shove him against the side of the front door with my beast's strength.

He thuds against it, but his right hand moves swiftly.

I already identified the dagger hidden at the back of his belt. I need to speak quickly before he drives it between my ribs.

"Promise me you'll look after her when I'm dead," I say.

Harrison trained Peyton for months. The way he followed her out this morning, watching her back, tells me he got close to her and cares about her.

He freezes at my words. A storm builds on his face, a surprising release of rage spilling out of him, his panther revealing itself in the animalistic gleam of his eyes.

"Do you mean Peyton or Kaitlyn?" He snarls. "You ripped both their hearts apart."

I jolt and let him go, backing away from him. *Peyton. Always Peyton.*

My world spins in a confusing spiral since I'm still on uncertain ground about my confrontation with Kaitlyn earlier and the possibility that I somehow hurt her long before she hurt me.

Harrison's fist clips my head, but it's a warning shot. "The only reason I haven't killed you already is because Peyton wouldn't forgive me. Get the hell out of here, Striker, before I do what I should have done the day I arrived and take a life for a life."

Rubbing my forehead, I don't waste another moment. Keeping to the side of the building, I race toward the fence where I bent it the first time, taking hold of the bars and pulling them apart with all my strength.

After squeezing between them, I drag them closed again. One side creaks and groans, refusing to return to its original position, but I'm sure the gap is too small for the creature to get through.

The forest is quiet and dark before me. It's the middle of the day, but the sunlight barely reaches the ground beneath the thick canopy of leaves and branches. I'm okay with that. My beast's eyes are better than mine.

I call him to the surface as I dart into the woods, my body shifting as I run, fiery light blurring around me from the molten fissures that rise along my arms and burn through the material of my sweatpants.

My vision changes with my power, the world taking on a burnished glow, every shadow and dark crevice between the trees revealing all the small creatures that live around me...

An owl quietly resting in the branches of a tree, waking as I pass... A fox darting away from me, its bushy tail flying as it flees. More surprising, deer scatter as the trees become slightly sparse toward the middle of the forest. At least, I think it's the middle. I don't really know. The deer leap and dart gracefully away from me as soon as I approach.

Twenty minutes later, I'm aware of another presence, one I

can't identify, also moving at a fast pace through the trees behind and to my right.

And also, surprisingly, a second presence, but that one is much farther back and won't catch up to me any time soon. Not unless I stop.

I speed up, telling myself I can't die here. I have to die at Hunter Cassidy's hand. If I die here, she won't hear about it.

If the creature has caught my scent, then I need to reach the edge of the Realm before it catches me.

Running through the seemingly never-ending darkness, I count my steps to stay focused, fear growing inside me that the forest will never end, that I've gone the long way, and that I'll never reach the Realm's edge.

My dread grows sharper as the presence on my right gains on me no matter how fast I run.

I can hear it now, the soft footfalls as it moves, but I can't tell if it's running on two feet or four.

Casting a glance to the right, I make out a shape about the same size as me, humanoid, but then it drops to the ground and its shape flickers between the trees, my surroundings too dark to determine what it is.

Its speed increases as it veers toward me.

Adrenaline bursts through me. *Beast! I need speed!*

Energy rages through my legs, but I've already burned through so much.

I dart to the left as snarls reach me through the darkness.

Passing too close to the nearest tree, sparks fly into the air as my fiery arm grazes across the tree's trunk, but I keep running, leaping over a fallen branch and between two closely placed trees into a small clearing.

The creature's breathing is too close. I'm not going to outrun it.

A blur of fury and claws hits me from behind, knocking me into the ground.

33. STRIKER DRAVEN

$\mathcal{A}$ heavy weight crashes onto my back, claws rip through my ribs, and teeth savage at my shoulder before I can push up.

The creature was clever and hit me from the side to avoid the deadly bones jutting from my shoulder blades and down my spine.

Only my beast's fire saves me.

The creature roars with pain as flames fill its mouth when it tries to tear through my shoulder.

Its weight shifts enough for me to twist, my claws slashing across its side.

It leaps off me just as I drive my claws toward its belly.

Its movements are lithe and agile, its body sleek black.

It's an enormous black panther that I estimate will stand at my waist height once I straighten. Its fur is matted with old blood, evidence of its defeated prey.

Glowing yellow eyes watch me without blinking. But there's something wrong with them and it takes me a moment to figure it out as I remain in a crouch, quickly checking my bleeding wounds—a precious moment of reprieve as it regains its balance, spitting out the molten lava it swallowed.

Its pupils are silver. So are its teeth as its lips pull back in a snarl.

My survival instincts kick in as the creature jumps toward me again, both of its paws slashing at me with extended claws, its big cat snarls a terrifying noise.

I retaliate with my own claws, roaring back at it, my hellhound in full fury.

One of its paws swipes close to my cheek and I'm startled to see a silver object wrapped around its claw.

I hit out with my fist, making contact against its side, sensing its ribs shift, but not enough to break.

We fly apart. The panther rolls and shifts its form, its fur fading into skin, its forelegs becoming arms, and its paws becoming fists and feet.

A human male rises up from a crouch, butt naked except for the dirt and blood covering every inch of his skin from his forehead to his toes.

His eyes might have once been brown, but now they're flooded with silver with only a hint of color at the edges and no pupils in the middle. The level of madness in his eyes is fucking insane.

He draws his lips back in a snarl, his voice scratchy, the sounds hissing between his teeth. "Striker Draven."

My beast roars back at him. "Who are you?"

He shakes his head, a quick, twitchy movement. "Get Striker Draven."

He launches himself forward, faster and more agile than I was expecting, his fists connecting with my cheek, chest, and chin in rapid succession.

Silver glints at the edge of my vision as his fist meets my jaw.

A silver ring on his forefinger rests against my cheek and for a sickening moment, it feels like it sucks the life out of me.

It's a sensation that is all too familiar to me. I felt it every time Raptor hit me.

My eyes widen as I duck his next fist.

This creature—this shifter—is wearing an assassin's ring.

I'm done being pummeled by wannabe assassins. I hit back hard, my fist crunching into his ribs, then his stomach, and straight into his throat in a blow that's intended to crush his windpipe, but he absorbs it without apparent injury.

Even so, he suddenly jolts, his entire body disappearing for a second that leaves me startled, but another second later, he reappears.

He grabs his head and screams as if he's in pain before he flickers out of view again.

It's weirdly like a flicker fit in reverse, as if he's sucking the light out of the air instead of intensifying it.

This time, he reappears closer to me.

I'm ready for him. It's been too long since I let my strength flow and now the fury rages through me. I kick my boot right into his face, sensing his jaw shift, but still nothing breaks. *Damn, this guy's body is like putty.*

What's worse, I can hear running footsteps approaching us, only moments away from reaching us.

If I don't make a move soon, my options are going to disappear fast. I flick my claws out, watching the shifter's movements as he comes at me again. I identify the gap between his right arm and chest, ignoring the pain as his left fist slams into my chest, waiting for the opening.

There.

I push forward, my claws shooting toward his chest, straight and true, sliding between his ribs into his lungs, deadly cuts.

I shove him away from me and he falls to the ground, but I follow him down, grabbing his head and preparing to drag my claw across his throat to end him.

He chokes, unable to breathe now that I've punctured his

lungs, but the way his breathing changes tells me—*oh, hell*—that his chest is healing fast.

The approaching footfalls stop at the edge of the clearing and Kaitlyn shrieks. "I won't let you escape, Striker! You—" There's a shocked pause and then she screams again, this time raw and emotional. "*Stop!*"

I blink hard to focus beyond my battle rage and the need to kill.

She races toward me, her blonde hair flying, her hands outstretched, and her features pale and desperate.

"*Stop, Striker!*" She launches herself at me, shoving me backward. My claw grazes across the creature's neck before my hand flies wide.

I fall backward with Kaitlyn on top of me as she hits at me wildly.

Nobody ever taught her how to fight. Let alone defend herself. I grab her hands, quickly flipping our position so that my full weight pins her down, my hands pressing her arms into the ground beside her head.

She screams at me, "Don't hurt him!"

"What the hell, Kaitlyn—?"

A fist hits me in the back of the head, pushing me down onto her so hard that my head smacks hers, knocking her unconscious.

I roll to the side, trying to shake off the concussion as I twist and hit back at the creature.

Now mid-shift, the panther man's claws rake across my chest, shredding the sleeve clean off my shirt before I make it back to my feet. His human foot connects with my stomach, kicking me so hard that I smack into the nearest tree.

As the impact jars through me, he turns away from me, focusing on Kaitlyn for all of a split second before he grabs one of her ankles, hoists her into the air, and throws her across the clearing.

Her unconscious body hits a tree trunk and drops to the ground.

Damn. She was trying to save him. My eyes widen at the savage treatment he gave her.

He continues to focus on her, crossing the distance between them, his claws extended as he leans over her and reaches for her head, as if he's preparing to rip out her throat.

Without thinking, I race after him, grab him from behind, and lock my arm around his neck to drag him backward. I punch my fist into his spleen, once, twice, and then his ribs, making him howl as he slowly lowers to the ground, forced onto his knees, his cries cutting off as my arm tightens.

Kaitlyn groans where she lies on the ground, trying to push herself up before she lets out a scream, flinching and grabbing her back in a way that tells me the nerves in her spine are on fire.

Even so, all she seems to care about is me and the creature, her gaze darting back to us.

Slowly extending my claws, I angle them toward the creature's chest this time. The only way I'll kill him is to rip out his heart.

Kaitlyn's eyes widen. "No!"

She scrambles toward us, but the creature bares his teeth at her, his growls harsh beneath my hold.

She stops in her tracks, staring wildly at him, her hands stretched toward me again.

"Please." Her voice breaks, tears filling her eyes, and sheer terror flooding her expression. "Please, Striker. I'm begging you. *I'm begging you.* Please, don't kill him."

My voice rises to a roar. "Why the hell not?"

"Because…" Her blue eyes are wide and frightened. "He's Jesse."

What the hell?

She inches closer. "I don't know how… but he's Jesse. He's Harrison's brother, Jesse."

Harrison's brother. That would explain why this creature is a panther—and why Harrison threatened to take a life for a life—but it doesn't explain Jesse's extraordinary strength or his ability to heal himself.

He struggles against my hold, his claws raking across my sides as far as he can reach. He's too strong. If I don't act soon, I'll lose my hold on him and Kaitlyn doesn't know the danger she's in. She wasn't conscious when he threw her across the clearing.

He suddenly lurches forward, trying to slip my arms, his claws raking across the space between him and Kaitlyn, narrowly missing her chest. He catches one of her buttons instead, ripping through the material.

She falls back with a shriek. "Jesse, it's me!"

I roar at her. "Whoever you think he is, he's not that person anymore."

The tips of my claws impale his chest, pressing beneath his skin, but Kaitlyn throws herself forward again, trying to stop me.

Jesse's left hand snakes toward her face, cutting across her cheek. She screams, but she doesn't give up, trying to dart between his claws to take hold of my arm.

As her gaze shoots left, following the arc of Jesse's nails, she suddenly freezes, gasping in air so loudly that it sounds like an inhaled scream.

"He's wearing an assassin's ring." Her eyes meet mine a second before she's forced to duck his claws again. "*Cut it off!*"

I don't have any choice. His strength is immense. I've already lost hold of him.

As he leaps out of my arms, all I can do is grab his left arm, wrenching him to the side and impaling his forearm with my claws so he can't pull away without shredding his arm.

My right hand darts toward his left. My claw slices neatly through his forefinger and it falls to the ground, taking the ring with it.

His roar rises into the air as he clutches at his hand and drops to his knees.

I back away from him, my chest rising and falling rapidly while I check Kaitlyn's position, prepared for Jesse to continue his attack.

As he looks up at me, his eyes shift, his pupils dilating, his focus coming to rest on me.

It turns out I was right: He has brown eyes.

His lips part, then close. He twitches forward over his wounded hand, a shocked groan of pain releasing from his lips as if he's only just now becoming aware of his wounds.

His lips purse, trying to form sound through lacerated vocal chords as his face contorts in agony.

I make out the shape of the word he's trying to speak: "*Where?*"

My jaw clenches. I have no idea how to answer the question of where he is in any way that will make sense to him, so instead, I ask, "Do you know who you are?"

His gaze casts around the clearing, his torso twisting as he suddenly becomes aware of Kaitlyn standing in the clearing behind him.

He freezes and inhales, his voice a throaty whisper. "Kaitlyn… baby?"

She chomps her lip, her cold exterior cracking and tears leaking from her eyes as she drops to her knees in front of him. "You remember me."

He presses his wounded hand to his chest as he reaches for her with his other hand, focusing on her bleeding cheek. "You're hurt."

A sob bursts out of her. "No. I'm all better." She reaches for him, shifting forward and settling into his arms, curling up against him. "I'm all better now."

He drops a kiss to the top of her head, cradling her close as he rasps. "Why are we here? What happened?"

"Too much," she whispers.

My warning snarl makes her startle. "Kaitlyn."

Her tear-stained face rises to mine as I loom over them both.

She must hear it too. So does Jesse, judging from the sudden tension in his body.

In the distance, boots crash through the undergrowth.

"You brought them with you." I snarl an accusation.

Kaitlyn shakes her head rapidly. "Not intentionally."

I don't believe her despite her open expression, but then... a long-ago overhead conversation suddenly repeats on me.

I hovered outside Lady Tirelli's office listening to Hadrix, Vulture, and Raptor talking the night after Hadrix first arrived. They said Kaitlyn shouldn't learn the truth about the creature in the forest, that the creature would be dead soon and they could close the door on her problems.

They knew.

They fucking knew that this guy—Jesse—was alive the whole time. They must have told Kaitlyn I killed him so she would come to the Academy seeking revenge. All of it to try to force me to show my power.

And now I can't fight the darkness threatening to engulf me. Hating Kaitlyn was part of my foundation and now it's been ripped away from me because...

She broke first.

As the crashing noises through the forest grow louder, I expand my senses and count the people coming for us. Maybe five.

I can beat them. I'm sure I can.

My jaw clenches as I take up position in front of Kaitlyn and Jesse.

"Striker?" Kaitlyn's question sounds small. "What are you doing? You should run while you can."

My response is brutal. "They'll kill him."

Her eyes grow wide when I twist to see her. "Why would they do that?"

"Because you weren't supposed to find out he was here. Nobody was."

"But… they thought he was dead. They'll be happy he's alive. Lady Tirelli must have brought him here… My family didn't have anything to do with this…"

"They knew."

"No." Her gaze grows hard. "My family's messed up, but why would they hide this from me?"

I narrow my eyes at her. "Because you were more useful to them broken."

The color leaves her face as she looks back at me. Her gaze passes from my face to my body. For a moment, I think she's going to throw up. She doubles over, groaning. "Oh, dear ancients. What have I done?"

Jesse must be attuned to her moods because he's already rubbing her back, easing his good hand into her hair in soothing strokes. They're both a mess. Kaitlyn's cheek is bloody and her forehead is bruised. Jesse's hair is matted with blood, his finger's bleeding, and his body is filthy with dirt and hell-knows-what-else.

I can only guess how he survived in this forest for the last three years, but I can imagine all the deer and fox his panther feasted on.

The assassin's ring had a terrible effect on him. Unfortunately, he's now as vulnerable as Kaitlyn is. And while I'm stuck here, Peyton gets closer and closer to her death.

My fists clench and my heart cracks, but I can't walk away.

Kaitlyn's family messed with her as badly as they messed with me.

"Stay down," I order them. "I can only defend you if you remain where you are."

A second later, Hadrix bursts into the clearing, rapidly digging his heels in as he takes in the scene before him: Me standing in front of Kaitlyn and Jesse, who huddle on the ground.

His face turns an awful, red color. He twists to scream an order behind him. "Vulture! Raptor! Send the others back."

Answering shouts sound from farther back within the trees. I hear the question in Vulture's voice as she shouts a response, although I can't make out what she says, but she's unlikely to question her husband's terse command.

Seconds later, she and Raptor appear alone behind him.

"Oh, hell." Raptor's upper lip curls. "You found him."

For a second, his disgusted look fades and he arches an impressed eyebrow at me. "It looks like you figured out how to beat him."

Ignoring Raptor, I narrow my gaze at Hadrix. "Your daughter deserves answers."

Hadrix tilts his head before he takes a step to the left to see past me. "How I treat my daughter is none of your concern."

Kaitlyn is pale, but as she looks from her mother to her father, her expression hardens. "You told me Jesse was dead."

"It was better that way," Hadrix says.

"For who?" Tears fall down her cheeks.

Jesse tries to speak as he pulls her tightly, protectively, against him, but I'm guessing he doesn't remember any of the events that brought him here.

A stone-cold expression falls over her father's face. "You want answers? Lady Tirelli came to me on the morning of Striker's twentieth birthday. She wanted Striker brought to the Academy but she knew he wouldn't come easily. She asked Raptor and Jesse to get him. Raptor still had his assassin's ring then, but Jesse needed to be stronger if he was going to take

Striker on. Lady Tirelli convinced Jesse to put on one of the rings she stole from the assassin's Guardian. Except it turns out that supernaturals react very badly to the rings."

He pauses for a breath. "At that time, she didn't know the effect it would have, and neither did I. Jesse lost it. He couldn't control the magic. So instead of going after Striker that night, Raptor had to go after Jesse. Jesse survived all attempts to kill him. Tranquilizers didn't work. We couldn't even cut the ring off. We finally managed to cage him and bring him here to let him loose in the forest. End of story."

"Why didn't you tell me the truth?" Kaitlyn asks.

"Why would we do that?" Vulture scoffs beside Hadrix. "You would have come after him and he would have killed you. Then what use would you be to us?"

Kaitlyn is ashen. "Why do you hate me so much?"

Vulture spits. "Because you're weak! You just wanted to be loved like every other little girl. You're exhausting."

She takes a step toward Kaitlyn, but my fist swings out and catches her on her chin.

Vulture shrieks and Hadrix rounds on me.

"You're going to let them leave," I say.

"Or what, Striker?" Raptor waggles his assassin's ring at me.

"Or you'll meet my beast." I always kept something back because that way I could tell myself Raptor hadn't beaten me. Even when he broke my bones and cut my skin, I still had my beast.

I allow a smile to break across my face. "C'mon, Raptor. Give me an excuse."

With a threatening smile, Raptor disappears from sight.

I remain where I am, closing my eyes, since they're no use to me in this fight.

Allowing my beast to surface, I welcome the hellish heat growing inside me, the bones protruding from my back.

Only another animal like Jesse would have the instincts to know how to attack my back. Raptor will stay in front of me.

I relax my arms and wait.

Crack. The impact of Raptor's fist is stunning, but I've spent the last four months practicing how to become numb to it.

With my beast's reflexes, my left hand snaps out at the exact moment of impact, grabbing, impaling and yanking his arm all the way past my side so that he jolts toward me.

He steps right into the waiting claws of my right hand.

They slide straight into his throat.

He can't even shout, let alone scream.

I pull him close and whisper to him. "Did you think I couldn't kill you all this time? I was waiting, Jake. You may have created Peyton, but I made sure she became strong."

As Raptor's knees fail, I speak over his head to his parents. "The minute I withdraw my claws, he'll bleed out. If you let Kaitlyn go, I'll give you the chance to heal him. It's your choice."

Vulture rages toward me. "I'll kill you!"

Hadrix yanks her back. "We'll heal our son either way," he says to me. "You don't get to call the shots here, Striker."

I open my mouth to respond, but Kaitlyn shouts from behind me.

"I have one last spell left." Her gaze passes across her brother with an odd sort of pity as she holds up her hand.

One rune remains painted on a fingernail.

"Kaitlyn!" her mother snaps. "Do not use that spell. If you run, so help me, I will hunt you down and kill you both."

Kaitlyn ignores her mother. She exhales and her whole expression changes, younger somehow and very human. "I'm sorry, Striker. I'm sorry for what I did to you. If I could take it back, I would. Promise me you'll run now."

I give her a nod—a quick but convincing one—even though it's a lie. I gave up my chance to run the moment I stood between her and her family.

She wraps her arms and legs around Jesse and just as quickly, she taps her finger against his back.

Then they're gone.

I can't help letting out a laugh—reckless, wild laughter—as I make a decision.

I could turn and run, leave Raptor to be healed, and see how far I get through the forest before Vulture casts a spell that stops me.

Or I can finally do what I should have done months ago.

Now that Kaitlyn isn't here to see her brother die…

I don't give her parents a second chance.

With a roar, I shove my claws deeper into Raptor's throat.

He jolts in shock. He tries to fight me, his survival instincts making him struggle harder, but I bury my claws so deep that I sever part of his spine.

He stops moving; only his eyes are focused on me.

Even in his dying moments, he doesn't stop hating me, but I can respect that. One monster to another.

"I'll see you in hell soon, my friend," I say to him as Vulture throws herself at me and Hadrix aims his gun and pulls the trigger with a roar of rage.

Bullets sweep my chest, but the impact only makes my next move more savage.

With a brutal wrench, I rip my claws through Jake's throat, half-severing his head before the bullets force me to the ground.

Hitting the ground, I'm cushioned in moss and mushy leaves while countless bullet wounds bleed across my chest. It's a miracle none hit my heart or my lungs.

Jake's lifeless body falls beside me, his eyes turned up toward the dark canopy above us.

The whole clearing is alive with screaming.

Vulture grabs at Jake, shrieking useless spells trying to heal him and bring him back to life.

Hadrix looms over me, shouting curse words so loudly,

they're indistinguishable from each other, his weapon pointed between my eyes, his finger shaking on the trigger.

I want to tell him to do it because then nothing will save him from Peyton, but I still have hope that somehow… I don't know how… I can stop her fighting Slade.

I try to speak against the blood bubbling through my teeth. "You need me. I make Peyton human. I'm her weakness."

"Kill him!" Vulture screams, but Hadrix shouts a final curse and lowers his weapon.

"Your life from this moment on will be nothing but pain," he promises me.

I raise my eyes past him to Vulture and give her a bloody smile. "You'll never find Kaitlyn."

Hadrix quickly blocks my view of his wife before his fist collides with my cheek and the world spins harder than it already was.

I slump against the ground, my vision blurring as he grabs my arm and begins dragging me through the forest to the waiting soldiers fifty paces away.

My body hits every tree, drags across every stone, and I'm forced to cage my beast before my jutting bones bury me in the earth, but all I can think about now is Peyton.

34. PEYTON PRICE

This can't be it.

I look up from the card on which the ringmaker's address is written to the pretty house with the well-kept lawn. It has a high wooden fence extending around the back, but like the neighboring houses, it's wide open at the front.

I'm in the middle of suburbia on the western side of Boston, having traveled by hitchhiking and compelling the young woman behind the wheel to bring me here.

Checking the quiet street, I make my way up to the tidy porch, noting the potted plants that are starting to bloom beside the door.

Before I can knock, the lock on the door clicks, the handle turns, and the door swings open all on its own to reveal a woman standing farther down a hallway. The corridor walls are lined with photographs, some of them black-and-white, stoic faces from long ago.

The woman is unarmed, standing back in the shadows, her arms held loosely at her side. "Who are you?" she asks, her voice carefully modulated, neither aggressive nor welcoming.

I swallow, maintaining my human form, reminding myself

that I have no aura that a supernatural can detect. Neither does she for that matter.

"My name is Peyton Price. I need your help."

Her gaze suddenly fixates on my bag and it rattles against my side. I'm startled to realize that it's not my bag so much as my whip banging against the inside of the bag as if it wants to fly out.

"You carry multiple weapons of magic, including…" Her lips part as she drags in a quick breath. "You have a feather!"

She takes a step into the light, revealing that she's average height, thin, with dark brown hair and unusual pale blue eyes, rimmed in black. They are bright with an intense interest, nearly feverish as she fixates on my bag.

I've seen those eyes before. A quick check of the photographs lining the walls around us reveal a family photo showing her and an older man standing with two children, both boys.

One of them is the young man from the vision I had when I touched the Keres feather, the man named Foster. The other boy is ten-year-old Slade Baines.

Holy hell. This woman must be Slade's mother.

"How do you know I have a feather?" I ask, unable to avoid the sharpness in my question.

Her mouth stretches into a smile that doesn't reach her eyes. "I have the power to sense metal that contains magic. I also have the power to bend it to my will." She takes another step toward me. "Right now, I'm deciding whether or not to kill you with your own weapons."

I shudder, remembering the way Slade nearly pulled my whip from my hands when he floated above the shield surrounding the Realm.

The woman doesn't miss my furtive glances at the family photo. "I see you know my son."

"What's your name?" I ask, without answering her question.

She arches an eyebrow at me in surprise. "I would think you'd know it already, since you're the one who came to me."

I give her a quick shake of my head. "I was given your address, not your name."

The smile finally reaches her eyes, but it's a treacherous glint. A cold, metal object presses up against my head, making me flinch. Refraining from making any sudden movements, I swivel my eyes to study the barrel of a revolver that floats midair beside me.

The hammer pulls back all on its own, preparing to fire.

"My name is Melinda Baines," she says. "And you have a Keres feather."

I opt for bluntness. "I want you to make me an assassin's ring."

"Well, then," she says as the revolver floats away from me. "You should come into the kitchen. That's where I do all my work."

She turns on her heel and the gun nudges forward in the air, as if it's trying to prod me along. She can't have figured out what I am, because otherwise she'd know the threat of the weapon doesn't alarm me.

Following her down the hallway and to the right, I find the kitchen is homely and warm but stuck in a moment in time. A faded child's drawing is affixed to the front of the refrigerator. Floral dish towels rest along the edge of the sink. It smells like cookies. Chocolate ones, judging from the chocolate-smeared tray cooling on the kitchen table.

As she walks past it, the metal tray rises up and floats across to the bench beside the sink.

She places both hands on the cleared table, tapping its surface impatiently, the feverish glint in her eye growing stronger as she fixates on my bag. "The feather. Be quick about it."

I hurry to unzip my bag.

As soon as it opens, the feather zips out of my bag and into the space above the surface of the table.

I grab hold of my whip, pushing it down and quickly zippering the bag before my whip can fly out too.

Melinda lifts both hands up into the air spaced apart, drawing them side to side. The feather twists in time with the gentle movement, catching the sunlight streaming through the kitchen window that overlooks a well-kept backyard.

"Oh." She sighs. "It's perfect." Without taking her eyes off it, she asks, "Will you use it to kill my son?"

The revolver floats up to my head again, but I don't lie to her. "I will."

"Then you don't want an assassin's ring," she says, still fixated on the feather. "Assassins train for years to learn how to control assassin's magic. You can't simply put one on and hope it will work. No… To kill Slade, you want a dagger coated with this feather." She glances at me, her eyes narrowing slightly. "It will need a strong handle to keep the Keres's magic in its place."

I can't help staring at her. She's talking so unemotionally about the death of her own child. "You're willing to create a weapon that will kill your own son?"

"I'm a ringmaker. I gave up fighting my compulsions long ago." She sighs and lowers her hands while the feather continues to float in the air. "Slade did what no other ringmaker has ever done—what his brother couldn't do. He mastered his power. He learned how to control the intoxicating need to manipulate feathers. He can resist the impossible pull, but I can't."

She gives me a frank look. "What you do with this weapon is up to you. I answer to the magic and that is all."

I suddenly recognize the look in her eyes when she talks about Slade, the tightening of her lips, the indifference.

It's the same way Vulture looks at Kaitlyn. The same way my mother looked at me before she took me to the Academy.

There is no love in it. And yet, a photo of Slade's older

brother is pinned to the refrigerator alongside the child's drawing and, between her speech, Melinda's gaze flicks to it.

All of her love is for her eldest child, the same way Vulture treats Raptor as an equal. The same way my parents treat my brother as if he were the light of their life.

One child is loved while the other is cast out.

It's a mystery to me how they choose which child to love. But of Melinda's two children…

Slade gave the feather back.

A feather that his brother ripped from the wing of a woman I know nothing about. She could have been evil or good, but if what Melinda says is true, then Foster Baines took her feather because of nothing more than an irresistible compulsion, which Slade fought and conquered.

I know which son I would be proud of.

"Do you have a dagger?" Melinda asks.

I drop my bag onto the table, opening the zipper just far enough for my hand to dive inside it, seeking the weapon belt Harrison handed to me.

I trust that he gave me the dagger I chose months ago—the one that best suits me.

Like the feather, it flies into the air as soon as I pull it out, its cover slipping to the table top.

"Perfect," she says, her gaze becoming distant while a satisfied smile grows on her face.

The copper feather begins to glow hot, its delicate etchings softening as it stretches into a perfect triangle.

Melinda's fingers deftly work the air as the flattened metal meets the dagger's blade, wrapping around the steel surface and conforming to its sharp edge.

She continues to work for another twenty minutes, perfecting the fit and the edges, slowly hardening the surface again until she takes a step back to admire her handiwork.

"I've made you a weapon strong enough to kill a Valkyrie,"

she says, a bead of sweat running down the side of her face, her hands shaking as she grips the edge of the table.

I reach for the weapon as it spirals in the air, but I hesitate.

Is there another way?

Can I back away from this weapon and find another path?

To avoid killing a man whose mother has no love for him. A man who loves his chosen woman more than anything else. An honorable man who fought his own destructive nature and conquered it.

A boy who gave back a feather.

This feather.

I snatch the dagger from the air, knowing my choices are already made for me.

"Strike true, Peyton Price," Melinda calls after me as I run from the kitchen and down her hallway. "Or my son's wrath will destroy you."

35 . PEYTON PRICE

t's raining by the time I reach Saber Lane.

I shiver without a coat to keep me warm as the icy sleet soaks my shirt and jeans. It even manages to get inside my boots. I thought about compelling someone to give me their coat, but it didn't seem like the right thing to do.

My hair is plastered to the top of my head by the time I reach the gray lampposts at the entrance to the Lane. It's mid-afternoon, but few passersby are braving the weather.

I know I can't breach the protective shield around the street, but I wanted to see it for myself, to get a sense of the people who live here.

It's the strangest, most eclectic mix of shops I've ever seen.

I'm not sure where the shield begins, or if I'll trigger some sort of alarm when I step near it, so I lean forward carefully, peering through the rain at the cozy assortment of buildings. Brownstones, a grocery store, a diner, and much farther along, the bookshop where Hunter Cassidy lives.

According to Vulture, the man who owned the shop was killed in a confrontation between the assassins and Lady

Tirelli's people. The witch who lives in the Brownstone—Tanzanina Grey—cast a spell over the Lane to protect it.

Vulture told me that Tanzanina's magic is damaged, but that I need to watch out for her instinctive magic because it's powerful if triggered.

A different shop beyond the bookstore makes me startle. It's an apothecary with a symbol of a silver star on the sign that is exactly the same as the symbol on the tubes of healing gel in Striker's room.

I edge forward, taking another careful step, wishing I could see the shop better.

A rush of water suddenly pours over me, but when I look up, the rain doesn't appear any different. Casting around for what caused the waterfall sensation, I'm startled to see a glimmer in the air much like the shield around the Realm.

Except that it's behind me.

Did I just step through the protective shield?

Vulture told me that nobody with ill will toward the inhabitants of Saber Lane could ever step through this shield.

I shiver, because my intent is purely ill.

Moving my feet, I take five more steps without resistance and the shimmering shield behind me doesn't change.

My inner Fury whispers at the back of my mind, reminding me what I am. I'm built to get through any defense, but how cruelly easy was it?

I'm suddenly aware that I'm standing in the middle of the street. If I haven't been seen already, then I will be soon. I throw my shoulders back and walk as purposefully as I can toward the bookshop, quickly assessing my surroundings as I go, my training kicking in now that my surprise has eased.

They won't expect an enemy to walk in like this. Anyone who sees me will assume I'm not a threat.

The dagger is tucked inside my bag. My first goal is to ascertain where Hunter is and if Slade is with her. Also how many friends she might have around her. She mentioned other assassins when I overhead her talking. They were all men, which doesn't surprise me.

I'm two weeks early for the deadline they set themselves, so I have no idea if she's rallied them to her mission yet or not.

Reaching the edge of the bookshop, I press against its corner, deciding there's no good place to lurk or conceal myself. If I'd known I'd make it through the shield, I would have come here at night. I consider whether or not I should walk away and come back later, but what if getting through the shield was a one-time thing?

Uncertainty makes me pause.

A sudden shriek from within the bookshop makes me turn and glance through the windows.

Four people stand inside the front of the shop. I recognize Hunter, but not the three others with her who all appear a similar age as her. One of them is a tall woman with honey-blonde hair, bright green eyes, and the aura of a witch. She's dressed in heels and a black dress. Her aura is so powerful that the hairs on my arms stand on end. She can only be Tanzanina Grey.

A man as massive as Slade stands beside her. He's all muscle with striking black hair. He's dressed in a tailored white shirt and navy blue pants that shout money.

The two women in the center of the room draw my attention. One is Hunter. The other is a curvy woman, also with long, blonde hair, although hers is paler than Tanzanina's, but it's her eyes that are truly startling.

They're violet. As if such a thing were possible.

A quick scan of their hands tells me that, other than Tanzanina, they're all wearing rings on the forefingers of their left hands.

They're all assassins.

Hunter throws her arms around the violet-eyed woman with another shriek. "Archer! That's amazing. I'm so happy for you."

I'm surprised. Archer was one of the names Hunter mentioned when she flew above the Realm. I assumed Archer was a man, but apparently not.

Hunter holds out her hand to the enormous black-haired guy, beaming at him as she draws him closer. "Cain, congratulations. You're going to be amazing parents."

I recoil. The woman—Archer—must be pregnant. Another surprise.

That assassins would even contemplate having children is a shock to me.

Archer tips her head back to meet Cain's warm gaze before she settles into the crook of his arm. They're so open with their affection, with their love, that it makes me shiver. The way Cain looks at Archer as though she's the most important person in his life strikes through me like someone's stabbing me over and over.

The pit inside me opens wider, so painful that I brace against the window before my sanity returns, and I veer off to the side and out of sight again.

My movement swings me face to face with a towering, furious mountain of muscle.

Slade Baines looms not three paces away from me, his hand twitching toward the back of his jeans, where he must carry a concealed weapon.

His pale blue eyes are so startlingly rimmed in black and his pupils flooded with silver that he doesn't appear even remotely human.

The rain doesn't seem to bother him, making his shirt and pants cling to his dangerously chiseled muscles upon muscles upon muscles…

The edges of his body blur with silver light as he speaks, his demand for answers a scarily low murmur that reminds me of a caged bear. "How did you set foot on this lane, Peyton Price?"

I'm surprised he knows my name, but I probably shouldn't be. Hunter said she was looking into the backgrounds of the students at the Academy. He's bound to have seen a picture of me.

I step away from the corner of the bookshop into the entrance of the narrow alley beside it.

I wasn't expecting to fight Slade so soon, but it looks like I won't get to choose my timing.

He's even more imposing standing up than when we floated in the air. I levitated to his height back then, giving me the illusion of being as tall as he is, but my legs will never be long enough to lift me to stand eye to eye with him.

I casually swing my bag to my front and reach inside it while keeping him in my sights.

He watches me remove the weapon belt and tie it around my chest. It crisscrosses so that it finishes off as a belt around my waist.

The Keres dagger is sheathed and sitting benignly beside an ordinary dagger on one side. Three handguns sit at intervals around my body—one at my chest and the other two at my waist.

Finally, I pull out my whip and test its weight in my hand.

I'm surprised when he doesn't try to stop me the entire time that I arm myself. His confidence tells me that it won't matter how many weapons I cast about myself. He must think he can beat me. After all, he crushes other assassins.

"State your intentions," he says, his command telling me he's unused to being ignored.

Now that I'm as fully armed as I can be, I tip my chin at him while raindrops slide down my face. "Do you know *what* I am?"

His response is immediate. "You're Unknown. You could destroy this entire street if you lose control."

A laugh tears out of me. "Yes, but not for the reasons you think. You see, I'm not Unknown anymore. I know exactly what I am."

My power surges through me. I leave my bag on the ground as I rise into the air, the familiar crimson haze burning across my vision. My hair rises around me in a way that tells me its color is changing, crimson streaks appearing in my tresses at the same time as my fingernails extend into blood-red claws.

"You've faced my kind before," I say.

"Fury." He backs up, but it isn't in fear. He will be trying to draw me out into the open.

The vision the whip gave me showed me that he's killed a Fury before. He has no reason to believe he won't succeed again.

Our location places us just beyond the visible edges of the bookshop windows. To see us, Hunter would need to deliberately step close and look in this direction, but the conversation I overheard indicates she's more likely to remain engaged within the shop.

I slip to the left, away from the shop windows, keeping close to the corner of the next building. It's impossible to miss the quick flicker of Slade's attention to the bookshop. He will be assessing how quickly I could change direction toward it.

As I circle out into the open, well beyond the shop windows, he takes up position between me and Hunter's location.

It's a protective stance that I can respect.

"I'm here to kill you both," I say. Slade because he can breach the Realm, and Hunter because she is the one who will try to kill Striker. "I hope that clarifies my intentions enough for you."

He nods, as though my threat doesn't faze him. "I sensed your power within the Realm. But it looks like you didn't heed my warning."

I give him a cold smile. "I understood you well enough. You plan to come back and slaughter us. I won't let that happen."

A slight crease appears in his forehead. "That's not quite what I—"

"Oh, so there are nuances to your threat, are there?" A storm grows inside me as I advance on him. "You'll only kill those whose names are in your ledger? But how am I to know who that is and isn't? How am I to know that someone hasn't written all of our names in your ledger to preemptively kill us in an act of self-defense against our future actions? We're dangerous Unknowns. That's why they put us away."

His brow furrows at that, a look of indignation as if I insulted him, but I don't allow him to respond. I lower my voice as I float right up to him, my whip gripped firmly in my hand. "How am I to know if the only man I will ever love is written in your ledger?"

I already know that Striker's name is written in Hunter Cassidy's ledger, not Slade's, but my question is intended to make my point.

The furrow in his brow deepens. "Tell me his name."

"Striker Draven."

The crease in his forehead clears. "It's true. His name is written in an assassin's ledger but his death is yet to be determined."

I falter. Striker's death isn't certain yet? Does that mean I could reason with the assassins? Change their minds?

But my fear returns. "What if it is determined?"

"Then he'll die." Slade takes a step back and his hand moves so fast that I hardly follow it.

There's a quiet *click*.

He holds a silenced weapon steady in his hand, perfectly aimed at my heart.

I pluck the tranquilizer dart from the top of my breast, unable to stop my face from screwing up in disgust as the bitter taste fills my mouth.

"Tranquilizers won't work on me." I drop the dart to the

ground. "But thank you for confirming that my name isn't written in your ledger or you would have used a bullet."

He shrugs, unfazed. "You're a different kind of Fury. It would be foolhardy of me not to try the simplest approach first."

He replaces his weapon behind his back, levels his silvery gaze with mine, and folds his fingers into fists. "It looks like I'll have to capture you the hard way."

I lift my whip, ready to unfurl it and attack him.

The rain suddenly stops.

Bright sunlight bursts around us, shining directly into my eyes and blinding me.

My free hand flies across my face to shield my eyes as I inhale the scent of thin air, clean and crisp. Strange birdsong fills my ears and I struggle to understand what the hell just happened.

The bright flare fades around Slade's silhouette, allowing me to finally see his electric wings shoot from his sides, wide and strong, electricity sizzling around them as they beat the air.

I force my eyes wide, shock striking through me.

The shops are gone. So is the street.

My stomach drops when I look down to find that we're floating high above a wide river that rages far below us, a dense jungle on either side of it.

My heartbeat races as fast as the water crashing across the rocks beneath us. *What the hell...?*

"I not only have the power to break into Realms, I can create them," Slade says with a challenging smile. "Welcome to my Realm."

36. PEYTON PRICE

I don't have time to respond.

The sound of gushing water is the only warning I have of the danger about to crash down around me.

Slade darts backward as a torrent of water hits me from above, colliding with my head and shoulders with as much force as a waterfall.

It *is* a waterfall.

Somehow, he's conjured it where I was floating and now I'm right in the middle of it. I suck water into my lungs before I can force my mouth closed against the force beating down on me,

The impact of the water is so intense that I can't escape it, can't fly out from under it. All I can do is fall.

Through the raging water, I catch sight of jagged rocks as I tumble toward the surface of the river, already choking on the liquid I inhaled.

Hitting the surface of the river is like hitting rock.

Every bone in my body shatters on impact.

A silent scream fills my mind and blood trickles from my mouth.

Every crack, every break, every shifted bone, every torn

muscle, all the screaming rages through me as my body is sucked up against the rocks at the side of the river, bashing against them, rebreaking the bones that are healing, shattering my collarbone and then my jaw as I hit another jagged outcrop.

All that matters now is that I don't lose the dagger in the wash. Clamping my hand around it, I fight the water, my vision turning black and then crimson red.

Harnessing every spark of fury inside me, I push toward the surface, breaking through the rushing water with a cry of agony that echoes around me.

Blood washes off my body, dripping from every broken, healing part of me as I shoot up out of the water. The waterfall is now behind me. A torrential river crashes along below me while rocky ground stretches out on either side as far as I can see.

Slade floats in the air higher above me, his arms raised at his sides. His shout confuses me. "Where are your snakes?"

I shudder at the thought, spitting blood as I speak, sensing it slipping between my teeth. "I don't have any."

For some reason, that seems to disconcert him. The blaze of thought—of truth—in his silver eyes tells me that he's suddenly uncertain. *But... why?*

His expression clears. "Then you aren't a full Fury yet."

Without a hint of regret, he flicks his hand.

A hard, gray object hits me from the side. *Crack!* The air whooshes out of my chest as I'm shoved across the air. I barely have time to look up to see another boulder flying at me from the other side, my momentum increasing its impact as it shatters across my head.

Rocks. Damn rocks!

My only safe place is right in front of him.

I dart forward, fighting and dodging my way between the stones he throws at me. He might be counting on my guns being waterlogged, but Harrison gave me the best weapons.

I pull both of them from their holsters, my training kicking in as I avoid the rocks flying at me and shoot forward, my arms outstretched, my aim strong and true as I pull both triggers in quick succession.

Bullet wounds bloom across Slade's chest moments before he takes to the air. I follow his flight, still firing, emptying both clips after him.

Despite my accurate aim, he doesn't fall.

Damn.

His healing powers rival mine. Well, almost. He's still bleeding when he charges back at me.

I throw my empty guns aside, freeing up my hands and ducking the fist he swings at my head. The power in his arm makes my senses tingle as the air rushes around me. I quickly retaliate with a fist to his stomach, then his jaw, followed by another kick to his stomach.

I'm shocked when his muscles tense and he absorbs the blows, grabbing my leg and twisting me so hard that I roll midair.

I kick his face with my free foot as I spin, but his fists come down hard on my knees, breaking both of my kneecaps and flipping me vertical again. I wobble for the mere second it takes my power to heal me, but it's enough for him to grab my shirt with one hand and pull me into his fist.

My cheekbone breaks and my vision shatters in my left eye.

My entire body is on fire with pain, hardly bearable, so deep that for the first time I'm not sure if I'm going to survive.

Tears of agony flow down my good cheek.

I retaliate on instinct alone, reaching for my whip, but it flies out of my hand and into his as he calls it to him.

I can't let him use it against me. I crash into him, a reckless, uncontrolled move, my claws extending and shredding his shirt, cutting across the bullet wounds in his chest, slicing through to his ribs before he leaps back from me.

If he's in pain, he isn't showing it.

With a roar, he darts in under my arms, his entire body hitting mine as he sweeps his wings and pushes me down toward the ground. His speed increases no matter how hard I struggle against him. It's like fighting a comet. There's no stopping the inevitable crash into the earth.

The ground cracks around me as he throws me against it, a savage beat of his wings stopping himself from crashing against me.

My spine breaks and now I can't form thought, nothing rational beyond the pain.

I can't move, can't fight back, my arms and legs not responding.

As I lie still, the water laps my thighs, swishing against my hips like a caress. It reminds me of how gently Striker cleaned the blood off me that one time. Just that once. Never again.

I can't stop the laughter bubbling up through my lips, blood leaking from my mouth as Slade glides to the ground to loom over me, my whip still gripped in his hand.

A boulder hovers in the air above my head, ready to drop on me as soon as he likes.

Forcing myself to speak, I try to draw air into my lungs. "You're just as brutal as Striker. Luckily for me, I'm used to his fury."

Slade's expression darkens, a moment of shock replaced with anger. "He hurt you."

"I have survived Striker Draven many times," I say, fighting the awful pain as I struggle to the side, drawing my wobbling legs under me to finally crouch and face Slade, the threat of the boulder following me.

His speech is full of rage. "A real man never hits his woman."

I'm surprised by such a declaration from an assassin, but I can't stop the broken laugh that tears out of me, so much agony that it becomes a scream.

"Striker Draven isn't a man! He's a broken piece of hell that found its way to the surface of the Earth."

Slade is incredulous, his arms lowering to his sides, the boulder lowering too until it settles on the ground. "Despite that, you're here to defend him."

"I'm not so different to him." I struggle to my feet, the pain fading enough that I can put weight on my legs. Despair and desperation are all I have now. Slade's own mother told me to strike true or his wrath would break me. "If Striker can't be redeemed, then neither can I."

Slade shakes his head, his denial absolute. "A man like that can never be redeemed."

"Really?" I ask, stepping toward Slade, testing my returning strength, my fingers twitching and my sight slowly returning to my busted eye. "Then how can you?"

I lift my arms from my sides in a deliberately helpless gesture, raising my finger to press it to my bleeding face. "You hurt me the same way. How is your conscience clean?"

For a moment, I think he sees me. As more than a Fury, more than a threat, but as a woman desperate enough to come after the Master Assassin himself.

Then his expression hardens, the silver flooding his eyes making him appear like a vicious animal. "I will do anything to protect my family."

Despite all his brutality, despite hurting me, he has a moral code, one he won't break. He fights within rules. He knows a Fury won't die easily, so he's fighting with everything he can.

I came to kill him and he's retaliating with all necessary force to subdue me, but now I've kept him talking for long enough to get close to him.

I've made him believe that I'm too weak to fight back.

This time, I won't try to use my whip and I won't rely on bullets, not even my fists.

There's no fighting Slade Baines with honor.

There is only a cruel blade between his ribs when he doesn't expect it.

"I will too," I whisper, my arm moving with deadly speed.

The Keres dagger catches the light before I ram it into his heart.

37. PEYTON PRICE

We hit the ground together, the dagger buried to the hilt in Slade's chest, me straddling him while I grip its handle.

The air burns, an awful scent, as his arms and legs twitch and his wings retract, disappearing behind his shoulders.

Copper light streaks from the dagger's entry point through his chest and shoulders and up his neck, pulsing across his cheeks.

At the same time, the Realm disappears around us, stretching apart in patches like a burning picture until Saber Lane reappears and the rain falls down around us again, lighter than before, a drizzle now.

We've landed right outside the shop in full view of its windows. All it will take is one of the assassins within the shop to focus beyond the glass and they will see us. We were concealed in Slade's Realm during our fight and now it's only because of the rain and the fading afternoon light—only because it's brighter inside the shop than outside of it—that they won't have already seen us.

I thought Slade's death would be instant, quick, but it isn't.

It's painful and cold, forcing me to face my actions and look him in the eye.

He drags in a breath as both of his hands dart to my face, wrapping around my cheeks and forcing me to continue looking at him. Disbelief and fear rage in his eyes as the silvery depths clear from his pupils, his irises becoming pale blue and all too human.

His speech is labored, hard words that sound as if they're wrenching out of him. "What… did you… do?"

A sob tears out of me.

I don't know why I'm crying. I succeeded in my goal. I killed him. That's why I came here.

Raindrops and tears drip from my face as I lean over him, my chest rising and falling rapidly as I continue to cry while his own breathing slows to become shallow and short.

I owe him the truth. "I fashioned a blade from a Keres feather to kill you."

Confusion floods his face. "What… feather?"

"The one you gave back."

His expression clears. "The copper feather."

His head turns toward the shop as if he's trying to see through its walls to the people inside it. Hunter is there. So close by.

Slade's gaze softens and his hands slide away from my face. I catch his arms before they hit the ground, placing them carefully across his chest.

It's quiet in the rain now.

I wait for his breathing to stop before I reach up and close his eyes, brushing his jaw with my fingertips.

Hot tears slip down my cold cheeks and I still don't understand why I'm crying, why I feel like I've lost something that was never mine.

Carefully pulling the dagger free, I rise to my feet, taking deep breaths and reminding myself why I'm here.

Slade was the only one with the power to breach the Realm. The assassins can't get in now that Slade is dead. Everyone who stays in the Realm is safe, but the threat to Striker remains. If Striker leaves the Realm, Hunter will come after him to kill him.

I harness my power, raise my voice, and scream. "Hunter Cassidy! Come out so I can kill you."

Then I stand in the rain over Slade's body and wait for the hell I've unleashed upon myself.

38. PEYTON PRICE

I sense the shocked silence from within the building before the door flies open and Hunter Cassidy bursts through it, her katana already drawn, her mahogany hair loosely tied at the nape of her neck, her focus fixed on me.

Her gaze flickers from me to the ground, to where Slade lies, and she freezes.

The blood drains from her face. Her weapon clatters to the ground, kicking up raindrops as it clatters to the pebbled surface.

She inhales, her lips parting for a shocked moment before her scream cuts through me. "*Slade!*"

I ignore the pain in her cry, ignore the tears that blur my vision, as she runs straight for us—for him—while I grip the dagger in my fist, my focus unbreakable.

I follow the precise movement of her arms, the angle of her body, the way she'll skid to her knees to reach his side, the way she'll leave her heart vulnerable to attack.

I drop at the perfect moment, ready to slash the dagger across her chest and end her.

Thud. Thud-thud.

I startle as I register the three daggers now protruding from my chest, one of them positioned exactly into my heart.

My focus switches to their source.

Archer whirls right in front of me, her booted foot hitting the end of the dagger over my chest and driving it deeper.

Pain and shock tear through me as I fly backward under the impossible strength in her kick.

I don't have time to wonder how the hell she reached me so quickly. The Keres blade I had so perfectly angled to ram into Hunter breezes past her as I'm thrown drastically off-balance.

Backflipping on the wet ground, I land just in time to leap out of the way as Archer slices at me again, two more daggers held expertly in her hands. They tear across the space where my neck was located a split second ago, vicious cuts that would have taken my head from my shoulders.

Her movements are quick and agile as she spins and slashes at me, forcing me to move evasively.

Her knife skills are superb. So superb I'm surprised she isn't a Master Assassin. She was certainly taught by someone even more skilled than Harrison.

It's a good thing I surpassed Harrison's skills weeks ago.

My Fury power rushes through me, lifting me and making me light and lithe in the air. I snatch one of the daggers from my chest before I whirl toward her, using my free hand to slice the blade across her arm and drive it into her shoulder.

Plucking the second and third daggers out of my chest, one after the other, I fling them at Archer at close range, keeping the Keres dagger in my left hand.

She deftly avoids the blades and barely flinches at the dagger in her shoulder, plucking it out before she comes after me again. I deftly evade every cut and thrust of her daggers, dancing and spinning away from her, judging the gaps in her defenses in infinitesimal seconds.

As I duck and avoid the blows, the opening I've been waiting for presents itself.

She exposes her shoulder again. It isn't her heart, but it will have to do.

I slam the Keres knife into her chest, sensing its power trigger and explode.

She lurches back from me, dropping her knives to grip the handle of the dagger in her chest, her violet eyes glowing brighter with every second.

I wait for the copper light to streak through her and take her life, but... she remains standing.

She glowers at me. "This knife won't hurt me."

As she takes a step back, new light explodes on either side of her, a blinding copper color that's so bright, it burns my eyes.

I struggle to keep my balance, my vision turning crimson, the color of my view blending with the golden rays shining around me to turn the world an awful bloody brown.

Golden wings shoot from her shoulders.

Keres wings.

I gasp in shock. Hunter and Slade are Valkyrie, but this woman is clearly Keres and she's defending them.

Keres and Valkyrie... friends?

Impossible. Enemies can't become friends.

Archer takes hold of the dagger, eases it from her shoulder, and roars at me. "You won't kill anyone today!"

"I already did." Despite my confident speech, anxiety rises inside me because I've lost control of the weapon and I'm quickly losing control of the situation.

Archer has driven me ten paces away from Hunter, whose screams strike through me, dragging tears back to my eyes as she bends over Slade's body.

As Archer continues to force me to backstep, I catch glimpses of Hunter trying to lift Slade up from the sodden ground into her arms, but he's so bulky. "No! Please, *please*, no!"

Just like Archer's wings did, Hunter's wings suddenly explode from her shoulders. Power ripples out from them, an explosion that beats at the air, causing me to stumble in the sudden whirlwind that blows around us.

She plucks at her right wing. "I can save him!"

The dark-haired man—Cain—darts around Archer's wings to Hunter, shocking me when he hurtles right into her, ignoring her sharp, metallic feathers to wrap his arms around her and pick her off Slade. "No, Hunter. You can't do this!"

"Let me go!" she screams at him, thumping her fists against his back so hard, I'm surprised his spine doesn't break as she tries to force him to release her.

"I won't let you kill yourself!" he roars back at her, refusing to release her, capturing her wrists and imprisoning her hands against his chest as she starts to sob and her wings fold against her back.

"Let me go, Cain." She's begging him, but he presses his left hand against her face, his assassin's ring glowing softly, and she suddenly stills, her knees wobbling as she collapses to the ground. "*Please*. He can't die."

Archer's shout cuts across their interaction, her attention divided between me and Hunter. "I can see Slade's soul!"

His soul? I turn in confusion, not understanding what she's talking about, but I don't have time to figure it out.

The blonde-haired witch stands at the periphery of my vision and I suddenly realize that the ferocious whirlwind isn't only a product of Archer's and Hunter's wings.

It's Tanzanina's magic. In fact, what I'm feeling now can only be a hint of the storm growing between her palms. An entire catastrophic weather event is held in miniature above her cupped hands just waiting to be unleashed as soon as Archer moves out of the way.

"Go!" Tanzanina screams at Archer before levelling her gaze on me. "I'll take care of the Fury."

I shake my head at the witch as my thoughts churn. I have to get the Keres dagger back but Archer is rapidly disappearing with it, and now Tanzanina stands between me and her.

If I can't get the dagger back and fight Hunter, then I'll have to flee with my mission only half-completed.

Is it enough? Have I kept the Realm safe?

"Your magic can't hurt me," I cry, hating the desperation seeping into my voice as I face Tansy with my claws fully extended and my vision blood-red.

Her eyes glow a deep emerald green and the hairs on the back of my neck rise.

"You haven't encountered magic like mine," she says.

She's right. I've never fought a witch who controls powerful instinctive magic before. Headmistress Osprey tried to use instinctive magic right before I killed her, but it was like a gentle breeze compared to the torrent of power I sense from Tanzanina.

Vulture told me that Tanzanina's magic was broken, but there's nothing broken about the storm she's about to unleash on me.

Lightning flashes between her palms.

I tell myself to move, to fight back, but I have nowhere to go. There isn't any training in the world that can teach me what to do now.

Move. I need to move. I came here to kill two assassins, and I've only accomplished one of those goals, but to escape, I have to get through Tanzanina and then Archer. Not to mention the male assassin currently restraining Hunter.

None of them will let me simply run away. I tell myself I simply need to survive. Survive, and then I can escape.

I stand my ground as the witch hurls her magic at me. The miniature storm and all its dark clouds and lightning expands, a giant sphere that engulfs me in darkness.

Thunder booms and the electrical crack of lightning shatters my hearing.

Blood trickles from my ears and even my nose. The wind rips at my clothing. I grab hold of my whip before it flies off my belt. The bite of electricity drives me to my knees, forcing me to hunch over, press my whip to my chest, and crouch on the ground, my hair slapping my face.

I'm vaguely aware of running forms outside the storm's sphere. It's difficult to tell who is human and who is supernatural, but I sense their combined power drawing together as their silhouettes circle around my location.

They're surrounding me.

A woody vine snakes through the storm, wrapping around my ankles. I try to hack at it with my claws while another vine wraps around my waist, narrowly missing pinning my arms to my sides. The vines are coming from a male silhouette outside the storm whose arms are outstretched.

A dryad? Like Lucinda?

Shock chills me. It has to be another dryad, but Vulture never told me about a dryad on Saber Lane.

At the same time, silver baubles of light float through the storm, glowing in the electrical streaks of lightning. They burst like fireworks, filling the space around me with such bright white light that tears stream from my eyes...

Not tears.

Blood.

Through the blur, a female form also stands with her arms outstretched, more silver baubles floating toward me. I don't know what kind of supernatural she is to create a force so close to starlight. Maybe another witch but Vulture didn't tell me about her, either.

At the same time, another male figure moves. He's large and burly, but he has a different physique to Cain. Fine silver daggers fly through the storm, straight and true, so many that I can't count them. Each one hits its mark, dotting my arms and legs.

The new baubles explode and another vine wraps around me, this time squeezing around my chest and constricting my breathing. Still the storm rages until I can't tell the difference between the wailing wind and my own screams.

Survival suddenly feels like an impossible feat.

"Stop!"

A man's shout rises above the chaos and I sense a deep shock ripple through the Lane's defenders.

A moment later, the storm fades, the clouds clear, and silence covers me, heavy and thick.

My ears buzz, damaged and unable to hear properly, as I remain collapsed on the ground, the vines still imprisoning my arms and legs.

A man I've never seen before walks steadily toward me, stepping past Tanzanina, whose arms remain outstretched in my direction, her power close to the surface.

The man's sleeves are rolled up around his large biceps and his black hair is slicked back. He has the most deeply chocolate-brown eyes I've ever seen and an aura I've never encountered before.

It's soft, calming, empathetic... But what's stranger is that he's carrying a bundle of blankets close to his chest.

"Dean!" Tanzanina grabs his arm. "No! What are you doing?"

He rounds on her. "I sense *fear*, not hatred. She's here because she's afraid."

A deep crease forms in Tanzanina's forehead, her eyes full of distrust and anger as she watches me with every step Dean takes toward me.

Blood drips from my eyes, mouth, nose, and ears. My breathing is ragged and distorted, my cracked ribs taking far too long to heal.

I moan out my pain, pressing my palms against the wet ground, collapsing onto it when the vines slither away from my body.

The man who conjured the vines stands tall nearby, definitely a dryad.

A few paces away from him is an elderly woman with starry eyes, her aura a strong, white glow around her cloaked form.

The man who flung the silver daggers at me is all human, straight-backed and stern, his black training gear revealing powerful arms and legs.

Tanzanina calls to them. "Christopher, Willow, Drake. Stay back from her."

Farther away, Archer's wings block my view of Hunter and Slade, but Cain stands beside Archer like a guard watching her back, never taking his eyes off me.

Like Tanzanina, he looks troubled, his alarmed gaze landing on the bundle in Dean's arms.

He takes a step toward Dean, but Tanzanina gives him a sharp shake of her head.

Dean kneels in front of me.

I try to wipe my eyes, smearing blood across the back of my hand, watching him carefully even though my vision is still damaged and my healing power is taking far too long to kick in.

Dean's eyes are warm and calm. "You need to know who you're hurting," he says, tilting the bundle toward me.

My world spins.

I start to shiver, uncontrollable trembling.

A baby girl sleeps in his arms. She fists his shirt, one hand escaping her blankets, her innocent eyes closed, her chest rising and falling deeply.

"This is Slade's daughter," Dean says, meeting my eyes. "I don't think you want to cause her pain."

I try to drag air into my lungs. Slade said he would do anything to protect his family. The baby explains the four-and-a-half-month delay in their planned attack on the Academy. Hunter must have been pregnant when she flew over us, but the electrical light that surrounded her at that time had obscured her body.

Flickers of the same light pulse through the baby's arms and cheeks.

I killed this baby's father.

I once asked Striker if we were on the side of good or on the side of bad.

He told me we would write our own future, but now…

I've written it.

I'm a monster.

A wail leaves my lips before I can stop it. "*No.*"

"You didn't come here by choice," Dean says.

"How do you know that?" I try to speak between my sobs, my vocal chords so strained and my teeth chattering so hard that I don't recognize my own voice. I drag my claws across the ground. "How do you know I won't cut your throat with my claws and prove you wrong?"

He considers me for a moment. "You won't."

I stifle another sob, hating him for reading me so accurately. "What makes you so sure?"

"Because you don't have claws."

My attention flies to my hands, to my perfectly human fingernails. Then I turn my focus inward to all of the pain in my body, all the torn muscles and bruised ribs that aren't healing.

Why?

I try to call my power, but it's slipping far, far away from me like a tide rushing out, and just as quickly, pain rushes in, so much pain that a scream forms at the back of my throat and I'm either going to cry or throw up. I'm not sure which will happen first.

Sharp footfalls strike across the cobbled street and I look up through the haze of agony into Archer's cold, violet eyes.

Without a word, she points a gun at me and pulls the trigger three times in rapid succession.

At the last moment, I recognize the tranquilizer darts protruding from my chest, the same kind that Slade tried to use on me before we started fighting.

I sway, hit the ground, and welcome the darkness.

39. PEYTON PRICE

"*B*e calm."

I wake to a hand pressed to my cheek. I struggle to open my eyes to see where I am or what kind of danger I'm in. All I know is that I'm lying on something soft. It might be a mattress, but its texture tells me it's without sheets. There's no pillow beneath my head.

My face hurts.

Everything hurts.

I try to speak but only succeed in moaning as I force one eye open a crack. My other eye doesn't obey my commands, remaining resolutely shut.

Dean's face comes into view, the stern expression in his deep brown eyes compelling me to stay still. His fingers gently stroke my cheek, filling me with a deep sense of peace despite the pain throughout the rest of my body. He moves a little to turn away from me without removing his hand.

"This would go a lot easier if Tansy would heal her wounds," he says, his lips pressing together in a disapproving line.

Behind him, four figures stand in a semi-circle several paces away from me, all of them dressed in black skintight suits that cover them from their necks to their toes.

They each hold one of my weapons.

Hunter grips my whip, her mahogany hair tied back and her glass ring sparkling like diamonds in the dim light from a lamp that sits on the only piece of furniture in the room: a small, round table. Her eyes are clear, but her cheeks are blotchy from crying.

Archer stands beside her, holding the Keres dagger clasped in her folded hands. She's at least six feet tall, but beside her, Cain is like a giant, his gaze piercing as he grips my weapon belt in one big fist, the Draven insignia on it turned toward the light.

Tanzanina—or maybe *Tansy*, since that's the name Dean used for her—is a force of anger at the end of the row. Her response is clipped. "Healing can wait until we determine if she's still a threat."

Dean sighs. "She's only a threat if you treat her like one."

"She either wants to kill us or she doesn't," Tansy snaps, her green eyes filling with light that tells me her power is rising again.

Dean turns back to me, his lips pursed into a 'shh' shape as if he senses I was about to speak. I'm not sure what he thought I was going to say. There's only one question I want to ask them.

Why haven't you killed me?

"A Fury reflects her surroundings," he says, startling me with this assertion. "Her true nature is peaceful. She hates violence, lies, and injustice. It's only when she's confronted by them that she is compelled to act with *greater* violence to confront evil with justified retribution."

He turns to Hunter again. "When you fought the Furies that time, where did you find them?"

"In a cabin hidden in the forest on Mount Greylock." Hunter's expression is shuttered and emotionless, but her body language is tense.

"Ah." Dean strokes my forehead. "Far away from everyone. Where they can find peace. They don't seek out evil, but they enact terrible vengeance when they see it." He twists and his voice becomes hard as he faces the assassins. "Not unlike you."

With enormous effort, I slide my hand along the mattress to touch his arm.

"What are you?" I whisper.

He gives me a soft smile, returning his attention to me. "I'm an empath. I can sense your emotions, but I can also influence them. I fear that when I stop touching you, you will feel like I've manipulated your feelings, but it's important that you stay calm right now."

"You're the reason I'm still lying here?"

He tips his head. "I'm keeping you this way. When I remove my hand, it's up to you what choice you make next."

He's the reason I haven't jumped up already, haven't sought the anger deep inside, the Fury that wants to kill them for threatening my safety and, if I'm honest, that hates them. Because it was the threat of these assassins that stopped me from killing Hadrix the moment he stepped foot inside the Academy.

If I'd ended Hadrix months ago, I would be far away from here now and Striker would be with me.

Tears burn at the back of my eyes, because despite all the hate, this is the first peace I've felt. Maybe the first in my whole life. "I don't want to stop feeling this way."

"I'm sorry," he says, drawing his hand away from my face until only a single fingertip remains pressed to my temple. He turns to speak to the assassins one last time. "Do *not* lie to her or she will react with punishing force."

He removes his hand and the cold rushes in.

The door clicks closed behind him as he leaves.

I shiver, realizing that my clothes are still wet from the rain and the reason my eye won't open is because it's swollen closed.

The compulsion to leap to my feet is intense. I fight the need to attack, forcing my movements to remain careful and slow as I slide my legs over the edge of the bed.

The assassins are dressed to kill, but they haven't brought any of their own weapons into this room. They also haven't moved from their positions, haven't given any indication that they're about to end me.

I guess, if I think about it, they don't need weapons. Their bare hands are enough.

I ask the question I dread. "Why am I still alive? Even if my name wasn't written into your ledgers before, my actions would warrant an entry now."

Archer turns the Keres dagger around in her hands. "You're only alive because you didn't know how to use this weapon."

I consider her warily. "What do you mean?"

"Keres power doesn't kill instantly. It forces the soul from the body. Your target doesn't die until you deliberately crush their soul."

I remember Archer screaming to Hunter that she could see Slade's soul. Then she'd worked over him, but I couldn't see what she was doing.

I grip the edge of the bed, suddenly frozen. "Is Slade alive?"

Strange, this hope that rises within me and crushes me at the same time.

Archer grows quiet, glancing sideways at Hunter, who allows my whip to unravel. The tips hit the floor with a *snap*.

"It's my turn to ask the questions," she says. "Why do you want us dead?"

"Because you have the power to breach our Realm. I can't let that happen."

She narrows her eyes at me. "What are you protecting?"

"*Who.*" I glare at her with my one good eye. "Every student at the Academy, including Striker Draven."

The light in Hunter's eyes takes on a sharp glow. "What about Adrian Hadrix?"

"What about him?" I snap.

She exchanges a quick look with the others. "Will you stand in our way when we come for him?"

I grit my teeth. She said *when*, not *if*.

Despair is thick around my heart. Nothing I do makes a difference to the path the assassins will choose. "Only if he makes me."

Now, Hunter narrows her eyes at me. "Explain."

"Will an explanation make a difference?" I challenge her, rising to my feet. "You plan to breach the Academy, kill whoever is written in your ledger, and then leave, but you have no idea how many innocent people you'll hurt in the process."

She straightens. "We never cause collateral damage. It's against our code."

"You already have!" I take a shuddering breath, trying to get my emotions under control as I step toward her, my healing power finally starting to flow again. The burning heat behind my eye eases with the increase of power so I can finally open my other eye.

My focus is drawn to my whip's strands as they sway from side to side at Hunter's side.

My whip. But it wasn't always mine.

She's about to speak, but I interrupt her with a demand for answers. "How did you kill her?"

She's puzzled. "Who?"

"The Fury who owned that whip."

She gives me a sharp shake of her head. "We didn't."

"You lie." My wounded eye opens fully and the pain in my ribs and back begins to ease as anger rises inside me.

"I'm not lying," she says, a crease in her forehead. "The Fury fled. All three of them ran away after we fought them."

I narrow my eyes at her in disgust. "She escaped wounded and you didn't bother to find out if she lived or died?"

Hunter looks as if I slapped her. "I—"

"She was no more than an animal to you. A creature who got in your way. A monster not worth saving. Like me."

She takes a sharp breath. The tension around us rises a thousand percent. Archer's grip on the Keres dagger strengthens, Cain takes a step forward, and Tansy's power glows around her silhouette.

I sense the energy ripple around Hunter, and I anticipate the release of her wings as she advances on me.

"You came to my home to kill my husband," she says. "Whether or not you're worth saving, either way, you're a monster."

"No more than you!" I snap back at her, rising off the ground to float forward and meet her in the middle of the room. "You plan to invade my home, kill what you can, and you call it *honor.*"

Her eyes widen and the blood drains from her face, becoming deathly pale. "No..." She shakes her head. "I call it *darkness*, and I fight it within myself every single day."

She takes a careful step back. "I'm Valkyrie. I seek death. I *want* death. I place rules around my behavior because without those rules, I have no boundaries, no limits to the damage I can cause."

She eyes me as I float before her and she suddenly appears incredibly wary. "You are a Fury and Dean is right. You punish what you see. So tell me... *truthfully*... why are you here to punish us?"

I sense the blood drain from my own face, even though my vision is crimson now.

I can see her thought processes as clearly as if she's speaking them aloud and I'm shocked by them. At first she thought I was perpetrating a senseless attack on her home, my purpose being the achievement of cruelty, possibly power over her and her family. She has many enemies who want to hurt her for the simple satisfaction of causing her pain.

But now, she wonders if I'm here as a Fury, to do what Furies do and punish her for a wrong she's committed in the past. Judging by the resignation in her eyes, there are many wrongs and she's prepared to face them.

But more shocking than knowing exactly what she's thinking…

I realize that for the first time in months, I'm finally seeing the truth.

Taking a quick breath, I release the firm grip I've held on my truth-seeking power and extend my senses toward the others—the witch first, surprised by what I find. Tansy is a protective force on the outside, but she's broken on the inside, the loss of love driving her not to lose anyone else important to her. She sees me in black and white: I am her enemy and she will protect her loved ones against me.

Archer is fierce; she can shut off her emotions when she needs to fight. A cold upbringing and violent past make her an aggressive opponent. But her heart is the polar opposite, warm and open and… recently healed, deep wounds mended because of the love she found in Cain… who fights his own darkness—a human darkness—that is dangerous in the way that a flame can either warm or burn you.

Hunter… She's complex. Far too complex to understand without a lifetime of interaction. Layer upon layer of emotion twines together inside her head and her heart—determination, love, distrust, warmth, anger, agony, and most surprising, a deep desire for peace.

I focus on that, hoping I'm not wrong when I lower myself to the ground. "You're asking me the wrong question. I don't want to punish or hurt you. What I want is my freedom and you're standing in the way of it."

"Then tell us how to get out of the way," she says.

It's such a simple request, but even with all the knowledge I have about their true natures, I doubt that she and the other assassins will do what I need.

"Kaitlyn Hadrix wrote Striker Draven's name in your ledger," I say. "I need you to refuse the mission."

"Why?" Hunter asks, speaking as quietly as I did.

"Because his safety is being used against me. As long as you're a threat to Striker, you're a common enemy that forces me to align with Hadrix."

"Striker Draven," she murmurs, as if he has already caused her a lot of trouble. She makes no sudden movements as she turns to Cain. "Would you mind bringing my ledger?"

He casts her a cautious look. "If you're sure?"

"I am."

He reappears within moments, holding a book bound in amethyst-colored leather, which he hands to Hunter while steering clear of my personal space.

Hunter presses the book to her chest. "Nobody but me should be able to read this book. My knowledge of Furies is sorely deficient, but now I wonder…"

She opens the book and holds it out to me, supporting it in her hands so I can see it without taking it.

"Can you read that message?" she asks.

Curvy, golden script, incredibly elegant, fills the entire page and then the next, curving across the pre-printed columns that would usually contain the names of targets and clients.

Hunter,

I've confirmed that there are five missing assassin's rings. I have no doubt that Lady Tirelli stole them. The rings must be found at all costs.

Oliver Draven has made powerful friends within the Magical Magnate and he's agitating for greater controls over the Factions of assassins.

He has personally threatened me that if anything happens to him, the Magical Magnate will be told about the missing rings. He says it will prove that we are unable to govern ourselves appropriately.

It's the excuse the Magnate needs to seize control of our operations. Of course, we know this is because many of them are corrupt and it's only a matter of time before their names are written in our ledgers.

However, I have no choice but to withhold sanctioning Oliver Draven's assassination by Slade until the rings are found.

In the meantime, he walks free and continues to supply weapons that kill innocents.

You must find the rings. I authorize you to make any deals required to get them back.

Catherine.

"Who is Catherine?" I ask when I finally look up at Hunter.

She closes her eyes briefly. "You *can* read it."

"Catherine is our Guardian." Hunter juggles the book so she can open it to another page.

This one contains Striker's name. And Kaitlyn's. And the reason she wants him dead: Because he took away the only person who mattered to her. I already know that's Jesse, Harrison's brother.

Hunter takes a deep breath as my gaze passes across the page. I guess she's trying not to make any sudden moves that might break our fragile truce.

"There isn't any proof that Striker killed Jesse Anderson," she says. "The Guardian asked me to find the truth. That's why we flew over the Academy that night. I need to know if he's guilty."

I swallow the turmoil of emotions inside me. "Why are you showing me this?"

She exhales slowly and gestures at the weapons they each hold. "Because you made a weapon out of a feather that Lady

Tirelli would have kept with her most prized possessions. You wear a weapon belt exactly like the ones that Lady Tirelli's thugs used to wear.

"And you carry a whip that was *stolen* from a Fury. A Fury whom I know for a fact is alive and well. It was stolen by Jake Hadrix. He used to be an assassin but spent the last three years torturing people on Lady Tirelli's whim." She takes another deep breath. "If you have all of these objects, then you might also know where the rings are."

The Fury is alive...

As I stare back at Hunter, something clicks into place.

Raptor seemed unconcerned about the assassins. He told me he has a way out. His family has all four rings. He must be planning to bargain for his life with them because getting the rings back is worth more to the assassins than killing him.

"You're offering me a deal," I say.

"Do you know where the rings are?"

"I know where four of them are." *Two of them are resting right beside the White Wand. One is on Raptor's hand, and the fourth is the one I hid.*

But what of the fifth?

I don't lie. "I didn't see a fifth ring."

Hunter pauses for a moment. "It's enough. Take me to the four you know of and I'll stop asking questions about Striker Draven's past," she says. "I won't go after him. I won't pursue you for trying to kill my husband. But be clear, this will erase the past. Not the future. I will come after you for anything you do after this point."

The irony doesn't escape me. Taking Hunter to the rings means inviting her to the Academy, which is exactly what I've been fighting to avoid.

"What a precarious deal." I'm unable to keep the sarcasm from creeping into my voice. "Especially since you're assuming

I'll continue on my wicked way and you'll have to come after me one day."

Her forehead creases. "That isn't what I—"

"It *is* what you meant," I say, but in the next breath, I make a decision. "I'll do it, but it won't be easy."

She gives me a nod, glancing at the others. "Tell us what we need to know."

40. PEYTON PRICE

I finally walk free from the room, having made a deal with the assassins and knowing what I need to do next.

Entering a narrow corridor, I'm surprised by my surroundings. I'm in a small apartment. Outside the sparsely furnished room I exited, I find a home with pictures on the hallway walls and a small kitchen ahead of me.

Hunter follows behind me, with Archer, Cain, and finally Tansy filing quietly behind her. They still hold my weapons and I have to respect that they won't hand them back until I reach the edge of the lane.

I'm supposed to leave now. I've agreed to go, and the faster I do, the less likely I'll do anything that will jeopardize our agreement.

As I pass the room on the opposite side of the hall, I catch a glimpse inside it through the half-open door, and my heart suddenly drops.

I thought maybe Slade was going to be okay...

The moment I stop moving, Hunter tenses behind me. She reaches out to pull the half-open door closed, but I stop her, placing my hand firmly on the wooden surface, my furious gaze meeting hers. "No."

Slade lies on the bed inside the room, a blanket pulled up to his waist, his bare chest rising and falling, his eyes closed, but my senses tell me he isn't sleeping an ordinary sleep.

Even from this distance, I can hear that his heart isn't beating. Magic is pushing the blood around his body, causing his lungs to expand and contract, keeping him alive.

The truth is hard to face. So much harder than I thought it would be. I'm the reason he's lying there.

"The damage to his heart was too great." Tansy's stern voice cuts through the silence. "I've done what I can. Now we have to wait to see if he wakes up."

Hunter is like stone beside me, but the force of her pain feels like being sucked to the bottom of a cold ocean, the icy waters pressing in on me, squeezing my chest. If our positions were switched…

I would have killed her.

I can't stop the truth from tumbling from my lips, even though it will hurt her more. "He won't wake up."

Slipping inside the room, I dart toward him before she can stop me. The tips of my whip shriek across the air beside me, forcing me to halt.

I whirl to face her as the silver objects slice through the air next to my cheek.

"Don't touch him!" she shrieks.

She wields the whip like an expert, but I stand my ground.

"It's my fault," I say, backing toward the bed. "I did this. But I can make it right."

The muscles in her arm tense, ready to flick my whip at me again. "Do *not* touch him."

Tansy storms into the room, standing on the other side of the door, her eyes glowing again. "You heard Hunter. Step away from Slade or our truce is over."

I force myself to remain as calm as I can, fighting my frustration as I search for a reason for them to trust me.

I'm suddenly amazed by the room around me. Family pictures sit on top of the chest of drawers with baby blankets folded next to them. A plush chair rests in the corner with a comfortable cushion and a well-worn dint in it.

This is the place where Hunter is a wife and a mother, not an assassin.

I shouldn't be in here—I'm an intruder—but I'm determined I won't leave without doing what I can.

"You don't have to trust me," I say, attempting to ward them off with my bare hands as I inch toward the side of the bed. "You can be ready to kill me, because I will be vulnerable. All I ask is that you wait until I've healed him."

Tension simmers like a heat wave around Hunter's silhouette, the power of her wings palpable.

"Tansy, be ready," she says.

My power to heal Striker was triggered because of all the hatred I felt around him.

When I transferred my healing power to him, I hated him with my heart and soul—but what I hated most was the thought of losing him. Now I focus on my self-hatred and the thought of being responsible for Slade's death.

I release my power, even my claws, as I rise up into the air and over the bed, then lower myself so that I float parallel to Slade's body without touching him.

Gravity causes my hair to fall forward, forming a curtain around his head.

There's no serenity in his face. He's fighting death with every breath that Tansy's magic compels him to draw.

I sigh as I realize that maybe hate isn't the answer here.

If I am a reflection of my surroundings—if the empath is right—then I can draw on all the love that exists in every part of this room, from the photos on the counter to Hunter herself, pulling it into myself greedily, remembering the way Slade looked at her the night they flew over the Academy.

Heat builds inside my body. My head, heart, and stomach all ache, but it will take more than I've ever given. I healed Striker because I was physically close to him. Crossing that boundary with Slade is an unwelcome idea, especially because Hunter will see any such move as a threat.

I lower my hands instead of embracing him with my arms, placing my palms side by side across his heart as I whisper inside my mind, over and over again…

I will heal you so I can heal myself. I will give you back your right to spend a lifetime with your wife and daughter. I will take nothing in return.

I will heal you so I can heal myself…

The power in my hands increases, a burning heat making my palms glow red at the edges, so hot that blisters form around my fingers, but I refuse to stop.

I will heal you so I can heal myself…

Pain strikes through me and I sense my power fighting itself, pressure building inside my chest. It's burning me from the inside and my Fury rages at me to stop.

But why? Why can't I heal Slade like I healed Striker?

A drop of blood drips from my nose onto his cheek. A deeper ache begins in my chest, my heart expanding far too much, beating far too fast. Energy rages through me with nowhere to go, threatening to consume me with the strength of what I want but will never have.

Writhing and gasping for breath, I scream. "I will heal you so I can heal myself! I will give you back your right to spend a lifetime with your wife and daughter. I will take nothing in return!"

Blood drips from my mouth. My head swims. My vision blurs. Darkness encroaches and I know I won't stay conscious for much longer.

"I will heal you—"

Dizzy and unable to stay in the air, I drop onto him, my chest colliding with his. I wrench him upright with a cry of effort and wrap my legs around his waist, my arms sliding around his chest after I pull his head against my shoulder and support his weight against me.

The burning heat in my body drains from me, flowing outward into him. Blessed relief fills me as the pain washes out from me. "Please, let me heal you."

The sudden beat of his heart against my chest is as strong as a drum pounding against my ribs.

His breath whispers against my neck. "Okay."

I close my eyes in relief. I don't have time to take a breath before a dagger presses against my ribs and I look up into Hunter's furious silvery-green eyes.

"Get the hell off my husband!"

Refusing to be intimidated, I check Slade's eyes, relieved to see that they are increasingly alert.

Quickly, I lower him back to the bed, sensing the resistance in his arms, the returning strength of his muscles, and the increasingly precarious position I'm in.

I lift off him, but my power fails me. I only manage to levitate down to the floor before I collapse, hitting the ground on my hands and knees.

I have no way of knowing what the consequences of my actions will be now.

Ever since I healed Striker, I become human whenever he's near me. Mallard told me I have to be human for love to exist in my heart.

But Dean said I reflect my surroundings, which would mean that I'm *reflecting* love when I'm around Striker.

Which is impossible because where would the love be coming from?

Unless…

Striker.

Dear ancients, could the love be coming from Striker?

The first time I was vulnerable to him was when he tried to defend me against Kaitlyn on the day she first arrived. Then again when he washed me in the shower afterward and asked me to let him take care of me.

Then when Raptor attacked me in the classroom and Striker wouldn't let me go. When he tried to leave after that, my power returned and I fought him; I thought my Fury came back because of how angry I was with him, but he hated me in those moments, hated that I stopped him leaving.

After that, when Ryan's wendigo attacked me, Striker came to my defense.

It's a miracle I maintained my power while the assassins flew above the Realm, but once again Striker was angry with me then, so agitated he was banging himself against the fence.

When I fought the soldiers in the combat area this morning, I remained part Fury because Striker was barely present—he was so blank he didn't even know I was there.

But when he *is* conscious of me, his feelings for me are so strong that they obliterate every other emotion around me.

I didn't become vulnerable to him because I healed him.

It was because he chose me.

It's not me loving him. It's *him*… loving me.

I can't breathe, can't process the heartbreaking truth now that I can finally see it, as I force myself to rise. I wobble toward the door, my heart in pieces as I bend to scoop up my whip, which Hunter dropped on the floor.

There's no need to push past Cain and Archer, or even Tansy, because they're all behind me now, crowded around Slade. Hunter is crying and Slade is holding on to her. Tansy is laugh-sobbing and Cain is hugging Archer.

I stumble from the room and leave the Keres dagger, my weapon belt, and all the happiness behind.

41. HUNTER CASSIDY

Peyton's gone by the time I look up.

I didn't expect her to stay, but I'm disconcerted that she slipped out so quietly.

When she wrapped herself around Slade, my protective instincts went haywire. I didn't trust her—*don't* trust her—but our paths are tangled now for better or worse.

I hug Slade on our bed while Tansy perches on the end of it and Cain pulls in two chairs from the kitchen for himself and Archer. Alexei—the Dominion Master—isn't due to arrive until later tonight, but this conversation can't wait.

Slade's voice rumbles in my ear. "Where is she?"

For now I choose to believe that he's talking about our daughter. "She's with Willow and Dean. She's safe." Even now that she's one month old, it's hard for me to let my little girl out of my sight. Despite the risk that Dean took showing her to Peyton, I know she's safe in his care.

Slade strokes the hair from my face. "Our daughter will always be safe because you will never let anything harmful happen to her. But you know that's not who I'm talking about."

I sigh against his strong jaw. "Peyton's going back to Bloodwing Academy."

Slade stiffens, his tone suddenly tense. "Did you send her back?"

I consider him with surprise. "No." I stop, rethinking my response. "We made a deal to get back the missing rings—"

"One that sends her back into hell," he says, the silver in his eyes becoming a deep disapproving gray instead.

My lips part as my surprise increases. "You're disappointed in me. Why? She *killed* you."

"She acted the same way a wounded and trapped animal will strike anything that approaches it," he says, a stern response.

I whisper, "I had to protect you."

His thumb grazes my temple and my cheek before he sighs and presses his forehead to mine. "You're the one who taught me to find light in the darkness. You're the one who opened your heart to Archer when you and she could have been mortal enemies."

"Archer didn't kill you," I object, a spark of anger growing inside me.

"Actually, I nearly did," Archer says from behind me, giving me an unhelpful shrug.

"Hunter." Slade's arms tighten around me. "If Peyton Price has spent a year imprisoned at an Academy run by Lady Tirelli —the woman who tortured, maimed, and killed to make herself more powerful—imagine what Peyton has survived. Now imagine what she'll do to protect the people she loves."

Oh, damn. She'll stop at nothing. She'll risk everything. Even her own life.

She's just like me.

"Can't you let me hate her, just for a minute?" I ask, giving him a fierce scowl.

A soft laugh vibrates through his chest. "Nope."

I press my cheek to his, soaking up all the forgiveness I find in his arms.

He and I haven't always walked a straight path, haven't always made the right choices, but we keep each other true. This time, he's the one guiding me back to the light.

"Now tell me," he says, pulling back a little. "What was the deal you made?"

"She will purge the Academy of Hadrix and his men. Then she will hand over four of the rings."

"In exchange for?"

"Amnesty for every student at the Academy. That includes Striker Draven. She also asked for amnesty for a man she calls 'Harrison.' She said he's Jesse Anderson's older brother."

"None of the students were targets," Slade says. "So you wipe a single name—Striker Draven's name—from your ledger and in return she takes out the rest of Lady Tirelli's organization *and* returns four of the missing assassin's rings." He shakes his head. "That's a bad deal for her."

I chew my lip. "It's all she asked for."

He seems to be done berating me because he says, "We can't let her go into that fight alone."

Tansy stands at the end of the bed. "I'll get a message to Alexei. He can meet you there. I'll stay here and watch over the Lane. I need to strengthen the protective shield and make sure a Fury can't step foot here again."

Cain and Archer rise to their feet. "We'll need the names of Hadrix's men written into our ledgers. It's time we all shouldered the burden."

Slade nods. "The final battle for peace."

I meet the determination in his eyes.

"We'll fight it together," I say, preparing my heart for war.

42. STRIKER DRAVEN

*H*adrix's men carry me past my room in the attic and dump me in Peyton's old room on her old mattress.

I passed in and out of consciousness on the way back.

Staring up at the scratched ceiling where Peyton cut through the rune that used to be painted on it, I estimate I have four bullet wounds in my chest and one in my left thigh. Three passed through me, but I sense that two are lodged in flesh or bone. It's those I'm worried about.

The two men laugh. One of them is Hugo, the guy who doesn't leave Tabitha alone. The other is Hodges. They're both burly with shaved heads, alike enough to be mistaken for each other.

"This room will do," Hugo says to me with a cracked-tooth smile. "We don't want you getting comfortable in your own space."

I swallow a laugh. They have no idea that this is the room where Peyton healed me. The room where I accepted her into my life and chose her.

There was a brief moment in time when I thought of asking

Lucinda to combine the rooms, but now I'm glad I didn't. This abandoned bedroom contains stronger memories of good things than my more comfortable bedroom where I pushed Peyton away from me time after time.

Hadrix walks in as they leave. "I promised you a world of pain and that's what you're going to get."

He lays into my wounded chest first, thumping each bullet wound so hard that I can't breathe, finally punching his fist across my cheek.

The scratched rune on the ceiling flashes in and out of view between hits, reminding me why I'm still holding on.

"Don't hold back, Hadrix." I spit blood, the world blurring in and out of focus, unable to fight back even as I taunt him.

He grabs my shoulder, pressing his thumb into one of my wounds so hard that the contents of my stomach threaten to see the light of day again.

"I won't," he promises. "I'll let you heal enough between beatings that you remain conscious for all of them."

He shoves me back to the mattress before sauntering from the room, yelling at the two men to guard me. "Shoot him if he tries to escape. If you kill him, so be it."

I sit up enough to spit over the edge of the bed so I don't choke on my own blood.

Survival now is simple. Keep breathing. Get the bullets out. Bind the wounds. Somehow.

Fighting the darkness, I extend a claw toward the bullet wound in my thigh—the first one lodged. The second one in my shoulder will be harder.

Five minutes and two blackouts later, the bullet drops to the mattress. I sink back to the surface, praying that I remain conscious, when a melodic voice sounds from outside the room.

"You will let me pass. You will not speak a word about my presence. When I leave, you will forget I was here."

A soft figure glides into the room and Bree's face comes into focus as she kneels beside the bed. Her aquamarine eyes pass across my wounds and so do her hands, her fingers pausing over the final lodged bullet. "Oh, Striker."

She slides her hand under my head, pressing the rim of a bottle of water to my lips. "Drink."

Like my stepfather's demonic power of persuasion, her siren powers have no effect on me, but I won't disobey her order, gulping the liquid as best I can without spilling it.

She stops me before I drain the bottle. "I'm sorry, but I need the last drops. My power wears off. Now give me your hand."

I do as she asks, her hand guiding mine to my shoulder.

"Now *claw*," she says.

I look away, trying to relax my hand as she uses my own claw to dig out the bullet in my shoulder. Blacking out in the middle of the process, I come back to find her blue eyes searching mine again.

"Striker? There you are…" She pulls back a little. "The bullet's out, but I'm sorry I can't do more to help you right now. Lucinda and Joseph sent me to tell you that we're done accepting captivity. We're fighting back. Tonight."

I catch her hand as she rises. "Peyton?"

Bree's expression fills with regret. "We all know she isn't coming back. We heard the soldiers talking. Hadrix sent her to her death. He wants to be rid of her. Nobody's strong enough to kill Slade Baines."

She is.

Strong enough to heal my heart. Strong enough to fight a legion of assassins. Strong enough to come back… to me and my fucked-up attempts to love her.

Bree glides from the room, pausing for a beat beside the guards. "My presence will be like a dream," she says to them before she's gone again.

Like a dream.

I press my hand to my forehead, reaching for my beast,

hoping he's the reason I'm becoming hot, hoping it's not fever setting in. If the other students are going to fight, then I'm fighting with them.

But for this fight I will need to become the beast, heart and soul.

His power—my power—will sustain me until it's over.

I sense my hellhound's voice deep inside my heart. *I'm already you, Striker.*

My claws extend and retract. I quickly roll off the bed before my back bones rip up the mattress. Molten fire burns across my skin, blistering heat masking the pain of my wounds.

Hugo and Hodges twist at the door, immediately raising their weapons. The gunshots ring out as I charge at them, taking the bullets at close range in my chest as I wrap an arm around each of their stomachs and hurtle forward.

The wide window smashes as we hit it, the ceiling-to-floor glass shattering as I throw them through it, teetering at the edge as they fall five floors to the ground below.

It's only because I dug my claws into the window frame that I didn't hurtle after them. I drop to the corridor floor before vertigo pulls me down. Peyton used to be afraid of heights, used to avoid this window. Now the early evening breeze rushes through the broken glass. The forest beyond the Academy is finally quiet.

I close my eyes, trying to sense if any of the new bullet wounds I sustained are lethal, but I can't be certain. My beast will keep me alive for as long as I need.

Thudding down the corridor to the fourth floor, I don't even try to take a stealthy approach. Meeting a rain of bullets from the four men guarding the students, I quickly retreat behind the corner of the stairs, stepping out of the path of the bullets and the wood chips that fly around me.

Shouts sound from the levels below. The gunfire, as well as the crashing window, won't have gone unnoticed.

Preparing to run around the corner and invite more pain, I stop when Bree's voice calls out. "Put your weapons on the ground."

Stepping out into the open, I find the men carefully placing their weapons at their feet. I'm not sure what Bree plans to do with them, but the time for letting these men go free is over.

I stride up behind them as she begins to speak, her voice dying in her throat as I twist the neck of the first one and swing his body into the next.

She looks away as I finish the others.

Lucinda and Joseph appear behind her. Behind them, the other students gather, some in the corridor, most still in the dorm, crowding at the door, including Lachlan and Ashley.

Over the last four months, their power has been quietly growing.

With a sweep of her hand, Lucinda commands a cupboard at the side of the hallway to rearrange itself, building a box around the bodies before she gestures for the other students to emerge.

They're all dressed in pants and workout tops, which is the only combat gear they have.

Lucinda approaches me, her steps purposeful, but she falters as her gaze sweeps my chest. "*Damn*, Striker—"

"What the hell are you waiting for?" I snap, striding away from her. "They know something's up now. We have to move quickly."

As I hurry to the top of the stairs, a wood panel slides down in front of me, blocking my way. I turn back to Lucinda with narrowed eyes. "Why did you stop me?"

She breezes up to me, her previous concern now hidden. "You're like a bull stomping through a field, Striker. Stay back a moment, will you? I'll let you know when we need you."

She turns to Lachlan and Ashley. "You're my backup just like we discussed. Check every room on this level and kill any soldiers you come across. We'll be one level ahead of you, so you don't have to worry about your power, Ashley."

She gestures to two of the other students—one a yeti, the other a cyclops—to come with her while Joseph takes up the rear.

Every other student with a power lines up between them.

"Just like you discussed?" I ask her as she passes me with the yeti and cyclops in tow. The cyclops snarls down at me and the air frosts as the yeti moves past.

"We've had months to plan this, Striker. We even had a plan to deal with the creature in the forest, but the soldiers said you killed it. Thank you for that."

I open my mouth to correct the facts, but she's already moving past me, her face set in determination as she glides down the stairs.

The others follow her, their footsteps quiet as they file down the staircase and take up position along the steps.

Ashley and Lachlan break off from the group and speed along the fourth-floor corridor to check the rooms.

I remain at the edges of the staircase as students transform before my eyes, taking the shape of every two-legged monster imaginable, from a minotaur with a human body and the head of a bull complete with deadly-looking horns to a stocky dwarf who looks like he could lift three times his weight.

Lucinda said she'd let me know if she needs me, and for now I'm willing to go with it, keeping a watchful eye on her as she descends down the stairs.

The moment she sets foot on the second last step, four men appear, but the cyclops and yeti are ready. The cyclops takes the two on the right, grabbing their guns, hoisting the barrels upward so the bullets bite the ceiling before he knocks both their heads together so hard, there's no way they're waking up from it.

The yeti grabs the other two, whose fingers click uselessly

on the triggers of their suddenly frozen weapons seconds before their eyes frost over, and they drop to the ground, their skin blue, each exhaling a final frozen breath.

Two more men run up between them, but one of the girls is ready. She springboards off the dwarf's waiting knee and leaps between their attackers, facing one of the soldiers, her back to the other.

As she flies past them, four long ropes of her black hair whip out as fast as vipers. Two of the ropes wrap around their weapons and wrench the rifles upward. At the same time, a third rope of hair snakes out to wind around the neck of one of the men, yanking him off the ground and choking him while the final rope of hair jerks the second man toward her back.

A mouth at the back of her head opens and the man doesn't have time to scream before she bites a chunk out of his neck.

She drops gracefully to her feet again, her focus shifting to the corridor ahead of her and pointing toward the east wing.

Two more students are already moving and I can only watch the beauty and synchronization of their attack as they peel out one after the other to fight with their teeth and claws, ending our enemy without a single bullet being fired.

The students are smart. They use their powers to their full effect. Much smarter than me.

Even Ryan contributes in his human form, grabbing a guy and pinning him for the second it takes for Bree to whisper in the mercenary's ear. Ryan lets him go and the guy immediately turns the gun on himself.

As half of the students finish off the men on this level, the other half swarm down the staircase with Lucinda, a wave of monsters who have waited for this moment for far too long.

One after the other, they clean out the third and second level, their efficiency breathtaking.

What's more, every time they end a mercenary, they take his weapon.

I thought the second level would be more heavily guarded because that's where Hadrix and his men sleep, but the rooms are empty and only a handful of men wait for us.

By the time we approach the first floor, we've taken out a third of Hadrix's force, but the remainder will have rallied by now. They'll be waiting to pick us off one by one as we exit the building.

Harrison waits for us in the entrance area, his arms splayed at his sides.

"I'm unarmed," he calls out.

Lucinda holds up her hand to the others to keep them back. "It's time to choose a side," she says to Harrison.

He gives her a smile, his eyes darkening. "I chose a side when I fought beside Peyton. But I want to be clear: When this is over, Striker and I have things we need to sort out."

I step out of the shadows. "Jesse's alive, if that's what you're talking about."

He jolts. "What did you say?"

I exhale. "Jesse's alive. He was the creature in the forest." I glance at Lucinda as she tenses beside me. Between her and Harrison, the tension is growing worse around me, not better. "I didn't kill him." My next words sound unbelievable. "I helped them escape. Kaitlyn and Jesse are free."

Harrison breathes out and all the tension leaves his body before it rushes back in just as quickly. He storms right up to me. "What proof do you have that you're telling the—"

His pupils suddenly constrict and his eyes shift rapidly to their panther form as he inhales. "Jesse's scent is all over you."

I remain very still as he circles me like the prowling cat that he is. "That wouldn't be possible if he wasn't alive."

He steps back in the nick of time. If he circled me once more, I was going to punch him.

"You smell like death, but not my brother's," he says. "I can't believe I'm saying this, but I believe you."

A loud clatter down the hall makes us jump.

A soldier holding a gun drops to the floor. Alison, the head cook, stands behind him, a heavy saucepan clutched in her hand. She gives the soldier another clobber for good measure. "All clear this level," she calls. "For now, anyway."

I spare her a smile that seems to disturb her more than anything else.

I guess a smiling hellhound isn't something anyone wants to see.

Lucinda recovers quickly. "Okay, then. We have twenty soldiers to worry about. Along with Hadrix and Vulture. But it's Raptor we really need to target. It's a miracle he hasn't blurred and attacked us already—"

"Raptor's dead," I say.

Lucinda's jaw drops. I point to my chest and the bullet wounds she noticed before. "This was my reward."

She swallows hard enough for me to hear it. "Is there anything else we need to know?"

"I may die when I shift back to my human form," I say, bluntly. "I'm not sure yet."

She nods, her hand rising and hovering above my chest. "I wondered about that shot near your heart."

The one I'm pretending doesn't exist.

"Your beast is keeping you alive?" she asks.

With a nod, I lower my face to hers, ready to do for the students what I promised months ago. "Whatever I need to kill, point me at it, Lucinda. The less blood on your hands, the better."

"Right." She's all business and for a second I have to admire what she's become. A cold-hearted commander who knows she's going to lose good people but is leading them into battle all the same.

She's come a long way from the tender-hearted girl she used to be.

She glances up at the first floor landing as Lachlan and Ashley appear and give her a nod that can only indicate the levels above us are now completely clean.

Then she turns back to Harrison. "Tell me what you can about their plan of attack."

"They're waiting for you on both sides of the building. Hadrix and Vulture are out the front. No matter what side you choose to exit from, the men on the other side will come up behind you and block any retreat."

"We'll be ready for that," Lucinda says. "Anything else?"

Harrison purses his lips as if he's choosing what to say. "Hadrix doesn't seem as worried as I thought he would be."

"Then he has a plan and he's prepared to sacrifice his men to achieve it," she says.

She turns toward the students but focuses on Joseph and a moment of warmth passes between them.

All the layers of strategy can't hide how they feel about each other.

I suddenly realize that he is her supporter, her backup. She might be the leading voice, but he's an important part of her decision-making process.

I watch carefully at the way he gives her a nod of agreement before she steps toward the front door.

"We will attack Hadrix and Vulture head on," she says. "Night is falling, but we have better eyes in the dark than they do."

Her footsteps are light as she approaches the entrance. I keep to the side as seven students line up behind her. The move makes me concerned. There's no way they'll all fit through the door in that formation—

Lucinda raises her hands and the wooden panels lining the walls on either side of the entrance tremble and crack at the cornices, lifting away before breaking into smaller squares.

Narrow strips of wood peel off next and attach to the backs of the larger squares.

My eyes widen in surprise as I realize she's making shields. She passes her hands over each one as they float past her.

The paneling changes color when she touches it, becomes dense and hard-looking.

A shield floats to each of the seven students.

"The shields will remain bulletproof for long enough for everyone to exit the building," she says. "You seven will lead the way."

She doesn't have to raise her voice as she addresses the others. "If one of your friends falls, you pick them up and carry them. Our goal is to get through the gate. We'll kill as many of these assholes as we can along the way."

With that, she swivels toward the door again.

I edge up to Harrison one last time. "You've known Hadrix for a while. He isn't completely human, is he?"

Harrison shakes his head. "He has power, but I've never seen it. I don't know what he is."

I step away from Harrison again as the entire front of the entrance trembles.

A surprised smile grows on my lips. It seems that Lucinda's going to rearrange the entire entrance.

The panels shift outward and to the sides, forming a larger shield around us. A barrage of bullets hits the wood on the other side but doesn't yet break through.

The students with shields step forward first while the others form a circle behind them, facing outward.

Those with weapons stand to the outside while those without stay closer to the center.

The moment that the gaps widen between the panels and the sides of the building, mercenaries run toward us, but the students are ready.

Joseph shoots down two men before a third gets through

and Joseph's forced to abandon his gun at close range. His style of fighting is much like mine—inelegant and brutal.

On the other side, the minotaur makes a shield of his own body, proving that the mercenaries will need bigger bullets if they're going to pierce his tough hide. The dwarf breaks a mercenary's kneecaps with his bare fists and the minotaur spears that man as he falls.

They're preserving bullets and that's smart.

Lucinda halts the panels with a wide enough gap to entice the mercenaries to try to come through it while siphoning them into certain doom.

Five more mercenaries meet their fate this way.

We've now taken down half of Hadrix's force, but there's a long way to go.

I told Lucinda I'd wait for her call to action, and I'm prepared to follow her orders, but the front of the paneled area won't hold much longer, especially when there's a pause in the gunfire and the next bullets pierce right through the paneling.

"Armor-piercing bullets!" Harrison shouts.

"Be ready!" Lucinda cries.

As the makeshift barrier splinters and breaks apart, the seven students with shields come together at the front, forming a barrier while those with guns take up position, weapons resting on their shoulders ready to fire.

We can finally see what awaits us.

Hadrix and Vulture stand just inside the gate while fifteen men are positioned in a semi-circle across the front. My heart sinks to see that two of them hold grenade launchers, each positioned on either side of us.

They could have easily killed us inside our protected area already.

They've been toying with us this whole time. It drives home to me just how little care Hadrix has for his men. He has already willingly sacrificed half of them.

Hadrix raises his hand for a ceasefire, shouting across the distance. "You don't have a hope in hell of making it out of here alive. It's a shame for all of you to die. So I'll give you a final chance. Hand over your leaders for immediate execution and the rest of you can join us. No more training. Only missions. I'll give you back control of your lives."

"Go to hell!" Tabitha screams from right beside me.

Hadrix smiles. "Is that your answer? I'll give you another moment to consider the firepower that surrounds you. How about you think about it a little harder?"

Lucinda's hand twitches and I can see her thought processes. The semi-automatic machine guns are a threat, but the grenade launchers are the most dangerous of all.

She's the only one with the chance to sabotage them from a distance. Even the girl with two mouths doesn't have hair long enough to twine around them from here.

Anyone else will have to get up close to the men holding them, which will draw gunfire from the others. A suicide mission.

I edge up to her. "I can do it."

She shakes her head immediately. "I can upset the earth beneath their feet, shift them off-balance, grow vines, or—"

"How many grenades will they launch in the meantime?"

"Just as many as they'll launch if you run at them," she snaps, swearing beneath her breath. "If we huddle together like we planned, we're a mass target ripe for bombs. They're trying to force us to break apart, but that's what we'll have to do." With a deeply exhaled breath, she capitulates. "Okay, Draven. You run for the one on the left. I'll handle the one on the right. You'd better not die before you neutralize it."

I scoff and meander through the students, determined to maintain my false bravado until the bitter end. When I saw the students fight like a highly trained unit inside the Academy building, I thought that escape would be possible, but now… all I see ahead of us is a bloodbath on both sides.

Lucinda raises her voice, waiting heartbeats between orders. "Get ready. Now… scatter!"

Gunfire breaks out in every direction, some of it ours, most of it theirs.

I run at the same time the others do, pushing every bit of my remaining energy into my legs as I dart between bullets.

Every student runs in a different direction. The strongest head straight to the unguarded parts of the fence, pulling at the bars. The cyclops takes a bullet in the back as he tries to block Tabitha while she runs through the gap.

Behind me, Joseph dogs Lucinda's heels, dropping to his knees and firing at every man who tries to take her down while she concentrates. Vines shoot from the earth and the mercenary holding the grenade launcher struggles to free himself from the greenery rising up around him.

I hurtle toward the man on the left, leaping upward and catching the grenade he launches at the crowd. I'm shocked that I caught it, so much that I nearly forget to hurl it back at him in time.

As the bomb explodes at his feet and blows a hole in the fence, I crouch to avoid the debris, uncertain whether all of it missed me.

My beast is keeping me pain free, which is a dangerous state to be in. I could lose a limb and not realize until I try to use it.

To my dismay, the launcher itself rises out of the man's hands, safely soaring up into the air all on its own so that the blast doesn't explode it.

In the distance, Vulture stands with a wand—Kaitlyn's old wand—raised in our direction, her attention on the launcher.

Damn. She's controlling it with her magic and now it's beyond my reach. Lucinda can disarm Vulture, but she's busy on the other side of the yard trying to disarm the other mercenary.

I run at the fence, use the bent section as a foothold to gain height, and launch myself at the hovering weapon, reaching out as far as I can to bring it down.

Just as my hands close over it, the launcher fires at the students escaping through the gap on the other side of the clearing.

No...

The explosion rings in my ears as I hit the ground.

The sudden bright flare lights up the encroaching dark. The buzzing sound it leaves behind is nothing compared to the screams.

Gripping the grenade launcher, I struggle to get to my feet, gasping for breath, unable to process the damage caused by a single bomb. I can't distinguish who was hit, don't know who's still alive.

I've seen a lot of bad, done a lot of bad, but this... Even my beast can't save me from the shock.

My body moves without control. I turn the launcher on Vulture's position, my finger ready to squeeze the trigger, when a new scream flows across the clearing and Peyton soars through the gate, her crimson hair flying around her.

Her scream washes across the entire space. "Stop fighting!"

A blast of wildflowers pulses across the clearing. My knees go weak and I hit the ground. Guns clatter to the earth as mercenaries and students drop to the grass. Lucinda collapses against Joseph. Far to the back of the area, Lachlan grabs Ashley before she falls, his body turning to smoke as the scent of compulsion washes through him. He's the only one who doesn't plunge to the ground.

That is, other than Hadrix and Vulture.

Peyton turns to them with a stern warning. "You, too!"

They simply smile. "No," they say in unison.

She doesn't look surprised. "Still immune?"

Vulture says, "We're glad you came back to die."

Without taking her eyes off Peyton, Vulture bends to the ground, taking a knee in a confusing way, because it looks almost as if she's bowing to Peyton, until I realize that she's reaching for a box on the ground.

As she rises to her feet again, she turns toward me. "Striker Draven, we promised you pain for killing our son. We thought that watching your friends die would be enough, but now you will truly feel what we feel."

A bright glow grows in the air around her as she lifts a slim, white object from the box at her feet.

"You were busy for four months!" Vulture shouts. "But so was I! I created a harness for the magic—a harness that allows me to control the greatest power on earth."

Bright, white light flows across the area, lighting it up like daytime.

It consumes the scent of wildflowers, leaving only a deadly silence, a calm in the air that quickly fills with tingling energy, making all my senses prickle. I stumble upright and take a step, drawn toward the source.

The White Wand.

Vulture's holding it within a special casing—made of what, I can't see from this distance.

She said she's harnessed its power, but that isn't possible. It can't be.

I wait for her to tremble, shake, anything that indicates she isn't in control, but her features remain composed, her hand steady, and my heart slowly sinks.

The grenade launcher in my hands is suddenly useless. The moment I fire it, she will deflect it onto the students. She'll do the same with bullets. Our bad situation suddenly got a million times worse.

The white light casts reflections across Peyton's face as she twists in my direction, her focus landing on me—on my beast—

her eyes widening as her gaze passes across my face and stops at my chest.

That damn bullet wound. She knows it's bad.

But the worst part is the way she falters in the air as soon as she sees me, the small dip that tells me her power is failing and she's fighting to maintain it.

"Do not turn your back on me, Peyton Price!" Vulture shouts, her voice carrying across the whole area. "This wand is hewn from the ancient bone of a primordial deity, Typhon, himself. He was the father of all monsters. With this wand, I control every monster in this place. Every one of these students you call a friend will rip you apart at my bidding."

I can't help the laugh that snorts out of me. Vulture's lost it. The other students would never turn on Peyton…

Twisting to the others, I expect to hear Tabitha shout profanities at Vulture and Hadrix again. She didn't exactly like Peyton, but she would never obey Vulture. My gaze lands on her body lying in the gaping, darkened hole in the fence where the grenade hit.

Nearby, Harrison sits propped up against the fence, a trail of blood leaking down the side of this face. The only reason I know he's still alive is because one of the mercenaries is holding a gun to his head, presumably prepared for when Harrison wakes up.

A scan of every living student tells me they're suddenly quiet and alert.

Focused on Peyton.

Even Lachlan stares at her, remaining perfectly still as smoke rises around his body. Joseph and Lucinda are blank, their monster forms more evident than before. Joseph's chest expands before my eyes, increasing in height and muscle. Lucinda's arms rise at her sides and the grass turns to thorny vines beneath her feet.

The minotaur snorts and stomps his feet, the cyclops knocks

his fists together, and the ground freezes around the yeti, his glacial focus unwavering.

Black ropes rise around the girl with the two mouths and far off to the side, a gangly wendigo—*Ryan!*—stands with thick claws poised and salivating teeth bared while a siren's song fills the air around us.

"Pretty Peyton," Bree croons. "Come to the ground and let us play with you."

Peyton twists in the air, her eyes meeting mine, and I can't decipher the depth of the expression in them, a new wisdom, a clearer understanding, as if she knows something, sees something, that she didn't know or see before.

The crimson glow around her disappears and she plunges to the ground without making a sound.

Vulture laughs. "Go on then, monsters. Tear her apart."

43. PEYTON PRICE

The truth is inescapable.

I hit the ground as my power fails, but I'm already running. Not away from Striker but *to* him.

Every monster in the clearing has a glow. Not an aura but a reflection of their nature. Some aqua, some emerald, some slate gray. But Striker's is the only crimson one like mine.

I always knew we were both creatures from hell, but I never realized what that meant.

He was always the most brutal, the coldest, the least vulnerable to emotion, the most likely to use violence as a means to an end.

He stopped me from taking the wand the day that Kaitlyn produced it. When I touched it, its power reminded me of Striker, a power that sent a thrill to my toes, a power I wanted more than anything.

Striker was the only one who remained truly unaffected by it. He struggles to love, struggles to let me in, fights his own nature to handle me gently.

Even his version of love hurt me.

When he first spoke about the wand, I saw the fear in his eyes—not fear of the wand, but that I would succumb to it.

I dart between the students as they fly at me with tooth and nail bared. Streaking between them with all my human strength, I try to catch Striker.

If I'd realized the true horror that awaited me when I came back, I would have struck Vulture down the moment I flew over her, even if it would have been a coward's kill from behind when she didn't anticipate it.

I'd expected to come back to the same hidden evil that I left, the same quiet manipulation, not the senseless stomach-churning carnage that she and Hadrix have unleashed.

Now, Striker has made it to the front steps already, attempting to get away from me and restore my strength.

I never realized before how hard it is for him to deliberately leave me to fight my battles alone.

Now that my power to see the truth has been unchained, clarity doesn't stop at the things I want to know. It tells me the things that hurt me too.

Striker does trust my strength, but he hates that he is my weakness.

Vulture shouts, "Lachlan! Ashley! Stop Striker and bring him to me."

Striker's fist darts out, but it flies straight through Lachlan's body. In contrast, Lachlan's hand latches around Striker's neck in a choking hold, lifting him off the ground and forcing him onto his back on the steps in one bone-breaking move.

Striker's hellhound form shudders as he groans on the ground, his body dangerously close to shifting back to his human form.

His eyes widen as he sees me coming.

Fear is my greatest enemy right now, but I won't let it conquer me.

I crash into Striker just as Lachlan is about to pull him up, the force of our collision loosening Lachlan's hold and forcing Striker to the ground again.

My hands rest on either side of Striker's heart, burning on the fire in his skin, but I refuse to let go until the monsters drag me away.

Striker shouts, wild and panicked, the flames in his eyes leaping. "Peyton! Get away—"

"The wand!" I whisper desperately. "You have to take it."

Claws rake at me from behind. Bree croons into my ear as her teeth snap at my neck.

"Striker, it's you!" I scream as she and Ryan pull me backward. "Let out your rage. Be who you are—"

Striker doesn't understand. His confusion is evident in the tension in his body.

He disappears from my view as Joseph looms between us, his fist snapping out against my cheek, making my world spin.

I slump in Ryan's arms as black ropes made of hair twine around each of my wrists, wrenching my hands behind my back. A third rope snatches my whip from my side, hurling it away from me across the grass.

Pain bursts across my shoulder as an icy hand freezes me, blistering my skin.

Joseph grabs at my feet, hoisting me into the air between him and Ryan as the others kick and bite at my sides. I try to hold in my screams as pain rips through me.

Through the gaps between their bodies, I see Striker launch himself down the stairs, leaving Lachlan's hands to grasp at air.

"Peyton!" He charges after me, knocking into the minotaur who is tugging at my foot. He thumps Joseph in his lower back and spins to gouge the cyclops's eye.

As the monsters continue to savage me, Joseph recovers and grabs Striker from behind, dragging him back. Lucinda's vines snap at Striker's torso as he struggles to get free. Lachlan runs in from the side, bringing both fists down on Striker's shoulders, driving him to the ground again.

Striker uses the downward momentum to roll, shooting to his feet, but this time, he pauses.

His focus shifts to the White Wand.

Then to me.

Maybe he realizes what I was trying to tell him. Maybe it's dawned on him that he's the only one unaffected by it.

But as I watch the emotions spin across his face, it seems that something else has broken his heart into pieces.

Emptiness fills his face, a fearsome resignation. The fire in his eyes burns brighter than I've ever seen it, leaking tears of lava down his cheeks.

He roars as he runs back to me. "Nobody kills her but me!"

The other monsters pause. Ryan's hungry teeth hover above my neck. Striker shoves the minotaur aside with an angry shout, looming over me, a fragment of hell that never should have risen to the surface of the Earth.

"She's mine to kill."

The ground rears up at me as the monsters drop me. Lucinda's boot presses against my chest, holding me down. Striker glares at her and she slowly lifts her foot.

He could always control them, keep them in fear, gripped stronger than any wand.

It's how he convinced them to lie to me for months. His power is in his ferocity, in his darkness.

He really is their leader. He just never realized it.

He catches my arm and wrenches me upright, his other hand swinging to grip my neck, his voice an angry snarl. "You were supposed to hate me, Peyton. You promised to hate me."

He's squeezing so tightly that I can't speak, but he knows what I'm trying to say.

I lied.

44. STRIKER DRAVEN

 $\mathcal{I}$ have no choice. I can't get away from her fast enough and they're tearing her limb from limb.

She was trying to tell me something about the wand, but all I hear is her final cry.

Let out your rage.

The only way to save her is to make her hate me, to destroy whatever feelings she has for me, break and crush them, smash them the way I'm destined to smash anything good in my life.

My hellhound warned me that this day would come.

I gave up all my alternatives because I was too selfish to walk away from her. I could have left her. I thought about it, nearly did it many times, prowling around the fence under the moonlight.

I promised her that I wouldn't hurt her. She promised me that she would hate me forever. We both lied.

In the distance, Vulture clutches the White Wand. She's controlling the students, but the path I'm taking will suit her for now.

She gives her husband a smile that turns my stomach as my hand closes around Peyton's neck.

If Peyton didn't love me she wouldn't be vulnerable, she'd be furious like she should be.

"You were supposed to hate me, Peyton," I snarl. "You promised to hate me."

Her eyes are clear, her lips pursed, but no sound comes out. As I squeeze harder, she starts to struggle, her human survival instincts kicking in.

The fingers of my free hand curl into a fist at my side.

I can't do it.

Yes, you can, my beast says. *You knew this day would come. If you want her to live, you will give up everything she wanted to give you.*

With a roar, my free fist cracks her ribs. Her body jolts with the force of the blow, her neck nearly snapping because I still grip it.

"You *will* hate me," I say.

She shakes her head, the slightest movement despite my hold around her neck. *No.*

My fist collides with her face, busting up her left eye with a single hit.

"You will hate me!" I roar at her.

Her one good eye reveals her shock, quickly replaced by anger. She kicks me. Hard.

Good.

I hurl her to the ground and the students move back to give me room.

My right foot stomps toward her where she lies on the ground. She attempts to roll out of the way, but she can't move fast enough. My heel hits her left shoulder blade, making her cry and arch. She's already covered in blood from all the bites and scratches from the other monsters and now there's a sickening crunch of bone beneath my foot.

She twists, grabs my ankle, and pulls, as if to wrench me off my feet, but I land lightly on my side, immediately shoving her with my upper hand.

She recovers and tries to leap to her feet, but I'm already close enough for my next strike to collide with her stomach, winding her.

I'm half-up on my feet now, risen enough to grab her by the neck again and throw her straight down. The *crunch* of her arm breaking as she lands on it echoes around and around in my head.

She hits out at me with her good arm as I shove her on her back and straddle her.

She has one good arm. One good eye. She's got nothing.

I draw on every shred of hatred inside myself, every jagged, broken piece and drag it through the love I feel for her, cutting my feelings, shredding them, tearing them apart so there's nothing left but *hate*.

Only hate like she should have for me.

Nothing. But. Hate.

I wrench her good arm above her head, pinning it there. She tries futilely to displace me with her kicking legs as I press my free hand, claws extended, against her collarbone, slowly and deliberately forcing it to move against its natural position.

Her scream is a bare hiss of air through her broken vocal chords. "Striker…"

I don't respond, glaring down at her as if she is nothing to me and never was.

Her breathing comes hard and fast as she looks up at me.

The look in her one open eye destroys me.

A single tear falls down the side of her face.

I sense the change before it happens, the moment when her humanity finally dies. The moment that I've killed it, along with any love she had for me.

Her uninjured eye clears. The bloodshot flecks in it disappear. Her irises become a lustrous brown instead. Her hair lifts around her head, rising off the ground a little, turning pure crimson-red, no longer streaked.

The ends of her hair suddenly extend in three places and my heart stops when three snakes dart from within the strands, sliding across her neck and launching toward me.

I leap off her, narrowly avoiding their fangs as I land in a crouch on the grass.

The snakes remain on her body, slithering around her waist and shoulders as she rises into the air, her broken bones snapping back into place, her eye healing, and every inch of her visible skin becoming luminescent.

The alluring scent of wildflowers wafts through the air as she inhales and exhales, the perfect curves of her chest, waist, and hips making me want to move toward her, be close to her, even though she'll never let me touch her again.

She considers me with the calculated gaze of someone adding up all my wrongs, computing the weight of them, and deciding the appropriate punishment.

"Striker Draven," she says, her mesmerizing voice making my heart burn. She tilts her head as if she's perplexed. "How did I ever love you?"

I sink to the bloody ground, my shoulders heavy.

My beast is quiet. And then: *You will not live to see her fury.*

I'm okay with that. Without her love, there is no life for me.

Across the distance, Vulture has jolted forward, the White Wand pointing wildly from me to Peyton.

Vulture's face is pale with rage as she screams. "Striker Draven, what did you do?"

What did I do?

"I released a Fury," I say.

And destroyed what was left of my soul.

But now Peyton will rage hell on our enemies. She will do what I couldn't. She won't stop until her vengeance is complete.

As I slide to the ground, my beast's power fades and the cold darkness of hell reaches up for me.

My vision fills with Peyton where she floats above me, her glistening hair framing her gorgeous face, a copper snake nestling against her shoulder while the other two hug her waist. Her eyes are crimson red, bright with power, and her lips are parted, as if she's inhaling fresh air for the first time in her life.

A smile flickers around my mouth before my muscles stop obeying my commands and my body lies heavy on the bloodied ground.

"I released a Fury," I whisper again as the darkness closes around me. "And she's fucking beautiful."

Find out what happens next in Rogue (Assassin's Magic 7).

Then complete the series with
Assassin's Match (Assassin's Magic 8),
the final book with NO cliffhanger
and a happily ever after.

ROGUE

(ASSASSIN'S MAGIC BOOK 7)

I am rogue. A vessel of wrath.

Love is my greatest weapon.

Content information: Rogue is dark urban fantasy romance, the seventh in the Assassin's Magic series.

Recommended reading age is 17+ for sex scenes, mature themes, and violence.

Ends on a cliffhanger.

ALSO BY EVERLY FROST

ASSASSIN'S MAGIC - COMPLETE

(Dark Urban Fantasy Romance)

1. Assassin's Magic

2. Assassin's Mask

3. Assassin's Menace

4. Assassin's Maze

5. Rebels

6. Revenge

7. Rogue

8. Assassin's Match

SOUL BITTEN SHIFTER - COMPLETE

(Dark Urban Fantasy Romance)

1. This Dark Wolf

2. This Broken Wolf

3. This Caged Wolf

4. This Cruel Blood

SUPERNATURAL LEGACY - COMPLETE

(Angels and Dragon Shifters)

1. Hunt the Night

2. Chase the Shadows

3. Slay the Dawn

4. Claim the Light

DARK MAGIC SHIFTERS

(Dark Urban Fantasy Romance)

1. Wolf of Ashes

2. Bond of Flames

3. Crown of Fate

KINGDOM OF BETRAYAL

(Fantasy Romance)

1. A Sky Like Blood

2. A Sin Like Fire

3. A Storm Like Iron

4. A Soul Like Glass

BRIGHT WICKED - COMPLETE

(Fantasy Romance)

1. Bright Wicked

2. Radiant Fierce

3. Infernal Dark

STORM PRINCESS - COMPLETE

(Fantasy Romance)

1. Book 1

2. Book 2

3. Book 3

DEMON PACK - COMPLETE

(Dark Paranormal Romance)

1. Demon Pack

2. Demon Pack: Elimination

3. Demon Pack: Eternal

MORTALITY - COMPLETE

ABOUT THE AUTHOR

Everly Frost is the USA Today Bestselling author of fantasy romance, urban fantasy and paranormal romance novels. She spent her childhood dreaming of other worlds and scribbling stories on the leftover blank pages at the back of school notebooks. She lives in Brisbane, Australia with her husband and two children.

amazon.com/author/everlyfrost

facebook.com/everlyfrost

instagram.com/everlyfrost

bookbub.com/authors/everly-frost

goodreads.com/everlyfrost